The Mirror of Freedom

Lois:

I hope you enjoy my book!

Russell A. Minar

10-10-12

The Mirror of Freedom

Russell A. Minar

TATE PUBLISHING
AND ENTERPRISES, LLC

Published by Tate Publishing & Enterprises, LLC
127 E. Trade Center Terrace | Mustang, Oklahoma 73064 USA
1.888.361.9473 | www.tatepublishing.com

Tate Publishing is committed to excellence in the publishing industry. The company reflects the philosophy established by the founders, based on Psalm 68:11,
"The Lord gave the word and great was the company of those who published it."

Book design copyright © 2012 by Tate Publishing, LLC. All rights reserved.
Cover design by Erin DeMoss
Interior design by Nathan Harmony
Illustrations by Elijah and Otto Shaw

Published in the United States of America

ISBN: 978-1-61862-271-6
1. Fiction / Christian / Classic & Allegory
2. Fiction / Family Life
12.03.08

Acknowledgements

I want to thank my Lord and Savior, Jesus Christ for granting me the ability, the imagination, and the desire to create this novel. Without the Lord's council, this book would have never developed into what it has become. I am forever thankful.

I would also like to thank all the people at Tate Publishing who helped and believed in me on this project; from Acquisitions to editing to concept design and marketing. Everyone who had a hand in making this book of mine a reality, I thank you.

Finally, I would like to thank my family and friends who encouraged me during the writing process to production; my wife Diane, Ann Minar, Brittany Minar, Scott Minar, The Shaw family, Henry, Wendy, and William Roberts, Terry Bailey, Donald Flowers, and the many others who gave me even a single word of encouragement, you know who you are, I thank you.

—Russell A. Minar

Dedication

This book is dedicated to my wife, Diane, who, without her, I could have never motivated the many emotions that were put forth to create this story. I love you very much.

Random House College Dictionary defines *dreamland* as "a pleas-ant, lovely land that exists only in the imagination."

Or does it?

When I was a child, I spoke like a child,
I understood as a child,
I thought as a child,
But when I became a man,
I put away childish things.
For now we see in a Mirror,
dimly, but then face to face.
Now I know in part, but then I shall know,
just as I am also known.

1 Corinthians 13:11-12 (NKJV)

Part One

Coming to Know the Mirror

Chapter 1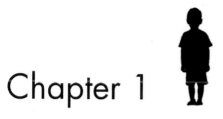

As I look back upon the waves of time that have passed me by, I am reminded of how my Master's hand led me to the place where I now am. My one act of obedience when I was young brought into my life a flood of blessings that I would not have been able to accomplish in the natural. It was destiny's call to me, and I had to make a choice. I struggled making the decision that I did, for my heart and my mind were not in agreement. The voice of my heart's conviction finally determined the path that I chose to follow. It seems very long ago that these events transpired, but as I write my memory in words, those images become clear, as if they just happened.

When I was a young boy of eleven years, I was living with my parents in Ohio. We lived in a small town along the banks of the Ohio River, just upstream from Marietta. It was summertime, a very hot and humid summer, and I, being a shy and lonely boy, began to have dreams in the night that were prophetic images of the events that were to come into my life.

I remember the dream I had the night before all that I am about to tell you started. With complete accuracy, I can visualize the concepts that were in my head as I slept. I was walking, but I did not know where I was or where I was going. I could distinguish that I was in a tunnel with a diminished amount of light. A thick fog filled the tunnel, so dense in its matter that I was barely able to see five feet in front of me. I felt like I was being escorted, but my eyes did not recognize their image, for the fog was so thick. I felt their furry paws, and what I could see of them looked like bear cubs that walked like humans. Glancing around, I noticed that the walls of the tunnel were almost completely covered by peculiar rust-colored ivy. It grew everywhere. Under my feet, I felt soft wood chips that covered the ground.

I became restless, wanting to know where I was being led to, when we came to a sharp curve in the tunnel, where we immediately stopped. What stood before us was a large, wooden door of gigantic proportions, approximately twenty feet tall, ten feet wide, and almost two feet thick. I briefly studied its ancient design, as I remembered what I had learned in history class, for the door that stood before me was reminiscent of the doors that were used during medieval times, except this one was a lot larger. My two companions walked up to the large door, and together, working as a team, using all of their strength, they pulled it open.

From beyond the other side of the door, a bright light cut through the fog as the door slowly opened loudly. The brilliant rays were almost blinding, and I had to lift my forearm up to my eyes to shield them from the intense light as I cautiously walked through the doorway and entered a region that bewildered my young mind.

What lay before me captured my sense of being in its peace and beauty. As I walked out of the tunnel, the blinding light was left behind. From where I stood, I could see lush, green fields that carpeted rolling hills that reached far beyond the conquest of my eyesight. A forest proudly stood on both sides of the rolling terrain, with trees so tall and enormous in size that it astonished me how something could grow that large. My two escorts led me partially across the fields to a designated place where we entered the woodlands. Following a wide path that scampered its way up and down rolling hills and cut back and forth among the trees and underbrush, I became aware of a glowing light in the sky. It sparkled like little jewels in the air through the leaves on the trees.

A fresh breeze mildly brushed my face with a familiar scent that reminded me of springtime.

This is what I felt, thought, and experienced inside the boundaries of my dream. I was in a world all my own, where my mind led me to follow the path that I had to follow. I could see the trees of the forest and the light that shined through them so vividly that I felt as if I was actually there. It was during those times, and only then, that I felt free from the world I lived in. The dreams carried me away from the emptiness that reigned over me, the result of being so alone. My parents were unable to give me security in love, and I did not have any true friends at school or in the neighborhood. Only in my dreams was I able to find contentment. It was there that I was transported to a world beyond the Earth and the stars, one that lived only in the boundaries of my mind. When I dreamt, I felt a distinguishable sense of freedom that I could not truly understand during that moment in my youth.

As I continued to walk through the woodlands in my dream, I became curious about the glowing light in the sky. It was much different than the sun. I looked up into the light, and at the same time, the sun separated the clouds in the sky outside the house where I slept as its bright rays of light shined through the basement window and landed upon my forehead. When the sunlight found its target upon me, my eyes immediately opened. Slowly, and with much caution, I surveyed the room. On the stained wood walls, I saw a Bugs Bunny poster along with various pictures of sports heroes that brought the recollection and the belief that the dream was over. I had returned to the real world, the life that I had to endure daily, which I occasionally referred to as the living hell.

"Why, tell me why, did it have to end? I was happy there. I was happy. I did not want to come back to this!" I yelled out to my empty bedroom.

Many questions troubled my mind as I became confused and miserably disappointed.

"I knew it was too good to be true. I was free from this life that has made me feel miserable for years," I softly spoke as depression and self-pity began to consume my emotions. The distinction between truth and fantasy was finally revealed to me like a slap on the face. Understanding and recognizing the real world rose up the motivation in me as I got out of bed. I tried to fight the despair that had captured my mind, but as I made an effort to push away those feelings with my mind, I became more vulnerable to them.

I could not find even a fiber of strength that might have helped release me from the morbid weariness that was controlling me. I carefully walked through my morning routine. After I got dressed in my usual summer attire, I prepared myself a small breakfast. My mom and dad worked full-time jobs, so during the summer, I had to discipline myself to be responsible. I ate a large bowl of Captain Crunch cereal, which was my favorite, along with toast, jelly, and a glass of grape juice. While I ate, I tried to read the comic section of the local newspaper. My mind kept drifting back to the dream that I had just woke up from. I believed that what I experienced was not just a dream but a revelation of an event that would happen to me in the future. What the dream meant, I was not sure, for I have had many dreams. Some were a bit strange while others were not. This dream was like a vision into a world unknown to most people, as I strongly desired everything that I saw in my dream to be real.

"I want to go back there, and when I do, I want to stay. I hope that what I saw in my dream was a real place, and if it is, somehow, I will find a way back there," I said aloud to the empty spaces in the kitchen with a voice of conviction.

Attempting to put the dream behind me, I cleaned my few dirty dishes. I stacked the newspaper neatly on the kitchen table. I saw a note left to me by my mother taped on the refrigerator door that I noticed when I put the milk away. It was a list of chores that had to be done before I could do anything else. As I read over the list, my mother's voice came ringing through my ears.

"Wash the basement steps, clean the bathroom tub and sink, and sweep out the garage."

My parents had sometimes accused me of being lazy. Actually, I wasn't, for I was a typical boy in many ways. During the summer I found it difficult to motivate myself to do the work assigned to me. What kid wants to spend half the day working around the house when he could be riding bikes?

"Who cares about school, good grades, and chores?" I often questioned myself when I was looking for a reason not to do the work.

Once again, I must emphasize that I was not lazy but did lack motivation and direction. Through the years, my heart felt rejected and insecure, as I alienated myself from the people that I loved. I felt totally alone at times and thought that no one in the world loved me. In my mind, I believed that I was a burden to my mom and dad. An orphan feels like that, for they never feel secure and have difficulty trusting and believing that there are people who care for them. I had many battles with depression through the years, and it blinded me to the purpose that was set before me.

I was born as Charles Alex Stormdale, on August13, 1959. My parents were two hard-working citizens who worked full-time jobs so that they could afford to create a good life for their little family. Money can sometimes grow into an obsession in people's lives, where its value becomes more important than people. My parents were captured and became prisoners to this ailment. Their main desire was the dollar sign, for it gave them satisfaction to have things most people could not afford. This disease caused an emptiness that led the unity of the family to fall apart, a consequence of their addiction. Stress came to live as an accepted companion in the home, for my parents were so overworked.

I was the real victim in the house, for I suffered alienation during the years that my parents pursued wealth. I became distant to them and lost myself in my own little dream world. In my make-believe existence, there were people who really cared for me, and I was happy. My parents did not approve of my tendencies to fantasize. When they would catch me daydreaming, I would be lectured about the importance of improving my mind. When they saw that I wouldn't stop, they used drastic measures, such as a paddling. The many times I was punished for lingering in my imaginary society never really sunk in, for I continued to dream on.

"No one understands me, for the only time that I'm happy is when I'm away from the conscious world," I often told my few friends at school.

I knew the work that was ahead of me, and I looked upon it with despair. I did not want to do my chores, for it was the end of the summer and soon, I would have to go back to school. It was a beautiful, warm, sunny August morning, and I wanted to be outside. Whatever my desire might have been, I did know better, for I could remember the pain from the consequences when I was disobedient. Many times over the years, I was rebellious, and when I was, there was always some kind of repercussion to endure. With those thoughts in my mind, it kept the motivation clear to achieve the assignments given to me.

I began my work with a stern concentration upon the completion of all my chores. I wanted to do a thorough job, but quickly, so that I could enjoy the rest of the day. My mind drifted away to a place of contentment after a few minutes of washing the basement steps with a small bucket of hot, soapy water and a sponge. I directed the sponge aimlessly over the linoleum tile without concentrating upon what I was cleaning. The dream I had just woke up from occupied my thoughts, and its memory had me spellbound. In the spaces of personal reflection, I could see the beautiful green fields, the large trees of the forest, and the bluest skies I ever saw. It was not an ordinary dream, for it felt so real, or was it a vision?

I became nervous when a seemingly eerie thought entered my mind. The possibility existed that I was really there, in another place, another world. With a speculative mind, I tried to recreate the dream, to understand what it meant. I must have looked like I had found paradise as I washed the basement steps, until something startled me. It was a ringing sound. At first, I did not know what it was, for it seemed to be quite a distance away. In truth, the ringing was near but could not be measured from the depths of my consciousness. The sound became louder, more distinct; and like a wet slap on the face, I was brought back to the real world. Suddenly, I realized that what I heard ringing in my ears was the doorbell. I immediately stopped working and ran to the door to greet the visitor.

When I pulled the door open, there before my eyes stood a tall man with extremely fair complexion. He was dressed slightly odd, as he stood out from the environment that surrounded him. He wore dark, baggy trousers that hung loosely upon him and a red-and-gray plaid short-sleeved shirt, both of which were years out of style, and in his arms, he carried a long, tan trench coat with dark stains randomly spotted all over it. Upon his head, he wore an extremely old fedora hat, and I noticed that his shoes appeared to be in the same condition as his hat.

This man walks a lot, I thought, *for where he has been, he wears on his shoes mud, grass, and pieces of wet leaves.*

"Come to the fair, my boy! Full of games, rides, and gifts for all!" proclaimed the man.

He stood tall over me, and as I looked into his eyes, they seemed to penetrate into the very essence of my being. I continued to look at him with fascination, speechless, with the intention of speaking, but the words failed to come out of my mouth. Finally, the visitor spoke up once again.

"My boy, there's much happening at the fair, with many interesting people to meet!"

I saw something very special about him through his eyes. Ancient prophetic writings tell that a person's eyes are the windows into their soul. What I saw in his eyes was a calming peace with a deep love for all humanity. Written upon his face and inside the confines of his being, he sent a message of love and joy without saying a word. It was quite foreign to me to come in contact with someone of that nature.

Suddenly, my young mind conceived a thought that raced like a bolt of lightning flashing through the summer night sky: *Fun!* My eyes became possessed with excitement from the possibility of going to a fair. I briefly stared at the man before me when I started to question what was developing in reality.

Who is this man? I asked myself, for he appeared to be like someone out of one of my dreams.

I sensed that I knew him. Random questions lingered in my mind for a few moments until I turned my thoughts back to the fair. I knew I had chores to finish or else face the consequences. My natural desire was to leave the work behind and go to the fair.

"I still have a few chores to finish around the house before I am able to come with you," I said, explaining my apprehension. "If you don't mind waiting, I can be ready shortly. I would invite you inside, but my mother told me never to let strangers in the house when I'm alone."

"I understand," he said with a sincere compassion in his voice.

I left the man standing at the door to quickly finish my chores, but I did not realize that there was a special element about him that made him extraordinary. As I walked away, he focused his attention skyward, when a strange bluish aura that was created from an inner passion formed around him. Transpiring at my doorstep was a divine spectacle without my knowledge.

The bluish glow that formed around my visitor was not from the world in which he stood. The sparkling illumination gave the man supernatural abilities and mental powers far beyond the ordinary man's intellect. After a brief moment, the bluish aura vanished as quickly as it had appeared when the man came out of his trance. A smile formed upon his face when he perceived what had been accomplished through him.

When I returned to finish my work, I witnessed what I thought was an unusual phenomenon. It was quick and almost blinding to my eyes when a flash of bluish light filled the stairwell. My eyes had to recover from the flash, and it took a minute or two for them to focus once again, and when they did, I was astonished by what I saw. The steps that I was about to finish washing were clean with a shine that was beyond the meaning of the word. I was quite mystified as I stared at the steps with disbelief.

Curiosity crept into me as I went into the bathroom only to find the sink, toilet, and the tub were clean with a shine reminiscent of the basement steps. I immediately went outside to the garage eager to see if the premonition inside me was true. A strong impression had suddenly come upon me that what I found in the basement stairwell and in the bathroom I would find in the garage. I was becoming quite confused, and what I found when I went into the garage was that it had been swept out and cleaned with a perfectionist's hand. It was a clean that I would have never done, for it had the look of being professionally cleaned.

I became completely dumbfounded as I stood alone in the middle of the garage with odd bewilderment that was beginning to torment me, not knowing what to believe. I assumed that I was either dreaming or some kind of miracle beyond my understanding had just occurred. When I carefully analyzed these happenings, my thoughts turned to curiosity about the peculiar man waiting for me at the door.

Or am I dreaming again? I asked myself as I questioned my sanity.

Up from the deepest desires of my heart, I quickly made a decision that would change my life forever. I chose to go to the fair and have some fun. In doing so, I thought it might answer some of my questions about the mysterious man who appeared at my doorstep. I was anxious to go to the fair as I quickly ran into the house. Once I got inside, I promptly dumped out the bucket of soapy water that still sat on the basement steps. I was completely unaware of the world I would soon enter when I left the house, and in a bold gesture, I began a unique excursion with my new friend.

Chapter 2

When I pulled the door shut and stepped outside, my new friend and I walked down the street towards downtown, with many thoughts lingering inside my head, causing me to become quite perplexed. I was apprehensive about the decision I had just made.

What am I doing, and where am I going? I asked myself as a disarray of many emotions came alive within me. I felt like a teenager on a first date: timid and fidgety, not knowing how to act or feel, what to say, or what to expect.

"What's your name?" I asked, trying to break the nervous tension that separated us.

He looked down at me with the appearance of misunderstanding the question, although after I came to know him, I realized that was not true. He was merely reading my thoughts, desires, and anxieties.

"Just call me Barnabus," he stated flatly as he softly peered at me through tender eyes. "My name means 'son of encouragement,' for that is what I do. My words motivate and amplify the spirit of man to greater heights. Learn from me, and you will find a unique way of viewing life that is a contradiction to how people look at their lives here. Through me may you find the wisdom, truth, and peace that your dreams have been desperately searching for."

I was quite astounded by what he just told me. I felt like he already knew me and my dreams. The words he used and how he used them were filled with a mysterious compassion, for I believed that it revealed his true nature. I immediately realized that this man was a rare breed, someone who could teach me above and beyond what I could learn at school.

"Where do you come from?" I asked.

He replied with a quick answer that displayed a certain degree of pride. "I live in a place that is so far away that it's probably beyond what your imagination could conceive."

I became anxious as we continued our quest, for my nerves had ignited insecurities that lived inside of me. It was tension of an extreme nature born from the reasons for what I was doing and why, which held me on the edge of emotion. I was facing a crossroads, and it was staring at me from a close proximity, but I didn't know it, for I couldn't see. At that time in my life, it really didn't matter because I just wanted to go to the fair.

My parents lived in the small village of Riversville, Ohio, just upstream from Marietta. Our neighborhood was on the northeastern part of town, which had been standing for more than fifty years. The homes in that section of town still looked good, although some of them showed signs of deterioration due to improper maintenance. I remember that the majority of the homes in Riversville were Cape Cod and Colonial style with a few variations, which many builders constructed throughout the country many years ago. Most of the houses were built on quarter or half-acre lots with two-car garages and various styles in landscaping, using shrubbery and gardens to beautify the appealing quality of the homes. Nothing much ever changed in Riversville. The Ohio River has always been there and probably always will be. The downtown area was small and consisted of a few insurance firms and doctor and law offices, along with banks, restaurants, stores, and factories. The nature of the town is peace and quiet, with the only attraction being the city park. It is located in the center of town, across the street from the town hall building, which is the tallest building in town, although it is only four floors high. A pond with a fountain is located in the center of the six-acre park, where, at lunchtime, people usually gather to feed the ducks.

Barnabus and I walked. It seemed to be a long and tedious walk, as the excitement of attending the fair had me captivated. I gradually became suspicious as to the true nature of our destination, for I had not heard that a fair was in town. I never saw any signs of advertisement either on a displayed poster board or in the local newspaper that I read almost every day. When we reached the city park, we sat down on one of the many benches to enjoy the mist from the fountain.

I became nervous when I noticed that Barnabus was curiously quiet. My thoughts continued to follow paranoia, as I wondered if he was really taking me to a fair. My mind was relentless in telling me all was not good as we got up off the bench and headed out of town. Finally, my curiosity could not be silenced anymore.

"I did not know there was a fair in town, for I did not see any advertisements that one was coming," I asked nervously.

When we got up to continue with our quest, Barnabus, who had been very quiet, did not reply immediately. He continued to walk like a man on a mission or a soldier marching off to battle. I could see the concentration in his eyes as I began to speculate if he even heard a word I said or if I was being ignored. Finally, he spoke up.

"The fair is located outside the city limits, deep in the woods. It is completely surrounded by trees in a beautiful clearing. The local media knows nothing of the event, and there was no advertisements displayed of any kind. Do not worry, my little friend, for word of mouth is the best promotional tool available. There will be many people at the fair, and a good time you will have."

Barnabus and I made our way through the downtown area as we headed toward the edge of town. I became temporarily satisfied with Barnabus's response. However, I became conscious of an eerie sensation inside of me. Ever since I left the house to follow Barnabus, my awareness to reality became slightly distorted, as if in a dream without actually dreaming. Turning directly west, we

walked past the warehouse and factory district, where a large percentage of Riversville's workforce is employed. Among the many
different factories and warehouses was where my father worked five
days a week, at Hopkins Plastics. When we passed the last brick
structure factory, a narrow path greeted us, lined with some ordinary
bushes and shrubs, decorated with pretty flowers growing alongside.
I followed Barnabus as he led me past some dried-up fields, until we
entered the domains of the forest. When our feet touched the dirt
path in the woods, I could hear the sounds of the fair coming from
an unknown source deep in the woods. I looked up at Barnabus with
joy and wonder in my eyes. It was the look that is only seen on the
face of a child when the truth far surpasses their expectations.

I became hypnotized by what I was feeling. All that was around
me, from the dirt path underneath my feet to the sunlight that was
filtered through the leaves of the trees, seemed to have come alive.
Ahead of us, I heard the fair, and with every step I took, the fair
became more real as the excitement within me erupted with an
urgent anticipation.

The trail led us to a place where I could hear the sounds of the
fair, as the mechanical thundering of the rollercoaster was vastly different than the musical rotations of the merry-go-round. I heard the
screams from the coaster riders as they sped up and down hills in a
minute version of euphoria. The sounds that rang in my head blended
together in unison. Several could have been identified individually,
although all of them had the origins of the same place. Barnabus
and I came to an exact point on the trail where we rounded a sharp
curve, and what lay beyond us was a long, gradual downhill slope. At
the bottom of the hill, I saw a clearing, and I believed the fair was
there. The trees arched their branches over the path, which gave the
illusion of walking through a tunnel. We passed through this corridor of natural design, as we were led to a destination that I thought
only existed in my dreams. The fair echoed through my ears, which
aroused adrenaline, causing my anxiety to practically explode. I had

been to several fairs and amusement parks over the last few years, but I knew in my heart that they were not like this one, for this particular fair felt like a dream even though I was not dreaming.

"There is something so familiar here," I said to Barnabus. "I feel like I've passed through these woods before."

Barnabus formed an ornery grin on his face, and through a weak laugh, he replied, "I can't even begin to count the numerous times in my life that I have felt like you do now, and however many times you try to analyze your situation, there is usually no explanation."

When we finally reached the gates of the fair, I stopped dead in my tracks, and my eyes opened wide with a childish fascination. Barnabus smiled, for in his heart, he felt my joy, which gave him much satisfaction.

"This fair is an original, Charles. When have you been to a fair or carnival that is in the middle of the woods, where you had to walk quite a distance just to get to its front gates? Have you ever been to a place like that?"

"Never," I said.

"Until now," Barnabus boldly replied.

With hope, but being timid in my heart, I walked through the front gates of the fair, which was a large arch made of stone that rose twenty feet over my head. I tried to look at everything around me, from the salesmen trying to sell their games of chance to all the wonderful rides. Most of them I had never seen before. The fair was crowded with people of all kinds—young and old, male and female, black, white, and Oriental—as they had come near and far to that remote place in the woods.

An explicit insight came alive and sprouted up in me as I passed through the gates of the fair. At first, this peculiar discernment did not carry the weight of consideration, but gradually, it grew, which eventually made me feel spiritually energetic. For years, I had merely existed without really living. I didn't have a purpose or any plans for the time when I became an adult, to give my life a focus or vision.

I suddenly realized that there was an objective planned for me, and somehow, I knew it was important. Never before had I encountered those feelings, as that presence in me was foreign, but at that moment, I knew I had a future and a hope. Using a clear and focused mind, I had to remind myself that I was not dreaming.

Walking around the fairgrounds, I looked at everything with wonder written upon my youthful face. I didn't want to play a game of chance yet, for I wanted to look, ponder, and observe all that was before me. Barnabus was watching every move I made while he walked at my side, trying to read what I felt. He knew that I was in a mystical world beyond my dreams, as I did not know where to go or what to expect. I wanted to experience it all, but I did not know where to start until my eyes fell upon the Ferris wheel.

"Wow!" I yelled very loudly. "Will you look at that Ferris wheel! It's the biggest one ever!"

Barnabus led me in the direction of the giant wheel as I continued to look at the many rides and exhibits. He had a smile on his face, happy to give me satisfaction, like a father would be of his son. Suddenly, he recognized a figure in the distance and immediately knew that his cargo had been delivered to the station. Without notice or reason and justification, Barnabus stopped while I continued to look onward. He turned around promptly, as he snuck away from me like a thief in the night, until he became a figure lost among the crowd of people. I didn't notice that he was gone initially, for I was captivated by what the fair had to offer. After a few minutes, I realized that I was alone.

I had the appearance of a lost little boy, when the impact of being abandoned sunk into my consciousness. I was searching for Barnabus in every direction as I walked hazardously through the crowd, until I bumped into something. The weak collision startled me, but I was not hurt. There before me stood an elderly black man with an old wooden cart packed full of all kinds of neatly decorated boxes. The gifts in his cart varied in size from very small to quite large. All of them were professionally wrapped, with fancy bows to coordinate with the multi-colored paper. The old man looked at me with curious eyes as a large smile that displayed his big, white teeth loomed upon his face. I was embarrassed by not paying attention to where I was walking, and I immediately apologized for running into him and his cart.

When he heard me speak, he realized that his package had been delivered. The old man who pushed his cart around the fairgrounds appeared to be elderly and somewhat frail, for he walked slowly. Appearances can be deceiving at times, for what the eyes see, another truth may be hidden in the mystical pathways that surrounded the fair. I did not know this to be true, for I looked upon him as old. He was not a large man, slightly shorter than most, but he did possess a slender and well-developed appearance. The assumption I had of his age was attributed to his bald head and the many wrinkles on his face. His big, brown eyes sparkled in the light of the day, and his smile made me feel comfortable in his presence. He looked at me, preoccupied by his thoughts, until a fragment of recall was triggered in his brain, like a distant memory from the past.

"Oh, you must be Charles!" he exclaimed with surprise.

I initially looked confused when I said with hesitation, "Yes, I am, but tell me, how do you know?"

His eyes seemed to penetrate deep within me. "Believe me, son. I've seen many things in my life. Some have been strange and unusual while others have been quite normal. Just trust me when I tell you that I know."

He was dressed very casually, wearing blue jeans and a gray T-shirt with an Oakland Raiders ball cap that caught my attention, for they were my favorite football team. I stood before him, exchanging glances, when my curiosity about his cart ignited questions in my mind. The stylish old cart probably at one time was used as a baby carriage. Renovation changed it for the proper use at the correct time, so it became what I saw before me. He had probably used it on many occasions throughout the years.

"So, what's in the cart?" I asked.

"Everything you ever wanted, any toy, book, or gift. Nothing is too large or small, for I have it. Just ask me for something."

I looked at his cart with many questions running in my mind while he smiled at me. I became distracted as the sounds of the fair whistled through my head and the weight of a decision pressed down upon me. I considered the fact that his cart was so small as I wondered how could it hold all that he claimed.

"All right, old man. Give me a remote-controlled, automatic toy jet that actually flies in the air. Don't give me one of those junky ones either," I requested, as I never thought that he would be able to find something that even closely resembled what I described in his cart.

He nodded to me and then turned his attention to the many boxes in his cart. My eyes got lost in sorting through all the activities at the fair. It was not the fair itself but the people in attendance that I noticed were out of the ordinary.

"Here you go, son. I believe this is what you asked for," he said as he gently handed me a box wrapped in maroon-and-gold paper.

I accepted the box with a bewildered look on my face, as if I was lost. When I finally realized the significance of what was happening, instead of thinking about the strange people at the fair, I was amazed with the reality of what I held in my hands.

"Wow! How did you do that?" I yelled out, surprised.

When I was asked what I wanted, I had just made up something out of my imagination. However, I did remember reading an article in a magazine that described in detail about the new and exciting toys of the future. I vaguely recalled that the article mentioned a remote-controlled jet toy that flew in the air. I had never seen one in a store, but in Riversville, the latest designs and technical advances were not very common, especially in the year 1970. I realized that this fair was quite peculiar to the effect of being seemingly unusual and that the man could be the key to the entire event. I accepted the gift with mild apprehension, trying to believe and convince myself that I was not dreaming.

The old man stood in front of me with a joyous smile.

"Go, my boy. Enjoy the gift I give to you, and have some fun."

When I heard his voice, I remembered the depression that greeted me to start the day. I left the demoralized mood that was stalking me earlier as I shook it off in my wake. We were in the midst of a crowd, and I needed room to test my new toy. Approximately fifty yards away, I could see a vacant clearing with a few picnic tables that were not in use. The old man followed me over to the unoccupied picnic area, where I started to play with my new toy, which gave him a delightful sense of satisfaction. He knew through knowledge and experience that giving was better than receiving, especially when it is into the hands of a child. Our eyes connected briefly as I constructed the small platform for my jet, and I felt an uncomfortable perception that he was trying to read into the depths of my heart.

The toy jet was set for launch. My eyes became fixed upon the airborne object when it took flight. Being a novice pilot, it took me a few moments to seize control over what had started as a very erratic orbit. I watched it fly when the realization dawned upon me that the design of the jet was similar to models used on some science fiction television shows. It flew around continuously, circling over many people's heads, and that was when I once again noticed the mysterious presence upon the people. Absent was their recognition of a toy jet flying overhead. I guided the jet to be in tune with the wind, where I almost hit someone. Again, there was no response from anyone. Confused, I turned my attention to the jet toy.

"How high can I make it fly?" I shouted. "Hey, mister, where did you get this thing? I've never seen anything like it before in my life. It's really cool," I said as I directed the toy jet around in a circle. When I accepted the positive results of the test flight, I gently maneuvered the skyward vehicle to land on the ground.

Chapter 3

Sincere admiration and appreciation flowed like a river through my consciousness as I faced the old man. In a place where emotions come alive, I was having a difficult time understanding why I couldn't feel that way about my parents.

I felt close to him, as if I knew him, just like I did with Barnabus.

We introduced ourselves to each other, and I learned that his name was Scatman. He appeared to be quite old, for he walked slowly, but still managed to get around quite well. I did not care how old Scatman was, for it was insignificant because he had become my friend.

Scatman Frost was a merchant of toys, books, and novelty items that could only be found in dreams. What he saw in me appeared as an obscure image of himself many years before. He remembered a time that transported him to a specific memory, when he was a little boy. His parents were not there for him, as his father left the family when he was six years old. His mother had difficulty managing the trials of separation. She ran away from the dilemma that confronted her, and as the years slipped by, she ran away only to find refuge in the warm solitude of a Wild Turkey bottle. She became an alcoholic, as the effects of the drink caused her to treat her children at times with cruelty and resentment. It depended upon how much his mother drank and the condition of her intoxicated self worth what person she brought forward on that day.

I put my new toy away in its box, and as I did, I noticed that Scatman was smiling at me.

"Well, how do you like it?" he asked, knowing that I approved beyond the measure of words.

"Like it? I love it!" I exclaimed favorably. "Thank you very much," I said with appreciation.

Scatman was glad that I liked my gift, and he wanted to continue giving to me for reasons that were unknown to me at the time.

"I know you haven't been at the fair long, so how would you like to go on some rides?" asked Scatman with a distinctly bizarre hint of a smile that seemed to change the attitude of his face.

"I would love to, but aren't you too old for that sort of thing?" I timidly asked.

As Scatman briefly looked upon my youthful face, an ambiguous expression formed on his, and as he continued to look at me, he became aware that I did not realize the nature of the situation that I was getting myself involved in.

"My body might have seen many years, but my heart is still young and beating strong. I'm sure that I can contain my composure during a few of these rides. I assure you of that. Before we ride, I must secure my cart behind one of those game sheds. If you would like, you can put your toy in my cart for safekeeping."

I gave Scatman my toy, and then we walked together to a place where he secured his cart. He told me to wait while he went in between a few of the game sheds. After a few short minutes, Scatman's figure came slowly out of the misty shadows.

"Shall we ride?" he asked with a juvenile excitement.

"Let's go!" I yelled with an agreed upon enthusiasm.

We casually walked around the fairgrounds to begin with, just like Barnabus and I had done. I looked with a speculative curiosity at all the activities and especially the people who were in attendance. My suspicions revealed to me that they were different, but I still couldn't figure out how or why. Scatman looked at me and wondered what it was that occupied my thoughts. I knew what ride it was that I wanted to ride. I had been hearing and feeling its vibrations, but until that moment, I had not laid my eyes upon the object of my desire.

"There!" I yelled, as I pointed in the direction of the rollercoaster. "I want to go on to the coaster!"

"Any ride you wish, my boy," said Scatman, desiring to grant my wish.

The entrance to the rollercoaster was a short walk, as Scatman followed me closely, where we took our places at the end of the line. I was both excited and slightly uneasy about riding the coaster. Scatman looked into my eyes, and knew what I was feeling, for it was the same thing that he felt when he rode a rollercoaster for the first time many years before at Myers Lake Park in Canton, Ohio. The nervous anticipation brewed up inside of me, and after a short wait, it was our turn to ride. We got securely strapped into our seats, and in a moment that seemed to last forever, the coaster train finally started to move as it entered a dark tunnel. Gradually, it accelerated and went around a sharp curve until the entire train jerked. The coaster track led us on a slow trek up a steep hill while it remained inside the confines of the tunnel.

I looked over at Scatman with an obvious panic-stricken face. The coaster continued to inch its way toward the top of the incline when I noticed that the light at the end of the tunnel was growing larger before my eyes. Fresh air and bright sunlight greeted us when we reached the top of the hill, with a view overlooking miles of countryside. I did not have much time to admire what my eyes were seeing when the coaster train began its powerful run down an extremely steep hill. The bottom of the abrupt slope came upon us in an instant, when we raced up and down several other large hills. I was quiet for the duration of the ride, as I just tried to hold onto the bar in front of me. I could hear Scatman laughing wildly while the mad wind screamed past our faces. The coaster ran with a mighty force over some smaller hills and around a few sharp curves until, at last, we reached the end of our three-minute journey.

"That was a great ride!" I cried out when the train came to a stop.

I stepped out of the coaster and walked down the exit ramp with Scatman following close behind me, in search of our next ride. "A Laugh in the Dark," was the name of the ride I chose to go on next. A short walk took Scatman and me to a line where we patiently waited for our turn to ride. On the other side of the tracks from where the passengers got onto the ride, I saw a life-sized mechanical mannequin that stood upon a small platform. Its head and arms moved in a gesture of extreme laughter. Out from behind him came a laugh that was quite creepy, which set the stage for the ride. The mannequin was dressed in an old, brown plaid suit; yellow shirt; black tie; tan trousers; and faded, dark shoes, which made him look like an old hobo. Upon his head, he wore an old fedora hat, which immediately reminded me of Barnabus. I wondered what had become of my mysterious morning visitor as I stood looking at the laughing dummy.

Our chance to ride came quickly, after a brief wait. The ride was a short jaunt of twists and turns with many florescent monsters, ghosts of many shapes and sizes, and dressed-up plastic dummies that seemed to have come alive just enough to startle and scare me. I enjoyed every second of the ride, and I believe Scatman did too. Even though he seemed old to me at the time, Scatman still possessed a child's heart.

The merry-go-round was the next ride of choice, which is always a pleasant but calm venture. I rode on top of a blue kangaroo while Scatman sat himself upon a yellow pony. An instrumental version of the song "Somewhere over the Rainbow" played over the loudspeaker on the carousel as we began to go round and round. I was reminded of the movie *The Wizard of Oz* and when it was that I first saw the film. It was a memory from a few years past, during one of my visits to my Aunt Rose's house in Cambridge, Ohio. I used to visit her for a couple of weeks during the summer. She was my favorite relative, as a deep loving feeling came upon me when I thought about those things. I loved her very much, and I only wished that my own mother was more like her.

When we got off the merry-go-round, Scatman suggested that we go on the Ferris wheel, and I quickly agreed. As we began our walk over toward the large wheel, I mentioned to him that it was the biggest one I had ever seen. We rode upon the rotating wheel, and when it stopped on the top, I looked out across the vast land that seemed to reach to the dawn of tomorrow. I saw the woodlands, the little town of Riversville, and the Ohio River. Finally, Scatman and I arrived at the bottom of the wheel, and the ride attendant assisted us out of our caged compartment.

"How would you like to try your luck at a game of chance? I'll buy!"

I accepted his offer with gratitude, as we found our way to the gallery of games. There were several rows of various games to choose from: the basketball foul shot game, coin in a bottle toss, the birthday game, among many others. All of the game salesmen had their own unique pitch that they thought would entice you into giving their game a try. At the end of the last row, I finally saw a game I thought I might have a chance to win. A fat man stood in front of a board lined with rows of inflated balloons.

"Break three balloons and win a prize!" exclaimed the fat man with a commanding voice.

He was large, slightly over six feet tall, and weighed approximately three hundred pounds. His wavy, short brown hair profiled his face, but the manner of his speech did not reflect what I saw in his eyes, for I believed he was like an actor in a play.

I stepped up with confidence to the line, which was painted on the ground just in front of me. Scatman paid the man the money, and I was handed the three darts. With the darts in my hand, I carefully aimed and tossed the three darts, one after the other, each with the same result. *Pop! Pop! Pop!* was the sound that we heard when I threw the darts. Of the three darts thrown, three balloons were broken.

"A winner!" shouted the fat man. "Your choice, my son," he said, ready and anxious to give me anything my heart desired that was displayed with all the other prizes.

I studied the many rows of prizes lined up on the walls of the game shed for a moment or two as I tried to decide what I wanted. There were posters; decaled mirrors; and stuffed animals of all shapes, sizes, and colors. My eyes were suddenly drawn to a small shelf in the back corner of the shed with the object of my desire sitting on it. Sitting on a platform, encased in a small plastic dome, was a baseball autographed by the World Series Champions, the New York Mets.

"I want the World Series baseball!" I yelled to the man impatiently.

He smiled at me, thinking that I was a big sports fan. When he handed me my prize, I thanked him with much appreciation, and as I turned to Scatman, I had a look of unparalleled amazement.

"Wow! Will you look at this baseball? It's signed by the World Series Champions, the New York Mets! One day, this baseball could be worth a lot of money," I said in the passion of excitement.

"It's very nice, Charles. Make sure you take care of it," said Scatman. "Now, how about something to drink?"

"I'm thirsty," I said in agreement.

A short walk through the fairgrounds led us to a crowded concession stand. I ordered a root beer float while Scatman got a pink lemonade. We took our refreshments to a nearby picnic table, where we sat down to relax and talk. We began talking of common things, from sports to history with many subjects in between. Little did I know that Scatman was leading the conversation in a specific direction. He told me about his life, how difficult it was, and how, on many occasions, he felt extremely miserable and wanted to quit, but he also told me how he survived.

"No matter how difficult life might appear to be, there is always a path of deliverance away from the horrible circumstances in your life. You have to be able to find that place of peace in the midst of your storm," Scatman told me as I looked up at him with a sincere admiration for the wisdom that he possessed.

"How old are you, Scatman?"

"I lost count of the years many moons ago, as I try to keep a healthy body and mind. However, if the light in the sky fails to shine through my eyes one day, I will know that I lived a good life. Yes, I must admit there were years of hardship and despair, but I overcame them, and later, I pursued a life that had a purpose that made me happy beyond my utmost expectations. I believe that the main ingredient that gave me peace and joy was helping people. My words of encouragement that I gave to many people became a focus in my life when I saw their hearts come to accept the word of truth. It gave me satisfaction to see someone's life changed who had been in misery and torment just by speaking a few words of what I perceived as truth."

"How do you get set free from a bad situation?" I asked with a sense of desperation.

Scatman looked at me with a disturbing appearance, and as he continued to gaze upon my outward image, he was, in fact, exploring the inner confines of my being. Before he answered my question, he probed my mind with questions of his own.

"Charles, you're not happy with your life at home, are you?" he asked, having been revealed the answer before I uttered a word.

"At home there is no peace, for my parents fight most of the time, and ignore me unless they need me to do some housework for them. I feel like I am raising myself, for if I have a problem, or try to seek advice from them, they always seem to be too busy."

Scatman continued to question me as his curiosity grew. His next question put some light into my eyes and made my heart skip a beat.

"Charles," he asked with hesitation, "how would you like to be happy with who you are and the freedom to seek after the desires of your heart?"

"Why, yes. Wouldn't everyone?" I quickly replied, knowing that his questions were leading to a climax with an ultimate purpose.

Scatman explored my heart through my eyes in a flash of a moment, until he looked away into the spell of the horizons. He became consumed by what he was seeing, until he began to speak. "Beyond the sky, even beyond your own mind, there is a place where complete happiness and contentment can be found."

"Where is this place?" I curiously queried with skepticism.

Scatman looked into my eyes, knowing that I did not believe. He turned partially away from me and focused his attention on a mystical sight that he caught a glimpse of but was hidden from my eyes. He began to speak like he was telling an ancient, mysterious secret that had been concealed from men's hearts for many decades. The manner of his speech changed in tone and inclination because the importance of what he was saying.

"Go across the fields of the countryside, to a place where eternal fog lies and the Earth buckles into a deep crater. Inside the crater, you will find a cave, and in its deepest corner lies the *Mirror of Freedom.*"

I stared at Scatman, who still had his focus skyward. His eyes had a mysterious fascination, and in them, I saw a genuine appearance of contentment. It was the impression of tranquility displayed in his nature that caused me to become slightly envious, for through Scatman, I saw and felt freedom. It was the independence to become that person who was buried deep within me. I wanted to escape from the life that I lived with my parents, and somewhere, I had to find the determination in me to break free.

"Go, my boy. Think about the gift I offer you, for in a day's time, if you believe in what I have told you are true, return to this place. If you should come back tomorrow, the chance to be happy and free will be yours to take. Before you leave, let me get your toy."

When Scatman walked away, I remained at the table as I watched my unusual friend slowly make his way through the crowd of people. Into a dark alley he slowly turned, only to emerge a short time later, pushing his old wooden cart. Many thoughts raced through my mind as he slowly walked toward me. I must admit that I was confused by what Scatman told me.

"The Mirror of Freedom," I said aloud to myself, realizing that it sounded like something from an old myth or fable.

I knew I had a decision to make, but I needed time to think, and that was what Scatman told me to do. It would be difficult to make a choice trying to use my limited knowledge upon a subject matter that I did not comprehend. The images that I had seen on this day seemed almost unreal. Only in the chambers of my heart deep within me did I truly believe.

Scatman walked up beside me and handed me my jet toy. "All you need is time to think, for I believe your decision is in destiny's hands. There is a master plan for all of us, and it is our job to find out what that plan is. We have a map that we should follow in this life. Sometimes we take a wrong turn, but eventually, we end up where we are destined to be. So, Charles, use your time wisely and meditate on the things that I have told you about, for the answer you seek lies within you."

With those words of wisdom, Scatman walked away and was quickly swallowed up by the many people who were walking around the fairgrounds. I remained at the table for a moment in time while I thought about the lessons that were revealed to me at this fair. I got up after a few minutes and put my autographed baseball with the toy jet into the box and began to walk in the direction of the fair's gates. I slowly made my way through the crowd, knowing what my destination would be: the town of Riversville. My thoughts were occupied with the peculiar experience of that day, and as they were, I looked once more at the people at the fair as I made my way closer and closer to the exit.

"Why do most of the people here look so empty and strange, like they were drawn by an artist's pencil?" I asked aloud, almost afraid that someone might hear me.

I knew from looking at many books in the library that an artist can capture many great images on paper, but they cannot bring to life what is written in a person's heart. With those thoughts lingering around in my head, I slowly left the fair and entered the domains of the woodlands.

A chill came upon me as my feet touched the soft dirt path that led me into the forest. An unusual sense of quiet was present in the woods that flowed like a wave of silent vibration, which was only felt but could not be seen or heard. When I was on that path before, on my way to the fair, the woodlands were full of life, with much activity by the creatures that made the forest their home. I felt many eyes on me as I moved down the trail with a nervous but steady motion.

The mysterious silence remained steady, until a large deer jumped out from the brush about fifty yards in front of me and stopped in the middle of the path. It was a mature male deer with big antlers, which revealed his age. Strength and grace were traits apparent in him as he turned his head to look at me while I walked up the trail toward him. I slowed down but did not stop as I became very apprehensive as to the reason behind the deer's motives. He quickly and gracefully jumped and ran into the thick of the woods when I started to approach him. Shortly after the deer ran off, I noticed two small squirrels running along next to me. I looked up into the trees that hung over my head only to find that a group of birds of different species were following me from the elevation among the highest braches in the lofty trees. I stopped, feeling uncomfortable from the events that were transpiring around me. Sensing something behind me, I turned around and saw two raccoons following me at a distance of thirty yards. I believed then, as I do now, that those animals were escorting me safely to the boundaries of their home. As I listened to the birds sing, I wished that I could understand their language of song. Finally, when I reached the end of the trail, I noticed that my animal friends were no longer with me. I stopped and quickly turned around, and I saw that all the animals that I had encountered were gathered together by a cluster of pine trees. The raccoons, squirrels, birds, and deer stood and watched as I walked away, waiting for me to turn with an indication of farewell.

"So long, my friends! I shall return!" I yelled back to them as I waved good-bye.

I knew that they did not understand my words, but they might have had slight comprehension of my gesture. I turned my back on them and then faced the approaching sight in front of me: the town of Riversville.

Chapter 4

The Unity Methodist Church bell tower rang twice as I approached the center of town, which told me what time it was. Upon entering the town, I now felt my normal self once again, which I thought was a bit strange. Did I just dream of the fair with my friends Barnabus and Scatman, or was it real? I believed it was not a dream, for I had the evidence that I carried in my arms. It was, however, a unique experience, one that I must return to. As I looked upon the town and the activities that were transpiring, the hunger pangs that came alive within me began to occupy my thoughts. I had hardly eaten anything, with the exception of my small breakfast and the root beer float at the fair. My desire was not to return home just yet. I knew that eventually, I would have to, but I decided to prolong my return for just a little while longer. I reached into my back trouser pocket and pulled out a five-dollar bill. I looked at it and realized that the money I held in my hand was just enough for something to eat. I walked slowly through the small downtown area, which would eventually lead me home. I suddenly stopped just past the front of the Mirage Coffee Shop, and as I did, I glanced through the window out of the corner of my eye. Making a quick decision, I turned around as I decided to have some lunch there.

The Mirage Coffee Shop was established in 1951. It possesses an old-fashioned theme, with many old booths, tables, and chairs. Scattered along the cedar paneled walls of the dining area were photographs of Riversville from many years before, along with a few select framed prints of some Norman Rockwell paintings. There were ten booths and ten tables that each sat four people, along with a wooden bar counter that also had ten seats. The Mirage was a popular lunchtime eatery for many bankers, lawyers, doctors, factory workers, teachers, and secretaries. Their specialty was the Ohio burger, which was their version of McDonald's Big Mac. Ice cream and coffee were also very popular, as they featured twenty different flavors.

I casually entered the eatery, approached the bar counter, and sat down on one of the swivel stools. Carefully placing my box with my souvenirs in the empty seat next to me, I nervously looked around and noticed the limited activity in the diner. During late afternoon hours, there was not much business, especially on a Saturday. Shortly after sitting down, one of the servers, whose name was Susan, approached me.

"Welcome to the Mirage! May I help you?" she politely asked.

"I would like to see a menu please," I said.

Susan reached under the bar counter and placed a menu in front of me while she inquisitively observed my actions.

"I'll give you a few minutes to look over the menu before taking your order," she said with a smile.

I read the menu from top to bottom, front page and back. The Mirage Coffee Shop features a wide variety of food, from chicken and burgers to fried fish and strip steak, with many other items in between to choose from. I took my time looking at the menu until, finally, I decided what I wanted to eat. Susan, who had been watching me occasionally, came over to me when she saw me set down my menu.

"So what have you decided to eat?" she asked.

"I would like the Little Ohio burger with a banana milkshake made with chocolate ice cream. Could you make sure the shake is on the thin side? I don't like them when they are too thick. You can barely drink them through a straw."

Susan looked at me as I spoke and, with a sweet smile, promised that my order would be made just the way I liked it. "Your order will be out shortly," she told me as she took the menu from my hands and placed it under the countertop where they were kept. She walked away and pulled out her order pad from the pocket on her apron and wrote down my order, ripped it out of the pad, and placed it on the order wheel.

"Order in!" she yelled, as she rang a bell that sat on the far right side of the service window.

In the distance, from inside the kitchen, a male voice replied, "Be right there, sweets!"

I took my attention off of Susan as my thoughts began to visualize my two friends, Barnabus and Scatman. Fear suddenly took hold of me and whispered into my ear that I imagined everything I thought was real. I remembered the jet airplane and the baseball that I had won, which I had brought with me. I looked over at the stool next to me, and sure enough, the box I had put them into was right next to me. I needed to see them, for my mind was creating false scenarios in my head. I took the lid partially off the box and peeked inside, and that was when I once again saw the airplane and baseball. It was a reassuring fact that I did not dream about my new friends and all that had happened to me at the fair.

"I really was at the fair, and the two souvenirs next to me are evidence to keep my dream alive," I said in a soft and refrained whisper, not wanting anyone to hear me.

"The Mirror of Freedom was what he called it, but I really wondered what he was talking about. He described it in a way that made me imagine that it was something not of this world. This day has been very unusual, but I knew in my heart that I was there, no matter what thoughts entered my mind," I slowly muttered to myself, trying to give encouragement to my conscious mind.

"Here's your food," said Susan as she placed my burger and milkshake in front of me.

I thanked her quietly, although I was not sure if she heard me.

I did not realize how hungry I was, for I ate my burger and drank my milkshake very quickly, along with a generous helping of coleslaw and potato chips. Susan was watching me eat my meal from a distance, and when I finished my last bite, she came up to me.

"It appears that you were hungry," said Susan.

"Very," I replied after I swallowed my last bite of food.

"Have you been enjoying the hot August sun today?" she asked.

"Yes, I have, and it has been a very strange day," I told her with a mystical wonder in my eyes that seemed to brighten my entire face.

I proceeded to tell her the story of my day, how Barnabus came to my door and how I met Scatman. I described to her in detail what I saw and felt at the fair and the manner in which the people acted, how they walked and talked. I concluded my story by telling her the strange occurrence in the woodlands, how those creatures escorted me to the boundaries of their home.

Susan was a very good listener and remained quiet for a few brief moments after I had finished telling my story. She seemed to be interested in what I was telling her. The manner in which I told my story gave her the impression that I was telling the truth or that I had confidence of what I might have conceptually imagined. Either way, Susan believed that I had the faith of my convictions.

"Your story is quite fascinating. Are you sure that you didn't fall asleep in the woods and dream everything that you have just told me?"

"No!" I yelled as I rose up off the barstool. "I was there, and I know that it was real!"

Many eyes became focused upon Susan and I, as curious minds wanted to know the meaning behind my yelling.

"All right, all right," she said firmly, trying to calm me down. Susan quickly gave me my check with my sudden outburst of anger and emotion.

I slowly sat down, glanced at what I owed, and gave her five dollars, which was enough money to cover the bill. She took the money to the register and rang up my check. I quickly got up, grabbed my box, and walked out of the restaurant without my change, being too embarrassed from my actions to look into her eyes.

I started to walk back to the house I had lived in all these years, after satisfying my need for food. Passing the many shops in the downtown area, I noticed that most of them seemed to be quite busy. A sidewalk sale was on First Avenue, which was the main street in town, where most of the stores were located. Many people were busy browsing through sale items in the few antique and novelty stores as well as Bailey Boys' Furniture and All-American Pro Sports. I saw the movie theater across the street as a young man was changing the sign advertizing the new movie to be shown. I slowly walked out of the downtown area and began to feel nervous about going home. I did not want the fun-filled day to end. I thought of Scatman and everything he had told me.

Who is he? I asked myself. *What are his reasons for giving me these gifts? He gave me a unique toy plane that flies in the air and offered me the chance to be happy and free. What does it all mean?*

Many questions seemed to linger around in my consciousness, which had captured my mind and put it into confinement. The idea that such a thing as the Mirror of Freedom could exist created a fear in me because it did not hold true to the natural laws of this world. The Mirror reminded me of the many fairy tales I had read in school, but the manner in which Scatman talked about it made me believe the possibility existed that it was real. Concentration became difficult, for the confusion clouded my reasoning capabilities and caused them to bounce from reality to fantasy in rapid succession.

I took my time getting home, for I hated my life at home so very much. I didn't dislike my parents, I guess I did love them, but I disliked the manner in which they treated me. I was their object of their frustrations most of the time. Just because their life did not turn out the way they had desired, they took it out on me. I felt so very alone, with no friendly face to greet me when I walked through the door. My parents were trying to suppress the passion that lay in my heart, which motivated me to become the person I longed to be. I had dreams, and those images were planted for a reason: to create and motivate the ability to accomplish those desires. Most people do not have the patience to chase a dream to its ultimate conclusion. I had a relentless longing to follow my dream, and if failure came knocking at my door, at least I would have the satisfaction to say I had tried. My parents never encouraged me, and usually, I was ignored, for the only time my presence was acknowledged was in the form of humiliation.

I finally came to the doorstep of the place that I called home. When I walked inside, I placed the box with my toy jet plane and the souvenir baseball on the kitchen counter. A strange silence loomed a stressful wave in the house, and when I entered the living room, I found my mother and father both reading the newspaper. I had a unique insight that led me to believe that my parents had just concluded with a heated argument. At first when I entered the room, they did not even acknowledge my presence. After a few moments, they put down their papers, and saw me standing before them.

"Hi Son," my father said, as he returned to his reading.

"Did you have a nice day?" my mother asked and, just like my father, went back to the newspaper. It almost seemed that they did not care, as if my presence here in their life was not the most important thing. My mother was a tall woman, just under six feet, and slightly overweight for her height.

She grew up dreaming of becoming an actress, going to New York City to pursue a career on the stage, but her dream never materialized. The fact that she never went to New York City wasn't because of her looks, talent, or dedication, but her life took a turn when she fell in love with my dad. It was her senior year at Riversville High School, when she was a cheerleader and my dad was the captain of the track and wrestling teams. One month after graduation, when she had plans to attend Columbia University in New York City to study theater, she discovered that she was pregnant. My parents got married at Unity Methodist Church in downtown Riversville, shortly after they decided to do the honorable thing. The pregnancy did not go full term, as my mom lost the baby in the fifth month, due to unforeseen complications. It was exactly three weeks after their wedding day when my parents lost their baby.

A few days later, Dave and Sharon privately committed their love to each other and pledged to remain married despite their great loss. My mom soon found employment at Ernie's Bar and Grill, located on River Road, which had a picturesque view of the Ohio River. She took the job to fill her empty days, to try to forget what she just lost. She was a waitress there, and even though she did not like the work very much, the money she received from tips was better than other places she could find employment at. Two years later, my mom got hired as a receptionist with her childhood doctor, Dr. Joseph, MD. Beginning with the first day on the job, her dedication was evident, and she has worked there since.

One year later, I was born. Shortly after my birth, my parents began to drift away from each other emotionally, as if two strangers were living in the same house. Affection between them became a rare occurrence, but constant arguments were not. Hateful words were spoken, but divorce never surfaced the arena of loud, harsh words. My mom gained thirty pounds and didn't seem to care.

My parents, at that time, did not share a close, personal relationship. The absence of unity within the family caused them to feel empty and frustrated as they spoke with hostility to each other and treated me with cruelty. I had to live with the stress that they had created day after day. They were not model parents, as love, understanding, and compassion was not present in the home. I stayed away a lot, whenever the opportunity presented itself to me. I was very lonely at a time when I should have had the love and support from my parents to encourage security in my life. They were not there for me, as they were too busy making money.

Silence filled the room, until I realized that I was bothering them, so I grabbed my box with my souvenirs, and went down to my room for the solitude of my own space. I almost started to cry, for I knew my parents would not change. I guess part of me had hoped that they would at least be concerned where I had been. I also was hurt that they did not notice how clean the house was; which Barnabus had a hand in accomplishing. I kept the truth about the fair to myself, knowing they probably would not believe what I experienced today. I believed that soon I would be away from my life that had been filled with pain and sorrow, for in my mind I knew I had to return to the fair.

Chapter 5

When I walked into my room, the memories of the day overshadowed the pain that I felt, and offered me hope. I stretched out on my bed, feeling slightly confused as I began to ponder about my two new friends.

I thought to myself, *Is it possible that an element of destiny is present in everything that has happened? A great force from beyond my imagination might be calling my name. I want to believe in the Mirror completely, for if I do, I might find that place of peace that I have been searching for. The reasons have become clear: the Mirror will be my guardian now.*

I stared at the ceiling in an oblivious state for quite some time as my mind became lost in time and space. I picked up a comic book from my collection that sat on an old pine end table next to my bed and began to read. I realized after several pages of laboriously trying to comprehend the words in front of me that I was indeed tired. I lay my head on my pillow, and within minutes, I fell off the sphere of the conscious into a place that wasn't a dream but where the mind and body could rest and get revived for the remainder of the day.

My mother's voice woke me up as I was called to dinner. I quickly got out of bed, and as I did, it felt like I was walking through a cloud. It was just a temporary sensation, for as I continued to move, I became increasingly aware of my senses. As I climbed the stairs from the basement, I seemed to be vexed with a nervousness that altered my rational thinking ability. It was a brief and agitated temperament that caused me to be blind due to the hostility that I held toward my parents.

I took my usual seat at the dinner table, and I noticed in the living room, I could hear the Cincinnati Reds baseball game being broadcast on the stereo radio. When I started to eat, I found myself in a disquieted mood, remembering the many times in the past when I was ignored by my parents.

It was a delicious meal that was set before us, featuring strip steak, barbeque style, served with oven-roasted potatoes and green bean amandine. My mother was a very good cook, for she learned from her mother and grandmother the importance of mastering the art of cooking. My great aunt Norma, who lived in Mobile, Alabama, told my mom years before she married my dad that the best way to please your husband and family was through culinary expertise.

Without my mother and I expecting it, my dad yelled out, "Way to go, Johnny!"

That sudden celebration came after the broadcaster reported that Johnny Bench had hit a grand slam home run. My dad was a dedicated Cincinnati Reds fan, and his favorite player was Johnny Bench.

"I think the Reds have a good chance of going to the World Series this year," he told my mom and me.

My dad was an avid sports fan and was a superb athlete in high school. Just like my mom, he had plans to go to college, except my dad had an athletic scholarship. As with my mother, my dad did not go to college and held a small measure of resentment in his heart from that day on. After my parents had gotten married, my dad went to work for the Hopkins Plastics Corporation as a general laborer and worked his way up through the company to become plant manager. It took him ten years, through hard work, the right words to the most influential people, to achieve success in climbing the Hopkins Plastics corporate ladder. He was a stern man at work, but on the inside, he was very sensitive. The caring and passionate part of him was hardly seen or heard; just the harsh, pragmatic plant supervisor was apparent. When he was at home, he wasn't much different, for most of the time, he managed his family like he was still at work. He was a handsome man, tall and thin with blue eyes and dark hair. At the factory, there were several women who found him quite attractive, but my dad was dedicated to his wife and son.

"May I be excused?" I asked.

"Don't you want some dessert? I made some chocolate pudding," offered my mother.

Her desserts were always delicious, and I was tempted, but I was still harboring a sour disposition, and didn't want anything more to eat.

"No thank you," I said.

"I want some," my father declared.

"Yes, Charles, you may be excused," said my mother.

I went into the family room, turned on the television, and changed the channels several times before I decided to watch the baseball game. I enjoyed watching sports of all kinds; I only wished that I was a better athlete. I often fantasized of being a professional athlete skillfully and gracefully playing my sport while thousands of screaming fans passionately watched. I became lost in my thoughts until I heard the doorbell ring and noticed my mother walking toward the door to answer the bell.

"Hi, boys!" I heard my mother's voice exclaim with surprise.

"Yes, he is here," my mother said, followed by her distinctive call. "Charles, you have company!"

At the door stood Joe Montgomery and Clyde Davies, my so-called friends who only came over to visit when they had nothing better to do.

"Hey Charles. What's up?" asked Clyde when I came into view.

My mom left to finish her dessert with my dad and to give me some privacy to speak freely with my friends. She vaguely remembered her youth and how she did not want her parents to involve themselves in her social activities.

"Nothin' much," I replied. "Just watching the baseball game."

"We stopped by earlier, but you weren't around. Where did you go?" asked Clyde.

He knew I had lived a lonely life and did not have many friends.

"I went to a fair today on the edge of town. It was really different," I reluctantly told Clyde and Joe.

"Oh yeah? Is it still goin' on?" asked Joe.

I was quiet for a short moment as suspicions formed in my mind that my friends seemed to be hinting around at something. They wanted to see this fair with their own eyes, to find out if it was real or was it a fabrication of my imagination.

"I think so, but I can't be too sure," I told them. "I got this really cool jet toy airplane at the fair. Let me run downstairs and get it so that I can show you guys. I'll be right back."

When I left my friends standing in the foyer to retrieve the toy jet airplane, my mother approached them.

"So, have you boys been enjoying your summer?" she asked with a smile.

"Yes, ma'am," said Joe. "I've been swimming and playing baseball a lot, and my parents took my sister and me on a vacation to Cape Cod, which was a lot of fun."

My mom had always liked Joe. He was her favorite of my friends, for he was always polite and his family was respected in town, which was important to my mother. Joe was a handsome boy, with light brown hair and a husky build for his age. His oldest brother received a football and baseball scholarship to play at Ohio State. Joe had aspirations to follow in his brother's footsteps. He was the son my mother never had, and over the years, she had made several references with cruel undertones since Joe and I had been friends.

"Why can't you be more like your friend Joe?"

Clyde Davies was completely different than Joe. Everyone who knew them often wondered why Joe associated with Clyde. For reasons unknown, Clyde and Joe had been close friends for many years.

Clyde had been labeled a troublemaker, as he talked behind people's backs and started arguments between good friends, as he thought it was funny to see good buddies fight among themselves. In spite of Clyde's many personality flaws, Clyde and Joe always seemed to have a good time together.

Clyde was tall and thin, with short, dark hair and brown eyes. His nose was slightly crooked, which was the focal point on his face. He was very insecure about the way he looked, and he tried to overcome his facial imperfection with the gift of gab. He was a talker, and he learned very early in life how to manipulate people to suit his needs.

I returned with my new toy, set it down on the floor in the living room, and carefully removed the lid. The toy airplane was unique, for its design looked futuristic, made of an unusual type of plastic. It was approximately eighteen inches long and six inches tall, as it imitated the Klingon spaceships from the Star Trek television show. The jet plane was black in color that sparkled with a glow that seemed to illuminate the area all around it. I felt a life force that came from its interior, and for a moment, fear gripped me. I knew the toy that I received from Scatman was special, one that could not be found in stores.

"Wow! That's really cool. Did you say you got this toy at the fair?" asked Joe, desiring one for himself.

"Yes, I did. I got it from an old black man who was very nice to me. Do you guys want to go outside and watch it fly?"

"It flies?" questioned Clyde, quite surprised.

"Of course it does. What, did you think that it was just a model?" I asked with a distinct amount of pride in my voice.

I took my two friends outside to the backyard to show them the marvels of my new toy. My parents' house stood on a half-acre lot surrounded by bushes and pine trees. Behind the two-car garage was a small basketball court, where I spent many hours practicing shooting hoops.

I set the toy upon the small plastic platform that came with it, and then I sat in the middle of the backyard. I slowly backed away from it with my remote in my hand as I prepared for liftoff. I pushed the green button on the remote, and immediately, the miniature jet came to life and it started to rise. It continued to ascend skyward until I pushed the blue button. I carefully controlled the toy's flight as it flew around and above us, following a circular path with a soft buzzing sound. Clyde and Joe watched the small jet with fascination and could not lift their eyes from the flying object.

"Can I try?" asked Clyde.

"Sure," I said as I handed Clyde the remote and showed him how to operate it.

When Clyde took control of the toy's flight, its path became erratic, but very quickly, he learned how to fly. He directed the small jet as it soared above us, just like I taught him.

"This is so cool!" Clyde exclaimed loudly, as he started to laugh, enjoying his moment of pleasure with the little flying machine.

After a few minutes of guiding the toy's path, he handed the remote back to me.

"Would you like to try, Joe?" I asked.

"No thanks," he replied, fearful that he might make it crash.

I maneuvered the jet around in a circle, and raised its elevation so that it flew just above the pine trees until, finally, I carefully and delicately landed the plane on the ground.

"That's really a neat toy, Charles. Is that fair still open today?" asked Joe.

"I guess it probably is. We could ride our bikes and be there in a very short time," I said.

Clyde and Joe looked at me with emotionless expressions, waiting for me to lead the way.

"Do you want to go, Charles, or not?" asked Clyde.

"I have to ask my parents if it's okay."

I carefully put my toy away in its box and carried it into the house. I promised Clyde and Joe to ask my mom about going to the fair. I went downstairs to my room and put the toy in my closet.

I quickly ran up the stairs, to ask my mother permission to ride with Clyde and Joe to the fair. When I found her, she was lying on the sofa in the living room, reading the recent edition of *Ladies Home Journal* magazine, which she subscribes to. An Elvis Presley record was playing on the stereo as I approached her. My parents loved music, especially Elvis, and I often heard them refer to him as "the king."

"Mom," I nervously began to say with an obvious apprehension in my voice, "is it okay with you and dad if Joe, Clyde, and I ride out to the fair that I was at earlier?"

She looked up at me from the black-and-white lines of the magazine. My mother did not like to be disturbed when she was reading. "Only if you get home by the time it gets dark. That gives you about two or three hours. Be careful riding your bikes in town."

"Thanks, Mom," I said with appreciation as I sped out the door like a race horse.

Even though my parents could be strict and insensitive most of the time, there were times when they surprised me, as they tried to remember what it was like to be young.

When I got outside, Clyde and Joe were patiently waiting for me. I told them that I got the green light to go to the fair, on the condition that I would be home by the time it got dark. I went into the garage and grabbed my bike and quickly jumped on, as Clyde, Joe, and I quickly rode out of the driveway and raced down the street.

Clyde and Joe had brand-new five-speed bikes while I had an old manual bike. My bike was not modern, but I loved it and I didn't want a new bike. It was purple in color, with a banana seat and handlebars that were shaped like the letter *U*. I liked the way the bike rode, especially down steep hills, and that was why I kept it for as long as I did.

"How far is this fair, Charles?" asked Joe.

"It's really not too far by bike, but if we walked, like I did this morning, it would seem to be quite far. The fair is a couple of miles from here, on the other side of town," I told them as we pedaled down the road.

The evening air was humid and sticky, so common were the conditions during the end of August. We began to perspire quickly from the heat and humidity as we rode our bikes toward town. My friends followed me past the movie theater, the coffee shop, and many other stores in town. On a Saturday evening in Riversville, there is usually not much activity. In this small town lived a sense of serenity to all people who lived there.

We finally made our way through downtown, until our bikes landed upon the path in the woods. Lingering in the air as it transcended down from the trees was a strange silence that made me feel like I was riding through a wooded morgue. Absent were the sounds of birds singing, or animals running about in the woods, or even the sound that crickets make. The vibrations that I had previously felt on my route to the fair were no longer present. I felt an impending doom coming closer to me as my friends and I rode through the calm of the forest with a river of perspiration that poured down our faces on our quest to find the fair.

My heart started to pound in my chest as fear took hold of my mind. I had a strong suspicion that the fair was no longer there. I heard whispers inside my head that were telling me that I had imagined everything, that nothing was real. The quiet in the woodlands triggered an apprehension that revealed to me the truth of the situation and what the consequences might become. I slammed the brakes on my bicycle when I finally got to the end of the trail, where just a short time before, a fair was in progress. What I saw before my eyes both amazed me and fulfilled the expectations of my fears. The fair was gone. It had vanished from the place where it had once stood. A wide-open field was the only thing before me; no roller coaster or Ferris wheel that towered high in the sky, no game vendors or people who had the attitude of a shadow. These things could not be found; just a meadow of high grass and weeds.

"What's this, Charles? Where's the fair?" asked Clyde, with animosity directed toward me.

"Yeah, Charlie. Where's this fair you bragged about?" questioned Joe with anger in his eyes that ripped through me.

"I don't know. It was here earlier. I swear it was," I said in my defense.

I got off of my bike and let it fall to the ground. I walked around the field with much confusion in my mind. I knew what was previously in the meadow just a few hours ago, and I could have never imagined the fair would disappear like it did. I saw in my mind where everything was and heard the many sounds and voices.

Clyde and Joe followed my lead as they got off their bikes and carefully placed them on the ground. They watched and followed me as I wandered through the field with many insects buzzing around me.

"Joe, I feel like we've been suckers. We rode all the way out here with the promise of a fair and a chance to get one of those jet toys. When we finally got to the place where this imaginary fair was to have been, we find nothing. I must admit, I'm angry. It was a long ride out here, and all we get for our efforts is an empty field of weeds and bugs," said Clyde with a rage that brewed up inside his veins and upon every word he spoke.

I knew my friends were mad at me, and I became fearful of them, especially Clyde. I knew that he had a violent temper, for I had seen it explode several times in the past. Joe was quiet, as he was just observing what was happening, not knowing what to expect from Clyde. I started to back away from Clyde when I became aware of his approach. He became possessed with a temporary hatred for me. Looking into Clyde's eyes, I knew that a fight with him was possible.

"You are sick, Charles!" yelled Clyde as he pushed me to the ground.

I timidly got up and faced him.

"I know you're really mad at me, Clyde, but I don't want to fight you. There really was a fair here. I know I didn't dream it," I said, trying to defend myself as well as my sanity.

"Oh, sure there was!" shouted Clyde in a humiliating tone that offended me.

I stared at the ground in shame, feeling bad that the circumstances made me look like a liar. Without expecting it, Clyde again pushed me hard to the ground, and I saw in his eyes that he wanted to beat me up, but Joe grabbed his arm, restraining him. Joe knew of Clyde's temper, and wanted to make sure it remained in check.

"Come on, Clyde. Let's get out of here. These bugs are eating me up," said Joe impatiently.

"You're right, Joe. Besides, I don't like to be around liars. You know Charles, I know you're alone, but if the only companionship you can find is in your fantasy-filled head, you really need some help. But in the meantime, maybe you can dream up a way for that fair to reappear!" mocked Clyde as he got on his bike and rode away with Joe laughing and making fun of me.

I lay on my back, looking up at the sky for quite a while. I knew I had some time before I had to be home, so I just sat there and pondered what had happened.

"Why?" I cried out loudly several times, desperately longing for an answer.

Patiently, I waited in silence for a response in a manner that I could understand. A stiff, cool breeze suddenly rushed upon me, cooling my sweaty forehead. The wind reminded me of the dream from this morning. While I meditated upon the memory, I looked down at my feet and noticed a crumpled-up piece of notebook paper blowing in the wind toward me. I thought it was a strange occurrence that a small wad of paper was found in a field out in the middle of nowhere, and as I picked it up and unfolded it, I learned the reason for my ordeal written in plain English. It was a note from Scatman, and it said:

"Only you Charles, for you are the one with the dreams."

Scatman

Chapter 6

I sat alone in the large field as the sun started its fall behind the horizons. The note from Scatman I held in my hand as I absentmindedly stared at it for a long time. I thought I was being called to and by the Mirror of Freedom, an object of divine nature that I did not totally understand in its significance. Memories began to flood my mind when I recollected being in a place beyond all human comprehension. Where I sat, I could visualize the seemingly mystical fair that I had been a witness to just a few hours before. Seeing the absence of what had been, I presumed that the fair was some type of illusion. There had to be an explanation for what had just happened, as the sincerity of Barnabus and Scatman's motives appeared to be genuine, blended with a slight fragment of the mysterious that kept my mind asking many questions.

"Why me?" I yelled. "Why me?" I asked again, almost a whisper.

"I don't understand," I finally said as confusion and discouragement started to consume my thoughts. "Barnabus and Scatman seem to be quite honest and trusting, but why are they interested in me? Or do they have alternative motives? My dream from last night is what started the events of the day. I believe the key to understanding the Mirror lies in my sleep," I said as I tried to analyze my current situation.

I had noticed that the dreams that I experienced over the last few months had become extremely vivid and realistic. Occasionally,

I felt like I was in another world, during a different time in history, as if I was living in the past. Distinguishing factors between reality and the dream became difficult to recognize during a few rare and authentic circumstances.

I really wanted to believe that I was being called to fulfill some important purpose. Deep in my heart, I knew that I had to have faith. Whispering in my ears, I could hear my parents' philosophical outlook upon the world. If hope was the map to follow to obtain faith, I knew I had to be aware of my inner voice and not my mind if I was to succeed in finding the destination of my endeavors. A war was being fought upon the battlefield of my heart and soul, which left me bewildered and confused.

I accepted the fact that the events that took place on that day would give insight to what my life would become. During my recent past, the months and years of personal history, my daily routine had been quite shallow, filled with numerous disappointments and much pain. Inside the Mirror, I hoped that I might find something that would give my life meaning. I desperately wanted it to be true, and as I looked across the field, the sun was slowly setting upon the horizons. The distinction of nature's timepiece made me recognize that it was time to return home; and I hoped it would be the last time I would have to call it that. I walked over to my bike, got on, and started to ride through the woods. Darkness had almost settled itself down upon the woodlands, and as I rode, I noticed that the strange quiet was still suspended; however, the silence was joined with a strong proximity of peace. I knew I had to return to that place once more, hopefully to find my friends, Barnabus and Scatman. There were many questions in my mind to ask them, and I believed that their answers would give me peace. I had to know in my heart if the day and the experiences that transpired were real or if I had dreamt them. In the patience of time, I hoped that the truth would find me.

I finally left the domain of the woods behind me, and I quickly approached downtown Riversville. The town was quiet, which was quite normal. The only activity seemed to be coming from Lucky Eddy's Tavern. It was the only bar in town, so it had steady business year round. I heard laughter and rock 'n' roll music as I rode past, which almost drowned out the *cling* clang of the pinball machines. It seemed to me that everyone was having a good time. When I finally arrived back home, I drove my bike into the driveway, and put it away in the garage. Since it had just recently turned dark, I remembered the promise I made to my mother. I hoped that she would give me credit for being close to the appointed time. When I walked into the house, my mother was at the dining room table balancing her check book. She briefly looked at me as I walked past her, not being too concerned of my presence.

"Did you have a good time?" she asked in a tone which almost seemed humiliating.

"Not really. Clyde and I almost got into a fight, but Joe was there to stop it. It was just a misunderstanding."

At that moment, I did not feel like talking about what had happened with my parents, for they would probably not believe me when I would tell them about the fair. I would probably be accused of fantasizing, like I had been many times in the past. A lecture from my father would follow, and for the next hour he would try to educate me on how to focus my mind on the important things in life. I did not want to hear it, so I went into the kitchen, made myself a peanut butter and jelly sandwich and quietly sat down at the kitchen table to eat. My mother continued working on her checkbook, and we sat there in silence. She did not say a word, and either did I. When I was done, I cleaned up after myself, went into the bathroom, and brushed my teeth. When I came out of the bathroom, I found my mother and father in the living room sitting on the couch, and I believe they were talking about me. Obviously, they did not find it necessary to discuss with me what they were talking about.

"I think I'm going to bed now, it's been a long day," I said.

Quietly muttering the words, "Good night," to them, I slowly walked away toward the basement steps. I heard my father say,

"Sweet dreams," which was a comical statement he often used when wishing someone good night. When I heard my father speak those words, a thought entered my mind that made me feel bad and also quite afraid. Those words became the last thing I would ever hear my father speak to me.

When I entered my room, I realized that it was still early for bedtime, especially during the summer, and the next day was Sunday. I was extremely tired from all my experiences on that day, and I was especially emotionally exhausted. I got dressed into my pajamas, climbed into bed, and started to read. After I had read a few pages, I realized that I didn't feel like reading, for the activities of a comic book superhero wasn't what I needed to be focusing my mind on.

Ideas and speculations ran swiftly through my head as my mind became disoriented to the choice I had to make, which caused a weight to press down upon me. In my heart, I believe that I had already decided. I began to think about my parents, as I thought they would probably be better off without me. Their selfish hearts controlled their motives and actions, and it blinded them to what love really is, especially my mother. My dad committed the majority of his energy to his job, and he just wanted to relax when he was home. I remembered the many times in the past when my parents treated me heartlessly, failing to appreciate the work I did for them around the house. As I examined the events of the day, from beginning to end, with every little or insignificant incident that took place, I could only imagine what the next day might bring, until the weight of the unknown became too heavy and I drifted off into the land of my dreams.

I felt myself fall into a sphere of a dream, and when I realized where I was, a sense of joy blossomed in my heart. Identifying wave after wave of an endless sea of florescent green that spread far beyond the scope of my eyes, I recognized the rolling hills being the same place from the night before. I looked around, noticing all the beauty in nature, until I saw Scatman's smiling face.

"Walk far and wide, my boy, for the Mirror is waiting. Hold onto your faith in your dreams, for it is your belief that will allow you to gain entrance into the Mirror."

Looking around at the place in which I stood, I saw the beautiful skies with their bright glow that penetrated warmth that came down upon me. I became firmly convinced of no longer being in Ohio when I saw all that was before me. Suddenly, I felt quite strange, as if I was walking without my feet touching the ground. I enjoyed this foreign feeling, until I realized that what I felt was actually happening. Fear entered me for a brief moment, until a voice softly spoke to my mind, which comforted my nerves to where I could relax and enjoy the ride. The voice belonged to Scatman.

"What a feeling!" I exclaimed.

I made my way across the hills to a place where thick fog lingered. Floating into the thick fog, my feet touched the ground once again. I found the crater that Scatman had spoken of, and I carefully walked down into it. I found a cave at the bottom of the crater, where a misty vapor had become extremely thick. Somewhere deep inside the cave, I immediately noticed a light. What I sought after I sensed was somewhere in the cave, but I was having some difficulty finding its origin. Finally, as I carefully walked down a long series of steps that emptied into a very large room, my eyes fell upon a massive-sized Mirror projecting a flood of bright-colored lights.

"The light is awesome!" I shouted out as I became mesmerized by what stood in front of me.

When I began to observe the object of my desire, I felt it slowly absorbing the very essence of my being. The Mirror was learning everything about me as I felt a peace, but at the same time, I was fearful until I heard Scatman say, "The time is not yet, but very soon. I promise."

Slowly, my eyes opened. The dream was over. My short vacation away from reality was planted in my dream to restore faith. It is hope that keeps dreams alive, the very nature that I had to believe upon to accomplish my desires for this day. I sat up in my bed and looked around the room as I tried to adjust my senses after being brought out of an extremely vivid dream.

"Just think. This could be the last day of waking up in this bed and this house feeling empty and alone," I said aloud to myself.

I got out of bed with an inspired sense of purpose as I grabbed a few clothes and went upstairs to take a shower. When I got to the top of the stairs, I looked at the oven clock in the kitchen and realized that it was quite early. I knew that on Sunday mornings, my mom and dad stayed in bed until almost nine o'clock, and I did not want to wake them. When the water from the shower rushed down upon me, I felt delighted and almost free from the many doubts that had caused confusion in my mind the day before. My dream answered some of the paranoid impressions that were haunting me. I quickly washed myself and got out of the shower with a new attitude. I was hoping that on this day, I might find the start of a new beginning. A few lingering doubts remained in my mind, and to return to the fair could quite possibly answer all those voices of uncertainty.

I quickly dried myself off with a towel and got dressed, wearing an old pair of blue jean cut-off shorts that I personally cut with a pair of scissors and a black Cleveland Indians T-shirt. I went into the kitchen and made myself some breakfast. I was trying to be quiet, for I did not want to disturb my parents while they slept. I wanted to be gone when they woke up. While I ate my breakfast, the memory of the dream was fresh in my mind. The words that I heard in the dream, "The Mirror is waiting," had a strong impact on me emotionally, for it gave me hope of the promise to come. After I had finished eating, I washed my few dirty dishes and set them on a towel to dry. I walked around the house from room to room, as if I was trying to memorize what everything looked and felt like. My eyes fell upon the many pictures that hung on the wall: my parents' wedding picture and several photos of me when I was a baby. I hoped and prayed that I would never have to return to the haunted dungeon that my parents called home.

I wrote a short note to my parents explaining that I woke up early and went for a walk. Taking only my Little League baseball cap and my father's moccasin wineskin filled with apple juice, I walked out the door.

I casually began to walk down the street, just like the many times when I would go down to the river to watch the boats. Unlike other mornings, I had a new attitude, with a distinct concept for what my future might become. I possessed a strong desire to find the fair, if it did really exist, along with my two friends, Barnabus and Scatman. I was hoping that I did not have to return from my walk with my dreams shattered. What I was searching for required me to have faith.

"Soon, I'll be free," I said, trying to encourage myself during an unexpected moment of doubt. A commitment was required of me to remain focused upon my beliefs, and, ultimately, my quest for the truth would find me.

I followed the same route that I had previously with Barnabus. The day before, I was innocent and naïve to where I was going or what I would encounter at the fair; but on that day, I understood much more. It was not clear to me the day before where I was being led because my mind was too focused on having a good time. At day's end, I was asking some important questions, and I later discovered many of the answers. One question remained unanswered, and it troubled me.

"Why me?" I shouted out as I continued to walk toward downtown.

The why was the one specific question that demanded an answer in my heart and mind. I couldn't find a logical explanation that would justify what I was experiencing. I had hope that Barnabus and Scatman could satisfy my hunger for what I was longing to find.

The search for the fair continued, which led me past the Mirage Coffee Shop, where I saw Susan, the waitress who had waited on me the day before, looking out the window. It was still early in the morning, but the Mirage was open for business. On Sundays, the breakfast crowd arrived later than most mornings, usually around 8:00 or 9:00, just prior to church services. When I walked by, Susan recognized me immediately, as she smiled and waved in my direction. I waved back, feeling bad about getting mad at her yesterday. She didn't understand what I was going through, but I still thought she was a nice person.

Walking through the town, I noticed that it was very quiet during the early hours of the morning. Most of the people in the town were still sleeping, but soon, the town would awaken, with several churches beginning their worship services. I took my time on my return to the fair, for I wanted to see Riversville one last time. I eventually made my way to the edge of the town and found the path that led Barnabus and I to the fair the day before. It would be the last time that anyone saw me in the world where I was known.

Chapter 7

I entered the woodlands with a considerable amount of hesitation, and I immediately tried to perceive all that was around me. A silence only the dead could fathom hovered over me the last time I had walked upon that trail; but it was a new day, and a change had come. The birds upon the lofty branches in the trees were the first of many things I noticed, and when I heard their melody in song, the musical notes floated in tune with the harmony in nature. I stopped and listened for a minute or two to appreciate what I was hearing.

I suddenly recognized my animal friends upon the trail ahead of me who had escorted me through the woods after the fair the day before. When I saw them, I was filled with a wonderful sense of joy. The sounds of the fair became familiar to me as I began to distinguish the roller coaster racing up and down hills and the merry-go-round singing out its songs of carnival. The mechanical sounds were distinct, although the absence of human voices was puzzling to me. Perhaps I was too early. The day before, I remembered the screams from the coaster riders as they quickly raced along the track. Today, those voices did not exist.

I was glad to see my animal friends, and I approached them without fear. I petted each of them individually, as a demonstration of how thankful I was to see them. Seeing them again was a revelation, for it told me that everything I had experienced from the time Barnabus showed up at my door was real. The fair of yesterday was not rooted in a dream, for it actually happened to me, just as I physically touched the fur on the back of the raccoon. Odd as it might have been, I began to suspect that these animals were actually waiting for me. As their eyes looked upon me, I thought they were trying to communicate in a way that was beyond my limited understanding. I started to walk down the trail with my animal companions as they escorted me once again to my destination.

"What a beautiful day!" I exclaimed with much joy.

I stole a glance at the raccoon when I observed that it was looking up at me. I suddenly assumed that the possibility existed that these creatures might have just understood what I had spoken by the manner in which they looked at me. I am not trying to convince you that these animals understood my language, but by tone and inclination, they could perceive joy and anger. If they could comprehend even a fraction of what I expressed, the language barrier was the only thing that hindered them from communicating with me.

Could this be possible? I questioned myself upon the prospect of extreme chance. "Did you creatures just understand what I said?" I asked as I looked into their eyes.

I believe that on a fractional scale, those animals probably did understand me, in a manner of speaking, for even though I was not within the confines of the Mirror, all that is a part of its existence is also controlled by it.

When I came out of the woods, my eyes fell upon the fair once again. I felt a peacefulness and contentment that flourished up within me, as I knew without any skepticism in my heart that what I had seen yesterday was planned for my benefit. The reasons were still a mystery, but no longer did I wonder if those images that played continuously in my head were real. I stood alone just outside the fairgrounds, looking with fascination all that lay just beyond my grasp.

"I know this is no dream," I said, trying to convince myself silently. Somehow, somewhere, I knew the truth with a strong conviction in my heart. For reasons unknown to me at the time, my mind did not want to believe what my eyes were seeing. "This is a real place, and as the belief in what I see is true, my focus will be controlled by a faith in the existence of the Mirror of Freedom."

The large, towering Ferris wheel rose high above me, beyond the large stone gates of the fair. Past the entrance, I could hear the many different sounds of the fair: the powerful rumblings of the roller train and the voices from the game and food vendors trying to sell their product. The lingering aroma of the carnival food smelled good, from the French fries and elephant ears to the sausage gyros and cotton candy. Even though I had eaten breakfast, the smell of the food ignited my appetite enough to make me feel hungry. I finally walked through the gates of the fair after meditating upon the sounds and smells for a few minutes. Being quite early in the day, I realized that it was not crowded like it was yesterday. The shadow people were still there, looking the same, as if they had never left. It was what I saw in their eyes that I knew they were different, for even though they participated in the events of the fair, what I saw in them captivated me with fear, for I sensed the absence of a living soul.

I decided to ride the rollercoaster, for the day before, I really enjoyed the ride. I immediately found my way to the ride's entrance, as I passionately desired to ride the coaster once more. Patiently, I waited in the short line until it was my turn to ride. The ride operator from the day before recognized me immediately, or was it that he was expecting to see me? I must have been a rare illumination among many bodies of shadows.

"So you decided to return for another ride, did you?" asked the ride operator.

He was dressed in the same attire that he was the day before: blue jeans and a black, collared, cotton t-shirt. I just nodded my head at him in agreement to what he had said. He was a nice young man in his early twenties, not overly handsome, although he possessed an athletically built frame, and I thought he was probably working at fairs to get money for college.

"Well then," he said, "let's put you in the very front."

He personally led the way to the lead car of the coaster, strapped me in, and made sure everything was secure. He quickly turned his attention to the remainder of the passengers, directing them to their appointed cars, making sure all was safe from any hazards from the ride.

When the train began to roll, I heard him exclaim, "Have fun, Charles!"

The coaster entered the dark tunnel, where it began to slowly climb up a steep incline. The constant sound of the train echoed in my ears when I thought to myself, *How did he know my name?* I did not have much time to think about the unusual occurrence when the long, steep downhill slope lay before me. The unseen force of gravity pushed the coaster down the hill, up and down a few smaller hills, and around several sharp curves while I hung on tightly, enjoying every second of the ride. Finally, the roller coaster slowed down and came to a screeching halt.

I got out of the car quickly and walked down the exit ramp of the ride as I started to curiously look around the fairgrounds. My mind was upon my two friends, Barnabus and Scatman, as I desired to look upon their faces, especially into their eyes. I went over to the Ferris wheel, for I remembered Scatman mentioning that it was one of his favorite rides. I waited in line when I distinctly knew in my heart that my two friends were close, for I felt their presence, but I had yet to see them face to face. After a short wait, the ride operator motioned me to get into the next caged cubical, and as I did what I was told, I found Barnabus and Scatman.

"Welcome, my son! Climb on in and sit down, for I know that there are many questions on your mind," said Scatman with his usual large smile on his face.

He was dressed basically the same as I remembered him from the day before, with the exception of his hat. I was happy to see my friends, and it was written upon my expression, for I realized that everything I had seen previously was no dream. I sat down in the seat across from Scatman as our door became secured. The Ferris wheel at the fair was slightly different than the traditional ones found at amusement parks throughout the country. This ride had an enclosed oval carriage with a fenced screen that could hold four to six people, depending upon their size and weight. When the ride began to rotate, Scatman looked upon me and saw a determination to find reality in the mist of what I had seen at the fair yesterday.

"I knew you would return," said Scatman.

"I also believed," added Barnabus.

"What is this place?" I inquired, not knowing who or what to believe. "I first saw this place when Barnabus brought me here, but then it disappeared when I wanted to bring my friends here," I said with a desperate hunger for answers.

"Those boys, whom you refer to were not actually your friends, and I think you realize that now. This was especially true of the tall boy who pushed you down. He is consumed by darkness and filled with a tremendous amount of anger. He inflicts pain on many people in a variety of ways. Charles, you were the target of his frustrations on that night. It is good to see you," replied Scatman.

"I want to find peace and happiness," I said with the voice of desperation. My mind was set upon the desires and passions that influenced my thoughts, for my life had not been what I had wished it to be. The Mirror of Freedom might be the door that I needed to pass through to discover this important element that would satisfy the longings of my heart.

"Charles, you can see with your eyes but fail to truly understand what is happening around you. You are entering the springtime of your life, a time when the need for personal revelations is very significant. You have a talent and a gift that you are just beginning to comprehend. Inside of you lies a strong creative force and it wants to come alive. Set the desires of your mind upon the knowledge that leads to wisdom. With guidance, the unveiling of mysteries that has been hidden from your eyes will become known. If Barnabus and I had left you in your present circumstances, the talents you possess might never have been discovered until it was almost too late.

"The fair that you see before you is not quite real. We heard what you said when you were leaving the fairgrounds yesterday, that the people looked like they were drawn by an artist's pencil. Charles, you are very close to the truth with that observation. The majority of people walk through life with their eyes closed. It's the explanation why there is so much darkness in the world. Here in this society, bigotry, jealousy, violence, murder, and disease can be found among other things that cause so much human suffering. Open your eyes far and wide, until you encounter the true light. Embrace it, and try to understand what it is that's really important. By faith, trust in the Mirror and surrender the hunger of the passions that could eventually destroy you, and in time, a mystical force will direct your steps. When faith is acted upon, the gifts that wait for you inside the kingdom will be yours. The convictions that have been holding you captive demand a confrontation or the opportunity to pass through the Mirror will never come to be. Do you understand what I am trying to tell you, Charles?"

"I think so," I timidly replied. "I must believe in the Mirror and trust in its leadership to lead me down the right path. My dreams have been like maps, showing me a faith that will guarantee my success in what I am led to pursue."

I looked out upon the vast landscape from the top of the large wheel as it continued to go round and round. The late morning brought some beautiful weather, and the smell in the air seemed almost intoxicating. I could see for miles as I noticed the Ohio River twisting its way across the face of the horizons. When the ride was over, the attendant immediately opened the door of our cubical to let us out. We began to walk around the fairgrounds when Barnabus quietly left us without Scatman and I being aware that he was gone.

"Are you thirsty?" asked Scatman.

"A little," I said.

"How would you like a frozen orangeade?" suggested Scatman with an eager desire to quench his thirst.

It was slowly becoming humid the older the day grew.

"Yes, that sounds refreshing," I said.

We walked to a nearby concession stand, where Scatman bought us two large frozen orangeades. I found a bench nearby to sit on and drink and talk. I suddenly became aware that Barnabus was missing.

"Where did Barnabus go?" I asked.

"He has left to prepare your journey to the Mirror," replied Scatman.

"Barnabus is very quiet and mysterious," I said.

"At times, he is, but he is my silent partner, who has great wisdom about the Mirror. I met him as a teenager, almost fourteen years old. I was naïve, irresponsible, and reckless. I don't really remember how I came in contact with him, but what I do remember is that it was at a Fourth of July parade. I first noticed his eyes, how they sparkled, and the manner in which he communicated with me without even saying a word. I was captivated by his pale appearance, for he looked like an albino, and he still does in a small sort of way. I was attracted to his personality, for the words he used were not like anyone I had ever met.

"When I met Barnabus, my mother, brother, and I were living in a deteriorated neighborhood in Akron, Ohio. Barnabus learned about me through the Mirror, and he saw my frustrated soul that hungered for deliverance. My mother was hostile and distant, the result of being an alcoholic. I stayed away from home most of the time and got involved with the wrong type of people. I started to drink myself, in spite of my mother. I was hurting on the inside, and I knew it, as I started to grow a root of hatred toward myself and other people. My mom loved me in her own way, but she was never able to cope with the consequences from the choices that she had made in her life. Consequently, my brother and I never realized how much she cared for us.

"Barnabus knew that I loved the outdoors, playing among the trees and animals. I tried to pretend that I was Robin Hood with my miniature archery set. I practiced a lot, and in time, I became quite a good shot. I had a target nailed upon one of the larger trees in the woods, where I routinely practiced my marksmanship. I would climb trees and play fantasy games that I was one of the men of Sherwood Forest. It was through my imagination that the Mirror revealed itself to me. Barnabus taught me the way, the truth, and the life, the essence of the faith in the Mirror of Freedom. The only truth that is essential in knowing and understanding is through the Mirror; everything else is secondhand information. You will learn these things as you grow in knowledge. Since the circumstances were similar that led us both to come to know the Mirror, I will be your guide, teacher, and friend."

Scatman had noticed that I was watching him closely while he told the story of how he came to know Barnabus. I must have had a tranquil, peaceful look on my face with a desire to learn about the place that had appeared in my dreams. He wanted to know what I, in my heart, really believed, for it was detrimental to determine if I would be able to pass through the Mirror based upon my inner convictions.

"Charles, how much do you believe in this fair and in me, who stands physically before you?"

"I know that you are real, but this fair seems like a shadow image from one of my dreams. But I know that I'm not dreaming," I told him directly.

"Only if you believe can you see, and only if you can see will you be able to believe," said Scatman with a slight apprehension in his voice, unsure if I could truly comprehend what he was trying to explain to me.

"I don't understand," I replied, confused about what hidden underlying symbolism Scatman was trying to reveal to me.

"If you can believe in something with all of your heart and mind without touching it physically, you have obtained a steadfast faith.

This is the basic truth that is essential to possess before you will be allowed to enter the kingdom of the Mirror. Charles, you have never seen the Mirror with your eyes. Except in your dreams, you haven't touched it with your hands, so how do you know that it exists?"

"I can't really explain it," I began to tell him, uncertain of my explanation. "It's like, how do I know that when I sit down in a chair, it will be able to support my weight? I'm not completely sure; I just believe it will. Just like I have confidence that the Mirror of Freedom is real and I believe it's out there, waiting for me."

"Charles, my young friend, that is exactly what I am talking about, the essence of faith," said Scatman with a large smile.

I took my last swallow of my drink, and then Scatman and I got up off the old wooden bench. We began to walk around the fairgrounds as he put his arm around me like a good friend giving advice and instruction.

"Try to understand, Charles, that this fair is not really here; its images have been planted in the deepest regions of your mind. Think of it as a mirage, for your physical presence is here, and so is mine, although the majority of what you see before you is not. The Mirror created this illusion just for you, Charles. This spectacular event was brought to life for one specific reason. It was to convince you to become an active and meaningful part of our little society, which, in turn, would deliver you from your personal turmoil. Life is so different there, although many of the pleasures of this world you will be able to find as well. The small tokens of happiness that humans cherish here on Earth, such as love and companionship and good food, among other things, are all important ingredients to the life in the Mirror. I will teach you in more detail about this when the Mirror allows you to pass into its kingdom."

Scatman and I walked to the edge of the fairgrounds, where a very old wooden fence stood. Beyond the fence, the ground dropped off severely and fell to the banks of the Ohio River. We looked upon the mighty river and across to the other side. I watched the boats on the water with the continuous sounds of the fair ringing through my head. Scatman looked down at me with a new sense of respect and love. He saw a faith that was growing in me, and he wanted to help, just like a father would encourage his son.

"When you enter the Mirror's kingdom, you will feel different," said Scatman.

"How?" I curiously asked.

"You will be washed clean by the Mirror. You will feel the same, and the same person you will be, but the emptiness that currently is inside of you will be gone. Charles, you will soon discover a love that has been destined to shape and mold your life. Inside the Mirror, people are recognized for their own unique character, not the worth of a person's wallet or their specific athletic abilities. A different person you will become, as you will begin to treat all life with love and become a child of the Mirror. Your flesh and blood will become clean, and you will be able to sense the world around you like never before. The physical essence of who you are will be altered, but you will not be able to distinguish the change at first, until you become one in harmony with the heart of the Mirror. Fixed inside your subconscious mind, the memories of this life will remain; however, your heart and soul will belong to the Mirror," concluded Scatman, trying to reveal facts that I would have to endure before I would be able to find the promise of my dreams.

"When will we be going to the Mirror?" I asked.

Scatman studied my eyes for a brief moment or two, wanting to find a desire and a faith of what had been foretold to me. Somewhere within the hidden chambers of my soul, he found what he was searching for.

"No time like the present," he finally said after being satisfied with what was revealed to him.

"This won't be painful, will it?" I inquired, fearful of the unknown.

"No, my son," Scatman replied through a weak chuckle. "It would hurt you much more if you decided not to come." He prophesied about my future without the Mirror. "Upon your skin and within your entire body, you will feel a distinct sensation that is not painful, just slightly uncomfortable."

"I understand, and I believe that I am ready," I said with an anxious anticipation.

"Charles, just close your eyes and hold your hands behind your back. I will now demonstrate what you have been waiting eagerly to see."

He looked down at me and saw the boy he once was in me so many years ago. Scatman had been a witness to the growth of my faith, as it was just beginning to take flight.

"Before we begin the first part of your journey to the Mirror, I must warn you that it is important to follow my directions. Keep your eyes closed, and focus your thoughts upon the Mirror. Do not open your eyes for anything. You might want to, especially when you feel a rushing, swirling wind all around you, but I warn you, do not. It would not be wise. Once the wind calms down and you hear my voice once again, the conditions will be safe to open your eyes. Do you understand, Charles?"

"Yes, Scatman. Do not open my eyes until I hear your voice," I said to verify what he explained to me.

Scatman looked out across the landscape with a mystical look in his eyes, and it seemed to me that he was trying to communicate with an entity that was beyond my comprehension. I became frightened with what I was seeing and feeling, and that was when I closed my eyes.

"Oh my Mirror, the time has come to make this fair disappear. Your own desire created it to illustrate a love and a peace that Charles will be able to embrace when he comes to know you. What he has witnessed here was by your own design. Now show Charles the real world within your glory. I thank you for your love, and I pray for your will to be done here in this boy's life."

I did not immediately recognize a change, for I still felt the presence of the fair nearby. Slowly and quite gradually, with my eyes firmly shut, I felt a cool wind that began to spin with a calm, swirling rotation that seemed to consume me. I knew that what Scatman had foretold to me was beginning, as the wind became so strong that I had difficulty standing. The sounds from the fair could no longer be heard as the blowing storm raged around me in a fury that was making it difficult to hear. This was a unique phenomenon that could not be compared to anything I had ever witnessed. I sensed that I was being carried through some kind of tunnel without any resistance to gravity. Being completely unaware, I felt a cool sting upon my skin as a foreign substance penetrated into the core of my being. Whatever it was that came upon me found its way into my bloodstream, as I felt an alien matter begin to wander among the pathways of my body. I felt cold, a bitter winter cold, as if ice water was being flushed through me. My flesh still felt warm, but on the inside, I felt like I was being frozen.

A few moments later, the chill decreased, and finally, I felt warm once again. I wanted to open my eyes just for a second, but I knew I could not. My desire was to see what was transpiring around me, but I had to obey Scatman's instructions. Voluntarily blinded, I began to feel the presence of a large entity that gently touched me; however, for some unknown reason, I was not afraid. Curious as it might have been, I felt an all-consuming love from this unseen specter. It quickly left, and I continued to ride the mighty storm with its swirling winds that blew past me in a fury. I was being carried by the powerful tempest, which was like being in the center of a hurricane or tornado. I was reminded of the movie *The Wizard of Oz*, where Dorothy rode the tornado. The fair was gone. I knew it to be a fact, for I could no longer hear or feel its presence. I believed that I was being transported from one plane of existence to another. Gradually, I sensed the speed of the wind that carried me begin to diminish when I suddenly felt like I was floating upon the waves of a tranquil lake. I sailed the peaceful wind for quite some time, until, finally, I heard Scatman's voice.

"Charles, you can open your eyes now. We are near the Mirror of Freedom."

I opened my eyes, and through my distorted vision, I saw Scatman's smiling face.

"Are you all right?" he asked, concerned for my welfare.

"Yes, I'm fine, but I must tell you one thing. That was better than any roller-coaster ride that I've ever been on," I told him, and we started to laugh, enjoying the pleasure of the moment.

Chapter 8

Shared laughter between friends can create a harmony uniting their hearts and minds. I knew Scatman as a man who gave to all who were willing to receive. Possessed by a divine wisdom, he always seemed to have a smile on his face. We rode the roller coaster and the Ferris wheel at the fair together, which I believe was a tactic to make me feel comfortable. He tried to teach me about a place beyond my dreams called the Mirror of Freedom. It was at that moment that I knew that Scatman was a unique person. I would never again meet anyone quite like him. Somehow, somewhere, I believe that I had met Barnabus and Scatman before, in a place beyond my comprehension.

I was sent on a wild wind ride that transported me from one plane of existence into another. I knew I was no longer in Ohio, and for the first time since coming out of the windstorm, I looked around to see what my surroundings were.

Scatman and I sat on a high ridge overlooking a deep canyon, and upon the other side, I could see a dense forest that covered many steep hills with a variety of many colorful and abnormal-looking trees. I noticed that quite a few of them grew in a strange and odd manner, being crooked or slanted as they pointed to the sky. I looked over at Scatman, and that was when I noticed something entirely different about him. It was not just his youthful appearance, but a presence had come to live in him that was not there before. At the fair, he seemed to be very old, but now, at the place where we would continue our journey to the Mirror, he had the impression of being forty to fifty years younger.

"What happened, and where are we?" I asked, not knowing what to believe.

"The first part of our journey to the Mirror has been completed, as we have crossed over into another dimension. You have also been cleansed, which will prepare you to physically enter the Mirror. This process of purification has cleansed you and the many channels that sustain your life. Thoroughly precise was the method of transformation so that when you enter the Mirror, the change will not cause any emotional suffering. The remainder of your cleansing will take place when you enter the Mirror and become a part of its kingdom."

"You were old at the fair, and now you appear to be much younger. What happened?" I asked, for I was confused about his new look.

"At the fair, I was my true age. What you saw of me at the fair is how I would have looked had I not gone to the Mirror. People live much longer in the Mirror, due to many factors, and the aging process is much slower. Barnabus was born in the Mirror, so the next time you see him, you will not notice much of a change. Once I came out of the wind tunnel, I regained most of my youthful appearance."

We got up off the ground, and as I began to survey my surroundings, the appealing quality of the images before me held my thoughts and emotions in a bewildered state. I stood virtually silent in the presence of such natural beauty, and I felt like falling to my knees in awe of it, for its creation and creator. Scatman watched me, as he was reminded of when he was in my shoes. Finally, he realized that it was time for our walk to the Mirror to begin.

"Shall we go, Charles? The Mirror is waiting."

"Yes, it is time," I replied with an utmost desire.

The trail that would lead us to the bottom of the canyon was long and slow, with numerous areas of unstable footing. Twisting its way through the wooded ravine, the path ran past dense sections of overgrowth, which had a wide variety of plant life. Scatman had walked on this ground before and knew what to expect, although it was expected of him not to reveal certain aspects of what he knew. From what I was told, it would be an exhausting walk that covered almost eight miles over rugged terrain.

"Charles, are you ready for this long journey?"

"I have faith that the Mirror will provide us with strength and courage. If we get thirsty, the Mirror will give us drink, and when we get hungry, we will find food," I said with an unknown source of confidence.

We followed a path that I believed would ultimately lead me to the origins of my dreams. The trail was made from a peculiar type of dirt that was black as coal, similar in structure to hard-packed sand. The path's dimensions were quite wide so that Scatman and I could walk side by side quite comfortably. When the thick of the woods began to surround us, I felt that we were not alone.

Voices in the forest started to quietly murmur the deeper into the woods we progressed. Birds sang and crickets chirped, and some unseen creatures ran about among the overgrowth. I became aware of the heat and humidity that was drastically increasing with intensity. Scatman and I realized that it would be necessary to begin taking frequent breaks from our walking so that we could maintain our strength.

I was fascinated by the sights I walked past, and I noticed that the forest was growing dark; but at the same moment, I sensed a glow that came from the ground we walked upon. The vast array of plant life interested me, for it was quite different than what I was accustomed to seeing. I had never seen anything that was even slightly similar to what I saw on top of the ridge. The trees and flora were similar in design and structure but much larger. A wide variety of colors captivated my eyes, and I recognized that some of the leaves on the vegetation were almost transparent, as I could almost see through them. I touched some of the leaves with my hand, and they felt almost weightless, like a piece of tissue paper. I inhaled deeply when a fresh scent that reminded me of my dream from a few nights before captivated my sense of smell.

Out from the desires of our hearts, Scatman and I came upon a small wooden bench to take a break from our walk. From where we sat, the view of the canyon was picturesque and exhilarating. My eyes looked out upon the deep ravine, and when I saw the bottom, I realized that I didn't remember seeing a lake there.

"I don't recall seeing that lake before, but maybe I didn't look close enough," I said, slightly confused.

"That's the lake of hopes and dreams. We will have to cross those waters at some time before we begin the last leg of our journey to find the Mirror," Scatman interjected as he got up off the bench and stood next to me. "You will be tested by the Mirror at some time near the lake. The manner of your trial, I have no idea when, where, or what it will be. It will be as much as a surprise to me as it will be to you. Keep your instincts sharp, and hold tight to your faith in your dreams."

As we continued our walk once again, I began to recognize unfamiliar emotions that were growing up inside of me as a foreign perception crept into my heart and mind. The passion satisfied me to search for the meaning behind my exploits, for in my mind, the measure of time was like a dream without the sensation of dreaming. Before me was a mysterious adventure in a strange land, where everything around me brought a deeper instinct to my natural senses. Scatman and I made our way down the trail, where it led us around the outer rim of the canyon and began an irregular descent toward the lake. In between the empty spaces of our conversation, our minds found the time to wander in the absent lapses of the moment. Understanding the concept of what the Mirror was would be a difficult obstacle, for I had to find a presence of humility, as Scatman had many years before. The Mirror would try to demand of me the gifts and talents that I possessed and find the best use for them.

Why? I thought with a presence that was trying to contradict what my faith was trying to believe. *What is the purpose behind the Mirror's pursuit of me? Why am I so special?* I questioned myself silently. My dreams, which were conceived in my mind, held the explanation that I could not seem to find, and it irritated the image of my own self-worth.

My senses were alert to what I was seeing and hearing in the natural all around me. I heard a constant buzz of insects, but strange as it seemed to me, the woods were not infested with them. I had always been slightly afraid of bees and wasps, especially since I was allergic to their sting. Fear caused my curiosity to question if the insects in this region were similar to the ones in Ohio. I took a deep breath to subdue my apprehension, and as the fresh air filled my lungs, what I felt could not be compared to anything back home. It was good to be away from civilization, surrounded by nature in its true form. The heat and humidity continued to intensify the farther we walked into the core of the canyon, as I felt the thick air being sucked down the walls that began to imprison us.

The path cut its way through a thick abundance of plant life, with many distinctive trees and bushes that looked like something out of a dream. Flowers with an unprecedented loveliness that produced a sweet, lingering fragrance grew in varied shapes and sizes along the trail. The leaves on the trees, shrubs, and flowers illuminated a glow from the color they possessed. They all appeared to be florescent, almost artificial and not quite real. I was suddenly attracted by some berry bushes, as the fruit had an appetizing quality to it, when I realized that I was becoming hungry. When I started to pick the berries, I immediately became slightly leery, as I wanted to know more about them.

"Are these poisonous?" I asked, holding in display the berries in question.

"No food that is grown near or inside the Mirror can be considered harmful," responded Scatman quickly in response to my query.

Hearing that information, I quickly grabbed some of the orange-colored fruit that slightly resembled cherry tomatoes in size only. Their texture had the likeness of blackberries, but they tasted just like an orange. I put one in my mouth and was instantly delighted by the delicious juices that awakened my taste buds.

"These berries are wonderful! What do you call these?"

"I believe they are called orangeberries," replied Scatman as he took a few berries from my hand that I offered to him.

I took another handful of the appetizing fruit as I continued to walk down the trail, with Scatman following close behind me. The bottom of the canyon was drawing closer with every step, and as I viewed the walls of the canyon rising above us, I realized how far it was that we had come. We stopped occasionally to sample different fruits and vegetables that grew alongside the trail. Eating is a passionate part of living, a necessity that most people find enjoyable. Scatman knew that it was important for me to have a healthy appetite and become familiar with the different types of food that grew wild within the boundaries of the Mirror. Just when the thought of being thirsty came into my mind, we came upon a small trickle of a waterfall coming down the sides of the canyon walls.

"Scatman, I was just thinking about being thirsty and how good it would feel to have a small drink of water splashing around in my mouth. Then, out of nowhere, we come upon a small dribble of water that formed itself into a small waterfall," I said with astonishment and curiosity.

"You might think nothing about this waterfall except by mere coincidence. However, when occurrences of this manner become more frequent, you will not think that way anymore. From a loving heart that created love, a weak waterfall appears to you when you are thirsty. How is this possible? This refreshment was given to us by the loving gratitude of the Mirror. Don't you remember what you said when we started this walk? If we get thirsty or hungry, the Mirror will provide. What do you think this waterfall is? It is provision. You spoke it, and now it has come into existence."

"Are you trying to tell me that the Mirror can read my thoughts and grant my every wish and desire?" I asked, being slightly skeptical.

"On some occasions, it can, when your thoughts, desires, and motives are in accordance with the will for your life."

"I think I understand," I said.

After a time of reflection of what had been said, we once again turned our focus to the call of the trail. The path turned and led us down a steep incline, with the sparkling lake becoming more visible on our left, and on our right, the stone wall that bordered the canyon rose up high above our heads. Scatman and I talked of many things, his life before the Mirror, and the many painful experiences where he almost lost all hope. We laughed and cried as we recalled the times of joy and sorrow. When we turned the last corner on the path that would lead us to the shores of the lake, I stopped dead in my tracks. I became frozen with fear at the sight that stood directly in front of me.

A large wild animal similar to a lion or tiger in physical characteristics only positioned itself in front of us. I knew this animal belonged to the cat family, although its fur and its eyes were out of the ordinary. The cold eyes sunk deep into the animal's face, a dark, deep blue that seemed to be reading the nature of my being. His coat of fur was black, with alternating stripes of faint red and white. Weighing over five hundred pounds and almost eight feet long, the cat was a very powerful creature.

"Try to stay calm, Charles, for the animal before you is a guardian of the Mirror. Fear not, for he will not act in violence unless the perception of deception against the Mirror alarms his senses. If you believe, Charles, no harm will come to you," explained Scatman as he leaned over my shoulder.

I cautiously approached the large cat as my heart pounded with a strong rhythm. Normally, I would have never tried such an act of courage, but I knew that I was in a unique place, as the circumstances and behaviors were different. The creature circled me quietly, as if he was stalking his prey. Possessed with unique and finely tuned instincts, the large cat did not perceive any danger from me. Finally, the large cat sat down directly next to me.

"It wants you to pet him!" Scatman yelled from behind me.

When I timidly touched the cat's soft and smooth fur, I immediately heard it begin to purr with delight. Against my better judgment, I was soon petting the large animal as I recognized the power and beauty that it magnificently possessed. I was nervous petting the massive creature, but at the same time, I enjoyed it. After a few short moments of being caressed, the animal rose from its sitting position and ran into the thick of the woods. I stood motionless in a temporary state of reverence when I realized what I had just done. When the large cat ran off, Scatman quickly came up to me and tried to calm my nerves.

"You have passed the first test that the Mirror has put before you. The success that you experienced here will give you confidence when the next test confronts your ingenuity. I can't tell you because I do not know when or what your next challenge will be. I can confidently warn you that I believe it will be soon, so be ready and expect anything."

"I have to admit, Scatman, that I was scared. Did you see the size of that thing? That's the biggest animal I have ever seen up that close. What do you call that type of animal? Is it some kind of cat?"

"It's referred to as a woodcat, the largest mammal that lives within the kingdom of the Mirror. Remember, Charles, you are no longer in the world you left behind. This land and the environment in which we stand is so peaceful, for everything here lives and thrives in complete harmony. We are all a finely tuned orchestra that lives and loves each and every day within the laws of tranquility."

"Where do we go now?" I asked.

"Do you see that canoe over there?" Scatman replied as he pointed to a small lagoon about fifty yards in front of where we were standing.

"Yes, I do," I said.

"The lake of hopes and dreams is calling for our passage to the other side of the canyon. Near these shores, you will be tested once more, which will allow you to gain entrance into the Mirror. Your strength and endurance, along with your heart and emotions, will be evaluated in this area."

We walked over to the lake shore, and when I looked upon the calm waters, I noticed how big the lake actually was. I felt a serenity that surrounded it, which gave me peace and joy that most people have never experienced. I helped Scatman get the canoe out upon the tranquil waters as he taught me how to maneuver the canoe properly. The boat floated away from the shore slowly but steadily, and I felt like the surface of the lake was like glass, extremely smooth. When we reached the middle of the lake, Scatman directed me to stop rowing as we let the calm current keep the canoe moving. I suddenly felt some type of mystical change come upon me from within, which made me feel very fortunate to be alive. I did not recognize its significance, but I knew that I wasn't hallucinating, and to this day, the presence that came upon me has never left.

Suddenly and quite unexpectedly, the canoe was jerked and the front section of the canoe where I was sitting was lifted out of the water. A powerful force from below the surface had Scatman and me desperately trying to hold on. Scatman had a better grip than I did, as I fell into the water with a big splash. I quickly swam to the surface and found that Scatman and the canoe were fine.

"What was that?" I yelled out to Scatman.

"I don't know," he replied honestly, but somehow, he knew that something was going to happen, and very soon.

A great wave from below the surface came upon me, as I was swallowed up in the core of its possession. I felt a thick, slippery coil being wrapped around me so that I could barely move my arms and legs. I desperately tried to hold my breath, as I was submerged under the water with an urgent need for air. I realized what had me wrapped up so tightly when it jumped out of the water just long enough so that I could take a deep breath. A giant sea serpent held me in its grasp as it twisted and turned in and out of the water. I was quite frightened by what was happening to me, but at the same time, I did not panic. I believed that I would not be harmed, for this serpent was taking me for a ride, testing me, just like Scatman had predicted.

After a few minutes of jumping in and out of the water, being twisted and turned in every direction, the serpent suddenly loosened its grip upon me and swam away. I watched with admiration as it jumped in and out of the water and finally out of sight. It was the largest amphibious creature I had ever seen, much larger than the woodcat I had encountered earlier. I stayed afloat as I turned my attention away from the great sea serpent to find Scatman and the canoe. I could see him as he rowed toward me about one hundred yards away. I swam as fast as I could toward the canoe, and with Scatman's assistance, I got out of the water.

"You're all right, aren't you?" Scatman asked, concerned.

"Yes, I'm fine," I said, "although I have to thank my mom and dad for those swimming lessons a few years ago. It was so unexpected to be taken for a wild ride in the grasps of a giant sea serpent. I will not soon forget that experience."

"The serpent was another guardian of the Mirror. Your faith was tested as well as the genuine desires of your heart. Charles, you have now passed the two required tests that will allow you to enter the kingdom of the Mirror. If those special trained creatures allow you to pass, the Mirror will accept you. Man can be easily deceived by other men, but those unique creatures are hard to fool."

"I'm soaked," I said when I finally realized how wet I was.

"You're quite lucky, Charles, for today, the air is warm, the light in the sky is bright, and there is a slight breeze, so your clothes should dry quickly. Do you see that small pier about a half a mile away on the right side?"

"Yes, I do," I replied.

"We will row this canoe over to the pier, walk to the edge of the woods, and find some wood for building a campfire. Along with the heat of the day, the warmth of the fire should be enough to dry your clothes. While we are here, I will show you how to make a fishing pole so that we might catch some fish for something to eat."

Chapter 9

The canoe slowly floated up to the pier, shortly after I was pulled out of the water. We carefully got out of the boat and secured it as we tied it to the pier. Scatman immediately began to teach me about survival in the woods. I was dripping wet, but I knew that in the heat of the day, my clothes would eventually dry. As I followed him around the waterfront and the woods that hugged the shore, we began to gather the essential materials that we would need to start building our fire in the sand.

"Charles, there are a few important items that you should always have with you. I always carry some fishing wire, along with a pocket knife, matches, some strong needles, and a very firm bobby pin. When I travel to and fro, I never leave without them, and in time, I will show you why."

Scatman was very thorough in showing me how to build a campfire. He dried out the bottom of a moderately sized hole in the ground that we both participated in digging and then put many dried leaves with large and small pieces of wood used to start the fire. Using a match, the dried leaves started to quickly burn. When I saw the flames start to grow, I quickly went into the woods to gather more fuel for the fire.

"Now that we got our fire started, let me show you how to make a primitive fishing pole," said Scatman with enthusiasm. Once again, I followed him into the woods, and as I watched carefully, he taught me about survival. There was a deep concern in his eyes for me, for he believed that one day, I would need the lessons that I was learning from him. It was many years before that Scatman was taught those very lessons by Barnabus's younger brother, Liam. I felt secure that Scatman was being patient with me and taking his time in showing me the proper techniques and methods used. I learned the proper wood for making a fishing pole: something that was firm, hard, and flexible that would be able to sustain resistance. I watched Scatman use a knife and a special fishing wire to assemble our fishing poles. He also demonstrated to me how to dig for worms down by the lake, which I thought was disgusting. I was interested in what he was showing me, and I knew that a day might come when I would be able to use what I was learning.

"You see, Charles, modern technology is not required to catch fish. All that is needed is some wood for a pole, some fishing wire, a hook, and worms and you will never go hungry when you are near a lake, river, or pond. Here you go, Charles, your first homemade fishing pole. Now let's catch some fish!"

Scatman handed me one of the two fishing poles that he had just made. I walked to the end of the short pier and sat down and threw my line in the water with anxious expectations to catch some fish. I had only gone fishing one other time in my life, when I was eight years old. It was on a camping trip with my parents in the Smoky Mountains of Tennessee. I caught two fish on that day, and so did my dad. I remember him mumbling that I had beginner's luck. Shortly after we brought the fish back to camp, my mom trimmed and cooked them over the campfire. I remember that it was the most delicious fish I had ever eaten. I recalled the memory in my mind as the last time I went fishing. At that time, I had a modern fishing pole with all the latest designs and features, for my dad went fishing occasionally with friends from work. I looked at the fishing pole that I firmly held in my hand with its primitive design when Scatman noticed that my mind was many miles from where I sat.

"What is it, my son?" asked Scatman, noticing the distant expression on my face. He knew that something was on my mind, and he wanted to discuss it so he could pacify any doubts that might have been troubling me.

"I was just thinking about the last time I went fishing. I was on vacation with my parents. I hope that I am making the right decision by following my heart and dreams."

"I had felt the same way when I was where you are now," replied Scatman as he looked into my eyes. "Let me assure you, Charles, that the life that you would have lived with your parents probably could have hindered your spiritual growth, unlike what you will experience with the guidance from the Mirror. Eventually, you would have walked down the wrong path and been led into a life of destruction. You will be saved from that now."

"I'm sure you're right, Scatman, but I still feel bad about running off like this," I said with a blank sadness that appeared on my face.

"In time, I'm sure that will change. You will learn to appreciate what the Mirror has to offer. When you begin to notice the changes coming forward into your life, you will be thankful for the choice that you made," Scatman told me as he gently touched my shoulder with a gesture of encouragement.

After a few moments of silence, I felt a tug on my line.

"I think I got one!" I yelled with excitement.

"Hold onto him, my boy, and start pulling him in," Scatman instructed me with pure pleasure of the moment.

He slowly and carefully showed me how to capture and bring the fish in with experience and expertise. I rose to my feet, firmly pulling on my line, as I reached out and forcibly removed the reluctant fish from the water and onto the wooden planks of the pier. I watched the fish struggle and gasp for his life. Scatman quickly grabbed the fish by its head, pulled out the hook, and put the fish in an old wooden bucket that we had found in the woods.

"Good job, Charles!" exclaimed Scatman. "Now it's my turn to catch something to eat," he said as he reached for his fishing pole lying near the end of the pier. It did not take Scatman very long before he had a catch of his own. I could tell that he was an experienced fisherman by the manner in which he pulled the large, struggling fish out of the water.

"Well now," Scatman said with a sincere enthusiasm in his voice, "let me show you how to cook out here in the wild."

Returning to our campfire, we saw that it had almost gone out, although it was still hot. I quickly went into the nearby woods and found some fuel for the dwindling fire. Using demonstration as his tool, Scatman showed me how to build a rotisserie made out of some small but sturdy tree branches. I also learned how to clean fish by both watching him and performing the task myself. After we had cleaned the fish, I followed him on a search for some seasoning spices. It didn't take him long before he had found some basil and sassafras. Using his knife, Scatman chopped, diced, and mixed the seasonings to form a unique blend of seasoning.

"It would help our cause if we had some cooking oil. Where would you suggest we find some, Charles?"

"I have no idea," I timidly replied, knowing that Scatman knew where to find some.

He rose to his feet, and with a keen knowledge that is only learned from experience, he began to walk to the tree line on the edge of the woodlands. Scatman looked among the trees and bushes for a few minutes, examining their leaves. Finally, he pulled out his knife and cut many leaves off of a certain bush that had large, dark green leaves. I did not understand what Scatman was trying to accomplish.

"Around here, Charles, there are many things that are not what they appear to be. These leaves are unique, and only when they are heated by fire does a perspiration process begin. They start to sweat, just like we do on a very hot day. The liquid they produce has the same characteristics as your mother's cooking oil."

Scatman took a few leaves and, for a few brief moments, passed them very gently over the tops of the flames from the fire. It did not take much time until they began to perspire, just like he said they would, producing a liquid. I watched Scatman as he caressed the fish with the leaves and then seasoned our fresh catch with spices. When he had the two meaty pieces of fish ready to cook, he secured them on a wooden skewer and placed them on the rotisserie. As the fish began to cook, Scatman sent me out to pick some fruit to accompany the fish for our meal. It didn't take me long to find the fruit, for I knew exactly where to find some. When I returned to the campfire, I saw Scatman manually turning the rotisserie and cooking the fish to the desired perfection.

"The fish is almost done cooking," he told me. "We hardly have any utensils, with the exception of two knives. Out here in the wild, sometimes you have to rough it. When you get inside the Mirror, eating will be a joy and everything you need will be at your fingertips."

The meal from the Lake of Hopes and Dreams was cooked to perfection. Scatman waited for the fish to cool for a few minutes before he placed my meal on a knife and handed it to me. I handled the knife carefully and then, with caution, sank my teeth into the thick piece of fish. I became delightfully satisfied when my taste buds came in contact with something that was vaguely similar to lake trout. We ate all of our food, and I devoured my first meal away from home on my way to the Mirror of Freedom.

"A very good meal, Scatman, unlike anything I ever ate before," I said.

After we had finished our meal, we washed our faces and hands in the lake and put out the fire as the time approached to continue our journey leading us to the Mirror. Our quest for food had been satisfied, and my clothes were not so wet, for slowly, they had begun to dry.

"I'm sure it would be nice for us to sit around the lake and talk for a while, but the day is growing short and we still have some distance to travel if we are going to reach the Mirror by nightfall. The Mirror of Freedom is waiting for you, Charles."

We walked away from the lake, and entered the woodlands, finding the same path that we had walked upon on the other side. The trail climbed steeply uphill, which made our pace slower, a time of the day that tested my physical endurance, mental attitude, and my faith. I learned a lot about myself, as I had to endure several precise tests. These examinations of the heart asked some important questions to the very essence of my existence. What did I feel on the inside that prompted me to follow Barnabus and Scatman? Time and endurance would reveal an unwavering truth found in the regions of the unknown. I wanted peace of mind, and I sought it earnestly, although it seemed determined to remain hidden from my eyes.

A climb that seemed to be endless was before us, which was becoming increasingly steep and treacherous. The path became extremely rough at that point, caused by much erosion that elapsed over many years. Secure footing was becoming rare, as our chances of slipping and falling became more possible with every step we took. We came upon two strong lengths of rope that were anchored to the side of the steep incline. Provision was once again provided to us in the form of assistance in climbing the steep cliff.

Fatigue was walking by my side, accompanied with a few aches and discomforts. I wanted to rest, but I knew that the Mirror was close and, somehow, I needed to find the strength to carry myself forward. I moved slowly, as if I was in slow motion, when I sensed the Mirror stronger than ever even though I could not see it.

What about my mom and dad? I thought to myself as I continued to pull myself up the steep hill. *What will happen to them when they discover that I am gone and might never come back?*

The opposing forces within me once again waged their continuous battle inside the boundaries of my soul. My parents had created an unpleasant world for me, which was either filled with hostility or alienation. My life had an ultimate plan, and I believed at that moment, during a crucial time in my youth, that I would only be able to find it by faith.

It was a hard climb for me, as I struggled pulling myself up the rope, until finally, Scatman and I reached the top of the cliff.

I was nearly out of breath when I immediately lay down on my back, and as I looked up at Scatman, I noticed that he was hardly breathing hard or even sweating after such a climb. We looked out upon the deep canyon, admiring the lovely sight that stood before us. Noticing where we had just climbed, I saw the spot where we had just eaten fish by the pier, and it seemed to be a long way down the sides of the hill.

"Tell me, Scatman. You are much older than I am, but you do not seem to get tired like someone of your age would. Why?" I curiously asked.

"Inside the Mirror, age does not matter that much. You might age one hundred years, but still have the same physical attributes that someone in their prime does. Young and old are physically almost the same, except when a person nears the end. What really distinguishes a person is knowledge and experience. It's not the physical that matters but the deeper functions of your mind. If you tell someone you are old, your confession will bring forth the reality of the words you spoke. I try to stay healthy in mind and body and use the Mirror as my guide to keep my life clean and virtuous.

"All I know," I began to say, astonished by Scatman's physical condition, "is my father and his brothers, who appear to be younger than you, could have never done what you just did. You climbed that cliff so easily, without the exhaustion that I experienced."

"Your dad does not have the power of the Mirror to guide him and give him an inner peace that could make his life feel meaningful. Most people do not have the pure motives that we embrace here in the Mirror. There really is a difference on how a person lives and the effect it has upon how you feel."

"I think I understand. So what you are trying to tell me is that I could live to be quite old and still be able to do many of the things I did in my youth."

"In most cases, that is true," Scatman said in agreement.

Looking away from the canyon, I saw a long tunnel of trees that seemed to reach far beyond my eyesight. A wide path divided a line through many large trees that lay just beyond us. Their enormous bearing reminded me of the dream from the other night, which I believed was the focal point that had brought me to that place and time. The trees were both tall and wide in diameter, similar to the Sequoia trees in California that I remembered seeing pictures of in a *National Geographic* magazine.

"This path will get us much closer to the Mirror," said Scatman as he pointed toward the tunnel of trees.

We got up slowly, having rested briefly from our strenuous climb. I was still a bit tired, but somehow, I found the strength to continue, especially since I could sense peacefulness in my heart that made it a pleasure to be in such a place.

"Scatman, I feel like I've been here before. Everything around and before me is a reminder of a dream. However, I know I am not dreaming. I am aware of where I am with no desire to turn and look back, for this place is very familiar to me."

"You were here, Charles, several nights ago. I was watching you. However, you are not dreaming now. This trail will lead us to the fields of the countryside that I have previously told you about. The entire region that surrounds the Mirror is truly an amazing place, for it has a mystical feel in the air and you almost can feel that something miraculous awaits you."

Scatman and I walked in silence for quite a while. The tunnel of trees seemed to be endless. I was quite amazed by the size of the trees, for they towered over us in a way that was beyond my conceptual understanding. Finally, we reached a point where we could see the end of the path after climbing a series of steep hills. I was tired both mentally and physically, beyond my own capacity to understand why. When we reached the end of the trail, I looked out upon the beautiful picture of nature that reminded me of some of the greatest works of art created by the premiere artists of yesterday.

"These are the fields of the countryside I told you about," said Scatman.

"This place is beyond beauty," I said in a mesmerized tone. "How far is the Mirror from here?"

"It's slightly over a mile. Do you see those rolling hills in the distance?" asked Scatman, directing my attention to a group of picturesque hills located not far from where we stood.

"Yes, I see them," I replied.

"Just beyond those hills, on the edge of the forest, we will find a crater, and on the bottom is a cave, and inside of its dark interior, you will find the Mirror of Freedom," explained Scatman with a distant and cryptic inclination.

The fields and hills were covered by a greenish-blue grass with high, flowering weeds and a variety of small bushes that gave it an appealing appearance. We began to cross the field, which gave me the feeling of great satisfaction, to have finally reached the destination of my dreams and desires. I felt good again, with my energy restored.

We walked up and down a group of lovely green rolling hills. Upon the top of the highest hill, I saw a small flock of birds hovering over a designated area. Seemingly, they were attracted to something.

"Those birds must sense that something is out of the ordinary," I said.

"Yes, Charles. The Mirror has captivated a sense of awareness in those birds; they can feel its presence."

When we reached the top of the third hill, just beyond its crest, we came upon a small crater partially hidden by a dim cloud of fog. I suddenly became spellbound with a staggering presence of fear, for during this quest to find the Mirror, I never really gave much thought to what I was actually doing. The reality of my dream, which began to close in on me, sparked the reality in me of what was actually happening. Slowly, I moved through the fog when I became aware of the size of the crater. It was made of some kind of rock embedded deep in the ground, almost sixty feet in depth and diameter.

"You have found it! Charles, the Mirror is located down there!" yelled Scatman, walking behind me.

The descent down the steep slope into the crater was slightly hazardous, as Scatman and I had to be careful. A thin layer of golden moss had formed upon the rock, which made it slippery. Once we successfully scaled the rock and found ourselves at the bottom of the crater, we entered a cave in between two massive granite boulders.

The cave was very dark inside, along with being quite wet. A misty fog was all around us, and as I started to move through the cave, the temperature dropped drastically. A chill came upon me and embraced me like a hug from a distant relative. I had a hard time sensing what was in front of me, if anything at all. The deeper I walked into the cave, I became increasingly aware of a distinctive white glow that came from deep inside. I felt a peculiar presence all around me, and it began to control my thoughts, sense of mobility, and direction.

"The Mirror must be at the source of the light. To find the Mirror, I will go to the light," I said quietly to myself.

The wet walls I used as a guide for my lack of vision. I slowly and carefully felt my way through the cave, walking toward the light. With the exception of the sound of our footsteps upon the surface of the wet floor, I heard nothing. When we came to the rear of the cave, I found some old, deteriorated stone steps that led us into a seemingly empty chamber. The fog slowly diminished, and the closer we got to the source of our desire, the mysterious glow welcomed us. Each step that Scatman and I took had to be delicately planted or the possibility existed to slip and fall, for every inch of the cave seemed to be wet with condensation. When Scatman and I reached the bottom of the long series of steps, I immediately noticed warm air. I stood in a very large room about the size of a small gymnasium. I knew that I was in the presence of the Mirror. The room was immaculately constructed, I noticed, just by the manner in which the stone walls and the ceiling were built into the cave. I was no longer in the dark, for I could see everything around me.

My eyes fell upon the source of the light, and I saw the bold, bright, illuminating glow that could be seen throughout the cave. Rays of distinctive light sparkled from the large, rectangular Mirror that was carved into the back wall of the large room. It was the largest Mirror I had seen in my life. Big is just a description; to actually see it up close and in person was to live in its presence. The Mirror itself was floor-to-ceiling high, approximately twenty feet, and it appeared to be twice as wide as it was high, which gave the Mirror a rectangular shape. A bright glow transmitted from its core, which was almost hypnotizing. The reflective images that I saw of Scatman and I were not clear and precise, but they appeared to be almost like a shadow. I stood before the Mirror, the object of my desire, with a bewildered mind and a peculiar expression on my face.

"Scatman, I had no idea that the Mirror was so big," I said as I turned around to face him.

What I saw at that moment fascinated and saddened me, for Scatman began to change right before my eyes. His once-bright image of life slowly began to vanish, only to be replaced by a figure of a weakly constructed shadow. Only a faint appearance of his face remained visible, particularly his mouth, eyes, and nose. I watched the miraculous phenomenon change my friend Scatman, whom I had grown to love and respect, into a pallid form of a man.

"Scatman, what is happening to you?" I yelled, frightened for my friend.

"This is the way of the Mirror, my friend. The human form and shape that you now possess is transformed, as it goes through an extreme change upon entrance into the Mirror. Once you are planted within the boundaries of the Mirror, an almost identical replica of who you are is formed. Don't worry. It's not painful, for you will be unconscious. Your current image of life on this world can never be restored once you pass through the membranes of the Mirror.

The benefits are worth anything you might lose. You have a choice, Charles, between a type of fantasy land, where practically anything you wish upon can become a reality, or human life on Earth, where many of the things that you desire will never knock at your door. The decision is yours, so take some time and think about it.

"However, if by chance you choose not to enter the Mirror, all you have to do is leave this cave. You will be immediately swept away through the wind tunnel once again. When you open your eyes, you will have been returned to your parents' house, just as if you never left this morning. All the memories of the fair, Barnabus, and myself will be washed clean from your mind. If you want to be satisfied and fulfilled, with the opportunity to see those dreams in your heart and mind come to pass, just walk through this Mirror. I believe deep in my heart that you will choose wisely. I will be waiting for you," said Scatman as his shadow stood and stared at me for a short moment, as if he was trying to memorize my face.

"Take care, Charles," said the faint image of Scatman, as he turned and stepped into the reflecting glass and was swallowed up by the giant sized Mirror.

Scatman was gone. I knew it to be a fact that I could not deny. Would I ever see his face again? I thought I might possibly, but I knew that there was a decision to be made. I felt alone and alienated, just like when I was young and I lost my mother in the women's department at JCPenny. Fear began to pull at me from within, a time when my faith that had brought me to this place in time began to fail me. I became depressed and frightened, and a deep chill ran through my entire body. I cried out for help, with a desperate need for guidance.

"What should I do?" I cried out to the large Mirror.

I reached out my hand to touch the giant reflecting phenomenon. My fingers passed through the outer membranes of the Mirror. Whatever its interior consisted of felt wet to the touch, but it was not water or any other type of liquid I could distinguish, for its density was thick. Suddenly, I pulled my hand away, frightened. Immediately, a thought entered my mind: *Mom and Dad, what will happen to them?*

A struggle of loyalty and freedom began a tug of war battle in the chambers of my heart and left me nervous and confused about what was happening. The majestic power of the Mirror suddenly initiated a flash of memories through my mind and projected those images upon its face, where I could easily see them.

I watched the Mirror with fascination as I saw past images that had taken place in my life. Betrayal, alienation, and physical and mental abuse that I had endured was being shown to me like I was in a movie theater. I remembered a time when I was younger, when I sang a solo in a choir concert at school. My parents told me that they would be there, but they never showed up. When I got home, I was depressed and hurt, and when I walked into the house, I found my mom and dad at the dining room table, drunk on wine and laughing hysterically.

The images quickly changed to a time when my father came to one of my Little League baseball games. I had a bad game on that day, for I was probably nervous about my father being in attendance. I struck out twice and committed two errors. Shortly after I got home, my dad started to yell at me on how embarrassed he was by my performance. I believed that he was not ashamed on my behalf, but my lack of achievement on the baseball field hurt his foolish pride because I was not a premiere athlete.

My eyes were glued to the Mirror as my past continued to be shown to me. It was another day, a moment that I wanted to forget. I was an acolyte at church, where it was my duty to light the candles that were on display in front of the worship center. My robe was too long, and just as I was about to light some of the candles, I tripped on the long garment. When I started to fall, I knocked over some of the candles to the floor as I tumbled to the ground. My mother embarrassed me that time, as she walked out of the church and waited for me in the car. I had to stay for the duration of the church service because it was an acolyte's duty to extinguish the candles at the end of the service. My mother and I never went to church again. On the drive home, she yelled at me how I had humiliated her in front of all of her church friends. My feelings were the farthest thing from her mind, for she never once thought of how I might have felt.

The pictures of my past life went dark at that point when they changed to the images of Barnabus and Scatman. I saw Scatman's smiling face and the mysterious Barnabus as he escorted me to the fair. It was the essence of how the actual events were lining up as truths in relation to the dreams that were planted inside of me. The Mirror was trying to make my decision easier for me by showing me the past and present. My thoughts raced back and forth continuously as the pictures on the face of the Mirror terminated, although I was still not sure which direction to choose.

"Should I try the Mirror, which could bring fulfillment into my life, or experience life in an earthly fashion, constantly experiencing ups and downs, living the life of a roller coaster?" I asked aloud as I stood in awe, looking up at the Mirror.

"What an incredible sight!" I exclaimed. "I will follow my heart. My dreams have been showing me the way. It's the guide that I must follow. If I regret the choice I make, I know there will be no turning back."

I stepped into the Mirror, and as I did, I immediately began to slowly fall. I felt a sudden sense of weightlessness come over me as I slowly floated head over heels with the sensation of being rolled like a large ball. My eyes were wide open, but the only thing I could see was a white glowing mist like a fog or a thick vapor. I became aware that my decent began to accelerate. An unknown power had me in its possession and seemed to be putting me to sleep, for my eyes grew heavy. I continued to fall for an unknown amount of time, for I was unconscious and under the control of the Mirror.

I had become a child of the Mirror.

Part Two

Inside the Mirror

Chapter 10

I slept. I don't know how long I was asleep, but it was rest that my mind and body desperately needed. On that day, I would be required to be aware of who and where I was and to believe that I wasn't dreaming. In time, it would be important to learn what the concept of life in the Mirror actually meant. The reasons behind my arrival would be revealed to me, especially what happened to my presence of life back in Ohio and the effect it had upon my parents.

I was put to sleep shortly after I began to fall through the Mirror. Dreams did not consume me though, for my mind and body were changed physically and emotionally to adapt to the environment inside the Mirror. My human shell was modified when it reached a specific chamber and was transformed into a transparent image just like I saw Scatman change into. I was totally unaware of what was transpiring around me as I fell through the Mirror, for I was unconscious. After being changed into a transparent image, a short process of altering my flesh was completed. This procedure is similar to the metamorphous that butterflies experience, for the Mirror alters every little thing that passes through its matter. This alteration, although extremely complicated by human standards, only takes a few moments. The stress and hardship that the body endures is completely exhausting both mentally and physically, and rest is needed to restore energy lost during transfiguration.

How many hours passed, I did not know. I did realize however, that I was no longer falling. The last memory that I could recall was falling through the Mirror with a cloudy mist or vapor all around me. When I opened my eyes and focused my vision, I found myself in a large room, and as my eyes consumed everything before me, I knew I was nowhere near my parents' house in Riversville. My short-term memories stuck to me like glue, and I remembered most everything that held a special place in my heart. I held on to those images just like a soldier's wife waiting for her husband's return from war. She grasps the memory of how he held her in her arms and kissed her good-bye. Entwined together were my thoughts and memory of the fair, along with my friends, Barnabus and Scatman, who played important roles that led to the events that placed me inside the Mirror. I knew that everything happens for a reason, but why? It was the one question that I could not answer, and it plagued my mind. I wanted all that I had seen and experienced to be rooted in reality, but at the same time, I needed to know why I was enticed into this world.

I looked around the room, and as I did, I tried to analyze where I was. My surroundings were very unfamiliar to me, as I lay on a bed with white silk sheets. The mattress was remarkably soft, which made me feel like I was lying upon thousands of cotton balls. As I noticed the ceiling when I looked up, I could distinguish that it was made from a stone I had never seen before. Bright yellow moss grew sparsely upon the red stone tiles upon the walls of the room, with blue ivy spouting out in between the cracks. The blend of colors caused a radiance of imagery that transformed and illuminated the room.

The ceiling was quite high, approximately twenty feet at its highest point. Upon the floor grew an abundance of bright green plants that resembled pachysandra. Four large plants that looked like cornstalks with bright red flowering buds grew in each corner of the room, and they almost reached the ceiling. A large wooden door stood along one wall. It appeared to be strong and heavy, the kind of door that might have been common during colonial times. I looked at the door curiously, becoming increasingly puzzled, for the door did not have a doorknob. I wondered how I was going to get out of the room.

I began to search myself, and I had a distinct impression of a drastic change that had come upon me without feeling altered. Physically, I felt different in substance and individuality, but I could not finger a definite change. I wore the same clothes that I did prior to falling into the Mirror, and I became aware of a precise contrast from what had been.

I got off the bed and started to walk around the large room. The feeling of being lost started to consume me, for I did not know what to do. I could not go anywhere, for I was trapped in the room without a way to get out. I believed that I had passed into some kind of wonderful but mysterious dimension. My hope was that where I stood was some kind of waiting station and, soon, someone would take me somewhere to be oriented into my new life. I continued to study the room and its contents until I heard a loud clanking sound from behind, which startled me. I quickly turned around when I noticed that the large, wooden door began to slowly open. I waited for several moments in anticipation until, finally, two small bearlike creatures entered the room.

I smiled and almost laughed at the sight of them, for they were so small and cute.

"Hello. My name is Charles," I said.

The creatures had shiny, yellow-and-green eyes that possessed a sense of gentle warmth within them. They were short and furry animals, just slightly over three feet tall, but appeared to be quite strong, evident by their husky appearance. Upon their perfectly round heads and behind their thick fur, I could see two small eyes, a nose, and a mouth. Their arms were long and muscular, and they almost reached the ground. The expression on their faces, especially within the scope of their eyes, was one of curiosity. The words that came out of their mouths were gentle in emotion but with a firm direction.

"Come with us," they said in unison.

The two bearlike creatures, which were called furtoes, approached me; took me by the hands, one on each side of me; and led me out of the room. I felt slightly nervous, but at the same time, I knew I was in no danger. We entered a dimly lit tunnel that was filled by a thick fog. Through the fog, I could see the walls of the corridor, which was covered by multi-colored ivy, and upon the ground, we walked upon wood chips that made a crinkling sound beneath our feet.

Silence loomed all around us, as if we were on a secretive mission, and I began to wonder where my two companions were taking me. I did not know where the tunnel was leading us to until we rounded a sharp curve, where a gigantic door stood before us. The door was quite large, almost twenty feet high, ten feet wide, and almost two feet thick, made of an ancient design and style reminiscent of colonial America. The two little furtoes walked up to the door and, working as a team, pulled the heavy door open. A very bright light that I had to shield my eyes from came upon me when the door opened. A fresh breeze met me as I walked through the doorway when I entered a paradise region if there ever was one. What I saw before me filled my heart with joy, for it was my dream coming to life. A magnificent sight stood before me, as I saw a vast variety of trees in all shapes, sizes, and colors along with many other plants, flowers, and vegetation displaying the splendor made from the creator's hand. The breeze ruffled the leaves on the trees that created a tranquil sound, which essentially was the symphony of the wind. Music in nature was being played, for its vibrations came alive in me as they rang through my ears. Each sound, such as the owls hooting, crickets chirping, and insects buzzing, had musical tones to me.

"This place is beautiful! It's just like the dream!" I yelled out with a deep emotion that filled my heart with a tremendous amount of joy.

My two escorts looked up at me with a curious but happy expression on their faces. We entered a thick forest, and as we did, I began to appreciate the simplistic peace and beauty around me. The woodlands were filled with a unique assortment of trees, peculiar-looking plants, and several varieties of wild flowers that had a characterization and distinction only found in the Mirror. Slightly ahead of us in the distance, I could see a family of animals that resembled deer but were not and ran quickly with an elegance of motion. There were many different species of animals. Their individuality in nature was distinct but altogether different than the creatures back in Ohio. Peace and harmony dominated this domain, together with all who lived to enjoy freedom that their natural instincts designed them to be. Only within the realms of the Mirror is man restricted from advancement that would benefit only mankind. His intelligence has given him supremacy over the other creatures, but man can only use that authority in compliance with the Mirror. The laws set forth by the Mirror have confined the way a man lives, and with obedience, he has survived in this manner for many years.

My two furry escorts led me down the path as I continued to passionately observe everything around me. We came to the top of a steep hill, where before me was a magnificent view displayed unto me like a giant mural. I briefly looked at the bright light in the sky when I realized that it was not the sun. The light that came down from above did not originate from a single source but was a global illumination from a power that was unknown to me. I looked beyond the trees to a region rich with lush vegetation and many farms featuring their individual farmhouses and barns. Just past the farmlands, a massive building similar to a castle caught my eye, for it looked like something out of a Walt Disney cartoon. The remarkable-looking castle was accompanied by a group of smaller structures that resembled factories and warehouses among many little dwellings that formed a small village. I knew that the castle was the heart of the community, for all activity seemed to center around it.

"I wonder if that is where I will live," I quietly speculated in my mind.

As we walked onward, we passed a few dark and secluded caves and several sparkling lakes. The waters upon the lakes appeared to be quite refreshing, as the rays of light bounced off its surface just as a Mirror reflected an image. After putting several miles behind us, hiking over some rugged terrain, we came to the end of the trail. The path emptied into a large meadow flushed in green. Springtime produced radiance through many lovely plants that reminded me of flowers back in Ohio. They grew in abundance around the edge of the large field and led up to a small stone house in the far right corner of the meadow. The house had a small front porch with an old wooden swing and a brick chimney, where I noticed a faint line of smoke flowing out of it. A black man stepped out of the house when we started down the stone walkway. A large smile planted itself upon my face as we got close enough to recognize him. I remembered the last time I saw Scatman. He was standing by the Mirror as he was transformed into a weak shadow. I recalled my emotions at that moment and how Scatman told me the way of the Mirror. Now, once again, he stood before me.

He watched me as I was led by the two furtoes up to his house. It was quite evident to me that he was expecting my arrival. Scatman understood, for he had similar characteristics when he was my age. When we came face to face, he looked deeply into my eyes and he examined my essence in life for a brief moment, knowing that I had gone through a distinct transformation.

"You finally did decide, didn't you? I know how you must have felt when I left you, for Barnabus did the same thing to me many years ago. The time of decision must have been difficult for you, but through the chamber of truth, the Mirror guided you to a resolution that you will not soon forget or regret."

I smiled at Scatman, for I was happy to see his face. He was my traveling companion to the Mirror, and he taught me many things while I learned some very important lessons about myself.

"I need to know one thing, Scatman," I declared in a serious manner.

"What?"

"My mother and father, I know there is an important reason why I was led away from them, for they probably would have caused much pain in my life if I had chosen to live in their world. What has happened to my existence back in Ohio?"

"You are gone. The remembrance of your life has been erased. Every person that you touched, from your first grade teacher, Miss Weinstein, to Clyde Davies, the boy who pushed you down, their memory of you has vanished. To those who knew you, your presence in that plane of existence never happened. You will always remember Charles, for that part of your life is an important fragment of who you are. Your parents are fine, but they are not mourning over your loss. Life goes on for them as if you were never born. Charles, there was no depressing funeral on your behalf, no tears, just a minor modification of the memory. The Mirror took care of everything. It always does in a situation like this. It will be important for you to remember your life back in Ohio, for there are valuable lessons that you have learned over the years that you will be able to use here."

"Why was I brought here? I believe that that there was a reason hidden from me that I was not told when we were back in Ohio. It really doesn't matter why I was not told, although I hope that you can tell me now."

"Yes, I can," Scatman replied quickly. "However, I imagine you must be quite hungry, so how would you like to discuss this over a nice, hot meal?"

"Sounds good," I enthusiastically agreed with a smile.

Scatman nodded to the two furtoes as they promptly turned around and began to walk back into the forest. I waved good-bye to them, for I believed that I probably would never see them again. Scatman turned his attention to me as we walked up to his house. When we got to the front porch, I smelled the pleasing aroma that poured out from the inside. It was the smell of old-fashioned cooking, and I reminisced of my mother's cooking while I anxiously awaited the meal that was forthcoming. When I walked through the door, my senses came alive, for everything that I could see, hear, and smell was at my reach. Scatman had a pot of stew cooking over the fireplace, which filled the house with a scent that seemed to talk to my stomach. I was indeed hungry, and my body craved nourishment. My eyes quickly traveled to and fro as I looked at the décor in Scatman's house. The fireplace had an active flame that radiated a soothing warmth while it cooked a stew in an old, cast iron kettle.

The walls of Scatman's house were made of brick and stone, with assorted items of memorabilia hanging sparingly from room to room. I noticed a photograph of Scatman and Barnabus that must have been taken quite recently next to a picture of Scatman with a very pretty woman, maybe an old girlfriend I thought.

"You will stay here tonight," said Scatman. "I will explain many things to you about the Mirror and the reason why you are here. Barnabus will be joining us later, and the three of us will talk, for you, Charles, have a lot to learn about your new life. First and foremost, let's see if our meal is ready to eat. I have some delicious stew cooking over the fire and some biscuits in the oven. Follow me, Charles, and I will show you around my simple little house, and after we eat, a bath is available if you want to wash. You will also find a change of clothes that I believe will fit you."

I followed Scatman as he began to show me around. We entered the kitchen to check the rolls in the oven. He opened the heavy oven door only to realize that the biscuits were not ready.

"Just another few minutes and we can eat."

The kitchen was a walk-through cooking compartment that connected the living room to the dining room. In the kitchen, I saw a wood-burning stove and oven and a small, antique-looking refrigerator in which Scatman kept the eggs, cheese, vegetables, and fruits. Strategically placed along the walls were several cabinets where he stored his plates, pots and pans, and his nonperishable foods. I followed him out of the cooking area, where he led me up a narrow flight of stairs to a small but cozy room. Inside, I saw a small twin bed, a dresser, and a nightstand with a small Victorian-style lamp on it. I noticed that the workmanship of the furniture seemed to be of such fine quality like I had never seen before. The majority of the furniture in Scatman's house appeared to have been made from a rare type of wood, one that I was unfamiliar with.

"This will be your room for the night," said Scatman.

"It's a small room but looks very comfortable," I told him with a smile of appreciation.

I knew that for the time being, I was Scatman's responsibility and it was his duty to teach me the essential lessons that would be important during my first few days inside the Mirror.

As I continued to follow Scatman around his house, he showed me the bathroom; the linen closet; and his bedroom, which was much bigger than the guest room. The floors of the upstairs creaked under each step that Scatman and I took. His house was extremely old but very clean. I remembered something my mother told me once when she would nag about keeping my room clean. She compared the cleanliness of a person's room or house to their personality. I think that I agree with her.

We walked downstairs to another flight of stairs that led us to the basement. I saw a large double sink made of stone with two washboards, one large and one small, that I knew was an old-fashioned method of washing clothes. I immediately noticed the absence of a washer and dryer, which was unlike the common household in Ohio. Across the room from the sink, I focused my attention upon a large bookcase that covered the entire length of the wall. Shortly thereafter, Scatman lifted his eyes in the direction of the kitchen, and as he did, his nostrils grew wide to allow the scent of food to penetrate his nasal cavity.

"I believe the rolls are ready," he said.

When we walked into the kitchen, I realized the degree of hunger that was within me. Without being asked, I assisted Scatman with setting up the dining room table by getting the plates and silverware and arranging them in their proper positions. I poured some fresh spring water into two tumblers, and Scatman brought the pot of stew and set it on a wooden pot holder. As he quickly returned to the kitchen, I patiently waited for him to be seated at the table. He appeared shortly after, carrying a small basket of hot biscuits.

"I know you're hungry, so dig in," Scatman told me.

I quickly reached for the basket of biscuits and took two of the warm rolls and put one, which I cut in half, into a bowl and poured one ladle of stew on top of the biscuit. I waited for Scatman to get his food before I started to eat. We ate our food in silence for a few minutes, and I enjoyed the quality of a home-cooked meal. The stew had been simmering for hours, which allowed it to obtain the best flavor from the blend of its natural meats, vegetables, and spices. Scatman watched me eat heartily, and he was reminded of his brother years ago, when he was young.

"This is delicious!" I exclaimed as I looked up for a moment while my bowl of stew disappeared. It had been a long time since Scatman had seen anyone eat as quickly as I did.

"You may have seconds if you want to, but slow down. Enjoy the food before you for the splendid quality of its culinary art," Scatman politely suggested.

I did eat much slower the second time around, and in fact, I did learn that it was better to eat slow and enjoy the flavor instead of acting like a starving animal in the woods. When I finished my second helping of stew, Scatman asked me if I wanted some Orangeberry pudding. The dessert offered to me was a special treat, for it was naturally made from orangeberries, fruit sugar, and Tislon's milk, an animal that lived in great numbers in the Mirror, which was similar to what I knew to be the Bison. It was just another example of the different types of foods that people in the Mirror eat. What I ate at Scatman's dinner table had similarities to the foods back in Ohio, with the exception of their freshness. In the Mirror, all food comes directly from nature. Even the preservatives that are used in canning are natural. People live much longer because of the superior quality of food and are less prone to illnesses and diseases.

When I had finished eating, I paid gratitude to the maker of the meal with a compliment. I promptly helped Scatman clear the table and clean our dirty dishes, being led by a considerate nature within me. The act of the chore reminded me of the numerous times I cleaned the dishes for my mom and dad, but I felt differently about doing it for Scatman, for I really wanted to help. My parents never really appreciated what I did for them, and as I helped clean the kitchen from our meal, I thought of how I was being treated like a person should be and not like a slave.

"I think I'm ready for that bath you mentioned," I said when I finished cleaning the dishes.

Scatman directly led me upstairs, where he got me a change of clothes and a few towels. I soon found out that Scatman was right, that the clothes he had for me did fit.

I turned on the faucet of the bathtub and adjusted the temperature to my own specifications. As I got into the tub, I immediately felt the warm, soothing sensation of the water as it captured my entire body into its melody of comfort. In just a few minutes, I was relaxed and satisfied with my decision during my moment of truth before the Mirror. What lay ahead in the future was unknown to me, but I felt a peace that I had never felt previously. Love and harmony ignited a passion from within, which had a purpose with a desire to learn from this land and the wisdom of its people.

Chapter 11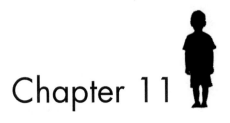

I had always loved to take a bath, for it gave me the feeling of being cleansed not only by soap and water but also of an invisible spiritual force. Soaking and meditating in the tub usually left me feeling exhilarated, with a fresh outlook upon life and myself in general. When I got out of the bath, my thoughts reflected upon what had transpired over the last few days. After I had dried myself thoroughly, I got dressed into the clothes that Scatman had given me. I didn't realize at first how comfortable they were, but as I examined them, I recognized the distinction that they were handmade. As I brushed my teeth and combed my wet hair, I felt clean and I knew, somehow, that I was different. When I finished dressing, I went downstairs to join Scatman. I was anxious to find out why my presence inside the Mirror was so important.

"Feel much better I hope," said Scatman.

"Yes. A warm soak in the tub always makes me feel refreshed."

"Very good," replied Scatman. "In a few minutes, we will go outside and I will show you around my little farm. I have animals to feed and many crops to look after. There is always work to be done when you live on a farm. You will notice, Charles, that our society here is limited in the amount of technology that is used. The manner in which we live, along with our morals and values, have not changed for almost one hundred years. We do not have television sets, fancy cars, or many other luxuries that you had back in Ohio.

But everything we need is here inside the Mirror, and there is no compulsion to become greedy or selfish."

I sat down on a small but comfortable couch that sat directly across from the fireplace, where I absorbed the warmth from its flames. My eyes moved around the living room, where, again, I noticed many of Scatman's possessions when I realized that there was not one item connected to his past life, before he came to know the Mirror. Objects of sentimental value were not present, such as family heirlooms, souvenirs from distant places, or other treasures that people hold close to their hearts. An old banjo stood upright on a wooden stand in the corner of the room by the front window that overlooked the front meadow. Several framed paintings hung on the wall. One displayed a beautiful landscape with a waterfall while another was a pencil drawing of a flock of birds flying in the air over a vast countryside. As I became quite absorbed by the images that stood before me, Scatman suddenly came into the room.

"Those pictures are a symbol of my life. What they mean to me symbolically is very significant. What you see in those pictures is probably different than what I see. Neither one of us would be right or wrong with our interpretation. It is the way you look at things that would be different than mine. From the way we distinguish some of life's situations to how we live our lives, it is important for us to analyze our actions, motives, and desires."

"Do you play the banjo?" I asked, changing the subject.

"Yes, I do," replied Scatman. "I will play later, but first, we must go outside and feed the animals. Remember how hungry you were just a short time ago? I'm sure that my little animals are getting very close to being as hungry as you were."

As we stepped out of the house and walked to the backside of his property, Scatman began to show me what life on the farm was all about. We walked through a large meadow filled with many trees, bushes, and shrubbery of many kinds, down a small hill to a barn that appeared to have been standing for many years. Scatman lived by himself, and although he had been removed from other people, he was never lonely. Scatman had been placed there by the Mirror for a chosen purpose, for he is the guardian of the gate that leads to peace and joy.

When I got inside the barn, the aroma of a farm greeted me very passionately. I saw many animals of various species. Most of them I had never seen before. They had similar characteristics to many farm animals that I had been familiar with, although they possessed their own unique signature in nature. I saw animals that looked like chickens but were not, as well as pigs, cows, goats, and lambs, all with distinct features that separated them from their distant relatives back in Ohio. Inside the Mirror, there were many things that appeared to be similar of things remembered but different and original in creation. I helped Scatman feed his animals, and I learned that it was just a part of Scatman's responsibilities in the Mirror but not his only function.

A peace in the air came upon me that made me feel unlike anything I had ever sensed before. As the breeze swept across my face, I was consumed by a specific emotion that filled my heart with an appreciation for what had happened to me that placed me upon this land. Scatman was showing me things that had to be done on a farm, as he saw a fascination in my eyes for all the various types of animals. After we had finished in the barn, he took me on a tour of his orchard and vegetable fields. By my standards, the vegetable fields were enormous, over eight hundred yards long and two hundred yards wide. It was very spacious, full of many types of vegetation resembling plants back in Ohio by their shape, color, and size. The corn, potatoes, carrots, onions, peppers, and lettuce grew in abundance, but once again, they had the appearance of being distinctly original, as they stood among other peculiar-looking vegetables. In time, I learned to accept and appreciate their unique color and shape, although their taste had characteristics that were vaguely familiar. As I looked beyond the fields, I saw a large orchard full of many kinds of fruit trees and bushes that lined a downhill slope for quite a distance. Scatman told me that his farm was one of the smaller ones.

"All food that is grown here on my farm can be used by everyone who lives here. Sharing is probably one of the most important virtues inside the Mirror. We could not have survived this long without everyone working and caring for each other, as well as the guidance that the Mirror provides. Only by working as a team could we possibly have been able to exist, for without the help of each other, we would be lost."

I followed Scatman around his farm, and we talked about many things that were important for me to know. There was much I had to learn, with numerous things I had to unlearn, such as learned personality traits within the very nature of my soul. What I was feeling in my heart was foreign to me, for my nerves were creating false impulses in my mind. I looked up into the sky and saw the light that shined down upon this land, and I sensed a rich energy in everything the Mirror possessed. I noticed the light was more of a glow, in which I identified was the origin of all life around me.

"Charles, here on this land, we work for each other, like the members of a championship sports team. Back in Ohio, there were many people who thought only of themselves. Here, we are all children of this kingdom with so much to learn. You will come to experience that life is so much more than performing a certain job, for you will see that living inside the Mirror is beyond many of your greatest expectations. The labor that is required by the farms is shared by everyone in some capacity, for we all enjoy the fruits of the harvest. This land sustains us through the food that grows in its rich soil. The Mirror also takes special care of its animals, allowing them to live in harmony, without man's intervention.

"This is quite a place," I said. "Even the clouds in the sky and the light that shines down upon us is different. I feel strange but altogether at peace, truly a special type of experience unlike anything I have ever known."

"That's the power of the Mirror working within you," said Scatman with a large smile that formed upon his face, noticing slight changes that were becoming apparent in me.

We walked back to the house through the vegetable fields. Faint thoughts of doubt quickly raced through my mind as impressions of dreaming came upon me. I was not totally convinced that what I was seeing, in actuality, existed. I hoped and prayed that what I thought I was experiencing was real, for I knew that if, by chance, I would wake up and find myself lying upon my old bed in the basement room that I left behind, depression would possess me. When I did hold tight to the faith that all that was before me was real, I felt lucky. How was it that all this happened to me? Surely the Mirror exists in some magnificent miracle of creation that I could not even try to comprehend, grasp, or touch during this time of my intellectual maturity. Life was so foreign to me inside the Mirror, for I still held on to the beliefs and concepts of earthly values. My outward appearance was basically the same, as the foundations were being planted within me to be totally cleansed and transformed for the purpose destined by the Mirror. This change could only have happened by direct intervention. A contentment of my own self-worth flourished from within, and even though I had doubts and questions, I seemed much happier than I ever did before.

"Charles, I'm going inside the house to lie down for a short nap. Barnabus will be coming over soon, and at that time, we will explain to you all that you desire to know. You can relax if you want or you can read. There are plenty of books in the basement to entertain and stimulate your mind. Since you have many questions about your new life here, may I suggest you to find *Reflections of Life*. It can educate you about this land and how it became what it is today. There is much information in that book. Most of it should give you insight on what you can't understand."

When Scatman went inside to lie down, I followed him and sat down on the couch across from the fireplace. I looked deeply into its flames, and I felt the heat from the bristling fire. My memories walked in meekness down that same road that passed the events that had shaped my life over the last few days. The question, "Why?" continued to influence my thoughts. I tried to relax, but I could not until some of the answers to my questions became known to me. I was suddenly motivated to find the book that Scatman had mentioned. My eager desire to acquire knowledge about my new home led me downstairs to the basement, where I lit a few candles, for there was not much light to read by. I examined the many books and stories that Scatman had collected through his years in the Mirror. None of the books were familiar to me, and I realized that there were no authors that I had read when I was in Ohio. I searched for quite some time through periodicals, religious doctrines, and medical and farming manuals until I finally found the book that I was looking for. I pulled out the large, hard-covered book that was almost twice the size of the traditional hardback, both in weight and diameter. I studied the ancient texture of the book's cover, for it was very old. When I opened the book, the pages made a crinkling sound that reveled the book's true age as I turned them.

Reflections of Life
A guide to understanding the Mirror
and the majesty of its kingdom

I noticed that there was no author noted, and as I was slowly turned each page, I tried to absorb every word that passed before my eyes.

The first few pages told the story of the Mirror, which dated back in time to just prior to the Revolutionary War in America. It was a time when man did not know about the physical existence of the Mirror, although they seemed to have overlooked that it had always existed in their hearts. The Mirror came to become the powerful, loving, caring symbol of promise and hope through man's desire for deliverance. There were many folks during those dark days who had great expectations of escape from their mental and physical hardships that they had to endure.

I learned that in each person, good and bad personality traits do exist.

However, neither good nor evil can dominate a person against their will. It has always been choices that are made over time that determine what harvest comes into a person's life. The Mirror began its physical breath of life from the dreams of those people who practiced morality that eventually led them into a place abundant with peace and harmony. Their dreams demonstrated symbolic pictures in which they saw a beautiful and tranquil land. After months of hoping and expecting deliverance from their burdens, a day came when they opened their eyes to a miracle that greeted them fondly. The sights that were bestowed before their eyes when they awoke from their dreams both frightened and held them in the state of bewilderment. What they had dreamt in the night had become a reality. Never again would they have to live under the influence of intimidation.

"This is incredible!" I exclaimed, amazed at what I had just read.

I continued to read, as I became fascinated with each passing word. I learned about the unfortunate circumstances of the American colonists as they struggled to feed their families and keep their homes. Many were desperate, and in their time of need, what came to life led them to a unique form of deliverance that had its design in their unconscious minds. It was not a single dream or even several but numerous dreams of the exact same content that were dreamt simultaneously that brought the Mirror into physical existence. A new world came to life through the oblivious will of man, as an escape from their battle with oppression. The first generation created the foundation on which people of the Mirror have been governed all these years, in a life that they managed to keep simple. Only when they understood what the Mirror was could they be able to trust and be led to the guidance of regulating themselves.

The words written in the book captured me unlike anything I had ever read. My mind seemed to be consumed by the subject matter, and I tried to experience the heart of the colonists and tried to imagine what it was like to live in those days. After pursuing that line of thought, I heard footsteps above me when I realized that Scatman must be awake.

"Charles!" Scatman yelled out.

"I'm in the basement," I answered back loud enough so that he could hear.

A few minutes later, he walked down the basement steps and found me reading by candlelight.

"Did you find the book that I suggested?"

"Yes, I did," I replied.

"Did you find the book informative?"

"It's truly amazing, especially the part of how the Mirror came to be; a group of people and their dreams, without knowing or realizing what they were about to accomplish, united together from their need to be free. Out of space and time, this world was created."

"This is a unique place," said Scatman. "However fascinating the theory behind the origin of this place is, here we are. We stand firmly in a place that is totally inconceivable by man's reasoning. You now live in a land that, only by a divine miracle, could it come to exist. What intrigues me the most is how we have grown and survived all these years. I believe it is only by grace and the Mirror's love for us, his children, that we have been able to survive. Charles, the three most important things to remember are, one, the Mirror loves you; two, it is essential for us to return his love by obeying what is revealed to you by his spirit; and finally, it is vitally important for each and every one of us to work united with the same cause. Inside the Mirror, people live a long time, and on most occasions, it is the result of being obedient to the laws of the Mirror, our diets, and the healthy environment in which we live. On Earth, man lives seventy years or so, but here inside the Mirror, the average age of a person, at the time of his death, is usually two hundred years old or more. I would almost be eighty years old on Earth, entering my final days, but here in the Mirror, I'm still young with lots of life left in me. When I was at the fair, I felt old and tired, but within the dominion of the Mirror, I feel good to be alive. It's the quality of life here, the unpolluted air, and the fresh foods that we eat to keep our bodies healthy."

"How many people live here?"

"Our population is almost at six thousand people. It is segregated between men and women, young and old, from all kinds of different backgrounds. Here, all the people you will meet, minus one, are good natured, as you will become acquainted with some of them in the days to come. Of all the age groups that are the most important, the youth carry the promise of the future. When you make their acquaintance, try to learn through them. And in turn, you will teach yourself what life in the Mirror is all about. Study and watch without being noticed, for you will find purity in their hearts. Enough reading for now, my son. We must start thinking about our evening meal, and we must go outside and pick some fresh food for our vegetarian spaghetti."

"Sounds good," I replied with keen interest.

"It tastes even better, and it is also much better for you than any pasta dish you ever had at your parents' dinner table."

Scatman and I went outside carrying two large straw baskets to put our vegetables that we would pick from the field in. We walked into a large area of tall stalks bluish green in color that towered over my head.

"You might think this plant is some kind of corn," he said to me, trying to acquaint me with what I was seeing. "I assure you that it is not."

"What is it?" I questioned him with curiosity.

"This is the plant we use for pasta. It's called noldomi, or string vegetable."

Scatman pulled a large knife out of the inside pocket in his jacket and removed it from its protective leather cover and, with one quick stroke, cut the stalk down. He cut the large stalk into four different sections and crammed them into my basket. Even though my basket was filled to capacity, I was still able to carry it, for the stalk was very light.

I watched Scatman as he picked several other types of vegetables. He found black onions that he told me had a tart taste. As I helped Scatman gather other vegetables, such as dark maroon carrots, white tomatoes, bright red squash, and lettuce that had a pale orange color, I became interested in the various types of vegetables that grew upon the crest of the land. When we had accumulated all the vegetables that we needed, Scatman and I headed back to the house. A familiar face was waiting for us when we walked out of the vegetable fields: my mysterious friend Barnabus. He was dressed casually and appeared to be much rested than he had been when I last saw him in Ohio. Immediately, he offered to help us bring the food into the house.

"Good to see you," said Barnabus in a warm greeting.

"It is also good to see you," I replied, remembering the morning that he appeared at my doorstep. My impression of him as he stood before me was one of improved health, for he even looked slightly younger than he had back in Ohio.

When we got into the house, I became one again quite interested in the vast difference of food compared to what I had seen in Ohio. I watched Scatman as he peeled the skin off the noldomi plant and pulled the string vegetable onto the counter. Observing the weight of the basket that I carried, I noticed that there really wasn't much useable vegetable. Inside the skin of the plant uncovered a vegetable that was similar to spaghetti noodles, except in color, for these noodles were white in color, but during the cooking process, they changed to a pale shade of yellow. Scatman worked in silence, and I watched him peel the maroon carrots and dice the black onions, tomatoes, and squash. He quickly and systematically got two pots, one large and one small, out of the cupboard and started to boil some water over a sharp flame. The vegetables he put into a smaller pot with a small amount of oil and started to cook them slowly.

"Come, Charles. Let us sit by the fireplace while Scatman cooks the dinner, and we can discuss the many questions that linger in your mind," said Barnabus, directing me into the living room.

Chapter 12

Barnabus and I went into the living room and sat down on the gray-and-red plaid couch across from the fireplace and seated ourselves at opposite corners, facing each other. Quietly, he sat, contemplating the significance and the importance of what he had to reveal to me. The serious manner in which he approached our talk made me slightly nervous.

"I know you are wondering why you are here. Why did we find it necessary to influence you to follow us into our world? This is just one of the nagging thoughts that trouble your mind. Am I correct?"

"Yes, you are," I said seriously.

"The realization must have dawned upon you by now that life here is quite different than it was back in Riversville. You probably have experienced many astonishing things since you have set your heart and mind upon the Mirror, with many more that await you."

"Yes, I have," I said with a desire to tell Barnabus all about my adventures. "I went through a wind tunnel, I petted a large wood-cat, I swam with a large sea serpent, and I fell through the Mirror." There was innocence in my voice and upon my young face that filled Barnabus with joy.

"What I am about to tell you, then, probably won't surprise you."

"Probably not," I replied.

"All right, Charles. As you have probably already figured out, there are many fantastic features about this place. The air is fresh and clean, the food is pure, and there is a freedom to be yourself. Life here seems to be as close to perfect as possible, but it is not. Something is not right, not now. A spectacular event took place several years ago, and at the time, we assumed that it was a blessing. As the years passed us by, we began to witness many specific events that unfolded when the realization dawned upon us that this 'miracle' was not anything that we hungered for. For whatever reason, the Mirror permitted these events to transpire. I do not understand, but I don't have to, for I am required to trust."

"What was it?" I asked in curiosity.

"Let me explain, Charles. When a person is brought through the Mirror, they are washed clean from many selfish ambitions and desires. These foolish intentions and emotions can pollute your spirit, such as pride, greed, and dishonesty, just to name a few. What we became a spectator to was totally unexpected, but sometimes bad things happen to good people to test them. Understand, Charles, that many of our heart's wrong passions, thoughts, and desires are eliminated shortly after coming into the Mirror. Almost three years ago, on a night when the darkness was just beginning to creep upon the land, a brilliant flash of light raced across the face of the horizons. It was similar to some kind of optical illusion that we occasionally see in the night skies. This was quite different though, for what we saw next was evidence of an amazing phenomenon. We ran to the spot where the flash was, and when we got there, we found a young boy, barely clothed, walking around as if he were lost. I told you at first we thought this boy was a blessing, a child of the Mirror. He called himself Kassar, which, in the ancient Mongol tongue, means 'archer.' He was of oriental decent, and his physical and mental maturity would have been parallel to a normal ten-year-old.

"One year passed, and as we had been observing him, we still thought he was a child of the Mirror. He was passionate about caring for other people, or so it seemed, along with possessing strong powers granted by the Mirror. However, there are times in our lives when circumstances are not what they appear to be. Shortly after this time, we started to suspect that Kassar was trying to pollute the minds of other people. He planted many harmful emotions within their hearts in a way that he could manipulate impressions upon their thoughts. These feelings were quite foreign to the people of the Mirror, and they did not know how to react. Kassar sowed the seeds of a rebellious nature into them, along with acts of violent anger.

"Slowly, a small part of the population began to act like the seeds Kassar had planted. Scatman and I were bothered by what we were noticing very much. Our ancestors came here to start a new life void of the many impurities that they left behind. For almost two centuries now, life here has been clean and moral. To lose it would be a devastating loss to everyone who has enjoyed peace and freedom for all these years. Scatman and I have watched and studied Kassar, and we are confident that he is manipulating people's emotions and eventual actions through their dreams.

"What he does is quite elementary, for he creates a bond with someone physically, emotionally, or intellectually. During the night, when everyone sleeps, Kassar plants himself into their dreams for the sole purpose of deception. This process, which is known as shadowtreking, has been a method of communication used only in the kingdom of the Mirror for several generations. I will explain the specifics of shadowtreking more thoroughly a little later. We tried to fight Kassar in the arena of the dream on several occasions, but it always ended tragically. He is quite clever and has learned how to use the dominion of the dream to his advantage. We became confused with not much hope, desperately seeking an answer to our dilemma when the Mirror showed us your image."

"I'm the one," I stated nervously. "I can faintly remember a dream from my distant past, when I heard a voice that said, 'You are the chosen one.' I did not understand the true meaning of those words at the time, but now that dream has revealed itself through time. You saw me, my life, and how unhappy I was. My dreams and my imagination and what I was capable of doing were revealed to you. I was the answer you were looking for, and I became your deliverance."

Barnabus smiled at me, and his pale blue eyes seemed to be reading the confines of my heart. He recognized how perceptive I was and how quickly I analyzed what their motives for attracting me into their world was.

"I believe you know more than we realize," he said with a smile.

"I had dreams about this place several times before I knew it to exist, even before you showed up at my doorstep. I have never met Kassar, but I believe I saw him in a dream about two years ago. We were playing chess, and just when I was about to declare, 'Checkmate,' he stood up and knocked the game over. When he walked away, he said, 'Stupid game.' I woke up at that moment, and it's strange how I remembered that dream."

Scatman, who had been listening to our conversation, came into the room. He looked at me briefly, until his eyes met Barnabus's.

"I believe Charles holds inside his vast imagination the key to finally defeat Kassar at his own game. We must train him to shadowtrek, to be like us and like Kassar," Scatman declared in a serious tone.

"Very true," replied Barnabus as he gently rubbed his chin and pondered what had been said. "Before Charles can learn to walk in the dreams of others, he must meet Kassar. They could form a mental and physical bond through competition. A game of basketball and chess or something similar would allow them to create that needful union. A basketball court is at the school, and I know there is a chess set at the school's library. It's possible that Charles's dream could come to life."

"Good thinking, Barnabus," said Scatman. "However, for the time being, I hope that everyone is hungry, for I have made more food than the three of us could possibly eat, so let's enjoy our meal."

We sat down at the dining room table for a meal of good food and pleasant conversation. It was a pleasure to enjoy a meal in the company of good people like Barnabus and Scatman. I was polite as

I ate, and I observed my manners, listening to my two companions discussing many common topics that really did not concern me.

"Barnabus and Scatman," I said in a very serious tone.

"Yes, Charles? What is it that troubles you?" asked Scatman as he noticed that I was concerned about something by the disturbed expression upon my face.

"I know that back in Ohio, when a person dies, their family has a funeral and they are buried in the ground. What happens here when your time ends?"

Barnabus quietly cleared his throat, and he looked into Scatman's eyes. It was not a question that they were expecting.

"Charles, on Earth, there are many theories and beliefs about what happens to a man's soul when his or her life ends. Each religion has written doctrines that claim that their belief is the only truth. Many spiritual scholars have done in-depth studies, but no one can claim absolute proof or give verifiable evidence to the mystery that has kept mankind guessing for years. It is only by faith that man can believe that their chosen religion is teaching the truth. Where there is no faith, one cannot believe. Here in the Mirror, it is quite different. When a person dies, their mortality is lifted out of them and transformed into a spirit of light. The glow in the sky that gives us light and warmth to live by comes from the Mirror and the people who once lived here. It is their love that shines through into our realm of life. The human remains are disintegrated in rapid succession by the power of the Mirror. There are no cemeteries here, for our loved ones are always near us. If we miss them, all we have to do is look skyward. Even though they can't respond back to us, their love can be felt in many different ways," said Scatman.

I finished my meal in silence, enjoying every bite. I also ate a bowl of apple cinnamon ice cream, which was delicious. When I had finished, I got up, rinsed off my dishes, and put them into the sink, and I joined Barnabus in the living room in front of the fireplace. I looked deep into the fire, and my mind traveled far from Scatman's house to some past memories. I recalled a dream about a boy from a couple of years before. I don't know why, but I believed that the boy in the dream was Kassar. He was a couple years older than me, physically bigger and stronger, had dark brown hair, and looked to be of oriental ancestry.

With the ability to see the future, the Mirror can change the circumstances of certain events, if it is deemed necessary. In legends of long ago, people had dreams of events that were to come, and even though the significance was never revealed, their patience waited for the events to unfold into their lives. Faith was alive in their hearts, and although it became a ritual to fight with many moments of doubt, they remained steadfast. I believed then, as I still do now, that everything that breathes, eats, evolves, loves, and eventually dies belongs to the Mirror.

Scatman finally joined Barnabus and I in the living room after cleaning the kitchen. He sat down in one of the chairs by the fireplace, and as they looked upon my face, it was evident to them that my thoughts were beyond their reach.

"So, where are you, Charles?" asked Scatman.

"I was thinking about Kassar," I said slowly as I made my way through a cloud of confusion after being interrupted from my deep trance. "Even though I have never met him, somehow, I feel I know him. I believe I had seen him in one of my dreams."

"Let's talk about dreams, Charles," said Barnabus very seriously, as he looked into the fire for a short moment, until his eyes fell upon me once again. "In dreams, there are times when the dreamer can see their image in actuality while on other occasions, they are themselves. In the case of shadowtreking, when the conscious life force enters the dream, the dreamer is always themselves. What Kassar has done and is still doing, we believe, is manipulating people's dreams, where he is in control of that dream. He can change certain situations and events in the dream, such as the weather, for he could make it rain or snow if he so desires.

"It is very similar to what a movie director does when he makes a movie, for a dream is nothing more than theater for the mind. Kassar has been influencing the dreamer to act in such a way that is a contradiction of their actions in the natural. Stories have reached our ears about an epidemic of strange and bizarre dreams. One man dreamt about setting fire to a field of crops that were ready for harvesting. Others have had dreams of stealing food, committing immoral acts with their neighbor's wife and daughter, and one such person dreamt about smashing the Mirror with a sledgehammer. Dreams like these have had an effect on many of our people during their everyday lives. They do not understand behavior of this manner while they are sleeping. Kassar's dream manipulation has created problems between people who normally get along quite well. There have been loud verbal arguments and fist fights, and some husbands and wives do not trust one another anymore. This behavior is a result of what Kassar has been doing when he probes the dreams of the night."

"What can be done, Barnabus?" I asked, very concerned.

Scatman got up from his chair and walked over to his banjo, which stood in the corner of the room by the front window, and he slung the instrument with its shoulder strap around him. He adjusted the banjo, put on his finger picks, and began to play. It was a soft but melancholy melody that floated out from his banjo, until Scatman began to sing. He was quite a good singer, and his voice reminded me of one of those Motown singers from the early '60s. The lyrics that he sang were directed at me to give me confidence. They spoke about not being afraid and being patient, until his words shrieked out at the conclusion of the song, which pierced the confines of my heart that if I did those things, I would *win*.

"Do you understand, Charles?" Scatman asked as he stared at me with a stern perception that made me a bit nervous, although I knew he was just trying to get his point across.

"Yes, I do. I must be like a fox," I said, smiling at him in response to his little song and verse about Kassar.

"Tomorrow," said Barnabus, "you will meet Kassar. He is often seen playing in the schoolyard such games as basketball, baseball, and soccer. He enjoys the great sports from Earth that we adopted as recreational pastimes. You should be able to compete very well with Kassar, for you are quite familiar with those games and you are about the same size. The dominant trait in Kassar's personality is jealousy, which, at times, turns into a violent temporary hatred. When he competes, there have been occasions when he does not play fair or, in a manner of speaking, he cheats. His pride is centered upon being the best athlete, chess player, or whatever else he chooses to engage his efforts into. Kassar has been accused of not playing fairly several times. This is just a warning to you, Charles. So in the event that you might play a few games with him, I want you to be aware of his little tricks."

"I will try, Barnabus," I said with confidence.

"You will also be given new living quarters tomorrow," interjected Barnabus, trying to make me aware of the plans for the next day. "We will move you over to the castle. I'm sure that you saw a large castle in the distance on your journey through the woods. In time, you will feel at home there, for you will be able to make some new friends. Some are the same age as yourself. We are not putting you in harm's way by placing you in close proximity to Kassar, but we are following the Mirror's destiny for you. Scatman and I will not be far away if you should need some guidance, and we will be watching your progress. There is much to learn before you can battle with Kassar in dreams. At the castle, you will have the chance to learn and mature with the companionship of others like you, who might share some of your interests. The youth of the Mirror is the future, our hope for a continuously peaceful and fulfilling environment in which to live."

Scatman started to play his banjo again, which brought music back into the dull quiet of the room. I smiled, as I enjoyed the sounds that came from his banjo and how they created an emotional river that flowed through me.

"Let's go onto the back porch for a while, as the fresh air feels so very good during this time of the evening," Scatman suggested to Barnabus and I as he continued to play.

When we walked outside and onto the deck, I realized that Scatman was right, as the early evening air did feel good, and as I looked out upon the farm, a comforting sense of contentment seemed to overwhelm me. The wooden deck was shaded by lofty trees, which made the air feel quite cool. A presence of serenity lingered, removing all nervousness and anxiety that was creeping upon me, desperately trying to seize control.

After Scatman had played some good music, he put down his banjo. I was pleased to be with my two friends, and I knew they would teach me much of what I needed to know about life in the Mirror. Realization suddenly dawned to my own sensibility: I knew that moment would be the last time Barnabus, Scatman, and I would be together under such carefree circumstances. Kassar had become a threat to the peace and harmony of life, and the Mirror designated Barnabus and Scatman's responsibility to stop him. They had tried countless times to reason with him and convert his manner of thinking to become one with the Mirror, but unfortunately, he had become a hopeless rebel. I was brought to the Mirror because my destiny had linked me to wage war with Kassar, for his sword had ripped a hole into the moral fabric of life inside the Mirror.

The night grew old, and as we began to grow tired, we went back into the house. After some brief parting comments, Barnabus wished Scatman and me good night as he walked out into the darkness and headed back to the castle. Scatman and I discussed for a short time what my tomorrows might bring until, finally, we both realized that it was time to sleep.

Almost immediately after my head hit the pillow, I fell asleep and found myself in a dream. I was walking through a large field with tall, green stalks of something that resembled corn that rose above my head. A hypnotizing breeze calmly tickled my face, which gave me the impression of everlasting tranquility. I did not know where I was going, and I really didn't care until, suddenly, a young girl appeared out of nowhere. I immediately realized a strong attraction that quickly formed between us as I noticed her beautiful blonde hair and blue eyes. We joined hands and began to walk the fields together, as our souls seemed to be in tune with the environment. In my heart, I almost believed that I had known the girl at my side my entire life. I looked upon her face, becoming spellbound by her youthful beauty, when she suddenly vanished just as she had appeared.

A faint melody came to my ears, and it began to rise with volume and intensity. My attention was focused on the song, and I continued to listen until I realized that what I heard was a chorus of chanting voices that sang out, "*Go away Charles! Go home! Go away Charles! Go home!*"

The voices sang the phrase continuously, and I began to shiver from head to foot. I felt unloved and unwanted, and I began to run frantically, having no idea where I was going. I ran as fast as I could with all my energy and stamina. My heart was pounding with much force, and I felt as if it was going to explode out of me when my eyes slowly opened.

I looked around the room, and as I recognized where I was, I became very thankful to be in Scatman's house. I took a deep breath, and security settled upon my heart. I knew that it was still quite early, for it was still quite dark. I rested for an hour or two, but I did not return to sleep, for I wrestled with the logistics of the dream.

Scatman eventually got up, knocked at my door, and told me that a new day had arrived. I felt rested, and I became excited about the new challenges that I would face. My thoughts focused on Kassar, which had me preoccupied, pondering the confrontations that lay in wait for me. I was motivated, but I knew that I had to have a firm grip on my faith.

Chapter 13

I felt quite anxious as I got out of bed and I went into the bathroom to get washed up and ready for the day. Without knowing what I was going to encounter in the hours and days that were waiting for me, my thoughts focused upon what I desired to accomplish. Ever since Barnabus appeared at my doorstep, my life had become filled with a mild sense of confusion, mental frustration, and extreme change. Believing that my faith would give me strength for what the future held, I walked downstairs with confidence, following the scent and sounds of a country breakfast. Scatman was cooking what he called grilled pickled bread, although it slightly reminded me of French toast; either way, the aroma was the same, and that made me hungry. Soon, we were ready to eat, and just before we were about to sit down, a knock on the door interrupted us. I went to the front door and opened it, and my eyes fell upon Barnabus, who was dressed very casually, wearing brown workman's pants and a yellow pullover cotton shirt. I stared at him for a quick moment as he stood before me just like he did a few days before, remembering that moment when he invited me to the fair.

"Come in, Barnabus," I said, happy to see him once again. "We are about ready to eat some breakfast."

He followed me to the dining room, where Scatman was putting the last of the condiments on the table.

"Hello, Barnabus," said Scatman joyfully. "Have you eaten yet?"

"Yes, I have. Thank you," replied Barnabus.

"How about some tea?" asked Scatman.

"No thanks."

While Scatman and I began to eat our food, Barnabus began to tell me the plans for the day.

"After you have finished eating, Scatman and I will take you to the castle. You will be taken on a tour of what will become your new home. Don't expect to remember everything, for it is quite a big place. Throughout the day, you will be introduced to many people, some of whom will make your transition into your new life much easier. We will also show you around the village that sits near the castle on our way to the schoolhouse. In time, you will become familiar with the castle and its village, until you will feel at home, as if you never lived anywhere else."

Scatman and I ate heartily until we had satisfied our need for food. When we had finished, we quickly cleaned the kitchen, along with the plates, glasses, silverware, and the large skillet. I went upstairs to the bathroom and brushed my teeth while Barnabus and Scatman discussed a few items of importance.

Upon leaving Scatman's house, we quickly found the path that led us through miles of lush vegetation. The weather was pleasant, just like the dawn of summer. The flowers were blooming, the light in the sky was bright, and the birds seemed to be singing in a most joyous disposition. When I left Ohio, summer was coming to its end, in the Mirror it seemed ready to begin. "Barnabus," I asked, "could you tell me about the weather here? Are there four seasons like there were back in Ohio?"

"We have all types of weather here," responded Barnabus very quickly. "Most of the time, it is similar to what you would call spring and fall. However, there are times when the air turns cold, like winter, and very hot, like summer. Usually, the weather is very temperate, and I'm sure that you will come to appreciate the climate here in the Mirror."

We walked quite a distance, and I looked at every little thing that passed before my eyes. Once again, I became fascinated by the unique characteristics of the landscape, with massive-looking trees that stood in size beyond my comprehension, along with many types of flora, shrubbery, and assorted vegetation. After climbing over a series of steep inclines, we came to a sight that held me captive. When I was younger, I had read stories of kings and queens who lived and ruled their kingdoms from grand palaces, which usually set my imagination soaring. I would have never imagined, even in my wildest dreams, living in one. A twist of circumstances had led me to a destiny that was beyond my understanding. Barnabus and Scatman smiled at me when they saw the look of bewilderment upon my face. I became quite enthralled by the appearance of the spectacular castle that was visible from where we stood.

The castle rested on a hill that so very slightly overlooked a small village. From what I could see slightly over a mile away, the village consisted of many simple family homes and a marketplace, along with a few factories that were operated to supply and furnish the needs of the kingdom.

The central government within the Mirror was located in the castle, where important meetings were held and decisions made that concerned the welfare of the entire population. Spiritual leadership was also at the castle, where worship services were held every Saturday night. Within the stone walls of the castle was where most of the elderly, widowed, and orphaned portion of the population ate, slept, played, and loved.

A large courtyard lay beautifully landscaped in front of the castle, which led to a long series of steps that ended at a large, ten-foot-high wooden door. Being artistically displayed, the courtyard had a large garden with a small stream that flowed alongside and under a little wooden bridge that led to the beginning of many white steps. A fountain sprayed streams of water in the center of the courtyard, where a species similar to ducks gathered in large numbers daily.

The picturesque setting truly enhanced the entrance to the castle. It was built from various types of brick and stone that was exclusive to the kingdom of the Mirror. The design was also original, especially since it did not relate to the time period in which it was built. The construction started shortly after people started to arrive in large numbers. The founding fathers had much help in those early days, from an essence that possessed a wisdom that was beyond normal humanity. It had been understood for many years that the castle was not entirely built by human hands.

I looked down at the castle from the hilltop, not totally believing that I was about to become a resident of the grand building. Never in my life had I seen a structure quite like the castle. I remembered a dream I had almost a year before, in which I was walking through the corridors of some large building. I didn't think much of it at the time, until my eyes came in contact with the majestic-looking edifice. I had been told what its exterior looked like and I had seen it from afar, but when we approached it, I was finally able to behold its size and dynamic elegance. The castle was truly a magnificent sight.

We finally started to walk down the steep incline, which eventually leveled off, as the entrance to the courtyard was through a small wooden gate. While I began to survey the complexities of the castle, I became hypnotized by its majestic bearing. Various emotions seemed to attach themselves to me. Some were quite strong. Their origin I did not recognize. But like a snowstorm that covers the ground, so I felt when consumed by that strange perception. I realized the reason behind what I felt, as I remembered what Barnabus had told me, for I was experiencing part of my final purification process. For a few moments, that consuming emotion kept my nerves on edge until, finally, a genuine peaceful feeling filtered in and seemed to engulf and crush what had lived in me before.

I walked through the courtyard with much fascination, as I saw a wide variety of flowers and shrubs that grew in artistic harmony. The gentle and tranquil sound of a small stream flowing through the courtyard comforted my nerves. The spray of mist from the fountain lightly touched my face, as droplets of water rose high into the air with the magnificent appeal of being magical to my eyes.

I turned my attention back to the castle, and the more I looked upon it, the measure of its size made me become increasingly mystified. As I looked skyward up at the lofty peaks of the castle, curious notions about the minds that conceived the plans for such a structure seemed to disturb me. To my own personal perception, a boy who had lived in Ohio in the year 1970, the castle had the appeal of being futuristic in design and dimension of its construction. Finally, we started up the steps that would lead us to the front door.

Forty-five steps created an illusion for me, as I felt like I was being lifted up and out of the courtyard to the castle's main doors. When we reached the top, Barnabus opened the heavy wooden door and gestured for Scatman and me to follow him inside.

We stood alone in the large foyer, until a very pretty woman in the prime of her natural beauty appeared and walked up to us. She had blonde hair with a radiant smile and wore a lovely red-and-white house dress. Women in the Mirror had retained many of the old-fashioned traditions from years past. To a woman, the family is the most important sustaining factor in their life, as most of their energy both in mind and action is spent taking care of it. Through the generations, these values had become very strong in women, as they gave thanks and praise the Mirror, loved their husbands if they had one, and tried to keep a pure heart. While all of these things are important to most women, it is an essential characteristic to maintain an attractive appearance as well as their feminine ways.

"Hello, gentlemen," the young woman said. "Barnabus, is this the young man you spoke so fondly of?"

"Yes, this is Charles," said Barnabus.

"Hello, ma'am," I replied politely as I offered my right hand in a gesture of greeting. Unlike the kingdom of the Mirror, I was raised knowing that it was customary to shake a person's hand upon being introduced.

"My name is Diana," she said as she took my hand while looking at me in a peculiar manner, until she realized the handshake was a custom to people on Earth. "I have a young cousin who could become your good friend. She's a very nice girl, although her life here has been quite sad. Her mother died shortly after giving her life, and her father raised her until she lost him in a tragic accident less than a year ago. Her name is Abigail, and she is twelve years old. How old are you, Charles?"

"Eleven," I answered her promptly.

"Perfect. The two of you would look cute together. Follow me, Charles, and I will show you around the castle."

Diana seemed to be a nice woman who possessed a friendly personality. She smiled and laughed a lot and had a deep concern for other people and their feelings. It was apparent that she was happy with herself and her life, although she was still looking for a love that she could share to make her life complete.

When I walked deeper into the castle, I seemed to have been captured by its size, beauty, and masterful design. My eyes were suddenly captivated by a large landscaped painting with many bright colors that seemed to be quite meticulously created. Among the various artifacts located in and near the foyer, I noticed several handcrafted statues made from wood and stone of different types of animals and birds, some of which were quite large and lifelike. My eyes roamed to and fro until I was drawn to an object that hung down from the ceiling in the adjoining foyer. It was large and preciously conceived chandelier that sparkled from the many jewels that were used to make it a wonderfully appealing object that caught my attention. From the stone walls to the wooden planks and the partially carpeted steps that led up to the second floor landing, it was obvious that mankind in the late 1700s did not construct the large edifice that I stood in. The castle was not created by man but for man as a blessing from the Mirror. I caught Diana starring at me, as I was in a temporary state of astonishment from the size and structure of the castle.

"Have you ever seen anything like this before, Charles?"

"No, I haven't," I replied. "The largest building I was ever in was the capital building in Columbus, Ohio."

Diana took me by the hand and led me on a tour of what would become my new home. We started in the basement, which was quite deep, and amazingly, it wasn't damp. In the basement, there were many leisure games, such as pool, ping-pong, and darts, among several others that I was unfamiliar with. It was explained to me that on a regular basis, card tournaments and chess and checker competitions were held, along with many other recreational activities to keep young and old minds healthy. On the other side of the basement, the music library and music practice rooms that had an assortment of musical instruments, from the violin to the piano, could be found. It was quite an extensive basement with large rooms and tall ceilings, which I thought was unusual for a basement. Diana also pointed out to me where the maintenance and boiler rooms were and suggested that I keep out of those rooms.

We went up to the kitchen next, where I noticed many of the kitchen and dining room personnel preparing for lunch. The dining area was very large and divided into several different large rooms with a variety of tables in size and style. The kitchen was busy constantly, as it catered to two separate dining rooms, with many special events held at the castle. Diana took me to the library next, where I saw more books than I had seen in my life. A large gathering room called the Waterscape stood down the hall from the library. It was called that because it had a miniature spring-fed waterfall and a stream in the corner, decorated by some rocks and artificial green and yellow plants. A fireplace with a small flame was located on the opposite side of the room from the spring, with several chairs, sofas, and tables. This room was the designated philosophical center of the castle, where many intellectual men and women of the community met regularly to discuss topics that affected the lives of all who live in the Mirror. Finally, we went to the very top of the castle, where Diana showed me the worship center. I found myself in a condition of bewildering awe when I saw the circular shape of the room and the many curved stained glass windows. After showing me most of the castle, she eventually took me to my room.

In the castle, there were five levels, but only two were used for housing. Designated east and west, each of the two wings housed sixty studios or apartments per floor. Most families lived in the village, although there were a few that resided at the castle.

"You will be sharing this room with William. Everyone just calls him Willy. He is a very nice and caring young man who is a few years older than you are, but maybe you could learn from him. Most of the kids your age are in school right now, and in a few days, you will be going also. Here in the Mirror, we try to make the learning process enjoyable, for you will find, in the proper environment and the guidance from a good teacher, that you can have fun while you learn. What you do not know can indeed be harmful to you. Just as a well-balanced diet is needed for the body, your mind needs a balance of stimulation through learning."

The sleeping quarters at the castle were very roomy and comfortable. Diana showed me my new room, which consisted of two beds, closets, desks, and dressers. There was also a large bathroom with a bathtub and a shower. I walked over to the bed close to the window and felt how soft it was, and then I opened one of the dresser drawers and noticed that they were packed full of clothes. They appeared to be brand new, without any signs of being worn.

"Excuse me, Diana, but there are clothes in here. Whose are they?"

"Why, they are yours, silly," she said with a cute smile. "They will fit you properly. The Mirror has assured us of that. We were informed prior to your arrival what clothes you would need."

"Are you trying to tell me that you were foretold of what clothes would fit me before I came here?" I asked, quite amazed.

"I myself was not told, but, yes, that is what happened," Diana said.

"Amazing," I said, stunned by the revelation of the truth.

I looked and studied the room for a few minutes as I tried to sort those facts in my own mind, until Diana took me downstairs to rejoin Barnabus and Scatman in the library.

"Enjoy your tour?" asked Scatman.

"Yes. This is quite a place," I replied.

"This is your new home, Charles," said Barnabus. "Take pride in it, and actively care for all who live here, for this building and the land it sits upon is the Magnus Opus of Mimetus."

"What is Mimetus?" I asked with a mystified curiosity.

"Mimetus is the name which the people here call this land. The founding fathers called it that because it slightly mimicked where they had come from on Earth. Through the years, the people have referred to themselves as Mimetians, even though it is a term that you probably will not hear too much of," explained Barnabus.

I briefly looked at the many shelves of reading material in the library, which seemed to ignite my imagination. In my mind, a good book was a tool to reach into the depths of my conscious mind, which links itself with another realm of existence. I saw many hard and paperback books of all kinds, encyclopedias, and many varieties of magazines and comic books. Although I was pleased to see a great assortment of literature, I was slightly discouraged that I did not recognize any of the titles. Absent was the name of one author or magazine title that I could call familiar. I later realized that the titles and names of the people who penned those books might have been different, but the stories themselves were slightly recognizable.

"Are you hungry?" asked Scatman.

"I could eat," I replied, although I wasn't really interested in food, for I wanted to research and study the various books and magazines in the library.

"Good. The first sitting is in about twenty minutes. After we eat, Barnabus and I will show you around the grounds and the village, and then we will go to the school."

"To find Kassar," I said, interrupting Scatman.

"Yes, to find Kassar," replied Barnabus with a downhearted tone.

"Until we eat," said Scatman, changing the subject, "why don't you find something good to read? I know there are books here that could stimulate your imagination. Some of the best minds to ever live in the Mirror, their thoughts are here on these shelves. The characters in many of these stories had strong faith and convictions in what they believed. Some of them were not that much different than you and I."

I eagerly turned my attention in the direction of the books, to search for the understanding that I lacked. It had been a long time since I felt good about myself, and I often wondered what it was like to be happy. I did recognize, however, that I had changed. It was slight, but it was apparent. I felt as if I was on a mission, with the burden of all that lay in the future dependent upon my belief in the Mirror for direction in my new life.

I looked through a few magazines for a few short moments, until it was time to eat. We left the library and took our places in the lunch line. When we finally entered the kitchen, I immediately noticed the magnificent aroma, which added to the appealing fact that the food had the impressionable quality of being delicious. The cafeteria line moved quickly, and soon, Barnabus, Scatman, and I were sitting down in the middle of a crowded dining room. I looked around before I started to eat, and I observed many other people eating their lunch and participating in good conversation.

How long is it going to be until I feel comfortable living here? I asked myself while Barnabus and Scatman ate their food and discussed topics that really did not concern me.

I tried to listen with interest, but I could not when I heard music that seemed to be vaguely intimate to me. It was a beautiful, soft melody with a perfect blend of harmonies that erupted together in unison, creating a majestic sound. The music was speaking to me, and I was being quite receptive. I had not heard music like that since I was in the fourth grade. Mrs. Jacobs taught music, and her class was my favorite. I learned to appreciate all kinds of music in her class, and I remember thinking that she was the prettiest teacher at my school. Looking back, I guess you could say I had a child's crush on her. The music I heard was classical, but the melody was different in a way that I did not recognize. The melody and harmony floated like a river, and I found myself sailing upon those waters, having escaped the conversation at the table, until Scatman reached out and pulled me back.

"Charles, where are you?"

When I heard Scatman's voice, I came out of my cloud of thought with a quick jolt back to reality.

"I'm really sorry, Scatman," I said in apology. "I was just remembering music class back in Ohio. The music that I hear sent me back to that memory."

"It is a very beautiful piece of music," said Scatman. "We have a music library here at the castle if you should want to listen to some. You can also learn how to play an instrument through instruction of one of our musicians. Occasionally, the choir and orchestra give concerts. Usually, they are quite good."

When we had finished our meal, Scatman, Barnabus, and I went outside and walked around the castle grounds for a short time. Soon, we found ourselves walking down a wide dirt road toward the village. On our way, I saw several large old buildings made from brick and stone that were used as warehouses and factories. We passed many lush acres of farmland and a few wagons packed full of fresh fruits and vegetables being pulled by what slightly looked like a horse, just as if I was living on Earth almost two hundred years before, with a few exceptions. When we got close to the village, I saw many log cabin homes in which many families lived. Many alleyways led off the main road to rows upon rows of primitive-looking dwellings. The amount of activity alongside the road increased the closer we got to the village. Men and women were busy at their trade, such as carpenters, clothing designers, potters, and shopkeepers, among many others. I observed all the work that was being done throughout the community, most of which I thought probably went unnoticed. We continued to follow the road as it led us out of the village and across some farmlands, where I saw people working in the fields, for it seemed to be spring harvest.

"It's time for you to meet your nemesis, Charles," said Scatman.

An unspoken agreement was upon us as we continued to walk down the dirt road. I had a role to play, and I would try to accomplish what was being asked of me to the best of my ability. It would become my responsibility to deliver people's minds from the chains of oppression. I looked up through the trees as I followed Barnabus and Scatman down the tree-lined road, and I thought I felt many eyes upon me just like an actor feels when he or she performs. I was insecure about what I would soon encounter, but at the same time, I had confidence that I would soon learn many things that were necessary to come to grips with peace.

We finally came to a fork in the road, and we followed the left side of the fork, which would lead us to our destination. It was a short walk until we were able to see the old brick schoolhouse on top of a small hill. The school was a large building made of brick, wood, stone, concrete, and glass. It was two stories high and had two wings of classrooms. Located in the center of the school were the administrative offices; the cafeteria; and the dining room for the students, an auditorium that was also used as a gymnasium. Outside the rear of the school was a playground with a large basketball court, teeter-totters, monkey bars, and several other pieces of playground equipment for the younger children. Beyond the basketball court was a large baseball and soccer combination field that was in use often for gym classes, recess, and many after-school activities.

We approached the school and walked inside. Two elderly gentlemen who seemed to know both Barnabus and Scatman met us in the large foyer. They talked briefly, until they took me inside the school's office to officially register me for classes. The current term ended in three weeks, followed by a five-week summertime break. I started the classes promptly, for it was advised to do so to get me familiar with other students, teachers, and the open forum style of education taught inside the Mirror. What I learned depended upon me, as the most important lessons came through association with others, along with circumstances and trials that led me to make important decisions. The basic elements taught were lessons of the heart: morality, compassion, love, and sincerity. I had to learn to adjust to this new life, and a change of schools was a foundation that was designed to create a change in me.

The registration process was quite easy. There were a few forms to be completed and a couple of tests to be taken, which was required by the school. The results of these exams were fundamental tools that the school used to determine mental aptitude. The test that I took gave the school's administration insight to what grade level to place me in. My grades were average at best back in Ohio; however, it was not because I lacked intelligence, for my focus was not on my schoolwork due to a stressful home life. In the Mirror, I believed my imagination would be challenged. The chance to grow spiritually, emotionally, and intellectually was here, for the knowledge that was deemed important was at my fingertips waiting to be possessed. Wisdom could create the development of my character and set the boundaries of my desires that grew up from inside of me.

Scatman showed me around the inside of the school, for he was quite familiar with where everything was because at one time not that long ago, Scatman was a teacher. It was a fast tour, and he quickly showed me the classrooms, the cafeteria and dining room, the library, and the restrooms. He knew that after a few days, I would be able to find where everything was. The many students at the school caught my attention, for it was a blended student body from various ethnic backgrounds. I smiled with the realization of what that school could become to me.

"Well, Charles, what do you think of our school?" asked Scatman with an inner curiosity.

"It's a nice school. I'm sure I will like it here."

"I know you will, Charles, for this school is very basic, but it is also very challenging. It's designed to teach the essential moral issues in life. Our community needs strong hearts and minds to become active participants in our society."

"Let's find Barnabus," I said, determined to meet Kassar.

Chapter 14

Scatman and I walked through all the seemingly vacant corridors of the school, past many empty classrooms, looking for Barnabus. It was the afternoon break, and the majority of the kids were outside. Our search became quite extensive until finally, we found him standing by a side door exit. He was looking out of a tall and narrow window next to the door, focused upon one particular boy. When we approached him, we both knew what Barnabus was so interested in. Revelation was ignited inside of Scatman's mind, as he knew that Barnabus feared Kassar more than anything he had ever faced. He knew to what extent Kassar could change the peace and harmony that breathed life into the community, although Barnabus believed that eventually, his manipulative plan would fail. The process of seduction was slow and gradual that Kassar was exposing the people of the Mirror to, but when Barnabus and Scatman discovered the truth, they began searching for a weapon that would stop him. In the months that preceded my arrival, several attempts failed to subdue Kassar, until the Mirror showed them my image. I became the one whom Barnabus and Scatman would take under their wing, to be trained in the ways of the Mirror, learning how to use my imagination in the vast chambers of the dreamscape.

"That is Kassar. He doesn't look any different than anyone else, but believe me, he is special, unique, and quite dangerous," said Barnabus, warning me to be careful.

Scatman turned and looked at me curiously, for I was watching Kassar through a window next to the door, and I appeared to be lost in thought. Through Scatman's eyes, I was a quiet but perceptive young boy intent on doing what was asked of me to the best of my ability. In my dreams, the Mirror came knocking, and through those tunnels of unconscious fog, I visualized many events and circumstances that had slowly begun to appear in my life.

"What about Kassar?" I quietly muttered to myself. I had dreamt about him on several occasions, long before I had been told about him. Within the dreamscape, Kassar had learned how to allure the people, but his motives were not with a pure heart but sang with a voice of selfishness. As I briefly meditated upon these things, I almost started to laugh when I realized that a similar technique was used by the Mirror to bring me to its kingdom and out of my own personal bondage. I was someone who needed help, as I was struggling in the muddy circumstance of human suffering.

"Charles, are you ready?" asked Scatman.

"Yes, I'm ready. I want to meet him," I enthusiastically answered.

"Keep in mind, Charles," cautioned Barnabus, "Kassar is not the innocent boy he will claim to be. He is also a liar. Don't believe a word that comes out of his mouth. The truth he will mix with lies to trick you, so it is best not to believe anything. He will defend his virtue and try to convince you that there are people, mainly Scatman and I, who hate him without justification. Don't let your defenses down, for he will try to find a weakness."

Kassar was someone who tried to imitate a normal, well-adjusted teenager. It was reported at the school that Kassar was thirteen years old, although he was not, for he was born of the Mirror just a few years before. His birth did not include a mother and a father, as he evolved from all the characteristics that the people of the Mirror are not. Kassar was superior both mentally and physically to the normal eleven, twelve, or thirteen-year-old, and he communicated in a very precise manner. He had partial oriental features that gave him natural good looks, with dark brown hair and brown eyes. A deep, dark stare was his instrument to gain access into the realm of a person's conscious. His dominion over the weak-minded he used masterfully, as they willingly allowed him to influence their dreams in the night.

Scatman and I went outside and onto the basketball court, walking in Kassar's direction. The presence of a battlefield came upon me as I approached him.

"Hello, Kassar. How are you today?" asked Scatman in a polite gesture.

"Fine, I believe," said Kassar, and he began to stare at me with penetrating eyes, which made me feel quite uncomfortable.

"This is my young friend Charles. He has just arrived here. The two of you are about the same age, size, and intellect, so I thought you could play a few games and get to know one another. Enjoy each other's company and the competition in the games you might play."

With those words of introduction, Scatman walked away and left the work required by the Mirror in my hands. A calming presence came upon him as he walked away, for he had faith in me to initiate the conflict that eventually would free the people of the Mirror from Kassar's mind control.

"How are you doin'?" asked Kassar as he bounced the basketball to me. "Do you shoot?"

"Sure, I play the hoops. I used to play a lot where I came from, as my mom and dad had a small court behind their garage."

I looked at the weather-beaten basketball for a moment or two and bounced it a few times until I lofted a shot from fifteen feet away. We silently watched the sphere fly through the air until it fell through the net without touching the rim or the backboard.

"Good shot, Charles!" exclaimed Kassar as he passed the basketball back to me for another shot.

We took turns shooting the ball until Kassar felt like my confidence was growing. I was making some difficult shots with a high percentage of accuracy. Kassar sensed that I was ready for a game, and just like a wolf, he seized the opportunity to stalk his prey.

"How about a game of one on one?" asked Kassar.

"Sure, why not?" I replied, as I had already anticipated the confrontation.

"Half court, ten points. The return line is the yellow line just beyond the foul line," explained Kassar.

Since I was the new kid, Kassar gave me the ball first. I dribbled the ball to the return line and looked at the basket when I averted my attention away from Kassar. He had his eyes upon me, trying to psyche me out to cause me to make a stupid mistake. I reacted quickly, for I knew the game he was playing, and it wasn't basketball. Without hesitation, I made a two-step move to the left when I turned and pivoted on my right foot, stepped up, and shot a quick jump shot, which surprised Kassar. I watched the ball sail through the air with anticipation, until it connected with the backboard and fell through the net. Kassar took the ball with poise and confidence, as his thoughts concentrated upon making his shot. He avoided eye contact with me entirely, until he quickly dribbled the ball past me and easily made a layup. He was bigger than me, outweighing me by almost twenty pounds and having a height advantage of a couple of inches, which made it difficult to defend him when he played a physical game instead of using finesse tactics.

The battle on the basketball court became a test of wills for the next few possessions. I made the long shots, and Kassar connected on the ones under the basket. The game went back and forth until I missed a shot. With an opportunity to gain control of the game, Kassar grabbed the rebound and powered himself past me, making a shot from five feet away, and he took the lead by the score of 8 to 7. When he knew he had the upper hand, he got greedy and he used a maneuver to intimidate and emotionally deter any hope that I might have had about winning.

During the course of the game, Kassar had been studying me, how I almost always took my shots from the right side of the court. He was hoping I would follow a pattern; so, without suspecting that he was a cheat like I was told, I tried to dribble past him, and as I did, Kassar extended his leg, tripping me. I fell to the ground, fumbling the ball as it bounced right into Kassar's arms. He quickly took the ball and raced to the basket for a score. I knew he had cheated, but I held my tongue. The score was 9 to 7, and I was mad and discouraged. I dribbled the ball once again to the return line and then raced to the corner of the court, but that time, I went to the left side. I shot the ball quickly but without confidence, and unfortunately, I missed. Kassar took the rebound with pride, sensing that the moment of triumph over me was at hand. Once again, he overpowered me by physically charging past my defense and shot an easy five-foot jumper that slowly rolled into the basket. Kassar won the game by the score of 10 to 7, although the game was won on a cheat. My enthusiasm for the game left the moment he had cheated. I felt sorry for him that he had to resort to such tactics just to win the game.

"Good game. We should play again sometime. Maybe with a little practice you might be able to beat me next time," Kassar stated coldly, gloating over his victory.

I did not say a word about the game, although I very much wanted to, but I decided not to give in to anger. A verbal war would have led me down a path that I did not want to walk upon. I realized that I was in a tense encounter with Kassar and I had to use good judgment. He was a master of games, especially the one that is played on the inside of the mind. He defeated me in basketball, as I allowed him to frustrate me through my emotions. I became angry, which took my focus off the game.

"Basketball is not the only game I play," I said with a return of confidence. I especially enjoy a good game of chess."

"I play chess," said Kassar. "However, I have a hard time finding anyone who could challenge me besides Barnabus and Scatman."

"Are they good?" I quickly asked.

"Yes, very good, and Barnabus is probably the better player. I have yet to beat him. He applies the knowledge for the game in a very studious manner, just like the game he plays in life. I get the impression that they don't like me, as if they think I'm sneaky and up to no good. I can't read their thoughts, but I can read the unspoken words written on their faces. What have they told you about me?"

I knew that Kassar was fishing. It was imperative that I responded quickly and in a manner so that he would not suspect anything. I had to conceal what I had been told about him. I cared enough not to lie, although I did not want him to suspect anything either.

"Barnabus and Scatman told me that you were alone and needed a friend. They also mentioned that you have a competitive spirit, which gives you your self-worth. The passion to win is strong in you, no matter what the cost might be."

Kassar looked at me curiously, slightly puzzled. He thought that maybe I was playing games with his mind. After examining my facial expression, he could not find any evidence that I was deceiving him. In truth, I wasn't really lying to him; I just did not tell him all that I was told.

"It's not a matter that I have to win every time. I just don't like to lose," said Kassar with a conceited heart, which was quite apparent.

"Yes, Kassar, it was a good game of basketball, wasn't it?" I said with a smile. "I haven't played competitively like that for quite a while. I made some shots that I normally would not."

"It just shows that the desire to win is strong within you also. When a contest is a hard fought battle like ours, it's quite normal to desire victory. You mentioned a game of chess. Would you like to play?"

"Sure," I said, knowing that I was more capable of achieving the desired outcome upon the chessboard, as opposed to the basketball court.

We walked back inside the school together, as we were not quite done with our competition. Instead of a physical contest, our game of choice led us to challenge each other's mind, for chess is a game of strategy and patience. It resembles life on a much smaller scale, for it asks us to make choices that potentially give birth to negative or positive results. I normally do not take many chances in a game, for I play defensively. Usually, I wait for my opponent to make a mistake. After observing Kassar play basketball, I believed that I had strategy that could be successful against him in chess.

When we walked into the library, I found a table suitable for playing chess while Kassar signed out a chess set. I looked around the library when I noticed Scatman talking with Diana near some very old and tall wooden bookshelves. Scatman smiled and nodded at me, and I immediately returned the gesture. I knew that Scatman wanted to leave me alone with Kassar, for what I was doing I had to accomplish on my own.

"Here we go, Charles," said Kassar as he placed an old chess set before me. "The best set they have, and my favorite too. If you observe carefully, my friend, all the pieces are delicately carved from stone. A masterful hand sculptured this set. Look at the detail, for you can actually see their faces, hands, even their fingernails. Charles, observe the unique color of these stones. One team is maroon while the other has the color of a pale yellow. This chess set is truly one of a kind."

"It's quite original," I said as I held a piece up to the light to examine it. "I remember I use to own a set similar to this one, except the pieces were made of wood and didn't have as much detail."

Kassar took one maroon and one yellow piece into separate hands and held them behind his back. "Pick which hand, Charles, for the color of the team that will be yours."

"Left," I said.

Kassar held out his left hand to me, and I believe that he knew which color piece was in what hand. He wanted maroon, and he manipulated the situation to make sure he got what he wanted. It was revealed to me when he opened his fist which color team I got.

"You get yellow, Charlie, and I get maroon. I think those colors are symbolic of our little game, don't you think?"

"Yes," I said in agreement, for it really didn't matter to me, for my dreams had revealed to me what the outcome would be.

"Light before darkness, or, like in checkers, fire before smoke," declared Kassar, smiling with confidence even before the game began.

I started the chess match by establishing my defense early, using my pawns and knights to defend the stronghold of my army. Kassar played quite aggressively, using his queen and castles in an attempt to intimidate me. At times, Kassar's attacks were utterly reckless, but somehow, he managed to escape my grasp every time. After several exchanges, I noticed that Kassar growing impatient, for he was having difficulty finding a weakness in my game. I was displaying a silent composure, patiently waiting for Kassar to make a mistake. He knew that it was almost impossible to cheat in chess, as the only way to manipulate the outcome was to break my concentration. I was holding on tight to the memory of a dream, which was what kept my motivation clear and focused.

Kassar was growing nervous and hesitant, for the confidence that he possessed to start the game seemed to have left him. Lost in thought he became as he studied the chess board, and for almost five minutes, his eyes did not wander away from the game. Finally, he thought he had found a weakness in my defense, and he captured my last bishop with his queen. His mind must have been elsewhere when he was studying the board, for he failed to notice the trap that I had set for him. I quickly took advantage of my opponent's mistake, which he probably made because of his lack of concentration.

I seized the opportunity expediently. For on my next two moves, I captured his queen and his remaining castle, which put his team in check. Despair fell upon Kassar in an instant, for he could foresee the inevitable without the ability to stop it. I was determined to end the game, and I closed in for the kill. Just when I was about to proclaim, "Checkmate," Kassar used a final act of desperation with a swipe of his arm, knocking all the chess pieces over, causing them to fall to the floor. Quickly, he rose up out of his chair and stared at me with animosity. Anger gripped him, and it projected displeasure toward me, the object and cause of his sudden outburst of hostile emotion. Kassar was a bad loser, and as he quickly left the library, I realized that he had difficulty confronting failure of any sort.

Scatman, who was talking to Diana when he heard Kassar's outburst of frustration that sent the chess pieces flying onto the floor, immediately got up out of his chair. When they approached me, I was on the floor, busy picking up the fallen chess pieces.

"What happened?" asked Diana as curiosity gripped her.

"I would have won, and he knew it, but he did not want me to have the satisfaction of victory like he did in basketball."

"Very well done, Charles," said Scatman, smiling with joy from my accomplishment. "Kassar is a very good chess player. I've played against him before. What we set out to do has been achieved, and a physical and mental bond has joined you to Kassar. The stage has been set for you to confront him inside the dreamscape. There will be much for you to learn before that will be possible, but you have taken that important first step. It's time to go back to the castle now, for we have finished here. You can have time to relax before the evening meal, and tonight, there will be much to do around the castle," said Scatman.

"I also want you to meet my cousin Abigail," Diana added with a lovely smile. "I'm sure that you will become good friends."

Scatman and I said good-bye to Diana, as she had to return to her duties as the school's guidance counselor. He told her that we would see her later. When we found Barnabus, he was in the school's office, talking to the headmaster of the school. He was the person in charge of the curriculum, polices, and obedience of the students as the official governing head of the school. Barnabus was making final arrangements for me to attend school starting on Monday. He immediately noticed Scatman and I enter the office and promptly introduce me.

"Charles, this is Mr. Morgan, he is the school's headmaster, which is the same as a term you might be more familiar with: *principal*," said Barnabus.

"Hello, young man. Your friend Barnabus has told me a lot about you. Don't worry, nothing bad. I was quite pleased to see that Barnabus and Scatman brought you here today. I hope you will like it here and, possibly for the first time, education will be a worthwhile experience."

Mr. Morgan was an older man with short, slightly graying hair that was growing thin on top. He had pale green eyes and wore thick, dark-rimmed eyeglasses. My first impression of him was that he cared for what was best for all of his students.

"It seems to be a very nice school, and I'm looking forward to continuing my education here," I said softly. I had a strong feeling that he was a caring, passionate person who, along with his other duties at the school, tried to direct students to the truth in life.

Scatman and I walked back to the castle for some rest and relaxation, which would revive us for the activities that were forthcoming. In my mind, the last few days had been an adventure. The circumstances that had led me to that point were unique in their development but possessed an unfamiliar scent which had a purpose that gave me hope.

When we got inside the castle, Scatman took me up to my room and introduced me to my roommate, William. He was reading a book when we walked in, as he had just returned from school a few minutes prior and was also intent on relaxing before evening.

"William," Scatman said, "this is Charles. He will be your new roommate."

"Hello!" said William in a joyous greeting as he put down his book. "Just call me Willie," he told me with a smile.

"I will leave you now, Charles, and I will see you later tonight. William, try to make Charles feel at home, and explain to him what it is like to live here."

"I sure will, Scatman," said Willie with his assurance.

Scatman left the room and closed the door. At first, there was a nervous silence between William and I, until finally, I broke the ice.

"How long have you lived here?" I asked.

"As long as I can remember. I know of no other lifestyle than what is here in the Mirror. Some of the people here had previously lived on Earth. Is that your story also?"

"Yes, it is," I replied.

"I grew up here in Mimetus," William started to explain. "Everything that I have learned about the Mirror has come from reading, listening and experience. On a daily basis, many wonderful events happen, and now you have the opportunity to witness them. My mom and dad loved this place until the Mirror called them home. For many months, I could not understand why they were taken out of my life, but now, I have peace in the destiny the Mirror has been showing me. It will be a pleasure for me to be an older brother to you, and I hope we can learn from each other as we become good friends."

William was a few years older than me, and I recognized immediately that he possessed a deep insight with a divine wisdom concerning the guidance that the Mirror provides for all his children. Just like me, he was short for his age but was still a few inches taller. He had bright red, curly hair; blue eyes; and a few faint freckles on his face. A quiet nature he carried with him, which always seemed to display a sensitivity that flowed through him.

"I have recently read about the history of the people on Earth and the different lifestyles and customs, and I tried to comprehend what it's like to live there. I'm sure there will be many things you will miss, Charles, while on the other side of the coin, there will be some you won't."

"I will miss the professional sports, movies, and live theater; for those are just a few of the many things that people on Earth use to fill their emptiness. However, with everything they have and desire, there is no peace."

"Life in the Mirror is totally unique," William began to say with genuine compassion in his voice. "However, I have never lived anywhere else that I could compare it to. But I have confidence that you will find a peace of mind that will come from within yourself. There are always many activities to get involved in, so boredom is never a problem. If you seek knowledge, companionship, or spiritual guidance, you do not have to look far. Sports and other recreational activities are plentiful. What you need to find is the desire of your heart. The food is good here, the accommodations are pleasant, and everyone who lives here is a part of a family, for you have now become a member of a large family with the love of a mother and father, coming from the Mirror."

When William had finished talking, he turned to his book and I lay down on my bed. In my heart, I believed I was lucky. I was quite comfortable with misery, but joy came into my life, making me feel a way that words cannot describe. I had to learn to forget most of my earthly pleasures so that I could concentrate upon what it really meant to be a child of the Mirror. My thoughts ran for an unknown amount of time until I fell asleep. I slept without dreams until William awakened me.

"Charles, wake up!"

Chapter 15

The moment my conscious mind was brought out of a light sleep, I had the feeling that was quite similar to being abruptly removed from an enjoyable swim in a tranquil lake. Slowly, I opened my eyes only to see my roommate looking down at me. His face was not entirely familiar, although I did remember making his acquaintance.

"Time to get up so that you can get ready," said William.

"How long was I asleep?" I asked, being disoriented and confused as to my whereabouts.

"About an hour."

I got off the bed and walked over to the window.

What I saw was quite picturesque. The beautiful array of colors had captured my psyche in its splendor until I finally turned my thoughts away from the view and went into the bathroom to wash my face and hands. When I had finished, William and I promptly left the room, only to be greeted by the lingering aroma of freshly cooked food. I was feeling quite hungry when I remembered that Scatman had told me the food was different than what I was use to, but a joy to eat.

My room with William was on the far east wing of the castle. The corridors were extremely long and wide, with rooms on both sides. As we walked down the hallway, I noticed a wide variety of framed artwork displayed upon the walls. I love art, although I lack the talent to draw or paint. Several times while we made our way down the hallway, I had to stop to get a better look at a particular framed piece of art. After looking upon several fine paintings and drawings as if I was in an art gallery, we finally made our way to the main stairway. I knew that it was going to take some time to adjust to my new life, but for the present tense, I temporarily imagined myself on an extended vacation during which I could learn and grow within myself. Inside the Mirror, there was new hope, wherein I could mature to accomplish whatever plans the Mirror destined for me.

When we got to the cafeteria, a quickly forming line greeted us, but as I found out, it did not take long for us to be served. The food looked very appetizing, for the menu offered was some kind of smothered beef with peculiar-looking potatoes and a vegetable medley. The meal was delicious in its own unique way, and after we ate, we went outside. Our short stroll led us to the large fountain, where we felt the fresh, cool breeze brush our faces. William and I talked of many things that were important for me to grasp and embrace to would make my life in the Mirror filled with fond memories and a deep, purposeful meaning.

As the day faded into night, I was suddenly surprised when multi-colored lights from several small pillars located behind where we were standing turned on and lit up the fountain, which reminded me of a rainbow.

I watched the blend of colors in motion, and I was filled with a joyous sense of promise. Finally, William and I walked back into the castle and down the wide basement steps to where the entertainment center was located. The bottom level of the castle was quite extensive, with many rooms that were connected to one another to form an uncomplicated labyrinth. I noticed that the ceilings were quite high in the basement, and I realized that the builders must have had to dig deep for the foundation. William showed me all the different activities, such as darts, ping-pong, card games, chess, and checkers, among many others. I saw a group of adults involved in a group discussion sitting on sofas and chairs in a semicircle. I watched many people playing all kinds of games, and as I looked upon them, I could tell that they were having a good time. William and I walked around this hub of fun when, out of the corner of my eye, I saw Kassar. He was playing cards with an older man. I became curious about him and wondered what motives were hidden in his heart. Would he cheat with anyone to get his desired outcome?

I was suddenly distracted by Willie to follow him, which took my mind off of Kassar. He showed me the music library, which had a large selection of music, most of which were unique in their origins. Many of the styles were foreign to me but, at the same time, had the voice of familiarity.

"Well, Charles, what do you think?" asked William.

"This is quite a place with a variety of things to do. There are many opportunities to get involved and many different people to get acquainted with. That is what I see from my eyes. I also could learn to play the piano like I had always wanted to."

A voice rose up from behind us, which caught both of us off guard, although we recognized the voice immediately and who it belonged to.

"There you boys are," said Scatman.

We turned around without hesitation, and I immediately noticed that Scatman was accompanied by Diana, who looked quite beautiful. Standing next to her was a very pretty girl with long, blonde hair who appeared to be my age.

"Charles," Diana spoke up quickly, "this is my young cousin Abigail, whom I told you about earlier.

"Hello, Abigail," I said as my eyes met hers.

"It's nice to meet you, Charles," she replied with a sweet smile.

I became focused upon Abigail's eyes, and I believe that even to this day, her eyes are the bluest that I have ever seen. She had a precious smile and possessed an innocence that was probably similar to what Scatman had seen in me at the fair. She wore a modern dress that night, which gave her the look of a young girl with the hope and promise of feminine maturity.

"Abigail, why don't you and Charles go somewhere and talk, get to know one another. Maybe you could play a game of checkers," said Scatman.

Abigail and I walked away and into the confines of the maze of rooms in the entertainment area, as we were both happy to find a friend. I sensed Abigail's presence as the girl I dreamt about last night. I became puzzled about those dreams and the frequency of truth behind their images.

"Do you like to play checkers?" I asked.

"Yes, I do, and I'm much better at checkers than I am at chess."

"Would you like to play a game?" I asked.

"Yes," she immediately answered.

Wasting no time, we found our way into the game room and located a checker set and a table, and Abigail and I set up the game.

"You can have fire if you like," I said with a hint of laughter under my words.

"Fire before smoke, correct?" she answered with a smile, looking deep into my eyes.

I believe that Abigail felt at peace with me from the very beginning, for I was someone she was comfortable being with. She also knew that I was lonely, for Diana had told her that I was new to the Mirror. Solitude was something she knew well, for she never experienced a close relationship with her parents. Her mother died giving Abigail birth, and even though her father cared for her to the best of his ability in her early years, he never came to terms with his wife's death. When Abigail was not quite five years old, her father died in a freak accident at the plant he worked at. From that day forward, Diana became her mother, her guardian, but more than anything, her friend.

Abigail started the game casually, and I played along just for fun. I was not really concentrating on the game, for my attention seemed to be focused on the pretty girl who sat across from me. It was a game in which I did not possess an alternative motive, for between Abigail and I, a friendship was being born. I felt good being with her, which was quite foreign to me because normally, I was quite shy around girls. In our hearts, hidden emotions slowly sprouted that, in time, would grow to satisfy our many needs and desires. Our conversation during the game was quite broad, and we talked about the Mirror, the dreams that inspired us, and the fear of change. I told her about life in Ohio and how afraid I was just before I entered the Mirror.

"In your heart, you knew it was the right direction to follow, which is what motivated your decision. Am I right?" Abigail asked in wonder.

"Yes," I told her.

"Do you regret your choice now?"

"I must admit Abigail that I was frightened when I woke up after falling through the Mirror. I became unsure of the decision I had just made until I saw Scatman. He knew what I was thinking and feeling, for at one time, he was in my shoes. It was not the words he spoke or how he said them, but the joy that lives in him is what gave me peace."

"I'm glad you are here, and I am looking forward to becoming your good friend," said Abigail with a sincere compassion. As she spoke those words, her hand touched mine in a gesture that said, "I care."

On the other side of the large room, I did not notice Kassar watching Abigail and I playing checkers and talking. A deeply rooted jealousy sprouted up from within him, not because he desired Abigail as a friend but because I was being accepted within the realm of the community. Kassar had never been able to fit in or feel the love and compassion that I was being shown by my new friends.

I eventually allowed Abigail to win the game, for I didn't really care who won because the checker game was just a tool to enhance our continued relationship. I was just trying to get to know her. After we put the game away, we went outside for some fresh air. She wanted to show me the wonderful place that she called home. The castle had become her home since her dad died, when she moved in with Diana and her Aunt Annie and Uncle Ed. We walked past the fountain, and I noticed the colorful change that had come upon it. The darkness had established itself into nighttime, so the unique blend of multi-colored lights really put a shine upon the fountain. We followed the cindered walkway that had dimly lit lamps intermittently placed alongside the path around the castle. Abigail told me in great detail about the grand design of her home. I had already learned about what she was telling me, but I let her explain to me anyway, for I sensed that it was a special delight for her to show me around.

When we finished our walk, we went back inside to the water-scape room. I was quite fascinated by the décor of the dark room, and my eyes moved from place to place with curiosity. It seemed to be decorated in the traditions of Old England, with dark cedar paneling and furniture and decorations that resembled that time in history. Abigail led me over to a small but comfortable couch in front of a bristling fireplace. Many other people were gathered in the large room, discussing many topics of interest. We were the youngest in the room, but that fact did not draw attention to us, as Abigail and I faced one another and began to talk amongst ourselves. It felt so natural to talk with Abigail, almost as if we had known each other for many years.

In the two days since I had been inside the Mirror, I listened and tried to comprehend what was being explained to me of what my new life would become. Abigail and Willie were trying to paint a picture in my mind that was very similar to what Barnabus and Scatman had illustrated to me. I wanted to use both the wisdom from my elders and the perspectives from my new friends to prepare myself. I would need to remember what I was learning and apply it at the correct moment. Since falling through the Mirror, I distinctly believe that I had somehow changed both in mind and spirit. When I was in Ohio, I had been possessed with much fear and anxiety, but those feelings seemed to have left me. Abigail was a calming presence, and I imagined how I could almost have a conversation with her without opening my mouth. I had never felt that way toward anyone, and I believed in my heart that it was rare to meet someone like her.

The room in which Abigail and I were sitting in started to get crowded as the evening grew old. Many of those who wandered into the room were seeking intellectual conversation and to become involved in some philosophical discussions. I could distinguish that a majority of them were scholarly types who studied a lot, as they debated over various issues that they found to be quite intriguing. I looked into Abigail's eyes while we talked with an uncanny feeling that we were alone in the room, although I knew it was an illusion.

Scatman suddenly entered the waterscape room after a long search for Abigail and me, realizing it was the lone room in which he had failed to look. He found us sitting on the sofa in front of the fireplace in the waterscape, talking the night away. In his eyes, we looked to be at peace together. It was the blossoming of young love. Pure and valuable are those emotions to the human heart. Scatman suddenly remembered his first girlfriend and the young boy that he was when he lived in Ohio. He was a lost boy at that time, until he met a girl who made his life worth living. During the trials of life, it is only through relationships that fulfillments and the reason to hope can be found.

"Here you two are. I was thinking that you might be in here, and I was right. Are you getting to know one another?"

"Yes, Scatman, we are," I said with a smile.

Hi, Scatman!" exclaimed Abigail, happy to see his face. We have learned that we have a lot in common."

"It's a good place to begin, enjoying common interests and understanding the value of friendship," said Scatman.

He looked down at us enjoying our time together with a heartfelt belief that the Mirror had pre-arranged for Abigail and I to meet and become friends.

"I hate to break up your first evening together, but Barnabus and I need Charles's assistance in an important project. You will be able to see each other tomorrow at breakfast."

"I understand, Scatman," said Abigail as we got up off the sofa and faced each other.

For a brief moment, our eyes became united as one, with an understanding of words not spoken transcribed into our hearts through visual contact.

"It was nice to meet you, Charles," said Abigail with a radiant smile that seemed to melt my heart, for I did not want to be apart from her. "I hope that we can spend more time together soon, and I will be looking forward to seeing you at breakfast."

"I will be there," I told her as she turned and walked away.

I felt a strange feeling rise up from within me: the infatuation of first love. We were both young, but that did not stop the emotion that was joining us together.

"She is such a sweet girl," said Scatman to me. "Be nice to her. I think she likes you very much."

"I like her too," I replied.

Part Three

Learning to Walk,
Learning to Fight

Chapter 16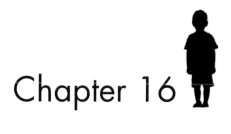

I always had a vivid imagination. With that gift, the Mirror brought me into its kingdom for one distinct purpose. The expectations that were placed upon me required that I would grow spiritually and acquire wisdom and knowledge to wage war with the one who torments within the realm of the dreamscape.

"I'm sorry I had to interrupt your evening with Abigail, but it is time for you to go to school," said Scatman, trying to be sincerely compassionate to the desires of my heart. "Not the building you visited today either, but the dream school. Tonight Charles, you will learn how to shadowtrek. I will walk you through it."

"Whose dream?" I asked.

"Barnabus's," Scatman stated with a firm seriousness.

I was silent for a short moment, studiously thinking about what I might encounter inside of Barnabus's dream. I was thankful it was someone whom I knew. I might not have understood Barnabus for his quiet and mysterious ways, but at least he was not a stranger.

"You will learn from this first shadowtrek, so be perceptive of the surroundings, your impressions, and what you feel physically as well as emotionally. Tomorrow night, you will walk in my dream. What you might experience in these two dreams can become vital tools necessary until you acquire the skills and patience to engage Kassar inside the tunnel of dreams."

"How was shadowtreking discovered?" I asked with curiosity, for it was a strange phenomenon and I wanted to know what I was walking myself into.

"Because you are about to enter the unexplained territory of dreams, I believe it is important for you to know its origins, for there is much to be learned from its history."

Scatman began to tell me as we walked out of the sitting room. He was leading me up to the tower, where the atmosphere was close to perfect for my first lesson on walking in dreams.

"Barnabus taught me about dreams and how to walk in them. His father and grandfather, who were the pioneers of shadowtreking, educated him as a boy. His grandfather, who's name was Stephen, discovered this amazing spectacle quite accidently. He later accepted the fact that this gift was predestined to him. It was just words from his heart that he had difficulty expressing that led him to discover a rare marvel in the realm of the supernatural. He just wanted to express the love and happiness that he was feeling to the woman who would become his bride. When he lay down to sleep on the eve of his wedding, he thought of his future wife continuously, and in his dreams, he dreamt about telling his bride to be what he felt. The next day, as he stood before her on the altar, she sweetly whispered to him how special the night before was. Barnabus's grandfather did not understand what she was trying to tell him. After the wedding, when all the celebration was over, his new bride, whose name was Martha, told him about her dream and how he came to her and what he said. Initially, he did not think it was possible that such a strange occurrence happened, but the more he thought about it, the visual image of the Mirror flashed into his mind. He knew that all things were possible within the proper framework of the Mirror.

"Through their years of marriage, there were times when they spoke to each other in their dreams, for occasionally, communication was hindered in the natural. Many mysteries about shadowtreking were unlocked during their years together. They taught their children at a young age about shadowtreking, in which they learned that having faith in the Mirror was essential to being successful in dreams.

"Charles, you have a strong bond with Barnabus, and so do I. That is why Barnabus's dream is the perfect testing ground for you to travel. The people here in Mimetus have used dreams as another form of communication since its discovery. In dreams, with the spirit of the Mirror as your guide, whatever can be conceived is possible. What Kassar is trying to accomplish must be stopped."

When Scatman and I walked up toward the tower, we discussed many things that concerned me. I had a deep desire to know the truth about dreams, what they meant, for I knew that there were occasions when dreams had a symbolic tone, which usually confused me.

"I am curious, Scatman," I began to ask, "why don't you and Barnabus battle Kassar? I do believe that together, you have the wisdom and strength to defeat him. Am I so special that I should be selected to wage war against him?"

Scatman did not answer initially, for he knew that eventually, I was going to ask that question. He suddenly stopped our climb up to the tower with a sorrowful expression upon his face. I looked at him, puzzled, for I knew that there was a good reason pertaining to the peculiarity of his facial expression.

"Barnabus is getting old, much older than you would imagine. Sending him into battle with Kassar in a dream could possibly kill him. We would rather not take the chance of losing him at this time. The Mirror showed us your image, and we believe that you are the one to deliver our people out of mental bondage. Barnabus is very wise, and he still can teach and motivate many people to come to a better understanding of the Mirror.

"Kassar has learned how to use many tools that are available in a dream against us. Inside our subconscious minds, we have many desires and tendencies that are normally buried, but that doesn't mean they don't exist. They are dormant, and what Kassar has been doing is putting a fire to those many appetites. To defeat him, we must put a shield around us in a symbolic manner. It is accomplished by first of all walking in love, which puts those hungers in chains. When a person walks under the Mirror's protective shield, evil will not come near.

"Almost one year ago, my wife died, and I strongly believe that Kassar killed her. The doctors who examined her body at the time of her death told me that she had died of a heart attack in her sleep. They do not know what was in her dream, and I suspect it was something unbelievably horrifying. It's true, Charles, that if you die in your dream, you die in life. You might ask, what were his motives? We were a threat, for we could have exposed him. Maybe Kassar didn't plan on killing her. Maybe he just wanted to scare her. I'm not entirely sure, but the one person closest to my heart is dead because of his selfishness. Her death created a deep sorrow within me for a long time, which prevented me from effectively confronting him. Never underestimate him, Charles, for he is very clever. He does not know you very well, which can become an ace in your hand. This is the reason why a stranger must battle Kassar. Come, Charles. It is time, for Barnabus will soon be asleep, and then his dream will begin. We must be ready."

Finally, Scatman and I reached the top of the stairs on the third floor. We walked down the darkened hallway to a small door, which appeared to be used for a closet. Scatman opened the door that led us to another set of stairs. As we climbed upon the old, narrow stairway, the wooden steps made a creaky sound that called notice to its age. Upon the walls, I noticed old fashioned lamps which shined brightly. After following several curves of the stairwell, we finally reached the worship center. The circular-sized room was an architectural rarity, and when my eyes fell upon its spectacular dimensions, I realized just how big it was.

On Saturday evenings, praise and worship services are held in the auditorium upon the top of the castle. Over two thousand people plus the pastor, the band, and the choir fill the cathedral to capacity at each of the services without the feeling of being overcrowded. Within its round configuration, the acoustics were perfect for praise services, plays, and concerts. When the choir sang, their voices blended together in perfect harmony, which gave the impression of something that was beyond the scope of the kingdom. Everyone in the kingdom was encouraged to attend the services and experience the love, joy, and peace to those who willingly open up their hearts. Behind the podium, where the pastor spoke from, I saw a symbol made of wood and glass. It was quite large, almost six feet high and four feet wide. Along its outer edges, illumining strips of silver and gold bordered the circumference. A triangle inside a square was the symbolic characteristic of the people's faith in the Mirror, which expressed both past and present in the hard, cold nature of the statue, vividly reminding all people that faith is eternal.

Scatman brought me up to the praise center for a reason, for he wanted my faith to be strong. With the Mirror symbolically close to me, I would have the guidance that I could not find anywhere else.

"Do you believe, Charles? Is the Mirror in your heart? Can you feel its presence close to you, dwelling in your spirit?"

"Yes, Scatman, I feel it inside of me, waiting to explode with a knowledge that has been concealed, but most of all, its presence is felt in my heart. This is what makes me believe the most; not the miracles that I have witnessed, but what I feel on the inside of me that was never there before. My faith is slowly growing. It's something I can't see because it's within me."

"This is a good thing," said Scatman. "Without your faith, we would never have a chance to defeat Kassar. Let us thank the Mirror for walking with us on our quest tonight."

We walked down to the symbol of faith, which was known as the Paraclete. It stood upon a small platform that was several feet high. We bowed our heads and gave thanks for our lives, including the obstacles and trials that stood in our paths. Scatman prayed for strength and guidance to help me learn quickly the essential fundamental nature of shadowtreking. When he finished praying, he looked upon the Paraclete. I was still in prayer when he looked over at me. He felt the faith in the Mirror growing within me. Watching me pray gave Scatman comfort, for he knew that the Mirror was working through me.

Scatman led me behind the Paraclete to the choir loft, where we sat down on the third row. He told me to look out upon the great room of praise and worship, and when I did, my mind released itself from the worries of the day. I was ready to learn and experience a unique dimension in this life that is quite unknown to the people I knew back in Ohio. Without realizing or understanding it at the time, I possessed a power that only select individuals have custody of. I did not truly comprehend the potential that my dreams would bring to my life. The wisdom and knowledge that I carried with me revealed the ability to alter specific circumstances.

"What you must remember about dreams is to expect anything. The possibilities are without limits, so let your imagination go free, for whatever can be conceived in a dream can be achieved. Your seed of thought is the only thing that is required to produce inner desires. The most challenging part of the dream link is the entrance into the other person's dream. Charles, your mind must focus upon that person and only that person. See their face, their expressions, the way they walk and talk. All their mannerisms must be visualized in your mind. When we get inside the dream, watch me and follow along and learn. These lessons will be a guide to remember while you're in my dream and many others in the days to come."

"I'm a little nervous about this, Scatman," I said, intimidated by my fear.

"I know you are, but let me reassure you that there is nothing to be afraid of. You are about to enter a world full of possibilities, and if used correctly, the outlook you have upon life will be greatly enhanced."

"Okay, Scatman. I believe that I am ready," I told him as I tried to gather up all the confidence that I could muster.

"Clear your head, Charles. Think only of Barnabus. Close your eyes, and see him with your mind as if he is sitting next to you. Paint his image just like a photograph. Now, with your mind, join me in Barnabus's dream."

Our physical presence remained seated on the pews of the choir loft, but the life force from within was lifted out on a quest through the vast dominion of the dreamscape. I felt weightless as I was being abruptly moved by a power that I would never even think of resisting. I was in some kind of narrow passageway with many bright-colored rays of light that buzzed past me, and at the same time, I heard many undistinguishable sounds that triggered my senses. As we continued to soar with much speed down the mysterious corridor, I knew that our destination was near. Without realizing that it had happened, Scatman and I found ourselves in Barnabus's dream. My eyes were immediately held captive to the surroundings. And as I looked around, I touched a hedge plant with my hand and I quickly noticed its authenticity. The birds sang, and the summer air gently caressed our faces with a peacefulness that completely confined Scatman and me in its serenity.

Barnabus and another man walked in front of us, and as I watched my old friend, I noticed that he was limping. I never remembered him having a hurt leg, but I did realize that I was in his dream. The man next to Barnabus was quite peculiar. He appeared to be a stick figure of a man, similar to something I might have seen in a cartoon. He had a large, swollen head and a long neck, and the rest of his body was short and extremely thin. He wore a brand-new black cowboy hat, and holstered around his excessively thin waist was a toy gun with plastic bullets.

"Are you sure this is the right time?" asked Barnabus, being skeptical.

"Yes, the time is now. No need to have regret or be remorseful about anything you did not accomplish," the man told him, trying to influence attitude toward the subject.

How many moments passed, I did not know, for I had no concept of time. In the distance, just above several rolling hills, I became aware of a dark red cloud approaching us. I knew that the cloud had some importance, but its significance was beyond my wisdom. Before I knew what had happened, we were consumed by the cloud and we began to walk through its thick matter. Scatman and I looked at each other curiously, wondering what the mysterious cloud could possibly signify.

"Wish the cloud away," Scatman said to me through mental telepathy.

I did not understand how I had just received instructions from him. I looked at him with a puzzled expression. He just nodded his head as if he was telling me, "Go ahead."

In my mind, I pictured the red cloud along with the thin man, and I saw it slowly and gradually vanish before my witnessing eyes. I did not comprehend the nature behind my mental suggestion, but the evidence of what I saw did not lie, as the cloud disappeared. I stopped in my tracks, bewildered, for I knew that I was not in Ohio, that it was a dream and many amazing things happened there. The physical laws which created this land were far beyond my prehistoric reasoning capabilities.

Scatman and I watched Barnabus as he continued to walk down the long dirt trail that seemed to lead into the mountains several miles away. I immediately became aware that Barnabus grew shorter with every step he took. I felt sad, but somehow, I understood.

Unaware that it was approaching, the strong and powerful force that had placed us in the dream took hold of Scatman and I and pulled us out of the dream and quickly down the tunnel. The invisible apparition that held us in its possession was quite strong and very consuming. The only thing that Scatman and I could do was to endure the discomfort of being detached from Barnabus's dream. As quickly as the dream started, it ended. When Scatman and I opened our eyes, we noticed that we had returned from where we had begun.

"Is Barnabus going to die?" I asked.

"I believe that in his mind, Barnabus is consumed with the thought that the end of his natural life is coming soon. No mortal can reliably predict when their end will come, but I think Barnabus can sense its approaching presence," concluded Scatman.

"What did that toy gun represent?"

Scatman smiled at the memory of the man with the toy gun and bullets.

"I'm sure that there is a symbolic meaning somewhere, what the gun meant and why, but I have no clue."

"Charles, you caused the red cloud to disappear. The main purpose with shadowtreking with you in a dream was for you to learn how to change the course of a dream just by your thoughts. In a dream, you are a conscious force in an unconscious mind. The person who is dreaming has only limited control over the events of a dream, as those images have the tendency to skip from one scene to another very quickly. However, when a conscious life force is also present, like your spirit was, Charles, it can alter its direction. When you wished the cloud away, you changed the dream. The possibilities inside the red cloud were without limits, but when it vanished, your conscious being became the stronghold of the dream. Barnabus was shrinking step by step because you thought the stick man was symbolic of death. What you did tonight and the images we saw are just examples of what can be accomplished in a dream."

"I was fascinated how real the dream felt. I touched one of the leaves from the bushes that lined the path we were walking on. For a brief moment, I thought I was touching one of the bushes near the castle."

"But you knew it was a dream?" queried Scatman.

"Yes," I said, "although I had to catch myself several times to remind myself of that fact, for when I saw Barnabus walking with a limp, I realized that I was inside of his dream, for he does not walk with a limp."

"Dreams are like puzzles," Scatman replied. "Within their mysterious passageways, a symbol of revelation or truth usually can be found. It's late, Charles, time for us to retire to our beds for some needed sleep."

Scatman and I got up off the choir loft and walked out of the worship center and down the narrow stairs to a place where we said, "Good night." Scatman always had a room available at the castle, even though he lived at his house most of the time. He was an important person within the kingdom and was granted special privileges.

I was very quiet when I got into my room, and I immediately washed my face, brushed my teeth, and changed into my bed clothes. As I lay down on the bed, I felt tired physically, but my mind ran with many thoughts from the events over the last few days. My eyes were wide open, staring out at the darkness that filled the room with a variety of images rapidly soaring through my head, which was preventing me from embracing sleep. Finally, after almost an hour of trying to analyze my plight, sleep came upon me and I fell into a dream.

I found myself in Ohio once again. I knew where I was, for I recognized the place quite vividly. A seemingly brand-new basketball I held in my hands, as I stood upon the small basketball court behind my parents' garage. I suddenly stopped shooting baskets and turned my attention to my parents' house, confused to the reason why I was there. I walked into the house and immediately noticed my mom and dad sitting at the dining room table. They were wearing ugly rubber masks over their faces. I felt the spirit of anger and resentment lingering among their presence as I walked by them. I was unnoticed, for they had the appearance of a mannequin, without the presence of a living soul within them, lifeless, like a portrait on the wall.

As I walked around the house, I felt quite strange, knowing I did not belong. I had a desire to leave, but for some unknown reason, I could not. The house seemed to be the same, just as if I had never left. Walking down the basement steps, I remembered the many times I had to wash them as one of my chores. I also recalled that it was the specific job that I was doing when Barnabus rang the doorbell. Since that moment, my life had changed, as I had been reborn, washed clean from the dirt that polluted my soul. I immediately knew in my heart when I was in my old room that I had to leave.

Quickly, I ran upstairs in a fury, and I tried to open the doors, but I found that each of them would not budge. I looked at the windows and noticed strong iron bars on them, as seen in jails. I felt trapped like an animal in a cage, and my heart cried out for rescue. I started to pound my fists on the door, desperate for release from the haunted dungeon I found myself in. My parents looked at each other, and I knew that they were curious about why I was acting with such hysteria. I watched them as they very carefully peeled off their skin-tight plastic masks in what I thought would reveal their faces. To my astonishment and horror, what I saw was not their faces but their skulls, all deathly white, all bone. They began to speak, being unified in words, tone, and emotion as they chanted, "There is no escape! You are our slave! Accept it!"

My parents, or what had become of them, spoke that phrase continuously in a monotonous tone, as each time it increased in volume, becoming implanted in my brain. I became perilously afraid, crying out for freedom. Falling to the floor, I cried very passionately with a hunger to return to my beloved Mirror.

"Set me free! Set me free!" I yelled out with an anguished heart.

The sound of running water coming from the bathroom woke me out of my nightmare. Looking around the room carefully with my eyes, I came to the conclusion that I was dreaming.

I was quite thankful that the Mirror rescued me from my nightmare, for it was the one fear that plagued my mind at times; to be returned to my parent's house in Ohio.

Chapter 17

The emotions that a person might experience when they awaken from a dream can impact their attitude toward themselves and other people around them. Dreams, at times, can be a result of decisions made in the past that have caused the heart to feel regret. I had been confused about what my emotions were trying to tell me. Most of the time, I believed that the choice that I made when I stepped through the Mirror was the correct path to follow. Occasionally, I had felt uncertain. Through time and faith in the destiny that pursues all men, I would come to the realization of the truth that shadowed me.

William walked out of the bathroom and greeted me good morning. I acknowledged his greeting promptly, and we talked briefly about the night before and what we had dreamt. William did not remember too much about his dream but was quite interested and concerned with why I was troubled about my dream. He was fascinated how I could recall my dreams with such detail.

"I can only remember my dreams once in a while, but never with such details as you have described to me," said William.

"My dreams are like this every night," I told him. "I believe some of the dreams are warnings while others I know are glimpses of the future. I also realize that some dreams are born out of our fears and desires. The insecurities to my presence here in this place could have triggered the dream I had last night. It's the explanation of the fear that I don't belong. Please understand William that I was very thankful for waking up inside the Mirror this morning."

"I am forever grateful to the Mirror each and every morning that I open my eyes with the realization of where I am. From what I have heard from people who once lived on Earth, there are many wonderful things there, although pain and suffering is also very abundant. I'm glad to have a roommate again. I had one for a while when I first came to the castle, but he had to leave. I never knew why. I believe the Mirror has been looking for the right person. Charles, I will try to be your big brother if you want me to, someone who is older but close enough in age so that we can relate to one another."

"I just want a friend," I said.

"Everyone who lives here will be your friend."

"Except one, and that is Kassar," I whispered to myself.

"Why don't you get washed up, and when you're done, we will get something to eat. The smell of breakfast cooking brought me out of my sleep."

"You must have a dog's nose, for I didn't smell anything," I said with a smile.

"I hope it doesn't look like one, but it sure works like one," replied Willie.

I went into the bathroom to take a shower, and when the water came splashing down upon me, I felt once again as if I was being cleansed from within. Certain aspects of the physical cleansing made me feel so very alive, much different than I ever did in Ohio. A few weeks before, I was living in a depressed state, oppressed in every area of my life. Inside the Mirror, I experienced a joy that ran triumphant through the core of my being. After I got out of the shower, I combed my hair and got dressed. Looking into the reflecting glass mounted on the bathroom wall, I noticed that a significant change upon my face was apparent, and I was happy to see it.

It is strange to say, but I knew what I had to learn. My faith had to be obedient for the welfare of others. As loneliness at one time in my life was a close friend, inside the Mirror, I would never have to feel that way again.

When I was finally ready, William and I walked down to the cafeteria for some breakfast. The aroma of food cooking in the kitchen penetrated my inner nostrils, which was like music to my empty stomach. A wide variety of breakfast foods greeted us when we entered the cafeteria, such as apple-spiced pancakes, waffles, eggs, and some type of meat. Although it did look similar to bacon, it did not taste like it. There were pastries and many types of regional fruit, some of which looked familiar but uniquely different. When Willie and I sat down to start eating, we were joined by Barnabus, Scatman, Abigail, and Diana. My eyes quickly lit up like candles when I saw Abigail's pretty face.

"It's good to see you again," said Abigail with a smile as her eyes met mine.

"It is also good to see you," I said as my heart jumped with pleasure. "I was just thinking about you, and here you are."

Scatman and Diana both noticed the strong fascination that was beginning to flourish between Abigail and I, and they smiled at each other, remembering what young love felt like. At times, it almost seems magical how two people meet and, over time, come to love. Scatman and Diana were just good friends, for she was a good friend of Scatman's wife. She was there for Scatman when his wife died, and they shared many nights of conversation into the early hours of the morning. Watching Abigail and I brought back memories to Scatman of the only woman he ever loved.

"Did you sleep good, Charles?" asked Scatman, knowing that I must not have slept very long, for he did not.

"Yes, I did," I replied.

"Any dreams?" questioned Scatman with curiosity.

"Almost a nightmare," I said. "Although I think I understand why I had the dream at this time. I will explain it to you later."

"When you start to realize what your dreams are trying to say, you will be able to apply those lessons into your own life. What you see in your dreams are symbolic puzzles, but when you put the pieces together and observe the picture before you, it becomes clear what is being revealed to you."

I ate my breakfast with my eyes on Abigail, and as I did, I noticed out of the corner of my eye Scatman and Diana looking at us. It was hard not to notice, in the days that followed when people would see us together, the close proximity of our chemistry. In Scatman's mind, an idea slowly developed while he watched Abigail and me talking. He realized that it might be beneficial for me to shadowtrek with Abigail for training purposes. The experience could serve to be quite rewarding to me, especially when it came time to battle Kassar inside the corridors of a dream.

Quality time in the scope of the family is usually during meal time, should it be breakfast, lunch, or dinner. It is also a time when concerns and issues among the family are discussed. Our small group was becoming close like a family, and as we ate our food, our main focus of conversation was the question being asked all over the kingdom; why has there erupted among the people so much turmoil?

Kassar was the problem, for Scatman knew that he was becoming distressed, apprehensive that his escapades in the night might have been noticed. In his future, Kassar could see a battleground emerging, as he knew that he had to be ready for a fight.

"I know everyone has questions, and Barnabus and I are working on a few solutions. I believe one major problem in our community is that a large percentage of the people have taken the Mirror's blessings for granted. I believe we are being taught a lesson, and that is why there is an abundance of discord and strife. Even our prayers have become more of a ritual than a desperate hunger to have a relationship with the Mirror," Scatman explained, using the voice of encouragement to motivate us.

Abigail and I listened to Scatman, but at the same time, we concentrated our attention upon each other.

"It's Saturday," whispered Abigail, hoping not to disturb the conversation upon the table. "Would you like to go for a walk later?"

"I would love to, but I must find out from Barnabus and Scatman what plans they have for me today. I am new here, and they are teaching me the ways of the Mirror."

"I have always lived here," Abigail told me with a sincere and compassionate voice. Her eyes were soft with emotion as she softly spoke. "I do not know, nor could I try to understand how you feel, for I have never been where you are now. At our young age, adjusting to a new life must be difficult. What you might see appears to be a peaceful existence here, but you must feel like a stranger in a strange land. The people whom you knew for many years cannot be found, and no one here can spark old memories. I feel bad for you, Charles, as I sense a sadness that lingers close to you. I want you to know that anytime you need a friend to listen, I am there for you."

"Thank you, Abigail. I will remember your words," I said as I gently touched her hand with a true understanding that united our hearts and minds.

After breakfast, Barnabus, Scatman, and I sat in the sitting room by the fireplace in the waterscape room. The main topic of interest was my perception of shadowtreking. It was important for me to remember the emotions and mental impressions that I felt during the experience. Barnabus shared with me his wisdom about dreams and the manner in which dreams work.

"When walking in a dream, your imagination has the ability to control the course of the dream. Be alert to what is happening around you, and use it to your advantage. Apply your knowledge and experience from your own dreams when walking in another person's dream. Anything that you can conceive and believe you can achieve in a dream. Depending upon your will and the focus of your thoughts, try to read what the dream's symbolic nature is. Create a pure heart in the dream's life, one that centers on morality and righteousness. A dream is the voice of the unconscious, for it plants negative and positive attitudes into a person's heart. Kassar is altering dreams in the opposite direction, by planting seeds of anger, resentment, and offense. This I believe is the root cause behind the problems we are facing. You must remember when you are in a dream that it is only a dream and that the power to take control is in your heart and mind."

"Tonight, when you are in my dream, Charles," Scatman began to tell me, "change the course of the dream. Remember, your thoughts can manipulate the events that unfold. Do not allow the circumstances of the dream to scare you, for being the only living conscious force that breathes life into the dream, it is necessary to utilize your imagination. Scenes and circumstances jump quickly, and you will be moved with the current of the dream. Don't be surprised when your conscious spirit is pulled out of the dream, so work fast and accomplish what you can. No one has ever been lost in the world of dreams. We do not know the origin of the power that pulls the shadowtreker back to himself, for it is something that comes quite unexpectedly. Be observant, Charles, and learn how to use that imagination of yours, for it is truly a wonderful gift."

"I will, and I am looking forward to the opportunity that tonight brings me," I said with confidence.

After lunch, Abigail and I went outside for a walk. When we stepped out of the castle, fresh air greeted us warmly as Abigail led me into the fields and woodlands on a bright and beautiful day. I felt at peace with her, while we quietly walked through a dense region of the woods with many tall trees that loomed high over our heads. I touched her hand, and then I firmly held it in mine, interlocking our fingers together. We were alone, with time to enjoy each other's company in the peaceful tranquility that lay in the domains of the forest.

Abigail was dressed in a light blue summer dress that was made of a lightweight fabric that gave her freedom of movement. She looked very attractive, as the dress highlighted her blonde hair and fair complexion. I knew I was attracted to her, for I felt a warm emotion come upon me whenever I was with her.

"Have you ever had a girlfriend, Charles?"

"No," I replied quite honestly.

"I never had a boyfriend either. Am I your girlfriend, Charles?" asked Abigail with a nervous hesitation.

"I want you to be," I said with the emotion of the moment being audibly apparent upon every word that came out of my mouth.

"I want to be your girlfriend too," she said with sincerity.

With those words, she stopped walking and talking, and we stood face to face, hand in hand, with smiles upon our faces.

"Then you will be my best girl, Abigail, and I will be your best boy, for I feel a warmth when I'm with you, as if something is joining our hearts together," I told her with loving tenderness written all over my face.

In an act of spontaneity, Abigail wrapped her arms around my neck with a joyful hug of tenderness. By her obvious actions, I knew that she was happy that we had committed ourselves to each other. We slightly separated from our hug and faced each other in close proximity when I kissed her briefly on the lips. It was my first kiss, not a mature, passionate embrace but a youthful one. I would remember that kiss and what we shared at that time all these years later. Abigail knew that the woman she would become was calling her name with that emotional moment in my arms. Confusion is typical during the transformation when walking upon the balance beam that separates children from adults. Abigail wanted to hold on to her youthful spirit, but at the same time, she desired to be a young lady.

Abigail suddenly let go of me, and she quickly started to run down the dirt path that led deeper into the woods. "Catch me if you can!" she yelled out to me, challenging my competitive spirit.

I was caught off guard for a brief moment, surprised by Abigail's playfulness. One minute, she was being a sensitive young woman filled with the emotions of young love, until suddenly her mood changed and launched me into a game of catch. I ran after her as fast as I could, amazed by her speed and the grace of her stride. She was a very fast runner, and I watched her long blonde hair blowing in the wind from the speed of her run. I considered myself a fast runner but was having a difficult time catching her. The trail spiraled and snaked through the woods under many mature trees, past an assortment of shrubbery until the path left the dark confines of the woodlands and emptied into a field lush with an assortment of vegetables.

I immediately noticed the abundance of greenery all around me that grew in stalks that rose several feet over my head. Many rows of various types of vegetable plants were planted with planned precision that grew upon rolling hills that, at times, were quite steep. Abigail knew the fields well, for she had played among the vegetable plants at times during her life. She ran with much speed up a hill and then suddenly turned up a pathway to the left, followed by another quick turn to the right as I desperately tried to keep pace with her. Eventually, her tactics won and I lost sight of her. I began to realize that I was lost, and I stopped running, for I did not know where Abigail was or where to find her. Quickly creeping back into my memory, I recalled a dream I had about holding hands with a pretty girl until she vanished, her image seemingly evaporated into thin air. Fear held me captive for a brief segment of time when I started yelling out her name, each second afraid that the authenticity of the dream might have slipped into reality.

"Abigail!" I yelled. "Abigail, where are you?"

I slowly began to run, with my heart pounding violently in the state of panic, fearful that I might never see Abigail again. Desperation momentarily became my companion, for I did not know what had happened to her, and I once again called out her name.

"Abigail!"

Without a hint of what was forthcoming, a force from behind me came upon my backside and pushed me to the ground. It was Abigail who had tackled me, and even though I was surprised, I was thankful that it was her. I wrestled her off of me, laughing in the comfort of the moment. It was a relief that it was just a game of

catch me and she had outwitted me. Although the dream had similar circumstances, it did not mimic the reality of the day.

"I thought I lost you, for you caught me by surprise. You are a
very fast runner, but you did have an advantage, for you know these
lands. You were like a quick and graceful deer when you ran," I said
with a complimentary voice, still trying to catch my breath.

"I did get a head start on you. And you're right, I do know these
fields," she explained, trying to comfort me.

We rested on the high grass among the flora that surrounded us
for we had just run fast and hard and we needed to catch our breath.
When Abigail and I got up, we walked out of the fields, returning to
the woodlands, where we found a small stream that emptied into an
algae-infested pond. We skipped stones for some time, until we built
a small boat made out of twigs from fallen branches. I set it to sail
upon the weak current of the stream, and we watched it slowly drift
away. I utilized my imagination when I followed the vessel along the
banks of the stream. Remembering an old war movie I had seen a
few years before when I was younger, I began to throw stones at the
small boat, pretending that it was being attacked by an enemy. Abigail
played along with me, and we tried to sink the vessel. Finally, after
many attempts by both of us, Abigail hit the boat with a direct hit
using a larger stone, and the weakly constructed craft broke apart with
a splash. The fun we were enjoying playing by the small stream, made
me realize how very peaceful I felt in Abigail's presence. Time gradually slipped by, and we both realized that it was time to return home.

We were in joyous moods on our return to the castle, singing
songs, laughing, and telling strange stories to each other. When I
looked upon the castle's walls coming out of the woodlands, the
term *home* started to become recognizably familiar in reference to
the massive structure. Awkward as it might have been to me, I was
adjusting to the lifestyle, which was completely different than what
I had experienced in Ohio. Not in my wildest of dreams would I
have ever imagined that I, Charles Stormdale, would one day live in

a castle. As slow as watching the hour hand move across the face of a clock, so was the sense of peace that came into my spirit as I began to enjoy my time in the Mirror. There was much to occupy my time, and I was making many friends.

"I had a good time today, Charles, and I am thankful that I met you. Are you going to the worship service tonight?" asked Abigail.

"I want to," I quickly told her. "I have never been to one or know what to expect. Scatman told me that they are quite an event. He said the music and choir are excellent."

"Yes, they are. And to give you an idea of what the services are like, I would probably assume that they have similarities to the church services back in Ohio. I'm sure that you will enjoy the music, and you might even learn something. The first service begins one hour after the end of dinner. Which one do you want to attend?" Abigail inquired, although I believe she really wanted to know if I wanted to go with her.

"The second one, as long as you are with me," I said after a quick moment of thought.

"I want to be," she replied with true sincerity and loyalty.

Abigail was making my transition into my new life much easier.

"Do you want me to come by your room when I'm ready?" asked Abigail.

"Yes. That would be great. Do you know which room I am in?"

"You room with Willie. I know where it is. Expect me shortly before nine."

"I'm looking forward to seeing you then," I said with the evidence of anticipation heard in my voice.

When we reached the front door of the castle, we had promised each other to go to the worship service together, as we were becoming close, with a bond and understanding that was so special to the heart. Young love can possess the commitments and emotions that are just as strong and meaningful as those found in mature relationships.

When I got back to my room, Scatman was there, talking with William. I knew in my heart that they were talking about me, but I also believed that it wasn't anything bad, so I did not take offense. William was lying on his bed, stretched out and relaxed, while Scatman stood by the door with a mysterious and unsettled look upon his face. They were discussing what they understood the will of the Mirror to be.

"Hello, Charles. Did you have a good time with Abigail?" asked Scatman.

"Yes, I did," I replied politely.

"I sense that there is a mutual attraction and a heartfelt affection between the two of you. I have noticed this when I see you with her. Am I correct?"

"Your eyes see very well, Scatman," I said. "For the first time in my life, I feel good about myself. I thank the Mirror for bringing me here and for the opportunity to know Abigail. I believe she has a lot to do with the way I feel, for I am at peace when we are together."

"Have you ever thought of shadowtreking her dream?" asked Scatman. "It could be an important test to try before you confront Kassar. Remember what Barnabus's grandfather did the night before he got married. His bride looked upon what had happened as a gift that became a very special memory to her. The next day, when he realized what had transpired, he became mystified of the miracle in his dream. Tonight, Charles, you will walk inside of my dream. Last night, we walked in Barnabus's. We are much older than you are, and it might be a good idea to walk in someone's dream who is your age. Kassar is a challenge, as he is parallel to you physically and mentally. He is very clever and remember that he was born from the Mirror. The spirit of divine purity never was developed in him, and now, darkness influences his motives and actions. You Charles are being led down the path of righteousness, and the light is eventually always triumphant. Charles, only with experience can you learn how to influence and change the course of a dream. Having a successful shadowtrek with Abigail could give you the faith that you need."

"It's a good idea Scatman, but I feel like I would be invading her privacy," I said, worried about the possible consequences it might have upon our relationship.

"Charles, here in the Mirror, no one has secrets. Everyone knows about each other. Do you remember the small little town of Riversville where you once lived? The kingdom of the Mirror is also like a small town, for all who live here know something about everyone. Because of this uninhibited lifestyle, the battles that are fought daily, through the power of prayer, deliverance can be found. People here do not hide behind masks that many people back in Ohio wear. Tonight, when you are in my dream, try to remember what you learned in Barnabus's dream and apply that knowledge to take control. The following night, I want you to think about shadowtreking with Abigail."

"Are you going to the worship service tonight?" I asked Scatman, changing the subject.

"I wouldn't miss it, and you are going with Abigail, correct?"

"Yes, I am. Is it that obvious?" I asked inquisitively.

"I just knew. Remember, I was once your age, and I had a girl-friend too. She was my best friend, so I know how you feel. I will see you in my dreams. Have a good night, and use your wisdom to take advantage in my dream."

With those words, Scatman left the room and walked away. I turned to Willie and inquired with curiosity what they were talking about.

"He was telling me about your life before you came here, how your parents and friends treated you, which led you to become quite depressed. Your dreams have become the avenue that the Mirror called for you to follow. Scatman wants to teach you about dreams and the life that we live here in the Mirror. Do not feel bad, Charles. We are family like Scatman said. There are no secrets."

"I don't feel angry or betrayed. I was just curious, for somewhere inside of me, I knew I was the subject of your conversation."

"You are very perceptive," said William.

Chapter 18

The afternoon loomed into the evening, and even though I tried to keep myself busy, my mind had great expectations of the time I would spend with Abigail once again. When the anticipated moment approached, I became quite diligent in getting myself ready for the evening. I washed my hair, brushed my teeth, trimmed my nails, and got dressed in some nice clothes that I had never worn. My new attire, what I would refer to as church clothes, made me look good. I was nervous, as I held a considerable amount of anxiety inside of me for my first real date with Abigail. My mind was filled with thoughts and emotions of nervous tension, for besides being jittery about making a good impression on Abigail, I was also concerned about the prospects of shadowing Scatman's dream. When I was in Barnabus's dream, it was like an adventure into an unknown world, a realm of existence that is only explored inside the Mirror. Inside of a dream, anything could happen, and I had to be prepared to meet any challenge. Suddenly, a knock on my door startled me.

I got up off my bed and opened the door. Abigail stood before me, looking quite radiant in a lovely pink dress that displayed ruffles at the shoulders and a high neckline. The dress wrapped spiral flutters from the waistline to the knees, revealing its dynamic appearance. Her hair was styled to perfection, with curls and waves to make her look very mature, the blooming stages of becoming a young woman.

"Hello, Charles. You look very handsome."

I was glad that Abigail liked how I was dressed, for I took a lot of care to look my best. I wore a navy blue casual suit coat with matching shirt, pants, shoes, and socks. It was our first real date, and we were both nervous. We had only known each other a short time, but during those moments, we had become close, with a deep understanding and commitment. Abigail was also trying to look good for me, and she was successful. She had help from Diana, who styled her hair and fixed her face, adding a little blush to give color to her cheeks.

"You are very beautiful, Abigail," I said with astonished eyes.

"Thank you," she said, blushing moderately, slightly embarrassed by my compliment.

"Are you ready to go?"

"Yes. Quite ready," I replied.

We walked out of the room, and I closed the door behind me and started to walk down the hallway toward the tower steps. I suddenly realized that I was having difficulty taking my eyes off of Abigail. Her beauty and elegant nature held me captive. She was not a woman yet, but soon, the petals of her femininity would mature. It is an expected part of maturity; just as a cocoon turns into a butterfly, so must a girl change into a woman.

We entered the spiral staircase that was slightly deficient of light, which made it difficult to see the steps before us. A beautiful melody embraced us as we started to walk up the narrow corridor. It filled our hearts with joy. A short, elderly man with thinning gray hair who was dressed in a gray suit welcomed us as we entered the auditorium. He gave us both pamphlets that listed the songs that were to be performed by the choir and orchestra, along with information about upcoming events around the kingdom and a brief message from the pastor. After Abigail and I sat down, we immediately focused our attention upon the violinist and the piano player, who were playing a duet. The music seemed to calm my emotions, which were still on edge, as it set the mood for praise and worship. My eyes scanned the worship center, noticing its size and unique design. I thought that it must have been an addition that was made years after the original castle had been built. Its shape was one of a perfect circle, with the choir and orchestra loft that rounded out the front of the sphere.

I watched the flow of people entering the auditorium from three different stairwells, filling the seats to capacity. The choir entered dressed in bright red robes. It was not a large choir. There were approximately forty singers, but when they sang, they produced a sound reminiscent of over a hundred voices. Downstage from the choir sat the band, anxiously awaiting their time to perform. It was a small ensemble made up of several violinists, a piano player and organist, clarinets, saxophones, and trombone players. Behind the main ensemble sat a person playing bongo drums, along with several guitarists and one banjo player. There was even someone who played the harmonica. Compared to some of the musical groups from the churches on Earth, what I was hearing had a creative blend of sound that was quite original.

Finally, when all the singers and musicians were in their proper places, the music director walked to the front. He raised his arms to get their attention, and as he delicately moved his arms in a circular motion, the music came to life. Slowly it began, like a turtle crawling along the sand, until the tempo increased, blending its unique sound with such precision. It was a joy to listen to when the heart of the choir rose its voices up and above the band instruments as they united together with perfect harmony. It was music I had never heard, and the choir with its supporting ensemble created a perfect composite of sounds. The entire congregation was mesmerized by what they heard, and at the conclusion of the inspired song, the music director motioned for the entire congregation to stand and sing for the next song.

After we had finished singing, we were directed to sit down by the pastor, and he approached the podium to speak. The symbol of faith, or Paraclete, as it is known, stood erect behind the minister, silently establishing its message of truth. My eyes were intently focused on the symbol, and I noticed a bluish glow that seemed to shine from its hard outer edges. It was a symbolic deity that became a comfort to the people of the Mirror.

The assistant pastor came to the podium next, a younger man with pallid, brown eyes. He was dressed in a green suit that was not very appealing; and as I looked at him, I knew that he was having difficulty sleeping. The few select announcements that he was given to read caused him great difficulty in pronunciation. However, he did clearly remind everyone in the congregation that a fair at the school was scheduled for the next day, with lots of good food, games, and a time of fellowship among all people of the Mirror. Upon completion of the announcements, the choir sang one more song, which was a very slow but lovely ballad, and when the song ended, the pastor led us in prayer.

"What beautiful sounds fill this room!" the pastor exclaimed loudly, and the echo of his voice seemed to linger for a few moments thereafter. "We must give praise to the Mirror for the many blessings that he has given us. Stand up and give a shout of praise!" he yelled out with a thankful spirit that bellowed out of his heart.

Immediately, everyone in the auditorium rose to their feet, raised their hands, and began to shout out praises of thanksgiving. The sound increased with intensity that became almost deafening, piercing my ears but at the same time filling my spirit with joy. The shouts of praise lasted for several minutes, until a spirit of peacefulness fell down upon the congregation and, slowly, they once again sat down.

The pastor returned to the podium, and he became the center of attention. "I am troubled by what I have been seeing and sensing in my spirit. There is a spiritual illness in the kingdom, and it is diminishing our faith from what it once was. It is only when we trust in the Mirror to rescue us from our troubles that we can find peace. We can't lean on our intellectual understanding, for our knowledge is nothing compared to the vast wisdom of the Mirror. All of us, myself included do not know what is best for us, as the Mirror does. When a measure of trust is in your heart, peace will eventually find its way to you and gradually will become a dominant force in our kingdom."

Victor Reuben had been the pastor for more than five years. He was a large man who stood well over six feet tall and was built like a trunk of a large tree. His eyes were deeply rooted in his face, and he possessed a look about him that made him appear to have a genuine passion for others. When he spoke before others, a passionate emotion sang out from the depths of his soul. His gift of speech he used to the utmost capacity, whether it was before a large group or in one-on-one counseling. Pastor Reuben was very wise man, as over the years, he had studied hard and prayed for direction in his life. He believed that he found his destiny when he was appointed the head pastor of the kingdom. Looking down upon the congregation, he noticed that all eyes were upon him, which made him feel good. The large worship center was very quiet for a few moments as Victor Reuben concentrated upon the mood of the people, trying to perceive in which direction to take his sermon.

"Do we trust the Mirror? I believe that our main enemy is our lack of trust and our shallow faith. Our inner desires have become more important than people. Our love for the Mirror and our neighbors has become cold, and its importance is now almost trivial. We must return to the ways of old!" he yelled out as his voice loomed and echoed, piercing and penetrating into the hearts of many.

"Our life here in the Mirror has been blessed because the trust we had in our hearts for the Mirror and each other. We were free from the stress that plagues the common man. Let us look back, and may history teach us a lesson. Our forefathers, who were the first inhabitants of this place that we call home, arrived here and were terrified, for they did not understand what had happened to them. They did not quite realize, at that time, where they were. The only thing they knew was that their homes were gone and they were in a strange land.

Those first inhabitants spoke freely of their fears and doubts, just as the Mirror was a trusted friend. Isolated in an obscure land, fear of what was to become of them stalked them day and night. It was their faith and belief in the Mirror to be their protector and provider that kept them striving for survival. Through an attitude and willingness to obey, the Mirror granted to them the desires of their hearts. But now, when I look out upon our community, I become alarmed by the actions that are motivated from our emotions. Be aware, people! Your thoughts can be very deceptive. If you allow fear to influence your actions, the deliverance from your own personal prison, as well as the blessings the Mirror has waiting for you, will be delayed. It is only through faith in the Mirror that can we reclaim the peace we once had. Let us give thanks and praise to the Mirror through our prayers. Remember one thing: the heartfelt prayer of thanksgiving can break bondages that might be holding many of us captive."

Victor Reuben led everyone in prayer, and we bowed our heads and prayed for deliverance. While we were still praying, the band began to slowly play a very beautiful melody. At the conclusion of the prayer, the choir rose up its voices, which blended in with perfect precision in accord to the sounds that the band played. It was a song that lifted my spirit, which followed a very dynamic message. At that specific moment, I knew that it was no accident or mistake on my part that I came to that place of peace in the Mirror. How the Mirror came to my unconscious state of mind, I thought, I probably would never know. Two messengers were sent to me, Barnabus and Scatman, so that a child would lead the Mirror's people out of distress. I knew that I was that child and my spirit would direct me to all truth, entrusting me with the courage to face the many challenges that were waiting for me in the days to come.

At the conclusion of the service, the congregation formed a long line which led to the front of the auditorium, to place their hands upon the Paraclete. The power of faith in the everlasting eternal spirit was unseen to them, although they still believed that trusting in the Mirror would provide them with peace. Abigail and I joined the long line to meet the pastor and to lay hands upon the Paraclete. When we approached the Paraclete, I apprehensively put my hand upon the hard symbol when I immediately felt a strong, powerful current run through me like a bolt of energy. The Mirror's power was injected into me, which lasted for a few short moments. And when the vibration faded away, its presence remained united with me like it never was before.

Abigail and I left the worship center after experiencing a touch of the Mirror's power. We walked down one of the spiral staircases, following the crowd until we got to the main dining room. A long table was set up by the food service workers, where cookies, warm spiced cider, and a few other snacks and drinks were offered. Through a variety of delicious snacks, people always seem to gather for fellowship. The table became very crowded, as many people ate their snacks and casually talked about random topics. Abigail introduced me to many people, and I took pleasure in finding common grounds with a few of them.

"What did you think, Charles?" asked Abigail with a dying curiosity.

Abigail was in tune with the Mirror and had been raised with a strong association that connected her spirit to its presence, and she gradually recognized its existence each and every day. I sensed that allegiance within her, and I realized in time that was one of the many things I loved about her.

"I learned, I felt, and now I am starting to really understand. The music held me captive through the beautiful sounds of the band and choir. I seemed to have been put under a spell when the singers and musicians united together to create such beautiful music. The pastor's message spoke to me as well, and I related to what he was trying to tell all of us. The Mirror was working through him, and it had the entire congregation focused upon a message that we needed to hear. This night has been quite an experience for me that opened my eyes and mind to a world that I thought was beyond my ability to understand."

"The lessons that we learn are necessary tools to keep up our strength on a daily basis," Abigail began to explain to me from her educated experience. "In our daily trials and what we learn from them, we grow strong in the Mirror. It's easy to forget what has brought us to this point in our lives, and for some people whose lives are filled with increased activity, their spiritual walk can become shallow."

"I have only been here inside the Mirror for a short time," I explained. "But ever since I have been here, a peaceful presence has been alive in me. I never felt like this in all the years that I lived in Ohio, and I believe it is something that is only experienced here in the Mirror. What I could not see before I do now, and through the dreams that I have dreamt, I am beginning to see the reasons why."

"I am happy for you, Charles. I am also thankful that I was able to share this experience with you. It makes me happy to see that you got a lot out of the service."

"Yes, I did, and I am also glad that you were there with me," I told her as I looked into her beautiful eyes, sensing the joy in her heart.

I took her hand in mine with a brief squeeze, expressing to her that I cared. We walked hand in hand to the sitting room, where we sat down across from the fireplace. In silence, we sat for a few short moments, just watching the bristling fire, until we began to discuss the pastor's message.

"It has been a challenge for me because I feel like I have been changed from the person I once was. I feel so different in every way. It's a good feeling, but a little strange and uncomfortable. I guess it will take some time for me to find contentment with the new person I have become."

"I'm not sure what to say, for I grew up here," said Abigail, trying to be compassionate for what I was feeling. "I didn't come from a different culture, where the Mirror had to transform me and lead me down the correct path. The spirit of the Mirror works its will in all of our lives. Charles, if you listen to your heart closely the soft voice of the Mirror will show you the way."

Abigail started to grow tired, and I knew that it was time that she retired for the evening. I escorted her upstairs to her room and kissed her good night. When I walked away from her room, anxiety came upon me like a dear friend, for I knew that the time was near to shadowtrek. I walked through the hallways of the castle for a while as I tried to calm my nerves. I finally returned to the fireplace, looking deep into its flames as fear gripped my mind. My heart cried out to the Mirror for help.

I looked into the sparkling fire with a gratitude words could not describe, thankful that I was brought into this world. I also appreciated having some good friends: Abigail, Barnabus, Scatman, and William. The Mirror used them to open my eyes to the knowledge of the truth. I was talking to and communicating to the dying fire in prayer, as if it was a real person. I asked the Mirror for guidance, wisdom, and protection on the strange and extraordinary journey I was about to travel.

I recalled the first time that I had laid my eyes upon Scatman. He was pushing that little cart around the fairgrounds. Slowly, he walked, and he appeared to be quite old. I did not know it at the time, but there was a mystical presence that surrounded him at the fair. In wonder, I watched Scatman grow younger in age the closer we got to the Mirror. I remembered the journey through the wind tunnel, and when I opened my eyes, I noticed that Scatman had regained much of his youth. During the course of our long walk to the Mirror, I became aware of how he walked differently, for there seemed to be more life in his step. He was happy, filled with much joy with every step he took that brought him closer to the Mirror.

I saw Scatman's face in my mind as I looked into the fireplace. I could visualize his smile, and his laughter I heard, which seemingly echoed through my mind, but most of all, I could feel his presence. Somewhere inside of me, I felt the measure of faith he carried with him every day. The Mirror had delivered him from a life that most probably would have been filled with much pain and hardship. He had become a dear older friend, almost like a father to me, and as I thought about him, it almost felt as if he was sitting by my side.

Suddenly, without realizing what was happening, I felt my inner spirit being lifted out of me as I entered a dark corridor. I was being quickly transported through a misty and mysterious tunnel of dreams. I sensed my heart pounding rapidly, as my nerves were reacting to what I was experiencing. The circumstances were very similar to the entrance into Barnabus's dream, and I traveled down an apparently endless passageway filled with a thick fog. I was being carried by an unknown force in nature leading me to a dream that lingered inside Scatman's mind.

Without noticing that it had happened, I became aware that I occupied a space in the dream. A fierce wind was the first thing I felt, as it almost pushed me to the ground. I saw Scatman's house, and I could see that it was having difficulty standing against the windstorm. Shingles on the rooftop were flying off, and the windows were starting to crack from the power of the typhoon-force wind. Every step that I took was a struggle fighting against the mighty storm, until I finally reached the front porch. I felt a lot of vibration under my feet and above my head, as the entire house shook. I pulled the screen door open, and as I did, the strong wind ripped the door from its hinges and almost knocked me off my feet. I finally got inside the house, shut the door, and started to look for Scatman, for I was quite concerned for his safety. I found him in the living room, sitting in his favorite chair, playing the banjo. His face had the look of despair that I had never seen before upon him. Hope and joy was always a predominant personality trait common to Scatman; but now, I saw that he no longer cared.

"It's all beyond me now. I've done all that I could. Let the Mirror inflict its wrath," stated Scatman with a voice of despair and doom.

I did not understand why Scatman was being so negative when the storm was ripping his house apart. I knew I had to make something happen. I could not listen to Scatman's words, for negativity can damage faith. I could see that the tiles and wooden planks on the floor were being uprooted. The entire house felt like it was falling apart. Even the foundation under my feet seemed to be sinking into the soil of the land. All of Scatman's pictures that hung on the wall began to fall to the floor, along with many of his precious books. Our eyes met for a second, and I saw depression and a lack of faith.

"Charles, don't try to fight the anger of the Mirror," he said through his dismal sorrow.

Immediately, I quickly ran out of the house and off the porch, fighting to stand against the violent wind. I knew what I had to do. I looked up at the sky, and everywhere I looked, I saw the dark storm clouds. It was deep from within my heart that a caring love for Scatman came forth, and I wished for a rainbow. The speed of thought quickly made the circumstances change. Inside the core of the storm opened a clearing, and down from that opening, bright-colored lights raced with a shine that illuminated the land. A big, bold, powerful rainbow stretched its arms of peace to the ground as the wind subsided. It was a beautiful sight to experience, with the colors of red, blue, yellow, and orange that came together to form an optical imagery in the sky. The rainbow grew in strength until the raging storm completely faded away. I felt peace in the air, and as I looked at Scatman's house, I noticed the obvious damage, but I also saw that it proudly stood.

Suddenly, without expecting it to happen, I was forcibly pulled from the dream. What had me in its possession I could not see, but I felt its power as my presence was pulled down the corridor of Scatman's dream. In my mind, I believed that some supernatural force beyond the laws of nature held me in its grasp. A brisk wind was biting my face as I traveled with much speed enduring the cryptic constraint that eventually returned me to where I belonged. When the realization dawned on me that I had returned to where I had started from, my eyes looked upon the small, withering flames in the fireplace.

"I did it!" I exclaimed loudly with the realization of what had transpired.

The room was empty, which made me happy to see, for it was quite late and I didn't need to be embarrassed by a spontaneous shout. The satisfaction of fulfilling my task was alive in me, with a thankful appreciation to the Mirror for granting me wisdom during the course of the dream. It was a test that I really needed to be successful at. If I had failed, it could have seriously damaged my faith in my abilities to meet the many challenges that I would, in time, encounter.

Looking back at the dream, it was evident to me what was happening to Scatman's house and that Scatman himself had lost his faith. The foundations of his life and his beloved world in the Mirror were falling down around him. My heart cried for him, for he was lost, with all of his dreams and desires gone. It was at that moment that I took control.

"It's truly amazing," I said to the fireplace as if I was talking to someone. "I would have never imagined that what I just experienced was possible had I not lived through it myself."

I remembered the effects of the storm as it shook his house. I ran outside to make peace with the raging wind and rain, with a very specific idea in my mind. With the faith of a child, I caused the mighty rainbow to calm the storm. The dream taught me a lesson that took root. Just as Scatman had told me, whatever is conceived in a dream can be achieved. When my analysis of the shadowtrek was complete, I felt a hunger for some needed sleep, and I got up and walked to my room.

Like a thief in the night, I quietly entered my room, for William was asleep and I did not want to awaken him. When I finally got to bed, I did not find sleep immediately, as my mind raced round and round with thoughts of the shadowtrek and the foundation of confidence I had just planted. My mind drifted to Abigail's image and what joy we embraced when we were together. She was unlike anyone I had ever known. She was my last conscious thought until I saw William standing over me, trying to wake me up.

"Charles!" Willie said in greeting as he pushed on my shoulders and arms, trying to awaken me. I became aware of William's face as he looked down at me with eager anticipation for the day to unfold.

Chapter 19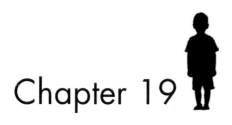

Anxious anticipation greeted me kindly as I got out of bed. I eagerly wanted to share the experiences of the dream walk with Scatman, as I was curious what he remembered. Abigail was also on my mind, and I desired to spend some time with her. With those feelings present, I could see the emotional landscape that set itself before me. William and I got dressed, washed our faces, and walked down the three flights of stairs to the cafeteria for an all-you-can-eat pancake breakfast. We were quite hungry, and I ate four large pancakes and some breakfast meat that looked like sausage patties, but tasted extremely different. During the course of the meal, William and I discussed our plans for the day. I specifically stated that I wanted to go to the library to read some books.

"If anyone asks where I am, point them in the direction of the library."

William promised he would, and I got up and walked over to the dishwasher window and gave the attendant my dirty tray. The dish machine operator grabbed my tray immediately and replied, "Thanks." I knew the people who ran the dish machine appreciated the consideration of bringing my dirty tray to the window. Quite recently, many people had seemed to forget that principal of courtesy in the dining room. In years past, there was never a problem of that kind; however, recently, many patrons of the cafeteria regularly had become inconsiderate to the people who worked in food service.

I left the dining hall and walked over to the library with one purpose in mind. I wanted to read and learn. My hope was to find a few books about shadowtreking. I have always loved to read, for a good book is more enjoyable to me than playing sports or other pastime games. Activities that require a certain amount of analytical thinking or using your imagination to enhance certain games always appealed to me. I had just started to read when Scatman walked in, looking for me. I was completely alone, and it felt good to enjoy the solitude. I knew that Scatman would find me that morning, for he wanted to discuss what happened during my shadowtrek.

"Good morning, Charles. You're up bright and early this morning. Did you sleep well?" asked Scatman with a certain degree of curiosity.

"I slept well, just not long enough. Willie woke me up and wanted to have breakfast, for he doesn't like to eat alone. I really didn't mind too much, for I am always hungry when I first wake up. So tell me about your dream."

"I was very depressed. I knew this, for I felt it. I wanted to cry, as frustration filled me with despair. Alone I sat as a terrible storm shook my house. I thought the Mirror was punishing me and was about to rip my house from its foundation. Out of nowhere, you appeared. We spoke a few words that I don't remember, and then you went away. That was the only time I remember seeing you in my dream. A few moments later, as my house was violently trembling from the storm outside, suddenly, it became quiet. I got out of my chair and looked out the window, and there before my eyes was the largest rainbow I had ever seen. It was a sight to see, as it almost took my breath away."

I smiled, and my heart was filled with joy when Scatman mentioned the rainbow. It made me feel extremely honored and grateful that I was able to have success in what I was asked to do. When I lived in Ohio, my parents gave me many assorted chores to do. Over the years, there were random instances when I did not perform my duties according to their specifications. As I remembered those times, it made me all the more satisfied with my accomplishment. It was just a dream, but I changed the events that could have transpired.

"When I woke up this morning, I felt good. A short time later, the Mirror spoke to me in its soft whisper, telling me that everything was going to be all right. At that moment, I knew that the kingdom would live in peace once again. There was still much work that needed to be done, but somehow, I know that the favor of the Mirror is upon us, watching over us as we seek to do its desired will. Tell me, Charles, what did you do to change the dream?"

"I think you know the answer to that, don't you?" I replied in question.

Scatman looked at me, noticing a glimmer in my eye. I wanted Scatman to guess what I did to change his dream.

"You created the rainbow, didn't you? It brought peace upon the land in the midst of the raging storm that could have destroyed my home."

"Yes, I did," I told him proudly, confirming the truth that was already evident in his heart. My confidence received a boost of my newfound abilities and what I have been called to do. Inside the Mirror, I believed there was an important role for me to play. My faith in action became a valuable tool that would alter the balance of success and failure.

"So you learned and experienced the abilities given to you and what can be accomplished in a dream. I am proud of you, Charles, but tonight, I want you to think about shadowing Abigail's dream. Out of each and every dream, you should learn something. This is how knowledge is acquired. The ability to understand something is not enough, for it is just as important to be able to apply what you have learned in every aspect of life. Only through wisdom can the circumstances in your life make any sense."

"I understand what you are trying to tell me, Scatman, and it is true that I had success in your dream. I will try to apply what I have learned to the future dreams that I might shadow. I know that it is important to be mentally prepared to encounter whatever might disturb the peacefulness in a dream."

"What made you choose a rainbow?" asked Scatman.

"For quite some time, I have believed that a rainbow is a symbol of promise for the good in life. When I lived in Ohio and a thunderstorm filled the sky with wind, rain, and lightning, I would always look for the rainbow when the storm had passed. I can never remember not finding one. The rainbow comes out when the peace has been restored. History has told us how ancient man used to look upon the rainbow with wonder and delight. Science has tried to explain the specific reasons why they appear. I believe there is another reason why they appear that I do not yet understand. It was for this reason, when I noticed that you and your house were in danger, I wished upon a rainbow."

Scatman smiled as he slowly got up out of his chair and looked deeply into my eyes. He knew in his heart that the Mirror saw things in me that he could not. My imagination, when trained together in the accordance set by the Mirror, could be used to change difficult situations. A battle was drawing near in the tunnel of dreams against a master manipulator. If I was to be successful against Kassar, peace would once again rain down from my victory. Scatman began to look at me with different eyes, for he sensed that somewhere inside of me was the ability to become more powerful with the Mirror than Barnabus or himself.

"Are you going to the fair today, Charles?"

"Yes, I am, for I promised Abigail that I would go with her. I suppose there will be a lot of food and many games. Are you going to be there?"

"I am planning on it, but be aware that Kassar will be there also. Use caution in the words you say around him, for if he suspects what we are up to, he will come after you the only way he knows how: inside of your dreams."

"Do you think he suspects that I know?" I asked with a sharp curiosity that troubled my mind.

"I can't answer that, for I have no clue. However, I would guess that he is suspicious," Scatman answered me truthfully. He looked at me and understood that I wanted to prepare myself emotionally, intellectually, and physically for Kassar. "All that I can tell you is to be careful at the fair and also at school, but do not avoid him. He knows that you talk with Barnabus and me daily, so if you begin to stay away from him on purpose, he will suspect something. Remember what I have told you about shadowtreking. A physical and mental connection must be made. I know you have already done that, but to win the battle in the dreamscape, you must go one step farther. With increased knowledge and wisdom about your opposition, you will have an advantage in the dream. Charles, don't forget that Kassar might appear to be friendly, but do not believe him, for his motives are not pure. Your best defense is extreme caution. I know that your faith has grown strong, but you must trust the Mirror more than your own abilities, for when you do, no weapon formed against you can succeed."

"Thank you, Scatman, for your wisdom and advice," I said with deep appreciation. "Your sincere confidence in my abilities has really helped me focus on what is important."

"You have learned quickly, Charles, but you had to. Something has to be done, for our situation is not improving with time but actually getting worse. Thank the Mirror for showing you the solution to the problem. Enjoy your books, Charles, and I will see you at the fair."

Scatman left the library with those words, and I was once again alone. I was not lonely, for I had the companionship of many books to keep my mind occupied. The library had a lot of reading material: fiction and nonfiction, reference books, and many texts on ancient philosophy. Upon the many shelves that filled the adjoining rooms in the library, there were over five thousand books. When I had my mind focused on reading and study, I just wanted to be alone. It was quiet beyond the meaning of the word, and that was just how I wanted it, with time to research unique rarities in dreams. What I was looking for, I thought might help me. Finally, I found a few books about dreams, telekinesis, and abnormal behavior in dream states. However, after many hours of study, I could not find anything substantial that could relate to what I had experienced over the last few nights. I believed that what Barnabus and Scatman had taught me specifically about dreams probably had never been written down on paper.

"Or has it?" I asked myself as a memory quickly entered my mind like a flash of light entering a dark room. I recalled a book that I was starting to read when I was at Scatman's house. *The Reflections of Life* was the name of the book, and as I thought about it, I believed that within its many pages, I might find some of the answers to the questions in my mind.

I quickly got out of my chair and started a search for the book of my desire. After an extensive search and not knowing where else to look, I walked over to the catalog file. Every book in the library was in the file, including magazines, pamphlets, and encyclopedias. I looked thoroughly, but finally, I realized that I would not be able to find it in the library. When my search ended up empty handed, I began to think of other places that I might find the book. I left the library and started to walk up the many stairs that would lead me to the worship center. I was using logical reasoning with the assumption that there might be at least one copy up where everyone sang praises to the Mirror. Once again, I was turned away in my pursuit, and I felt completely discouraged.

Before I left the worship center, I went down to the Paraclete. I placed both hands upon the glowing figure and prayed quietly in my own mind. I asked the Mirror with a humbled spirit where I could find the book of my desire. I stood quietly, thanking the Mirror continuously for the answer, and then, suddenly, it came. I slowly walked away from the symbol, satisfied with the knowledge of where I could find the book that I sought to find. In my spirit, the Mirror told me to find Barnabus or Scatman, for they were two of only a handful of people in the kingdom to own a copy. A new direction had been established in my heart, and I set out to find Barnabus, for I knew that Scatman's copy was at his house. Barnabus lived on the second floor of the castle, so with the desire to locate the book that could help answer some of my questions, I found myself knocking on Barnabus's door. He opened the door after a short moment, and with a look of surprise written all over his face, Barnabus noticed a stern desire in my heart looking up at him.

"Hi, Barnabus! Can we talk?"

"Sure. Come on in," he said, curious about my motive.

Barnabus lived alone. He had had the same room in the castle for the last twelve years. It had been that long since his wife, Martha, had been gone. His heart had missed her for all those years, especially the friendship that they shared. Although she might have not been with him physically, her light continued to shine down upon him every day.

Barnabus and his wife Martha had lived in a small, three-bedroom bungalow located between the castle and the school with their son, Gabriel. Their house stood upon several acres of land that was filled mostly with trees. Barnabus would play with Gabriel among the trees when the boy was in his youth. It was a happy time for Barnabus, a time in his life filled with precious memories that were dear to his heart. He moved into the room at the castle shortly after his wife died, as his son was married with two children. He did not want to impose on his son's marriage, although his son built a spare room at his house just for Barnabus, in the event that he might want to spend the night. He did not want to be alone in the house that he shared with his wife, for the memories would keep him stagnant in his past. Peace found him in his new life, which allowed him to demonstrate love to all people. He was sought after for advice on a variety of matters, for Barnabus possessed great wisdom. Most everyone in the kingdom knew his name and gave him the respect of a person with great knowledge. Barnabus found contentment, but never a day passed that he did not miss his best friend, wife, and companion. One day, he believed that he would be with her again, but only the Mirror knew of each man's destiny.

Barnabus's room was a large efficiency apartment. It had a small kitchen area, a bookcase, a desk, a dresser, a bed, a small sofa, a large closet, and a bathroom. The apartment seemed very spacious for its size, and it had everything that a single person might need. Out of the two windows of his room was a beautiful view of the back side of the castle.

"What can I do for you, my friend?" asked Barnabus.

I looked up at him, as I remembered that it was Barnabus who was the first person of the Mirror to come to me. It was Scatman who became my teacher and good friend, but Barnabus was the first one I met.

"I was in the library, reading and doing some research about dreams and other things that I thought might be able to help me when I shadowtrek. I could not find too much information about what I have experienced over the last few nights. I was about to give up when the Mirror reminded me in prayer about a book that I was reading at Scatman's house. The book is called, *Reflections of Life*. Have you ever heard of it? I have been looking for a copy over the last hour, and I thought you might have one."

"Well yes, Charles, I have a copy," said Barnabus.

"Could I please borrow it for a day or two?" I asked with enthusiasm.

"Yes, you can," replied Barnabus with a smile, a characteristic that I rarely ever saw upon his face. It was not that Barnabus wasn't happy; let's just say that his mind was focused upon more serious matters.

Barnabus looked into my eyes and saw a strong desire to learn. I was eager and willing and was growing with strength that only came from the Mirror. Barnabus knew the book and had studied it very thoroughly over the years. He knew that I really did need the book, for it could open my eyes and teach me how to fight the battle I was about to engage myself in. Barnabus nodded his head as a gesture of granted permission, and he walked over to his bookcase. The books were arranged in perfect order, just like his room and, for the most part, his life. He always tried to follow the laws written upon his heart by the Mirror and treat his fellow man with kindness and respect.

Barnabus looked over the many titles of books that stood in front of him. For a couple of brief moments, he surveyed the bookcase until at last he secured the book he was looking for. It was ancient looking, a faded, white, hard-covered book that seemed to have seen many days. Barnabus looked at the old book as if it was a treasured possession until he turned and looked at me.

"About ten years ago, I tried to get this book reestablished into the worship services. The spirit of the Mirror is with us always and stronger than life itself, but outside the worship services, there is a need for spiritual guidance. Most people, even the most spiritual of souls, have weak moments. This book is not used in our community anymore, and I believe that the decision not to use it is a mistake. My great grandfather helped write a large percent of what is written here. Upon these pages, Charles, you will learn the history, foundations, and the glory of the Mirror. The power of this book is in the word. When you read it, revelations of truths are disclosed to your spirit. They can bring peace, joy, and love to live inside of you. I read this book often, and it has helped me through many difficult times. And I believe that without this book, I might have been lost."

"I promise to take good care of your book, and I will seek to find meaning in its words," I said with complete sincerity.

"I know that you will, Charles. And if you believe that this book can help you, I want you to read it and receive some of its wisdom."

"Why isn't this book more involved in the worship services?" I asked, curious why such a valuable book was no longer an important part of the spiritual growth of the people.

"The administrators of the worship services have been blinded from the truth by no fault of their own. They believe that this book is outdated, and they replaced it with what they thought was something better. What they do not realize is that this book is eternal and speaks the divine, inspired word of the Mirror."

"I think I understand," I said.

"Charles, a clearer, more precise comprehension will be revealed to you when you read the book," said Barnabus with a seemingly distant and literal statement that almost spooked me.

Barnabus handed me the book, and I curiously looked at its ancient cover only to notice how worn out and faded it was, just like Scatman's copy. I was thankful to have finally found a copy. I looked back at Barnabus and thanked him as I walked out of his room.

I held the book firmly in my arms, as if I had just found an ancient relic. I walked to my room, which was located on the other wing of the castle. When I finally got there, I was happy to find it empty, and I shut the door behind me. I found peace and quiet in the room, and I now had time to spend reading the book that took me so much effort to find. I hoped that I would not be disturbed when I sat down on the edge of the bed, and I casually began to scan through the pages of the book. Beginning in the index, I began my search. I knew what I was looking for, and it did not take long for me to find it: a section about dreams. It was there where I found specific information about dreams and shadowtreking. The purpose and reasons for shadowing dreams were written in the book, and as I continued to read on, I remembered what Barnabus and Scatman had been teaching me.

On page 488, it was written, "To conceive and create a bond in dreams, a physical and mental connection must be established in the conscious world." The next line jumped off the page at me, as it opened my spiritual eyes: "It is impossible for the natural man to accomplish anything without faith in the Mirror. When the inner desires of a man's heart are present, all things are possible to those who believe."

I knew that to be true, and I read on. I found myself being pulled into the contents and substance of the book. I discovered how to change the course of a dream and cause the destination to emerge differently than what would have been. To alter what is transpiring in a dream, the shadowtreker uses his conscious spirit against the dreamer. The conscious life force has dominion in a dream, using its own brainwaves to control the dream's life. I was becoming totally fascinated, and I also found out what happens to the projected being when it is pulled out of the dreamer.

"The outward contraction," is the term that describes the act of being removed from a dream. To understand it, I imagined the shadowtreker as a particle of food that gets caught in the throat. The fragment remains for a short time until, at last, it is physically removed, and sometimes with great force. I accepted what I was reading, although I did not completely comprehend. Scatman told me that no one had ever been lost shadowtreking. *The Reflections of Life* did make a strong warning pertaining to the elements of dangers:

> Within a dream, if there is a conflict between the shadowtreker and the dreamer, such as a fight, and there is an injury, the effects that were suffered in the dream carry themselves to the present. If either participant dies in the dream, their life ceases to exist in the conscious world. Do not approach the dreaming entity with the intent of causing physical harm. The dreamer will do anything possible for self-preservation.

I suspected that to be true. Barnabus and Scatman had told me once that they had tried to confront Kassar inside of his dream. The result from what Scatman told me was unsuccessful. I suddenly looked away from the written word as a thought came to my mind. "So there is a danger. I knew there had to be," I said to myself. In preparation of what I would soon be involved in, I had to motivate my mind to be clear and focused upon what was important. I knew that when the time was right, I would face Kassar in the dreamscape. I wanted to be ready and motivated for what would soon confront me.

Chapter 20

A knock on the door startled me just as I was growing weary of the words on the page before me. I put my book down, got up off the bed, and casually walked over to answer the door, knowing who was on the other side. When I pulled the door open, I found that my suspicions were correct, as Abigail, Diana, and Scatman stood before me.

"Are you going to read all day?" asked Scatman with a big grin that formed upon his face.

Looking at my friends, I suddenly felt guilty about reading and studying for most of the day. I knew that it was time to put my research away and indulge in the enchanting fragrance of the beautiful day.

"I apologize," I said. "An idea formed in my head, and I needed to find the truth. My mind would not rest until I found what I was looking for. The quest for knowledge was calling out to me."

Abigail quickly walked over to my side, put my hand inside of hers, and reassured me that everything was all right.

"Are you ready to go?" inquired Scatman.

"Yes, quite ready. I just need to put on my shoes."

I was soon leaving the castle with my friends, and we walked through the lush gardens that lay just beyond the courtyard. It was a lovely day with bright skies, warm air, and a gentle breeze that caressed our faces. Distinctive-looking flowers grew in abundance at our feet, displaying the beauty and grace through their splendor.

Looking over at Abigail, I remembered my walk through the forest on my first day inside the Mirror. Abigail seemed to be happy, and I noticed a glow within the sphere of her eyes. She was quite content to be with me, which made me feel good. Whenever we were together or if she even thought of me, her heart was at peace.

We followed a path for about a mile or so, through an area thick with small trees and underbrush. Finally, the path ended abruptly only to be emptied out upon a large meadow that was surrounded on all sides by some distinct-looking little trees. On the other side of the meadow, we followed a path up a long, steep hill, and as we climbed to reach the top, the school grounds came into view.

From our new perspective, we could see the grand fair in the distance. The aroma of food reminded me of another fair I had attended recently, and because of that particular fair, I came to reside inside the Mirror. When we finally reached the fairgrounds, Abigail and I went off by ourselves, and she told Diana and Scatman that we would see them later.

Abigail and I casually walked around the fair, looking at all the people, displays, and activities. I took a deep breath, inhaling the scent of all the wonderful food that was calling out to my stomach. I became quite tempted, especially when I smelled the many types of grilled sandwiches and fried potatoes. Along the south side of the school grounds stood numerous food stands, and in their midst stood an extremely large tent with many picnic tables. I watched the cooks preparing the food and noticed how systematically they performed their job. What they were creating smelled delicious, and if they had any indication of how the food tasted, their cooking had become an art form. Abigail and I walked up to a specified food stand that specialized in grilled sandwiches and fried potatoes. We both agreed to get marinated elk steak sandwiches, which were made fresh, with onions, peppers, and melted cheese. We also got some spicy fried potatoes and some lemonade with our sandwiches.

I found an empty picnic table for Abigail and me to eat our food at and to enjoy each other's company. During the time that we ate our sandwiches, our discussion covered a wide range of topics. I was interested in finding out what it was like growing up inside the Mirror. We shared memories of experiences when we were younger, as Abigail also desired to know about my life back in Ohio. The sharing of our pasts seemed important to both of us, for it made us both understand our painful moments along with those special times of accomplishment. I felt close to Abigail, and I reached my hand across the table to touch hers with a demonstration of a special love. I knew that I found a dear friend in Abigail, and I hoped that we would always be close.

Just when we had finished eating our sandwiches, Kassar approached our table. He was dressed in yellow-and-black athletic attire, ready to engage in some sort of competition. Envy was written all over his face, for in just a few days acceptance came to visit me, something that Kassar had never seemed to obtain during the few years he had lived within the Mirror.

"How have you been, Charles?" Kassar asked with obvious resentment in his eyes.

"Good," I quickly answered.

"A one-on-one basketball tournament starts in about thirty minutes. I thought you might be interested. It would give you the chance to even the score on the basketball court with me. I know you want to. There are also some running races later on if either one of you wants to participate," Kassar boldly stated as if he was offering up a challenge.

"I would like to run in one of those races," Abigail quickly spoke up.

I suddenly realized that I was being inconsiderate.

"I'm sorry," I said to Kassar. "This is Abigail. Abigail, this is Kassar. On my first day at the castle, Barnabus and Scatman brought me to the school to show me around and introduced me to Kassar.

We played basketball and chess on that day. Kassar won the basketball game while I won at chess."

"It's nice to meet you," Abigail said sincerely, smiling graciously in Kassar's direction.

"Likewise," Kassar replied, looking briefly into her eyes until he focused his attention upon me. "I do plan a rematch in chess," he fiercely asserted with a short, piercing glance that seemed to penetrate deep within me.

"I think I will decline to play basketball at this time, but I believe Abigail and I might be interested in one of the running races. We can play chess and basketball some other time. Just tell me when and where."

"Suit yourself, but I will be running also, so depending on the race you choose, you might not have much of a chance to win," Kassar said with an attitude of superiority as he walked away.

Kassar desired to be the best in everything that he put his hand to try. I was good competition for him mentally and physically, for our strengths and weaknesses were in balance with each other, which ignited our competition to a higher level. The advantage that I carried was that my relationship with the Mirror was growing closer every day.

Abigail and I sat for a while after we had finished eating, and we continued to discuss Kassar so that she could possibly start to understand just a fraction of what I was beginning to encounter in my relationship with him. I tried to explain to Abigail that I believed that Kassar's heart was not very strong in faith and seemed to be distant from the teachings of the Mirror.

We got up off the picnic bench and began to walk around the school grounds, which had been converted to a summertime festival. There were many displays to look at, with many performers presenting their art form. One young man with a thick beard and mustache was playing a guitar and harmonica while a few yards away, Abigail and I listened to a vocal quartet that was singing songs of their faith with a modern sound that had its foundation in gospel music. Without giving it much of a thought, we walked past many different displays such as jugglers and gymnasts, both of which were illustrating their grace and balance.

Finally, we came to the baseball field, where a softball game was in session. The game did not keep my interest for too long, so we began watching the basketball competition. Kassar was playing. He was a very good player, although he lacked the size and strength of the other players. The tournament was divided into several different categories so that the younger players did not play against the veterans of the game.

As I watched Kassar play basketball, I realized that he was quite a talented athlete for his size. What Kassar was able to achieve against bigger and stronger athletes I thought was quite extraordinary. Kassar must have used an unseen weapon that gave him an advantage. What he lacked in size and strength Kassar made up for it with speed and shooting accuracy. He never missed a shot from the time Abigail and I sat down to watch him play. I watched him make shot after shot, and I noticed how he concentrated upon the ball after he released it.

I began to wonder if Kassar had that much command upon the gifts given to him by the Mirror. Each time Kassar's opponent shot the ball, he quickly turned his head and concentrated all his mental powers to the sailing sphere. Was he controlling the ball's direction and velocity with his mind? I knew that was an incredible idea, but inside the Mirror almost anything that is conceived can become reality. If Kassar had the ability to manipulate the outcome of a basketball game, he was indeed more dangerous than Barnabus and Scatman had realized. Before I would play Kassar in basketball again, I wanted to try that little trick myself to find out if it was possible.

Time passed quickly for me, and I felt like a stranger watching a play at an outdoor theater. It seemed a bit odd to me how people in the Mirror reacted to each other. Everyone appeared to be sincerely friendly, and as I recognized these mannerisms, something tugged at my heart. In the short time that I had lived among those people, I realized that the behavior I observed was the expected courtesies to all who resided in the kingdom of the Mirror. What I had witnessed back in my hometown of Riversville was a conduct among a large percentage of the men and women that had its roots in pride, envy, jealousy, and hatred. I felt like I was a foreigner upon the land, but I knew not to put too much trust in my feelings, for they could be deceptive. I realized that everyone there was not perfect, but each and every one of those people had their own special gift. Since my arrival, I discovered that even I had a specialty that the Mirror was using for its own desired will. Inside the Mirror, I was becoming less socially awkward. My friends that I had made since my arrival had a positive influence upon me. In only a few short days, the significant perspective that I was becoming a man was revealed to me, leaving my childish insecurities behind me.

Minutes turned into hours as Abigail and I enjoyed our time together at the fair. An announcement that captured everyone's attention was lifted up over the small rumble of voices at the fair from the loudspeaker mounted on top of the school building.

"Anyone interested in participating in the one hundred, four hundred, or three thousand meter runs, please report to the baseball diamond."

Abigail looked into my eyes with eager anticipation, and we got up from where we sat. On our way over to register for the race, we discussed which race held the most promise of success. The distance race we agreed suited us best, for we both had good endurance, having faith that our abilities would enable us to be competitive. I knew it to be true of Abigail, remembering the game we played, catch-me-if-you-can, when she lost me in the fields near the castle. Just like in the basketball tournament, the races were divided into different categories depending upon age.

A small table was set up by the heavy-duty aluminum net behind home plate at the baseball field, where two pretty young girls sat organizing the registration of the races. Abigail and I both entered the three-thousand-meter run, and the girls gave us a piece of paper with a four-digit number on it and two pins each to attach to the front of our shirts. The girls told us that when the one hundred and four hundred meter races were over, the participants of the three thousand meter run would be called to gather by first base.

Race time approached quickly, and Abigail and I began to loosen up our muscles in preparation for the race to prevent injury and to enhance our performance. I saw Kassar lying on the ground by the dugout in a carefree position, watching everyone. He won the basketball tournament easily, and he hardly broke a sweat. His shooting accuracy controlled every game that he was in. Kassar rarely missed a shot in five games. I looked at him, and he displayed pride in the relaxed language of his body. I hoped and prayed that his overconfidence would lead to his defeat. Of course, I wanted to be the one who would outrun him, for I wanted Kassar to eat my dust.

The shorter races preceded ours, and it did not take long for them to come to their conclusion. At that moment, I saw Kassar get up off the ground, and he immediately began to stretch. In close proximity to the starting line, almost fifty runners anxiously congregated to receive instructions. The course followed the perimeter of the baseball and soccer fields, along with a short run following a wide path in the neighboring woods. The race was run on grass and dirt, the last five hundred meters of the course coming out from the woods, with the finish line being in the middle of the outfield. A painted white line was provided for the runners so that they would not take a wrong turn. The race officials called the attention of the runners lined up in a double line and spoke a few brief instructions. I was very nervous, but I knew that it was the excitement of the race that made me tremble. The race official saw that the runners before him were ready. His assistant, a short and slightly overweight man with short, dark hair, lifted a horn to his lips in preparation to the beginning of the race.

In an extremely loud voice, the race official shouted out, "Get ready, get set, go!"

The horn sounded instantly and erupted with a blast into the air.

I heard the fury of many feet rumbling as the race began. Kassar quickly ran to the front of the pack and established a fifteen-meter lead. Abigail and I got caught up in a group of runners, and just before the course entered the woods, we maneuvered around the pack of runners so we could pursue Kassar. I followed Abigail closely, with confidence in our strides, with one thought in mind: to catch Kassar. He had about a twenty-meter lead on us until, gradually, we decreased his lead to only a few meters. Kassar seemed quite confident at the beginning, but, at the halfway mark, his lead had diminished. Abigail, Kassar, and I had distanced ourselves from the rest of the runners by almost twenty-five meters. It had virtually become a three-person race, with only six hundred meters to the finish.

When we came out of the woods and saw the long stretch to the finish line, I knew what I had to do. With almost three hundred meters remaining, I passed Abigail and Kassar with a quick burst of speed and started to sprint toward the finish line. Kassar was surprised by my tactics and tried to catch me; however, he could not. With almost eighty meters to the finish, I had increased my lead over Abigail and Kassar to almost fifteen meters. People were yelling and screaming at us, but I did not understand whose success they were targeting their concern upon. In my mind, I believed that I was going to win, not knowing what was coming behind me. Abigail, who ran fast and strong, swiftly burst into a mad sprint and passed Kassar and I, and she broke the tape at the finish line just a couple of strides in front of me.

My initial reaction was frustration when I realized that I did not win, until I had realized who it was who had finished ahead of me. I was quite happy that Abigail and I both defeated Kassar. When the race was over, I found Abigail, who was tired and breathing hard, and gave her a big hug. I wrapped my arms around her and offered my congratulations on a great race, as the victory was truly hers.

"I did not know I had it in me," she said through her deep breaths of exhaustion.

We both immediately and spontaneously started to look for Kassar, but we could not find him anywhere. Finally, I spotted him walking away from the fairgrounds, in the direction of the castle. I suddenly remembered the chess game, how he got mad when he was about to lose. I believe that when Kassar is defeated or does not achieve according his standards, his pride becomes hurt. We watched him walk away with his head lowered, and as Abigail and I looked at each other, we smiled, realizing that it was Kassar's pride which made him fall.

Many of the other runners came up to Abigail and congratulated her, speaking highly of her strategy. They told her what she already knew, that her patience paved the way for her victory. It made her feel good to hear such compliments, although she was slightly bashful about people praising her. Diana and Scatman, having seen the race, made their way through a small crowd of people to congratulate the winner.

"You looked like a beautiful and graceful horse as you ran past Charles and Kassar. I watched as you ran, and I observed your elegant stride, for in those last few meters, you glided past Charles and Kassar like they were in slow motion. The manner in which your legs moved in harmony with the rest of your body, as your long hair blew in the wind, was a pleasure to watch. Who said that the male is the physically superior species? Not here, not today, for a young woman outran them all! Good race, Abigail!"

"Thank you, Scatman. You ran a good race too, Charles," said Abigail, trying to comfort me.

She knew that I was disappointed that I did not win.

"I am so thankful that I was able to win, for it surprised me when you passed Kassar and me as you started your sprint toward the finish. I saw Kassar trying to catch you, but he was unable, for he did not have the strength or speed remaining in him. I wanted to beat him just as bad as you did. When he said to us, 'Don't plan on win-ning,' I thought to myself, 'What a little creep!' For those words, I wanted him to eat our dust."

"He did," I said, and I looked at Abigail with joy and content-ment in my heart. "I did not win the race, but I did beat Kassar, and that was my main desire. I wasn't sure if I could beat you, Abigail, but I tried. I never met a girl who could outrun me until now."

Scatman put his arms around the two of us, for he was happy about our success. "It really does not matter who won, but what's important is how you ran the race. Both of you ran with all of your heart. Defeating Kassar was the objective, and I believe that each of you wanted to beat him for similar but different reasons. Kassar's attitude toward winning and losing has its root in pride, as Charles knows and, Abigail, you found out today. He did not even have the decency to congratulate the winner. Do you see what I have been trying to show you about Kassar, Charles?"

"Yes, I understand," I replied in quiet agreement.

Scatman and Diana walked Abigail and me over to the refresh-ment area for something to drink. Just beyond the basketball court was a small picnic area with a stand offering lemonade, fruit punch, or spring water. Two elderly gentlemen with thinning gray hair, who appeared to be slightly older than Barnabus, were handing out the liquid refreshments. Scatman knew that Abigail and I were both thirsty after our physically exhausting race. While we rested for a short time, our drinks served as a platform to discuss what we had just accomplished in the race.

The moments in time eventually slipped away and into another spectrum, and before long, the fair became a memory. Its favorite moments would be replayed in our minds occasionally, and all who attended seemed to have a good time. The many volunteers who had assisted the fair committee in the day's events were satisfied with their efforts and the results. But as the fair's end approached, much work remained: the cleaning and security of all of the equipment.

Many of the people who had remained at the fair offered their helping hand to clean up from the day's events. It only took slightly over an hour to clean and put everything away with almost one hundred people working as a team. While Abigail and I helped with the cleanup, my mind was upon the next day, for in that building, I would resume my education, hoping that school would be vastly different than the one I had attended in Ohio. I was looking forward to what I could learn about the Mirror and the life it had to offer me. My attitude had to be positive, for the key to success or failure lay upon everything I set my mind to accomplish.

Chapter 21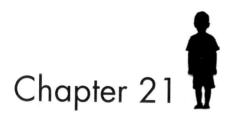

Abigail and I started to walk back to the castle after all the work was done. The trash cans were emptied, all food and display stands were broken down, and everything that was used for the fair had been put away into storage sheds. On our way home, we began to discuss the significance of defeating Kassar in the race.

"I hope the memory of that race will teach Kassar a lesson," said Abigail.

Even though I quietly agreed with her, I knew better.

"You are very competitive with him Charles," Abigail firmly stated with a deeper meaning to her words than were initially apparent. "I notice a strong determination between the two of you, as if you have something to prove. When I participate in sports and games, I try to do my best, but it does not compare to the passion and intensity that you share with Kassar. What is so important, Charles, where you lose the fun of the sport? Is it pride that was never completely washed when you entered the Mirror, or is it something else that I am blinded to see?"

"Abigail, you don't understand, and I had promised Barnabus that I would not tell anyone what is so important about what you see as a rivalry between Kassar and I. Abigail, I promise that when I can tell you, I will."

"I understand, Charles," Abigail respectfully acknowledged, "and I respect your agreement with Barnabus, for I believe that he must have his reasons."

We walked in silence, hand in hand, as we enjoyed our time alone in the peaceful solitude of the woodlands. The glow of the day was starting to weaken, and soon, the light would diminish only to be replaced by darkness. We felt comfort in each other's presence, and in the few short days since we had come to know each other, a greater and much more significant essence had its sights upon us.

When we reached the castle's doors and walked inside, a low rumble of voices could be heard coming from the entertainment center in the basement. Abigail and I walked downstairs with curious minds to investigate. It was more crowded than the audible voices that we heard upstairs would indicate, with people playing cards and throwing darts, among other games. I saw Kassar watching a dart game between two older men. When our eyes met, he immediately walked over to us with a desire to redeem his failure in the race.

"I just wanted to congratulate the both of you for a good race. I always feel bad when I lose, and I wanted to be alone. I'm too hard on myself when I don't win. I guess I'm just a perfectionist," said Kassar, trying to be sincere, although I suspected that he was up to something, but I was not sure what it was. "Would you like to play a game of chess Charles? We don't have to wait until tomorrow, do we?"

"Of course not. Sounds like fun," I said with confidence.

"I know one thing, Charlie," Kassar said in a casual tone. "This game will be much different than the last time we played."

"No two games are alike," I stated with a cold poise that made Kassar nervous that I might know something that he did not.

Abigail walked with me as Kassar and I acquired a chess set and a table on which to play. Kassar had found a chess set in an old trunk that sat in a dusty old closet where many old-fashioned games were kept. I located a small table on which to play, and we immediately began to set the stage for combat. Abigail found a chair and pulled it next to me and sat down to watch the battle of the minds. It was my belief that Kassar might become a vulnerable victim for me in a game in which I might find victory quite easily. However, I did not want to become overconfident, causing me to lose my edge, something that Kassar might have experienced at the race. He immediately grabbed the black pieces without asking, not that I placed much significance upon it, for I knew that it was a psychological preference for Kassar. Exactly as Kassar had spoken a few moments before, that game became quite different.

I approached my initial attack against Kassar with a contrasting eye to the one I had last time we played, which immediately caused him to be on the defense. Using my queen, bishops, and knights, I quickly trapped his team. My offensive tactic benefitted my defense, for it made Kassar befuddled at what I was trying to accomplish. Before he realized what had happened, I had captured his queen, one castle, and both of his knights, along with a few pawns. The only piece that Kassar had captured of mine was a knight. Quickly, and without mercy, I moved in for the kill and ended the game with an astounding checkmate.

Kassar looked at his dethroned king with bewildering eyes, mystified by what I had just accomplished. He rose up out of his chair with anger and frustration that surfaced from the core of his heart and, with one quick swipe of his hand, knocked the majority of the chess pieces against the wall and onto the floor.

Angry and frustrated, he looked at me and yelled, "Stupid game."

Once again, I had defeated Kassar, and he stomped out of the room. He began to wonder, *Who is this kid they call Charles? Why are my powers ineffective against him? I possess the ability to manipulate almost everyone in the community, and out of thin air, he shows up, and my life changed. I believe Scatman brought him here from somewhere because I lost my sense of control when he arrived.*

Kassar drifted into confusion, with the desire to think and meditate. The Mirror had been generous in the gifts given to him, but those talents were for a distinct purpose that never took root. The distinction between right and wrong was alive in him, although for most of the time, he chose to be disobedient. He had matured in strength through the Mirror; however, he had been created from the spoiled fruits of man's inner nature and desires. Kassar could have become a decent, moral young man, but he was never washed clean when he had arrived in the kingdom. It was quite the opposite of what I had experienced, as Kassar grew into sin with evil thoughts and actions that ruled his inner being. The desire to dominate and control took flight in him, but only for a season, as the Mirror heard the prayers of desperation from its people. Those prayers grew wings that waged a war against the power that created what Kassar had become.

A foundation of jealousy and resentment for Abigail and I rooted itself among all of Kassar's inner desires. In his twisted, manipulating mind, he conceived an idea that promised to inflict pain upon me in the worst way by attacking what was so dear to my heart: my relationship with Abigail. When the idea was initiated, a memory suddenly came to him which had taken place over a year ago, when he had done a bad thing to Scatman. Kassar believed in his heart that it was an accident that Scatman's wife died. He did not intend to kill her; he just wanted to scare her. Ever since that day, Kassar believed that Scatman has had an eye for revenge.

Retaliation was not a motive in Scatman's heart and mind, for he knew that when the time was right, justice would be served. In the known universe, for every action, there exists an equal reaction. Scatman knew that Kassar would one day suffer the repercussions for his actions, but his foresight could not determine when that day would arrive. Forgiveness was a complicated matter for him, for he still experienced moments when his anger would grow strong and he would have to subdue it with a strong hand. He had even offered up deep, heartfelt prayers for Kassar to be cleansed, trying to have faith in a day when he would see Kassar living free from his evil ways. Whatever the reason might have been, his supplications went unanswered. Kassar continued to emerge as an agent of the darkness, becoming more insensitive as he pursued retaliation upon anyone who opposed him.

The chess game was over, and I saw the look of disbelief shouting from Abigail's face from Kassar's reaction that she had just been a witness to. I was not surprised, for I almost expected the events that transpired. Once again, Kassar had failed to beat me in chess. It was just a game, but in a small way, the manner in which we play each and every game should be the perspective upon our daily lives.

"Kassar has a serious problem," said Abigail as she helped me pick up the fallen chess pieces.

Almost everyone in that section of the room where we were playing chess had their eyes upon us, wondering what the cause of the commotion could be. Finally, after the small echo of murmuring voices faded, the many curious onlookers resumed their activities.

"I'm so glad you are not like him, Charles. He gets angry over everything. When he loses, it does not matter if it is in athletics or a challenging board game, his pride becomes hurt and his emotions dictate his actions. How did he ever get like that? He doesn't have the love and compassion that most of us embrace. He's not like us."

"You are beginning to see the mystery that is Kassar. I really feel sorry for him though, and I believe he needs our prayers. The Mirror could purify his heart, wash him clean, but only if he really wants to change. If Kassar fights the will of the Mirror, he might fall, and very hard. It's good to see that you are beginning to notice what Kassar really is."

As the evening grew into its darker stages, Abigail grew tired from the long day and needed some rest. I was still quite alert, for I knew what was required of me, and that kept my motivation strong. My desire was to shadowtrek Abigail's dream. I believed that it would be quite easy to obtain passage into her dream, for we shared a personal friendship that had united us and seemed to be growing stronger every day.

I escorted Abigail to her door and held her in a tight and tender embrace as I wished her good night. She told me that she would see me at school the next day. I replied that I was looking forward to learning the many things that I never learned in school back in Ohio. For a few short moments, our eyes connected in a symbolic gesture of affection that was more satisfying than our previous hug. I finally turned my eyes away from her and walked down the hallway as Abigail closed the door behind her.

After Abigail retired to the apartment she shared with her aunt, uncle, and Diana, I tried to focus upon what was important. I walked back to my room and found the book that I was reading earlier, the one that Barnabus had loaned me. William was in the bathroom, getting ready for bed. It would probably be an hour or longer before I could enter Abigail's dream, so I went down to the sitting room to spend some free moments waiting in anxiety and found the room almost empty.

I sat down on the couch by the fireplace and started to read about the guidelines that the Mirror expects his people who live in his domain to follow. I found the most important virtues I already held in my heart, such as forgiveness, honesty, love, giving, and sharing. When I read those words, I became aware of the few things in my life that were once there but had disappeared. I remembered how I once lived before I came to know the Mirror. In the past, I used acts of deception and manipulation to get my way. The majority of the time, my heart would feel guilt and convict me of my wrong motives and actions. The memories of what had once been made me realize that I had drastically been transformed from the boy who once lived in Ohio. The Mirror had given me a new life with the promise of many blessings to come forward in the future. I put the book down, only to realize that I was alone. I finally had my solitude and the appropriate atmosphere to reach out to Abigail and walk her dream.

I knew it was time. I placed my face into the cup of my hands, and earnestly prayed for a successful link with Abigail. When my mind came out of prayer, I looked up with my focus being upon the flames in the fireplace. Suddenly, I could visualize her face, hear her voice, and distinguish the attitude of her walk and the expressions she wore on her face when she laughed. In my mind, I saw the many things that made Abigail such a unique person, which was what pulled me into her dream.

I felt her presence all around me, and as I continued to look into the fire, I became slightly timid as I felt a slight vibration when I was lifted outward and down the long tunnel of dreams. I was becoming very familiar with the method of travel that transported me into the dream of the dreamer. The tunnel was the link that connected our two minds.

Briefly, the moments passed when I began to distinguish the fact that I occupied space in Abigail's dream. She made her presence known to me when, out from behind a red maple tree, she appeared. It seemed to me that she was waiting for me. We faced one another, looking with intensity into the deeper regions of our hearts, until we began to walk into the forest, following a narrow trail. Abigail stopped suddenly; stared at me curiously; and with an ornery smile, turned and started to run away from me down the trail.

"Catch me if you can!" she shouted back at me with a voice of encouragement to pursue her.

I knew from experience that Abigail was a fast runner, but I also knew that I was in her dream. My desire was to catch her and to run at her side. Quickly after the thought entered my mind, I caught up with her effortlessly. I turned to look at Abigail as we ran through the woodlands when I wished that we could fly and be changed into birds of the air. Once again, upon conception of thought, we were transformed and a weightless sensation came upon us and we began to glide upward into the air. We flew above the great trees of the forest and entered a pathway of eternal sky. I glanced over at Abigail as we flew only to see that we had been changed into a species of an eagle that I was unfamiliar with. Our feathers were light brown with many small freckles of white. It was so very graceful, the manner in which we flew the skies, as we spread our mighty wings.

Abigail and I flew higher, rising to an elevation that enabled us to see the land of the Mirror like never before. I did not realize how large the kingdom was, for only in dreams could I ever see what birds do. We were at peace flying the skies when I flew above Abigail and placed myself several mere inches above her, until our feathers touched. United in body, mind, and spirit, we flew together, and we were changed in an instant, becoming one bird. With amazing speed, we flew the endless sky as one, soaring over the castle, the vegetable fields, and all that lay beyond. Without thinking the idea, we fell into a dive, accelerating to a speed that was almost beyond my comprehension, with our eyes focused upon a sparkling blue lake. Just before we would have splashed into the water, we drastically changed our velocity and direction, and our belly skimmed the surface of the lake until we once again reached for the heights of the sky. Above the tips of the trees we flew until we separated and became two birds once again. Abigail and I gracefully extended our wings to full capacity as we glided ourselves on a slow but gradual decent. Just as we were transformed into birds to fly the skies, when we touched the solid ground, our humanity found us once again.

Seemingly mesmerized by images in our minds that we were birds, we looked up into the sky with wonder in our eyes. Abruptly, we turned our eyes away from the scope of the horizons and our focus became glued upon each other. Our arms spontaneously became entangled in each other in a tender embrace until we kissed. I looked at Abigail with love in my eyes and in my heart as I passionately tried to tell her what I felt.

"I love you too, Charles," she said with watery eyes from the emotion that came from deep inside of her.

Having honestly expressed our feelings toward one another, I was suddenly pulled out of her dream and down the dark, misty tunnel until I came to realize that I was looking into the dying flames of the fireplace. With a speculative curiosity, I surveyed the room, knowing that I had returned from Abigail's dream. I looked down at my feet, and I immediately noticed that there were several brown and white feathers lying on the floor. I reached down and picked them up and held them in front of my eyes. A smile came to my face as the realization of what I held in my hands became a souvenir from the dream that would remain in my heart for many days to come.

I got up off the couch, took my feathers and my book with me, and walked upstairs to my room. I felt blessed with what I had been able to accomplish inside Abigail's dream. Upon the completion of the dream, I knew that we shared a special type of love that I hoped would not be easily disrupted. When I got inside my room, I took off my shoes and lay down on the bed without changing clothes, for I was very tired. I immediately began to drift off from the conscious world and eventually found myself in a dream.

The sensation of flight came upon me initially in my dream, for I believe its image was still present in me from the shadowtrek. I knew that I was some kind of small bird during the beginning of the dream, just flying around without any direction, until I passed through several other transparent waves in the sky. As I passed through these strange ripples, I experienced numerous alterations from a cardinal into other types of birds flying over maple and pine trees and overlooking streams and ponds during what would seem to be autumn. I finally became a large seagull with a large wingspan, and I soared over a grand body of water such as an ocean or a bay, and upon the coast of a large land mass, a forest stood proud with an appearance that was so serene that it was artistic. The sky was a brilliant shade of blue everywhere I looked, until something caught my attention in the woodlands.

I quickly flew down into a tunnel of trees made by natural design, led by a mysterious force that had captured all of my logical reasoning capabilities. Beyond what I could measure, I began to notice a dimly flickering light in the distance, which I thought might have been the end of the tunnel. My desire to learn the origin of the flickering light multiplied, and as I flew closer, it began to resemble a torch. Just prior to approaching the flame, out of the shadows, Kassar suddenly appeared with both hands consumed with fire. He smiled at me, emerging with an image written upon his face that seemed to be possessed by an entity that was drenched in the fathoms of evil. I was only five feet from his burning hands of fire when he yelled at me with the inclination of extreme hatred and envy, "Burn, Charles! Burn!"

Chapter 22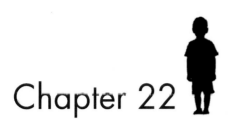

I impulsively sat up in my bed with a quick jerk of my upper body. Silence loomed around me, and for many minutes, I sat in its presence, just listening. Sweat poured down the side of my face, and my nerves trembled with an eruptive emotion as I wondered if Kassar had been in my dream. I pondered upon the idea as rationally as I could until I finally lay back down on my bed. The possibility existed that Kassar was trying to learn what my true intentions were. He knew that Barnabus and Scatman were my mentors and would eventually teach me to walk the dream. Thoughts of confusion drifted like waves in my mind when I realized that it was possible that the dream could have been the result of an unconscious fear.

I rested in my bed for another hour or so, not really sleeping, for my mind was skipping randomly among diverse images. When I was about to fall asleep once again, William startled me and told me that it was time to get ready for school. A bold determination had my mind focused upon the new day, a new beginning, as I was starting in a new school. The thought of facing new teachers and classmates whom I had never met before made me slightly nervous. The memory of my first day of school in kindergarten all those years ago came upon me. I remembered how I experienced many fears and anxieties that made me tremble with a temporary violent emotion. I hoped that I would be more relaxed than I was back then, for I did not want to panic like I did when I was younger.

When I finally decided to get out of bed, I knew that I did not get enough sleep. I was tired, and as I slowly walked into the bathroom, I desired to return to my bed. Stepping into the shower, I desperately hoped that the spray of the water would lift me out of my drowsiness. After a few moments, I felt revitalized as the water sprayed down upon my face. I quickly dressed for school after thoroughly washing and drying myself. As I brushed my teeth, I looked at myself in a reflecting glass that hung on the bathroom door. What I saw looking back at me appeared to be a drastic contradiction to the image that I once was. I sensed that I looked different, much more mature for my age than I had been before. The new perception that I had of myself gave me poise and confidence that I would need to pass tests that would prove my faith. I knew that Barnabus and Scatman had taught me well, but from that point forward, I had to provide the substance and desire to stand upon my beliefs with evidence of my actions in accordance of the values that the Mirror had placed in my heart.

William and I wasted little time getting breakfast, and we ate just pastries, fruit, and juice. When we had finished, we disposed of our waste and left the castle. The fresh morning air greeted us as we stepped outside, and a familiar scent that reminded me of sassafras was dominant in the air. I remembered that smell from Ohio when I used to play in the many wooded lands near my parents' house. The memory had the inclination of being a long time ago, but I knew that in reality, it had been less than a week. Since I had come to the land of the Mirror, I had various peculiar encounters and met a few interesting people, so, as a result, I felt that my absence from my earthly home had been much longer.

When we approached the school, I began to become nervous about what I was about to encounter. As we walked through the school's doors, William immediately directed me to the school office to pick up my class assignment. Barnabus had given him specific instructions to assure that I was properly situated on my first day of school. The office secretary, who was an attractive woman with long, red hair, greeted me when I stepped into the office. I looked at her apprehensively until I timidly told her that I was new and it was my first day.

"You're a little nervous, aren't you?" she asked with consideration for my feelings.

"Yes, ma'am," I said, as I notably demonstrated my anxiety.

"My name is Julie, and you are?"

"Charles," I replied.

"It's nice to meet you," she said as she glanced down at the many papers on her desk, pulling out a couple and placing a few papers in front of me that she said required my signature. After I had signed my name to the papers, she handed me my assignment sheet, which she told me to give to my teacher. I took the paper, folded it in half, and thanked her for being so nice to me on my first day.

"You're welcome," she replied. "But calm down. School isn't so bad here. You might even come to like it."

"I'll try," I said as I walked out of the office.

William was waiting for me as I concluded my affairs in the office. I quickly followed him through the crowded hallways of the school, and I noticed many kids getting books and other school materials out of their lockers, randomly talking with friends while they proceeded to their first class. I handed William my class assignment that instructed me on which room to report to. He looked at it briefly until a smile came to his face.

"You have Mr. Schneider," Willie told me. "He's a good teacher with a strange sense of humor, as he makes learning fun. You should enjoy his class, and he will teach you many things. I was in his class two years ago. His room number is sixteen, down to the end of the hallway, up the stairs, first room on your left. I will walk you there, but then I must get going."

When we arrived at my classroom, Willie looked into my eyes, and he knew that I was nervous.

"Relax, Charles. There is nothing to be afraid of. Just remember that you possess a great talent, so draw from your experience and school will be quite easy."

"Thanks, Willie. You have been a great help to my confidence, and I appreciate your moral support," I said with gratitude.

With those words, William walked away quickly, and I turned and faced the door with the number 16 carved in the wood with silver numbers. I reached for the doorknob with trembling hands and grabbed hold of it, turned it, and pulled it open. I walked into the classroom and quietly pulled the door shut behind me. The curiosity of thirty sets of eyes fell upon me. I felt so alone, like an alien creature on a strange and hostile planet would. Somehow, I found the strength and courage to move forward.

Mr. Schneider's room had more than thirty small wooden desks lined up in rows, facing his large desk at the front of the classroom. A large rectangular blackboard with a bulletin board next to it was mantled on the wall behind his desk. The bulletin board had various magazine and newspaper articles from the school's weekly and monthly publications, along with pictures of all the students in his class.

"May I help you, young man?" asked Mr. Schneider, who sat at a large, wooden desk with many books and papers that sat in a disorganized manner. He seemed to be a tall man in my eyes, with dark brown hair, green eyes, and a full beard and mustache that needed trimming. He appeared to be approaching middle age, for I noticed his receding hairline and several faint wrinkles that had formed around his eyes and upon his forehead. He was dressed quite properly, wearing a suit vest and tie that gave him the appearance of a person in authority. I walked over to his desk and handed him my class assignment sheet. He looked over my paper briefly, until his eyes met mine.

"Class, today, we have a new student. I want you to welcome Charles to our class. Charles, take a seat in one of the empty desks in the back of the classroom," announced Mr. Schneider, directing me where to sit.

I walked to the back of the class, and as I looked through a sea of curious eyes, I saw a familiar face. My eyes fell upon Abigail, dressed in a very pretty blue-and-white flowered dress. The feeling of being alone no longer accompanied me, for I had a friend in the class. She looked at me with loving eyes, and I knew that my eyes were probably showing her the same affection that she was showing me. I wondered if she knew that I was in her dream the night before.

"Charles," said Mr. Schneider in a loud voice, giving direction, "Could you stand up and introduce yourself to the class? Tell us a few things that would give us a brief glimpse of who you are."

I slowly and timidly stood up and looked around the classroom, and I noticed that all eyes were upon me. I was nervous and felt quite awkward, but somehow, I found the inner strength to do what was asked of me.

"As you have heard, my name is Charles," I said, being quite bashful as I spoke. "I just recently arrived here a few days ago from a place I used to live called Ohio. Life was very different there, and I am very thankful that I am here now. I love sports and games of all kinds. I like to run, read, and play chess. I believe that it is when I am in the fresh air, among the trees that I find my place of peace," I said as I finished my brief introduction of myself, looking around the room at all the young faces until I sat down.

"Thank you, Charles," Mr. Schneider said in appreciation. "You will learn that our curriculum here is probably much different than what it was back in Ohio. We learn the essentials of life here, the important principals of our existence and what we have been called to be. We learn morality and the fundamental laws of nature, man, and the universe. Today, we are going to discuss the responsibility that each of you has to the family of the Mirror and how faith interacts with that obligation."

Mr. Schneider taught in a very personal but unique manner. I liked him from the start, for he talked to us rather than lectured, and the ability to learn was enhanced because of his style. He encouraged class participation, for he wanted us to express our thoughts and beliefs concerning certain issues. The morning seemed to pass quickly, as my attention was focused upon the topics that were being discussed in the classroom. Just before the lunchtime break, we had a lesson in mathematics and how it is applied to life in the Mirror. I had never liked math. It was always my least favorite subject. However, I did notice that Mr. Schneider taught only what was necessary and vital in mathematics, which could be used in our daily lives.

Suddenly, I became aware that I was beginning to enjoy that school, as I was learning about the many virtues held close to the human heart. Basically, I understood most of what was being taught, and I began to perceive what the role of man inside the Mirror is composed of. Traditionally, it is supposed to be service to each other that places us in accordance to the laws of love set in place within our hearts. Available for everyone's benefit are abundant resources used for the enhancement of the many gifts and talents that the Mirror bestows upon his children. School was just another tool; its purpose was for the distinct development of young minds to gain perspective of what the will of the Mirror for their lives to be.

The lunchtime bell rang, announcing the end of morning classes. I got up out of my seat, found Abigail, and walked with her down the stairs to find the lunch line. She introduced me to a few of her friends while we waited. Many of them had great plans for their time off from school, and, being curious minded individuals, they asked Abigail what her plans were.

"I just want to spend a lot of time outside, in the woods and fields, being alone in nature. I want to walk in the fresh air, swim, and canoe. I really don't care what I do as long as I'm close to nature, for there is peacefulness there that I can't find anywhere else," said Abigail, and her friends looked at her curiously until they quickly changed the subject.

We finally got our food and found a comfortable small table for two to eat at. The dining hall, which was quite large, had many different-sized tables, some that could seat up to twenty people while others were more intimate and could accommodate only a few.

"Did you have a good a night's sleep last night?" I asked, curious to hear Abigail's interpretation of her dream.

She looked tenderly into my eyes when she fell into recall. Just the thought of those brief moments upon the dreamscape filled her heart with joy.

"I had a wonderful dream. We were birds flying as one, with the presence of one another alive in our hearts. We could see regions of the kingdom in the dream that only birds have the chance of seeing."

"It sounds like quite a dream," I said. "What kind of birds were we?"

"I believe we were some kind of an eagle. The feathers on our wings were light brown in color with white markings from what I can remember when we flew as birds."

I reached into my pocket and pulled out a feather while I listened to Abigail as she vividly painted mental pictures about her dream. I held it in my hands on the table in front of me, gently caressing its delicate hairs. Abigail did not discern what I was trying to tell her by the display of the feather in my hand.

"I was there, Abigail, and this feather is proof," I said, looking into her eyes, searching the depths of her soul.

Her eyes grew large with astonishment when she realized what it was that I held in my hand. The recognition of the dream recalled the emotion that had surfaced within her, which was equal to what would have been had it actually taken place in the natural. I could read her face as she thought about the dream and the intensity of what she felt when we confessed our love. Abigail gently touched my hand that held the feather, and we passionately looked into each other's eyes. A flood of various types of sentiment erupted from within her that she could not control. She began to cry tears of joy with the memory of the dream, especially the words that I spoke.

Through her tears, she began to look at me with new eyes and a deeper love in her heart.

"Did you really mean what you said to me last night?" Abigail asked as happy tears ran from her watery eyes and a faint smile came to her face.

"I meant it last night, as I do in this moment when I tell you that I love you, Abigail. I believe that I lost my heart to you the moment my eyes fell upon your face," I said with complete sincerity.

"I love you too, Charles," she said with restrained passion as the tears continued to trickle down her soft face. "How is it possible that you were in my dream? I had heard rumors of a few select people with the ability to do what you did last night, but I was not convinced that it could be done."

"I can't tell you right now how I was able to do what I did, but I promise I will, and soon. I wanted to be close to you last night and to speak those words that I was having difficulty expressing in the natural."

Abigail dried her eyes with a cloth napkin on the table, and we started to eat our lunch. We looked at each other in love as we ate our food, for nothing around us was important enough to distract us. It was both scary and exciting for Abigail and me to encounter love, and even though we knew we were not quite ready, we realized what was happening to us.

Just as Abigail and I were finishing our lunch and were about to get up, Kassar approached our table in a desperate attempt of confrontation.

"You beat me in chess twice and you outran me in a race. Now I want to see if you can beat me in basketball. I know you want a rematch, don't you?" asked Kassar, offering a stern challenge.

He was testing me, for he wanted to find out how much of a competitive spirit I possessed. He was searching for a weakness in my character that could become an easy target. It was his plan to humiliate me in front of Abigail, which, in turn, he thought, would damage my fighting spirit.

"I must be honest with you, Kassar. I really don't feel like playing basketball, but I did promise you, so I will be true to my word. Just don't get mad if you lose. It's not healthy mentally or physically," I said with truth and compassion.

"I won't lose," Kassar said slowly, with a voice filled with stern pride.

"If you say so, Kassar," I said. "I'll meet you outside on the basketball court in a few minutes."

"I'll be waiting," said Kassar as he projected a hateful stare in my direction.

The games that we played were more than competition to Kassar, and everyone who played games with him knew it.

I allowed my food to digest for a few minutes before getting up from the table. Abigail walked with me outside to the playground basketball court to face Kassar in a game of confidence and concentration. I knew what I had to do, and I trusted in the Mirror with all my heart. In athletics, the victor is not the one with superior talent, although occasionally, the circumstances will arise to allow it, but it is usually the individual or team that has a focused mind.

When Kassar saw Abigail and I walk out of the school's back door, he was thankful for the opportunity to restore his confidence. I stepped onto the basketball court with strong faith as Kassar passed me the ball. I took a few practice shots, and I made each one, using the technique that I saw Kassar use in the one-on-one tournament the day before. Watching the ball sail through the air, I controlled its direction and velocity with my mind as it fell through the hoop. What I observed Kassar demonstrating at the basketball tournament required total concentration to be effective. When Abigail and I helped clean up after the fair, I tried a few shots on the basketball court. I wanted to find out if what I suspected was actually possible. I made five shots using that method, and I even made shots that I tried to miss on purpose. I discovered that Kassar's technique worked perfectly. I felt bad, for in all truth, it was actually cheating. My father's voice rang in my mind at that moment, quoting an old saying: "All is fair in love and war." Kassar did not know that I had discovered his secret.

I looked at Abigail, who stood alongside the basketball court, and just by being there, she gave me moral support. We smiled at each other until I focused my attention on the game. Kassar let me have the first possession to begin the contest, and I was determined to take advantage of the opportunity. I dribbled the ball slowly, never taking my eyes off of Kassar. When I turned my focus to the basket, I quickly launched a jump shot from fifteen feet away. My eyes concentrated on the ball going through the basket until I heard it swish through the net for a score. Kassar grabbed the ball expediently and dribbled the ball back to the return line. I guarded him very closely, and when he shot the ball, I immediately turned around and tried to prevent the ball from going through the basket.

My heart jumped for joy when I saw the ball hit the front of the rim and bounce into my awaiting arms. I immediately dribbled the ball back to the return line and, without allowing Kassar time to recover, quickly attempted a long-range shot, concentrating on it as it fell through the net. When my lead reached 4-0, Kassar began to grow frustrated and confused, for he could not comprehend what was happening. I noticed Kassar growing impatient, desperately trying to make something happen. I felt slightly guilty about laughing under my breath as I watched Kassar frantically trying to get back into the game. I was teaching him a lesson about manipulation and the proper way to use power given to us by the Mirror. Without wasting any time, I quickly ended the game with a domination that looked almost elegant, as my mind control was more effective than his and I won the game by the score of 10-2.

When the game was over, Kassar could not even look at me. He just walked away with his head lowered, feeling humiliated.

Depression fell upon him, for I had defeated him in yet another one of our competitions. He desired to be alone and try to analyze why all his plans had failed him.

"Why? Why? Why?" he shouted out, terribly confused.

Abigail gave me a short victory hug, and then we promptly walked back into the school, returning to our class. We briefly discussed Kassar and how he reacts when he loses. I felt good that I defeated him, but at the same time, I felt sorry for him. Kassar did not know how to accept defeat, so when he lost, he departed with a resentful taste in his heart. I knew that I was making him even more dangerous, for out of his frustration, his wrath might unleash upon the innocent. The time had come to confront Kassar upon the landscape of dreamland, using caution and wisdom of what I had learned about him personally, united with my limited knowledge of shadowtreking.

Chapter 23

Abigail and I returned to class just in time before the bell rang after an eventful lunchtime break. As the afternoon classes began, I tried to focus my attention upon what was being taught and discussed. For most of the day, I succeeded in paying attention even though part of my mind had concerns about Kassar. It was impossible to run away from time, and I knew that the moment was approaching that I would have to confront him in the scope of a dream. Although I had been successful in two dreams, I seemed to lack the faith that I needed. The Mirror was with me in more ways than I could understand at that time, but doubts continued to jump up at me when I was trying to believe. Being hesitant was the evidence of not completely trusting, which could open the door to failure. I had to try, for I did not want to disappoint Barnabus and Scatman, who had spent so much time and energy training me.

I enjoyed my first day of school, and as the day ended, Mr. Schneider was teaching on sincerity. He emphasized the importance of the words we speak and how they should reflect our actions. The mannerisms that we portray on a daily basis reflect the motives of our hearts. Mr. Schneider began to slightly alter the subject and began to talk about having respect for one another. He believed that respect had three main categories: feelings, property, and reputation. I remembered in Ohio how it felt to be ridiculed and be the target of a joke with the intention of being cruel. Hearing Mr. Schneider teach on this subject reminded me about the few times I went to church with my mother. I learned about the Ten Commandments: do not steal, do not kill, honor your mother and father, and all the others. Again, here in the Mirror, I was learning those same foundational rules in a similar but different manner.

The bell rang to end the school day, slightly startling me, for I was quite absorbed by what Mr. Schneider was teaching. Slowly, I left the classroom, put a few things in my locker, and found Abigail as we casually made our way out of the school building.

"How did you like your first day?" asked Abigail as her radiant blue eyes flickered in the light of the day. As I didn't already know it, my eyes focused upon just how delicately beautiful Abigail appeared to be.

"I enjoyed it. This school is much different than the schools I attended back in Ohio. Our teacher seems to be a good man, for I think he cares about our thoughts and feelings. I could feel his compassion this afternoon as he taught us about respect. He wants us to be able to think for ourselves, and to be considerate of everyone who lives here."

"I'm glad to see that you understand what our school is trying to teach. This is not a school to learn how to add and subtract, to learn and read history, even though we do learn those things. We learn how to live and what it is in this life that will bring us happiness."

When Abigail and I returned to the castle, I looked up at the massive structure and how it seemed that those old brick walls were looking down at me. I was still having difficulty accepting the fact that I lived in such a grand building and becoming comfortable calling it home. Abigail and I agreed to take a walk later, and we went to our separate rooms to relax until dinnertime.

I sat alone in my room, looking up at the walls for a few minutes, until I decided to go downstairs to the library to find something to read. As I walked among the many aisles of books stacked neatly upon old wooden bookshelves that were desperately in need of dusting, I became aware that I was in the fiction section, just where I wanted to be. Deliberately taking my time, I found a book that interested me, a collection of fantasy short stories that told tales of extraordinary and marvelous places where strange humanoids lived. I sat down on the floor; crossed my legs; and with the book that sat lazily on my lap, I got lost in the mist of the bizarre narrative.

With my mind captured and suspended in the cloud of time, I began to think about what my life had become, like one of these strange stories that I was now reading. I was perplexed to realize that I was living a life full of adventure with many unexplained phenomena similar to the many images I used to dream of. In the brief amount of time since I had come to live in the Mirror, happiness became my new friend. When my thoughts began to lose their focus, I instinctively felt someone's presence near me before they placed their hand on my shoulder. I looked up, and there stood Barnabus and Scatman.

"We thought we might find you here. So how was your first day of school?" asked Scatman with his ever-present smile on his face.

"I hate to admit it, but I liked it, for it was different than any school I had ever attended. I also beat Kassar in a basketball game. I figured out how he was able to win the basketball tournament yesterday so easily. He cheated without anyone knowing it, using a mind control technique to win. I used the same method, without any hint of his suspicions, and I beat him very easily. The image of him walking away frustrated and defeated lingers in my mind, as I felt his sorrow."

"That's the good nature in you that makes you feel other people's hardships. Don't let your heart become weak when you face Kassar. He will be able to see it and try to alter any circumstance that he can. Remember Charles, Kassar can't be trusted no matter what face he reveals. You have done well and been obedient to what we have taught you," said Scatman.

"Did you dream with Abigail last night?" asked Barnabus.

"I shadowed her dream, as you suggested," I told them as I got up off the library floor.

"What happened?" questioned Barnabus as his curiosity occupied his mind.

"When I entered her dream, we started to run through some woods, and I wished we were birds of the air. Before I could realize what was happening, we had changed into birds and were flying as they do. At one point, we were flying as one, with the physical presence of each other alive in our hearts."

I looked at Barnabus, who immediately turned to look at Scatman. They both smiled, as they knew what the one bird symbolically meant.

"The power of love," said Barnabus with his explanation.

"A strange occurrence happened when I came out of her dream," I said. "I didn't notice it at first, but somehow, I brought something back," I told them as I reached into the back pocket of my trousers and pulled out two feathers. "These two feathers were among others that lay next to me on the couch as I came out of Abigail's dream."

Barnabus took the two feathers from my hand and studied them with a curiosity short of amazement. He looked back at me with a puzzled expression on his face, and he passed the feathers to Scatman.

"I don't believe this has ever happened before. The Mirror probably wanted you to have these feathers as a physical reminder of the dream. In symbolic terms, the Mirror could be telling you that Abigail is your chosen partner in life," said Barnabus.

"I want to ask both of you about something else that happened last night," I said with a puzzled expression of nervous fear that appeared upon my face.

"What is it?" asked Scatman, concerned from my frightened expression.

I led Barnabus and Scatman to a small wooden table near the front of the library and sat down. Hesitation kept me quiet and still for a few moments as I began to reminisce about the dream that woke me early from my desired sleep. I was searching for the correct words to explain my mysterious plight from the night before and the suspicions I had that Kassar might have been lingering within my dream to put fear in me.

"How can you tell if someone has been shadowing your own dream?" I asked, desiring to know the truth in a way that I could understand.

"Usually, you can tell through your heart's convictions. If you suspect in your heart, nine out of ten times, you're probably correct," Barnabus stated flatly.

"I believe Kassar was in my dream last night," I said.

"Tell us your dream, Charles," Scatman insisted with authority.

"It was similar to Abigail's dream in the fact that once again, I was a bird. I realize that I might have dreamt about flying because of the shadowtrek I had just experienced with Abigail but also the freedom I feel from my previous life that I left back in Ohio."

"I believe a dream of flying usually symbolically represents some type of freedom, physical, emotional, or spiritual. Or, as the old saying states, 'Free as a bird,'" Scatman said, interjecting his wisdom.

"As I flew high into the sky, I could see the beautiful mountains that covered the land for miles. I saw something out of the ordinary or slightly peculiar among the trees that sparked my interest. When I allowed myself to be engulfed by the trees, I flew through a large tunnel made of natural design by pine trees. It was quite dark in that corridor of the woodlands, but I was not blind, for birds use their natural sensory instincts to see in the dark. In the distance, I saw a small, flickering light waving in the gentle breeze. I became extremely nervous, which made me cautious and apprehensive, and I slowed down the speed of my flight. When I was almost on top of the flickering light, I realized that I had been tricked. Out of the shadows emerged Kassar; his hands had become torches of fire that I had seen in the distance. He held up his hands of fire and shouted with rage that consumed his anger that was written upon his face, 'Burn, Charles! Burn!' A short moment later, my eyes opened, and I was awake."

"Kassar is trying to get to your mind. He is after you. He blames you for what you have been taking from him and is envious of what you have become. Divine wisdom has been steadily growing from inside of you. Reverent compassion for others coupled with a sincere love has filled your spirit, and even though you can't notice the change, Charles, everyone else has. Tonight, I want you to link with Kassar inside the dreamscape. Seek and find his consciousness, but be aware that he might be shadowing another person's dream. If that is what you encounter, try to change the dream in which he has control. You have been victorious in the games you have played with him. You can win inside the dream also. The Mirror knows that you can do this, and so do Barnabus and I, but you must convince yourself and confess the victory that is already yours. This is the beginning of your destiny. It is the reason you were brought here," explained Scatman, trying to build up my faith.

I put the book that I was reading back in its proper place, and I walked out of the library with Barnabus and Scatman. We walked over to the cafeteria, for it was time for the evening meal. A castle favorite was being served: smothered steak. When I sat down, I quietly looked down at the food on my tray, watching the steam rise up into the air from the hot food.

Mankind has made the art of cooking into a passion, not like the wild animals of the woods that eat to survive. Eating is essential to all living organisms, but man is alone in creating various cravings for an assortment of different tastes. When I had almost finished my meal, I began to discuss Kassar and how I should approach the shadowtrek with him with Barnabus and Scatman.

I learned from the two masters of the dream that it is your mind that gives the shadowtreker the advantage. A thought by a conscious entity could alter a dream significantly. Barnabus and Scatman were veterans of the dream world, so anything that they had to say on the subject, I listened to with much interest. Understanding how to influence and dominate the life of the dream was what I pursued to find the answer to, and although I did not receive specific insight, I did gain knowledge for what I needed.

I promised Barnabus and Scatman that I would be cautious as I got up from my seat. I assured them that I would only shadow Kassar either in his dream or one that he was attempting to control. Without even considering what was to come, I assured my two dream coaches that my plan was one of just observation. With those words, I picked up my tray, wished them a good evening, and walked away.

I made my way from the cafeteria into the hallway, which led me to the foyer. My walk was quicker than usual, for my mind was anxious of meeting Abigail. The beautiful landscaped grounds around the castle appealed to my senses before me, and as I looked beyond to the forest, I became aware of the drastic change of events that brought me to the place in the Mirror in which I stood.

When my mind was summoned back to reality, I noticed Abigail sitting on the brim of the fountain, looking up at the sky. She was watching the birds flying back and forth with no apparent direction or intention. I noticed the many birds that were hovering about, and as I approached her, I began to think about the prisons that birds are trapped in, the chains of the skyway.

"Hi, Abigail!" I exclaimed as I walked up behind her.

"Hi, Charles," she said with joy that lit up her face.

"Were you waiting a long time?" I asked.

"No. Just a few minutes."

"I see you have a new fascination with birds," I said, being slightly sarcastic. "Did this curiosity for our feathered friends have anything to do with your dream from last night?"

"I think you know it did," Abigail replied with a tone that was equally filled with sarcasm. "I really felt like we were flying last night, for we had become creatures of the air, completely free, totally at peace."

"I felt the same, Abigail, but as I noticed you watching the birds, a question formed in my mind. Are birds really free?" I asked with a sense of mystery.

"I don't really understand what you are trying to say," she said, puzzled.

"Birds symbolically represent freedom. In actuality, birds are prisoners of the sky. Their ability to fly is the security that they need for their survival. No living thing is totally free, for we are all caged to our own creation."

"You are so right, Charles. However, to us humans who are confined to the ground, birds appear to be peaceful and free, without a care in the world. I am not speaking in truths, but out of my emotions."

"Shall we go?" I asked. "Where would you like to go?"

"The lake," Abigail responded enthusiastically with a smile.

Chapter 24

Hastily leaving the castle grounds, Abigail and I entered a region of the surrounding forest that would lead us to the lake. We walked hand in hand, which seemed so very natural, believing the Mirror brought us together at this certain place in time for a reason. Our relationship had its core in faith, and its significance was never questioned, which brought unity to the companionship that called us.

When we reached the end of the trail, the large lake smiled reflections of radiance at us. It was partially surrounded by trees, and upon the opposite shore were a series of rocky cliffs. As we came out of the woods, we started to run upon the beach, which was not that large, approximately fifty yards long and twenty yards wide. A small pier with several small boats tied up to it partially divided the beach. We sat down upon the wooden pier with our legs hanging over the side. The smooth-flowing waters of the lake appeared to be very gentle in their current, as they rippled with signs of laughter. The light of the day was beginning to fade, and as I noticed dusk approaching, a beautiful portrait was displayed. All who saw it recognized the Mirror's signature by its paintbrush. I desired to go out on the lake in one of the boats, and I knew that we still had time before it got too late.

I looked over at Abigail, and as she looked back at me, our eyes tried to find the intentions in each other's heart. Suddenly, as if it had been staged, we said to one another in unison, "Want to go out on a boat?"

It seemed to be quite extraordinary how our minds were so in tune with one another, with the ability to decipher the passions that lay within our hearts. We quickly rose to our feet and walked off the pier to where the boats were tied up. I quickly observed several of the rowboats and canoes to find out if they were watertight. By my perception, I thought they would be. Abigail spontaneously climbed into one of the boats, and as I untied the line, I quickly got into the boat myself and began to row away from the pier. Without too much effort, we found ourselves upon the calm current of the lake.

"What a day!" exclaimed Abigail. "Charles, are you feeling what I am? I can feel the Mirror so strongly here. What a joy it is to feel its presence in our hearts and everything that surrounds us. I can't truly explain what I feel, but I know that the Mirror is here with us," said Abigail as she excitedly shared what she felt with me.

"I agree," I replied. "I stand in complete astonishment, as I believe in my heart that the Mirror chose me to come into this grand kingdom. Look around us, Abigail, everywhere the eyes can see, you find evidence that the Mirror had its hand upon the creation of this place."

Abigail and I let the boat drift for an undesignated amount of time, as we were content in tranquility upon the waters of the lake. Alone in nature and on the lake, we felt like early mankind during the great awakening. In those early days, there was only one man and one woman. They had a good life until the destroyer came to deceive and manipulate them. The choices that were made during those days mankind has been paying for ever since.

I began to row the boat back to shore, as we began to sense that the light of the day was fading and would soon be replaced by the dark of night. When we reached the pier, I tied the boat up, and we carefully got out and walked out upon the beach. Leaving the lake behind us, we entered the woods on our walk back to the castle. I sensed that Abigail was troubled. At first, I could not discern what it might be until the Mirror revealed to me the answer. She was quite concerned about my secret oath that I had with Barnabus and Scatman, which I had promised to tell her about soon. This agreement had her worried, for Abigail thought that I might be getting myself entangled in something that might be beyond my understanding. Inside the Mirror, there were some primitive symbolisms to be found which led to the essence of life that, I eventually learned, took time and wisdom to appreciate their significant basic elements. She knew that the Mirror would protect me no matter what fearful thoughts might be conceived inside her mind.

When we reached the castle, the darkness loomed over the kingdom. A mystical stillness within the castle walls was present, and we perceived that something was not right. It was more than a slight awareness of the senses, as if an unseen entity was trying to warn the people in the kingdom of something that was forthcoming. Abigail and I walked over to the sitting room, where Barnabus and Scatman were sitting by the fireplace. They both turned around just as Abigail and I entered, almost as if they were anticipating our arrival.

"Come in, Abigail and Charles!" exclaimed Scatman with a joyous disposition. He seemed to be in a jubilant mood, although his spirit seemed to be carrying a burden, but I could not signify its meaning.

Abigail was at my side as we walked into the room to talk to Barnabus and Scatman. My curiosity ran deep when I perceived in my mind a strange and solemn sensation that seemed to be lingering in the castle. I felt nervous and apprehensive, for I knew that something was coming, an event that would change the course of life in the Mirror as people know it. Whatever it was that I felt, it raced through my spirit, and my senses were acutely aware of the puzzling emotion that had become stagnant around the kingdom.

"Where is everyone tonight?" I asked. "The castle seems to be empty. I know that there are a few people downstairs, but it feels unusually quiet, like the calm before a storm."

"Usually on the first day of the week, it is very quiet," replied Scatman, "although I believe that tonight, the Mirror is probably convicting people to pray, for there is a heavy burden alive in the air tonight, a call for all of us to get upon our knees and pray."

"I have felt a disturbance in my spirit as well, Scatman," stated Abigail with a facial expression that revealed fear. "I really don't know what it means, but I have faith that the Mirror is in control of all things."

"The Mirror is definitely working on something," added Scatman.

"Well, Charles," said Abigail when she turned to me and looked into my eyes for a few brief moments, until she gave me a big hug. "I'm off to bed."

Upon her departure, she suggested to me in a loving way not to stay up too late, for we had school the next day. I watched her walk away with deep love in my heart for her, and then I turned my attention to Barnabus and Scatman.

"We both have felt a nervous energy running through the air tonight, just like Abigail mentioned, and I believe that it centers on you, Charles. Tonight, when the castle sleeps, you will have the chance to begin the end of the many hostilities that have captured our community. Try to somehow give Kassar opposition to his evil plans. Charles, you have grown strong with the Mirror. We have taught you to the best of our abilities. I know that you lack experience, but Scatman and I have accepted the belief that you will end Kassar's reign over the kingdom within the dreamscape. Be patient, Charles, and use the Mirror as your guide and seek its wisdom," concluded Barnabus as he looked into my eyes, trying to find my state of mind.

Barnabus knew that what he asked of me was no easy task, but he believed in me, which made me feel good. I had been trying to understand the significance of the circumstances that were shaping my life and what they really meant.

"Restoration is what we seek. I am praying that our way of life to be restored to the days of old. There is an evil wave that has swept like a flood over all of us, manipulating the manner in which we live into the hands of a boy named Kassar," expressed Barnabus with a desperate hope written upon his face.

Scatman approached me and reminded me of something I read in the book *Reflections of Light*.

"Anything can be accomplished in a dream, for within the desires of your heart, joined with your imagination, miraculous events can occur. Do not restrict the Mirror to just guide you. Ask for its divine wisdom, and you will find the solution to the dilemma that has been set before you. Charles as a suggestion go to the Paraclete when you begin your shadowtrek, for it is your comfort and shield. Conceive in your mind the victory that is already yours. Speak it, for with the confessions of the heart comes possessions," said Scatman, as he wished me good luck.

As Barnabus and Scatman walked away, they left the work of the Mirror in my hands. I was nervous about my upcoming task, but I knew that it was something that had to be done. When I shadowed Abigail's dream, I began from in front of the fire, but the shadowtrek that I was confronted with would be drastically more challenging. I sat in front of the fire for quite some time, just meditating upon my thoughts. With a concept of reality tugging upon my mind, I desired some assistance that I knew only the Mirror could provide. I decided to go up to the worship center just as Scatman had suggested. Pulling myself up off the couch, I made my way out of the sitting room and began my walk up to the tower. It was the Paraclete that I needed to be close to, for I realized that it was the one place in the castle where, through faith, I would receive the maximum amount of support and protection from the Mirror. My mind was focused as I climbed the many steps to the chapel.

When I finally reached the worship center, I noticed that the large, circular room was almost completely dark. The only light was coming from the Paraclete. From within the symbol of faith, a blue illumination glowed from its presence and the small area around it. I slowly walked down to stand next to the Paraclete until I placed my hand upon its hard but smooth surface. I spoke boldly about my fears and doubts, but at the same time, I knew that the Mirror could see everything that was possible for me in the future. I stopped talking and stood in silence for a few minutes until at last, a soft-spoken word like a whisper came into my mind.

"Be still, and know that I am with you. Where you walk I walk. Trust in me, and I will never leave you."

I immediately looked up, wondering who was talking to me. Suddenly, I knew without any doubts what I was hearing: the encouraging voice of the Mirror. A strong river of confidence rose up through my spirit when I heard those words. I believed that the will of the Mirror would be done on this night.

"My Mirror," I began with my eyes closed tightly in an earnest gesture of prayer, "Protect me upon my quest tonight. Give me confidence and wisdom to overcome any obstacles that I might encounter. I thank you my Mirror, for your love and for every little thing you have brought into my life. And in your name, I seek the truth."

I lifted my head out of prayer and walked over to the choir loft and sat down. With a quiet I had never experienced, my mind became focused upon the task that called for its completion. Listening to the strange silence that lingered around me, I was granted a few moments to retrieve my thoughts until I began to concentrate upon the assignment that was set before me. Once again, just like I had previously done, my mind created images of the person I desired to shadowtrek. A few short moments passed, and then I began to hear Kassar's voice and feel his presence just as if he was sitting next to me. Minutes later and before I could realize what was beginning to transpire, I was quickly pulled down the dark, misty tunnel of dreams. My mind was fixed upon Kassar, and as I sped down the ominous corridor, I sternly gave my mind direction so that I could find him.

"Kassar! Kassar! Kassar!" I shouted out as I was pulled by an unseen force through the tunnel. The traveling time to the actual dream seemed much longer than usual, without the sound of muffled voices that normally made it hard to concentrate. Finally, I arrived at my destination.

Cold air with a brisk wind was the first thing that I sensed in the dream. I knew that it was cold, but I myself was not. Snow steadily fell from the sky, which reminded me of sled riding at Shelly's Farm Park located near where I once lived in Ohio. Halfway up the snow-covered hill, I noticed two sleds speeding down the hill. I recognized one of the kids as Kassar. I knew it was him, for I identified his eyes and his Oriental ancestry. Only a handful of individuals had that type of heritage in the Mirror. He was wearing a dark robe with a hood similar to the ones that the monks of the medieval church would have worn. When the two sleds came to a stop, Kassar quickly jumped upon the other person, and they started to roll around in the snow, laughing. My heart started to pound when I heard the laughter of the other person. I recognized the voice as belonging to Abigail. My heart began to throb and pound at that moment, for I knew that I was inside of Abigail's dream. Kassar was tricking her, and I knew it.

For a few short moments, they lay on their backs in the snow, holding hands and trying to catch snowflakes with their tongues. I quietly watched them when I began to feel a deep pain in my chest that grew with earnest intensity. The love I felt toward Abigail was being betrayed, but I knew she was not consciously aware of her actions, for Kassar had control of her mind.

Looking at Abigail in a caring fashion, Kassar climbed on top of her. My biggest fear since realizing that Kassar was in Abigail's dream began to transpire, as Kassar started to move his face towards hers in a gesture of a kiss. Realizing what was about to transpire, I quickly wished for Abigail to see what Kassar really was. Speed of thought travels faster than the speed of light, and as the thought had been conceived in my mind, Kassar was immediately transformed into a large, black snake. Instantaneously, Abigail was changed into a white owl with a glow of purity and flew away into the snow-filled sky.

I immediately began to laugh, and very loudly, for the expression upon Kassar's face when he went through the change was hysterical. Quickly, I was pulled from the dream as my laughter grew. Kassar was unable at the time to change from his snake form fast enough, and he watched the owl fly away with beauty and grace. In the distance, he could hear laughter; and he knew it was my voice, which made him extremely angry. Kassar realized what I had done, and without noticing his image in the dream change, he was returned to consciousness.

My eyes opened, and when they did, I saw the dark confines of the worship center all around me. In my mind, I knew what had happened, and I was still laughing about it. Fear came to me uninvited, for I became afraid that Kassar had heard my laughter. After I pondered upon the dream for a few minutes, I walked over to the Paraclete and placed my hand upon the hard structure. It felt good, what I had accomplished, although I had a bad feeling about Kassar, for I knew he would seek revenge.

"I thank you, my Mirror," I began to pray, "in guiding me to the right way to alter the dream. Fear had my heart in its grasp when I saw Kassar with Abigail. I love her, and I don't want anything to come between us. Please, my Mirror, show Abigail what Kassar really is, and give me wisdom on how to deal with his anger. He is filled with so much bitterness, jealousy, and selfishness. I only wish there was a way to lead him down a different road. Work out your will, my Mirror, for you know what is best for us all. I thank you for your love. In your name, I seek the truth."

I walked out of the worship center, thankful for the guidance that the Mirror gave me. I thought about the next day while I made my way toward my room, desiring rest. Waiting for me were the consequences from what I had changed in the dream. I was protecting Abigail from Kassar's deception, and I had no feeling of regret because of it. Before school in the morning, I would talk to Barnabus about what took place in Abigail's dream. It was also my belief that

Abigail needed to be informed, for she had become involved. Kassar would probably threaten me in some manner during the day, trying to plant the seeds of fear in me. Barnabus and Scatman would know what to do, for I knew that there was a solution to the problem that seemed to be out of my control. They had much knowledge and wisdom and a greater understanding of the concepts within the Mirror. When I finally arrived at my door, I crept into the room like a thief in the night. I cautiously found my bed in the dark, took off my shoes, and lay down on the bed. I did not want to awaken William, and before I knew it, I fell asleep.

Chapter 25

I slept, but I did not dream, for my body needed rest. I was probably only asleep for a few hours when the light of day awakened me. I felt quite rested, even without much sleep. Eager and anxious I was to face the many challenges that were waiting for me when the cloud of sleep faded from my presence. Willie was already awake and getting ready for school. I got up off my bed, went over to the window, and looked out upon the courtyard below. Thoughts of uncertainty came upon me in relation to where I was. I remembered that Scatman had told me when I first met him that the land of the Mirror was beyond space and time. I knew I was in some kind of unique dimension, but my curiosity was getting the best of me.

When Willie came out of the bathroom, he startled me, for my mind was far away from where I was standing. He immediately felt my troubled spirit as I looked out the window.

"Good morning, Charles," said William in greeting. "What is on your mind this morning? I sense that something is troubling you."

"I feel lost," I said with a certain amount of desperation. "I know I'm at the castle, but I'm not really sure where that is."

"Charles, you remember how you got here and what brought you to this place. There are specific reasons for the many things in life that we cannot explain. It is our faith that has put us here and keeps us here. Don't try to fight the master's hand. You are here for a reason. Try to accept that fact in faith."

"I know what you are trying to tell me, Willie, but when I lived in Ohio, there was a bright star in the sky that we called the sun that gave us light and warmth. There was a moon that I could see at night, with many planets and distant stars. I learned about them in school, and I could see them through a telescope. Here in the Mirror, there is a peculiar glow that shines down from above us that gives us light. This place has the feel of a dream without actually dreaming. Sometimes I am afraid of going to sleep at night, as the fear of waking up back in Ohio torments me."

"I sympathize with you, Charles. I do not know how you feel, and I'm not going to tell you I know. All I can do is pray to the Mirror to help you understand. However, you must learn that there are many mysteries in life that have no explanation. If we try to logically comprehend them all, we open the door to confusion. Charles, your faith must be in the Mirror. Ask your many questions in prayer, for if you ask, you will receive the answers you seek. I realize that you feel uncomfortable about where you are, especially in your mind, but just remember where you have been and try to focus upon where you are going. The first inhabitants of this land were very confused. It was their faith that allowed them to survive. The Mirror saw their heart's intentions, and, in response, created miracles that were humanly impossible. You were promised a better life than the one you left back in Ohio. Charles, you can have that life, and all it takes is a strong commitment to this family of the Mirror."

"Willie, you are so right. Thank you, for I believe I needed to hear something like you just said to give my confidence a lift," I replied, happy to have a friend like William.

"I'm glad I was able to cheer you up," William said with a smile. "Scatman and Barnabus need you and your gifts for a specific task. I was asked to keep watch on your moods so that you would be able to concentrate on what is important."

"Thank you, Willie, for being a friend and pointing me in the right direction. At times, I become troubled because of what I have been going through. Almost every day, something new happens, but I am learning about myself and the ways of the Mirror. I'm afraid that I'm not ready for what Barnabus and Scatman ask of me."

"Charles, I do not know what they have you involved in, but I believe if they have confidence in you, you're ready. Try to be strong and put your faith in the Mirror, for all things work out through his hands."

I briefly gazed into William's eyes and felt the sincerity in his heart and once again thanked him for his wisdom and inspiration. I quickly went into the bathroom and washed up and changed clothes, and when I was ready, we walked down to the cafeteria for some breakfast. I ate just a sweet roll, a banana, and some juice, for I wanted to talk to Barnabus before going to school. Willie noticed that I hardly had anything to eat and was curious to the reason why.

"Why are you eating such a small breakfast? We have plenty of time."

"I need to talk to Barnabus this morning before going to school. It's very important," I said to Willie in a hurry as I got up, grabbed my tray, and started to walk away. I turned around on impulse, looked at William, and yelled back at him that I would see him at school. "I'm sorry, but it's just something that I must do."

William nodded his head in my direction with a mouthful of food and waved good-bye. I left the dining room with my mind focused upon what I wanted to discuss with Barnabus.

I was troubled by my thoughts, for the experience in Abigail's dream with Kassar had me concerned. The clouds of uncertainty had me confined to my own emotional prison, and out of it, arose an attitude of doubt to come alive in my heart. I knew that I could not make a rational decision based upon the emotional analysis of my circumstances. Barnabus was someone I could trust for sound advice and directional navigation. Old and wise he was, with the experience of many years in fellowship with the Mirror. He was the one person I believed could help me the most.

Ideas and images wandered inside of my thoughts as I walked up to the second floor landing and then down the hallway to Barnabus's room. When I approached his door, I looked at it briefly and, with my nerves on edge, gently knocked. A few brief moments of silence passed, which seemed to be an eternity to me, until I heard Barnabus approaching the door. He slowly opened the door, and when he saw my face, he was surprised beyond my expectations. Knowing what was expected from me the night before, his astonished facial appearance quickly changed into concern.

"Hello, Charles. What brings you to my room so early? Shouldn't you be on your way to school?"

"I know I need to be, but I had to talk to you."

"Please come in," said Barnabus with a suggested amount of concern in his voice. He offered me a place to sit on his couch, while he remained standing. "Now tell me what happened last night that is so important that you come to my door early in the morning," said Barnabus.

"I'm sorry for knocking so early, but something happened when I tried to dreamtrack with Kassar," I told him as I tried not to show him my fear.

"What?" inquired Barnabus with a desired curiosity.

"I went looking for Kassar, and when I found him, I knew he was in another dream."

"Whose dream?" asked Barnabus, although in his heart, he already knew what my reply would reveal.

"It was Abigail's," I replied with a deep emotion.

"I understand," acknowledged Barnabus with a sense of compassion that lodged itself within the root of his soul. Barnabus knew the emotions that come from a love relationship. His realization also included the possible complications that could develop from a dream with two conscious entities, each with a different motive, all inside of one dream.

"I know that what we asked of you was extremely dangerous, and I am thankful that nothing serious happened to Abigail. With each mind transmitting energy and all three forces emotionally involved in some way, do you understand why this was a hazardous situation? I know we did it when you first dreamtracked my dream with Scatman, but that was a training dream, for you were learning how dreams work. Your desire in that dream of mine was not to stop or harm me. Scatman was there as well, watching you. In the dream with Abigail and Kassar, there were two different motives in one dream."

"I understand what you are trying to tell me," I said with relief that nothing bad happened, especially to Abigail.

"So tell me, Charles, what happened in Abigail's dream?" asked Barnabus, curious and slightly anxious for me to explain myself.

"I believe that because of last night, Kassar might know what our plans are. It was snowing, and Kassar and Abigail were riding sleds and playing in the snow. When Kassar began to move his face toward hers, with the intention of kissing her, I quickly wished that Abigail would see what Kassar really was. When the idea was planted in my mind, Kassar was instantly changed into a snake, and Abigail was transformed into a white owl and flew away. Barnabus, you should have seen the expression on Kassar's face the moment he began to change. It was quite funny. He was not expecting the transformation to come upon him. I could not help myself, and I started to laugh quite loudly just as I was pulled from the dream. Do you think it was possible that Kassar might have seen me and heard my laughter before I was pulled from the dream?" I asked with curiosity.

Silence entered the room for a brief moment as Barnabus thought about how Kassar might react. He knew of his compulsive and impatient personality traits that have led him in the past to make foolish decisions.

"Kassar probably knows that we are after him, and we most definitely are. His knowledge of the dreamscape is extensive, and he is a master at planting sour apples into people's minds. He must be stopped, but until he is, you must be careful, Charles, for he will most definitely come after you."

"What shall we do, Barnabus?" I asked, seeking guidance from my wise friend.

Barnabus pondered the problem for a brief minute, as he knew I was young and lacked experience. I did not know the best way to handle the circumstance that I faced.

"If you do not hear from Scatman or I during school hours, take Abigail to Scatman's farmhouse, and we will be waiting for you. Abigail must be told what is happening, for she is now involved. I have felt a strong presence of the Mirror around her, and I believe that her faith will grow strong even though, at this time, it is undeveloped. This will be a team effort, Charles, for the future of our community as well as the mental stability of the people who live here is in danger. Remember, Charles, that praise and thanksgiving directed upon your love for the Mirror can change certain events in our lives. Use caution at school, and try to stay away from Kassar. Don't let his threats scare you, for it is only a game to create fear. But it is he who is afraid. Don't forget that you have outwitted him in everything, even in dreams. Kassar hates to lose, and even though this is not a game of basketball or chess, the Mirror can give you wisdom to confuse him. He fears losing his power of manipulation, and he will fight desperately to hold on to it. I know you must go to school now, but keep your mind focused upon what Scatman and I have taught you, for no weapon formed against you will succeed."

"I understand, Barnabus, and I will try to be careful. So if I do not hear from you or Scatman by the end of the school day, Abigail and I should walk to Scatman's farmhouse," I said as I looked into Barnabus's eyes with a desperate need for some reassurance. Even though I had a considerable amount of apprehension, it made me feel good that I would not be alone. Expediently, I left Barnabus's apartment after I said good-bye and quickly made my way out of the castle and ran all the way to school.

I arrived at school on time, for I even had time to go to my locker and the bathroom before I went to class. Just when I was about to sit down in my seat, the bell rang. I looked over at Abigail, who sat two rows across from me, and I saw her smile at me. She quickly wrote down a note on a small piece of paper, folded it, and then told the boy who was sitting next to her to pass the note to me. The slightly overweight boy with curly brown hair passed the note just as Abigail requested. After he had handed me the note, he looked back at Abigail in a peculiar fashion, as he sensed the extent and circumstance of our relationship.

> I need to talk to you, very important.
> Love, Abigail

The night before, when I came out of the dreamscape, I knew that Abigail would have to be told everything. That morning, Barnabus confirmed what I had thought the night before. Abigail had become an important figure in the battle which had become a team effort. It was my desire to tell her sooner, but I was protecting her as Barnabus and Scatman had advised me to. I looked at the note, and I knew what she wanted. After a few moments, I wrote her a note of my own.

> I promise you will know everything. Talk at lunch.
> Love, Charles

I folded the note quickly and passed it over to her. Abigail read the note with much interest, and when she was finished reading, winked at me, which was acknowledgement that she approved. Mr. Schneider took a few minutes to get his class plans organized. He began the morning by teaching us about specific types of animals. I was extremely interested about the various species that lived within the kingdom of the Mirror. He picked me out of the class to tell everyone about the many types of animals that I had seen on Earth compared to the ones that lived within the Mirror. It felt good to be participating in class, for I seemed to have developed a desire for knowledge. Most of my life, I had longed to be accepted, and now it felt that I was beginning to. Contentment began to settle into my life, for even though I might still have been confused about certain issues in my life, I tried to keep my mind focused. It was a bit funny, but for the first time in my life, I really wanted to learn. The morning classes passed quickly, and before I knew it, the moment was upon me to tell Abigail about the night before.

After the lunchtime bell rang, Abigail and I went and stood in the lunch line and waited for our food. Compared to the school cafeterias in Ohio, the food at this school looked quite appetizing. When we got our food, Abigail found a remote table to eat at to discuss what was heavy upon her heart.

"Charles, please tell me what's going on. I know something is, for I had a very disturbing dream last night in which Kassar was the central figure. Do you know if Kassar was in my dream?" she asked with a demanding expression on her face, desperate for the truth.

"Yes, he was," I replied in a slightly timid voice.

"Were you, Charles?"

"Yes, I was, but I promise that it wasn't supposed to happen," I said, trying to explain.

"Charles, I love you, and I believe that you love me to, but please be honest with me."

My eyes focused upon her face, where I could almost feel the innermost region of her soul. I knew that she needed to know what was happening between Kassar and me, for she was now involved. I was the wrong person to explain those extraordinary circumstances to her in a way that she could understand.

"I had an assignment given to me by Barnabus and Scatman last night to find Kassar and confront him in a dream. I finally found him, but when I did, I realized that I was in your dream. When I saw that he was trying to kiss you, my heart started to pound hard. Quickly, I wished upon the Mirror that you would see what Kassar really was. When the idea entered my mind, Kassar was immediately changed into a snake. We were both in your dream, but it was not intended to be so."

"Charles, I know what happened in my dream, and I do appreciate your love and concern for me, but what I want to know is what is going on. You guys can't be playing around in my dreams unless it has a purpose that the Mirror has authorized."

"I know, Abigail, and I am sorry, but you don't realize what is at stake here. I talked to Barnabus this morning about what happened last night, and he told me that you should know everything. He wants me to bring you to Scatman's house after school. You will be told everything and learn what I have gotten myself involved in over the last few days. I can only tell you what I know, but Barnabus can teach you in a way that I cannot, for I have just learned all of this myself."

"Learned what?" Abigail asked with curiosity.

"Abigail, please be patient and wait until we get to Scatman's house for those answers. I am not the right person to explain everything to you."

"Okay, Charles," she said with a smile. "I understand, and I will wait. I trust you, Barnabus, and Scatman to explain this mystery to me that you guys got me involved in."

Abigail looked at me across the table with love in her eyes but also with concern. She knew that I did not quite understand what I had gotten myself into and I was just starting to comprehend the ways of the Mirror. She was quite thankful, however, that she was an important part of my life. In the week since we had met, I had grown spiritually mature with a genuine loving faith. Just as we were about to finish our lunch, Kassar pulled up a chair to our little table and sat down. A sudden nervousness came upon Abigail and me, as we both realized that we were in the presence of something that had become absolutely wicked. A dire presence sat at our table which felt so heavy that it sent chills up and down my spine.

"You think you're pretty clever, don't you?" Kassar questioned me with a tone that sounded threatening.

I quickly looked away so that he could not capture my thoughts with his mind control tactics. I believed that Kassar was the one who was fearful and he was trying to hide it. He had a reason to be afraid, for his time was short, and somewhere inside of me, I knew that he knew.

"Kassar, you are the problem here, for you are a threat to all of the people who live here and cherish their simple little lives. You know nothing about love, joy, and peace, along with the trials and struggles that produces faith," I said, trying to use a philosophical approach to my enemy.

It was a game that Kassar knew, and the more I spoke, my words seemed to frustrate him.

"Charlie," Kassar began to say, "you might have outsmarted me in those games we played, but you do not realize what you're getting yourself into."

"Oh, I understand," I quickly responded, "for you can try to intimidate me, but I can read your face, and what I see is that you are the one who is really afraid, not me."

"I'm not afraid of you," Kassar said, boasting with pride; but as he spoke those words, I sensed that the manner of his tone and inclination did not match what I saw upon his face.

"Maybe you should be," I said calmly, trying to control my emotions.

"What lies in your dreams can kill you, Charles. Just ask Scatman. One can never tell what will happen in a dream. It's possible to die in your sleep, or your brain could be fried like an egg on a skillet. Barnabus and Scatman can't always be around to protect you. I must admit, that they have taught you well, but what you lack is experience. If I were you, I would think twice about sleeping and entering a dream, for what you don't know can kill."

Kassar had issued a threat with those words. He got up from his chair and gave me a long, penetrating stare that sunk into the root of my consciousness. I did not falter under the weight of his intimidation for

I was mentally prepared. Kassar walked away from the table, knowing that the stage had been set for a battle within the domain of dreams.

I turned my attention to Abigail and looked upon her face, thankful that I had her support. I knew she was confused about everything, with many questions in her mind. Kassar's threat had also involved her indirectly. I tried to comfort her by caressing her hand, for I sensed her nervousness.

"I had the feeling that he was going to do that, but I was ready for him. I think I handled his attack pretty good, for I didn't let my emotions get away from me. I can tell that he is afraid. Did you see his face? It had fear written all over it."

"Charles, I believe Barnabus and Scatman know what they are doing, but I need to know for my own peace of mind," Abigail said, pleading with me.

"I know, Abigail, and you will learn these things after school, when we get to Scatman's house. I promise. Barnabus and Scatman can explain things to you in a way that you can understand much better than what I could," I emphasized, trying to calm her fear and doubt.

When the lunch break came to an end, Abigail and I got up, took our lunch trays to the dishwashing window, and went back to class. The afternoon seemed to be quite long, for my spirit was filled with much anxiety. It wasn't that Mr. Schneider's class was boring or what he was teaching was tedious; I just wanted to get far away from Kassar. As the classes were finally dismissed for the day, I was faced with a situation that made me feel uneasy. I did not hear from Barnabus or Scatman, so I knew what my instructions were.

Chapter 26

Abigail and I quickly left the school and headed for the woodlands, walking in the direction of Scatman's house. Peace and tranquility surrounded us, for only in the Mirror had mankind found that dominant presence of peace that comes from an everlasting love. It is the law of nature and the law given to man centuries ago to love one another.

I could have walked to Scatman's house blindfolded. In my mind, I had done it several times when I had felt alone and afraid at the big castle. Scatman was a special friend, and in my heart, there was no one like him. His journey to become one with the Mirror had similarities to the path that I had just walked upon. I sensed pain in his heart that lingered from years past, which I knew made him sympathetic to what I was feeling.

Abigail and I made our way through the woods to the large fields of vegetation. I knew when I saw those fields with the large assortment of fruits and vegetables that grew in abundance that we were near Scatman's house. We walked alongside the tall Noldomi plants that rose many feet over our heads. Finally, after walking several miles, Scatman's house came into view. I saw the smoke coming out of his chimney, and I immediately knew that he had a fire burning with a pot of stew simmering, filling the house with a mouthwatering aroma.

"There's his house!" I yelled with eager anticipation.

I quickly recalled those pleasant memories of the day that I spent with Scatman. I was a baby in the Mirror at that time, being taught the way, the truth, and the life. Looking back, I realized just how much I had grown in such a short time. It was a miracle that only the Mirror could produce.

I took Abigail by the hand as we walked up on Scatman's creaky front porch. Just when I was about to knock on the door, it opened, with Scatman standing there with his ever-present smile on his face.

"I was expecting the two of you. Charles, I am glad that you remembered the way to my house. Do you also remember the deer stew you enjoyed so much on your first day?" asked Scatman.

"I sure do. It was delicious. I also remember how hungry I was," I replied with memorable thoughts of the tasty stew, which started to make me hungry.

"I made another pot of it today as a special treat for the two of you. I hope that Abigail will enjoy the stew as much as you did," said Scatman, looking upon Abigail's youthful face.

"I'm sure I will, Scatman," she told him. "I like stew very much."

"Splendid," replied Scatman. "Come in and rest from your long walk."

Scatman led Abigail and I into his house, and we followed him to the sitting room and sat down on a couch across from the fireplace. Scatman excused himself, returning to the kitchen to finish the final preparations for dinner. A knock on the door interrupted our thoughts, and as Scatman answered the door, I soon realized that Barnabus had arrived.

"Are they here yet?" I heard Barnabus ask.

"Yes. They just arrived. You will find them sitting by the fireplace."

Barnabus slowly and curiously walked into the sitting room, and as he looked upon our faces, he hesitated, trying to read our disposition. He sat down in Scatman's favorite chair, feeling the nervous tension that surrounded us, but he also felt hope, which made him feel good.

"I'm glad that both of you are here. It gives me the opportunity to explain to Abigail what has been happening and what Kassar has become. Did you have any problems with him today at school?"

"Not really," I said. "He did threaten me and warned me about entering a dream tonight."

"I told you that he might do something like that. Abigail, I know that you are probably wondering what this is all about," said Barnabus with sympathy.

"Yes, I am," replied Abigail, curious about what I had gotten involved in.

She cared for me very much, enough to realize that there were many mysteries that lie within the Mirror's deity, knowing that I lacked the understanding of its many symbolic definitions. After we had arrived at Scatman's house, she began to feel better, realizing that we had found some help.

"Kassar is not one of us," Barnabus began to tell Abigail, and he started to tell the story of Kassar and why he had to be stopped. "He was not born from human flesh. He was created from the Mirror, but not the bright, shining source of light and inspiration that we have come to know. Kassar is a strange product of man's impurities that the Mirror finds offensive. He was never washed clean by the Mirror when he came to us, due to an oversight on my part."

"Why?" Abigail curiously inquired.

Barnabus explained in detail to Abigail about how Kassar came to be. He tried to paint mental images in her mind about the bright light and how Kassar had walked out from that illumination.

"Our hearts were filled with so much joy that the Mirror sent us a child, or so we had thought. During those days, we did not think that Kassar needed to be cleansed since he was born of the Mirror. I blame myself quite often, looking back at that time, for I was blind. However foolish it was, I now believe that it was the permissible will of the Mirror that allowed this to happen. Nothing can come into our lives without the authorization of the Mirror. I know this to be true, and when I look at the events that have unfolded, I can see those loving hands that allowed all these things. It's a test upon our faith, for we must need the Mirror in our lives each and every day.

"Kassar has been filled over the years with so much anger, selfishness, and evil tendencies that I believe it is probably almost too late for him. It would take a special act of intervention to save him now. Kassar possesses many lusts and desires that are in contradiction to the laws of the Mirror. He is a wildfire raging out of control in the forest, and we must fight to put out that fire. It was also a good thing that Charles was inside your dream to protect you last night. If Kassar had been successful in manipulating you, he could have gained an important ally. It was so important that Charles stopped him," concluded Barnabus.

"I am also very happy that he was there, Barnabus," said Abigail, looking into my eyes with tender affection. "Although, I must admit that when I awoke this morning, I was confused and slightly upset. I thought Charles and Kassar were fighting amongst themselves and using my dream as their battlefield. At that time, I had just woken up, and I was still under the influence of sleep and not thinking clearly. I am no longer angry, for I now know what Kassar has become and that Charles was just acting as my protector."

"Abigail, try to understand that you are not here by chance but by design. Charles is also here for a purpose. He followed us here, where he discovered a new birth, with a passion and a vision to seek the truth. Destiny has brought the two of you together, and I believe the Mirror had its designs on both of you. I am old, and the journey to bring Charles here inside the Mirror has exhausted me and left my days numbered. I know that my time is close at hand, for the Mirror has revealed it to me in several dreams. My purpose here in my last days is to be a teacher of the faith and, as my name means, to be an encouragement to others. I will not get involved in this situation any longer. Scatman is your teacher and guardian. He will watch over you on this very important task. Seek his knowledge, listen to his words, and apply what you have learned."

Scatman entered the room after Barnabus had finished talking, and he curiously looked at everyone until he announced that if everyone was hungry, dinner was being served.

The meal was cooked to perfection. In the land of the Mirror, there is no other dish that has the vast appeal that deer stew has. In certain regions from my past, there were distinctive dishes that defined the heart of the community. Deer stew is the signature dish inside the Mirror. Just as we did last time, we ate the stew with some freshly baked honey biscuits.

When everyone had finished eating, Barnabus rose to his feet and looked at all of us with tender and loving eyes. He felt a tugging upon his heart to return to the castle. Barnabus knew that he had to follow its direction, which would give Abigail, Scatman, and I time to prepare ourselves for the battle that was waiting for us in the tunnel of dreams.

"I'm returning to the castle. What I was called to do here is finished. I feel an urgent desire upon my spirit to return there. I know I must find Kassar. It's also getting dark, and I don't like walking in these woods after dark. It is my plan to retire early tonight, for I am quite tired," explained Barnabus in a slightly depressed tone that had suddenly came upon him.

"Good luck to all of you," Barnabus said, knowing the burden he had placed in our hands.

"Thank you, Barnabus," Abigail and I replied in unison.

"Are you all right?" asked Scatman, concerned for his friend's welfare, as he felt that something was troubling him.

"I'm fine. You do not have to worry about me, for you have enough to occupy your mind," Barnabus told him as he expediently walked out of the house and into the cool, moist air.

Scatman watched Barnabus walk away in the direction of the woods, and a sudden chill came upon him. At first, he thought it was just a nervous apprehension brought about from the anxiety of the events that would transpire on that night. He knew that something was amiss, for his spirit was not at peace, and he felt in his heart that it had to do with Barnabus. At that moment, Scatman released Barnabus's fate into the hands of the Mirror. Barnabus walked to the castle slowly and cautiously, as the darkness was soon to fall down upon the land. He knew what he wanted to do when he returned to the castle: find Kassar. It was not his desire to talk to him; he just wanted to look upon his face.

When Barnabus entered the castle, he immediately tried to locate him. He searched everywhere, from the entertainment area and the library to the tower, but he could not find him anywhere. Frustration started to rise up in him until he stopped when the realization dawned on him like a new day that he must have over-looked him somewhere. Being ever so cautious, Barnabus retraced his steps until he finally found him in the music library. He had not searched there previously but knew that he should have, knowing Kassar's love for music. Barnabus looked upon Kassar with fascina-tion, watching him sit peacefully in a chair with headphones on, listening to music. His stare was casual but almost hypnotizing until Kassar turned his head and their eyes met and became entangled. When Kassar saw Barnabus's face, the hatred he held in his heart for the old man leaped out from his eyes and held Barnabus in its grasp. Kassar had blamed Barnabus more than anyone else for the events that had shaped his way of life. He believed that it was Barnabus and Scatman who were responsible for bringing me to the Mirror, and he was right.

Kassar held Barnabus in the grip of his penetrating stare for a few moments, and Barnabus tried to fight off the stronghold inflicted upon his mind, but he was too old and weak to stop him. Years ago, Barnabus would not have fallen victim to Kassar's manipula-tive schemes. Finally, Kassar released him and Barnabus began to walk away, as if in a daze. Slowly, he went to his room and began to feel normal again, although he realized just how exhausted he felt. Barnabus washed up and then prayed for protection over his three friends who would begin an important quest. He asked the Mirror for guidance, as the battle with the evil forces that controlled Kassar's heart and mind had not yet begun. When Barnabus had finished praying, he climbed in bed and pulled the covers up upon him, and in a few short moments, his eyes grew heavy and he drifted off into a deep sleep and fell into a dream.

Walking upon an endless sea of sand was the first thing that Barnabus noticed. The sky was a perfect blue, not a cloud in sight. At his side, he recognized the familiar stick figure man, remembering him from a previous dream a short time before. The man possessed an almost morbid appearance, as he wore his familiar attire—blue jeans, green-and-yellow plaid shirt, and cowboy hat—with a toy gun in a holster wrapped around his tiny waist. His face had almost no color, except his eyes had a mysterious golden orange glare, and his facial expression seemed to be without emotion.

"I know you know who I am and why I am here. Do not fear, for there is nothing to be afraid of. Your friends will be fine. You have done more than was expected. It's now time to rest," the stick man told him, speaking in comfort.

Barnabus looked around at his surroundings, for the only thing he could see was sand. For miles upon miles, it dominated the landscape, and above him, no birds flying or clouds drifting could be seen. It was a region where there was no life, and the peculiar stillness of the hot afternoon air was filled with a consuming presence of peace. When he casually looked back at the man, a deep, frightening chill ran through his veins. In horror, Barnabus witnessed a bizarre transformation that slowly developed before his eyes. The face of the stick man changed completely, as a dark veil covered it, so Barnabus could no longer distinguish any features. Characteristics of his face slowly began to reappear, and when Barnabus saw who it was, fear gripped his mind and held it captive, for the image before his face was Kassar.

"What are you doing here?" Barnabus demanded to know, growing angry.

"My old enemy and friend, I am here to make certain that you do not interfere with my plans anymore. You brought Charles here to try to stop me. You gave him extra strength with the union he has with Abigail. Your friend Scatman knows too much, thanks to you, and he must be silenced, as will all of them. Barnabus, I am making sure you do not wake up," concluded Kassar with a wicked expression that projected itself from the depths of his tormented soul.

"Kassar," Barnabus began to say in a calm voice, "I was on my way to my final resting place. The stick man, whom you replaced, was my escort. This was my final journey."

"I know who he was and where you were going. But I wanted the pleasure myself of watching you die. You were always against me, and in a way, it is your fault that I became what I am. So, just for my own selfish reasons, I want to end your grip on my path in life," Kassar said with the eyes of vengeance that made his youthful face gleam with delight.

"Your battle will never end, Kassar, for Charles and Scatman will receive my faith and wisdom. You will never be able to defeat all three of them. Their powers will increase when they receive what I give them. Charles will destroy you, for he will become stronger than you could ever imagine," prophesized Barnabus in a warning to Kassar.

"We will see, old man," replied Kassar with bitterness that captivated his soul.

Barnabus read Kassar's heart and mind and knew what his motives were. He prayed in the hidden chambers of his mind for the will of the Mirror to be done. Kassar studied Barnabus's eyes, and even though he tried to conceal what he was praying, Barnabus could not conceal his thoughts from Kassar. When Kassar recognized what he was praying, he grabbed a hold of the toy gun. With the power possessed by his mind, just one thought transformed the harmless toy into a blade of destruction. An evil smile appeared upon his face, and he felt the plastic toy change into a weapon that would ultimately end Barnabus's days. The destructive tool that Kassar had changed the toy into was a blade almost a foot long and nearly an inch thick, and it sparkled when it was held up to the light. In a quick act of wrath, Kassar stabbed Barnabus near his heart. Slowly, he pulled the knife out, enjoying every moment as Barnabus moaned a weak cry, and fell upon the sand, apparently dead.

Barnabus lay on the bed in which he had slept in for many years, alone and lifeless. His eyes became sunken inward toward his skull, with the expression of mortal fear. Focused upon the ceiling, Barnabus had the look of something so dreadful that words could not describe. Kassar killed Barnabus in his dream. When he was lifted out of the dream, Kassar was determined to eliminate Abigail, Scatman and me, hating everything that we believed in and lived for.

Chapter 27

The stage was set, and the battle upon the dreamscape would be acted out inside of my dream. Kassar wished for nothing but my destruction, along with anyone else who might get in his way. He masked his apprehension with anger and resentment that consumed his being, and it alienated him from fear. I welcomed fear, especially of the unknown, for without fear, how could I be aware of the dangers in my environment? I was especially afraid of what was going to happen when I fell asleep. I knew what I was fighting for: the protection and prosperity of everyone who lived upon this land.

Abigail, Scatman, and I spent the evening talking about dreams, and we tried to paint a picture in Abigail's mind of the experiences one feels when walking in a dream. Scatman explained to her the original concept related to shadowtreking, and he told her the story of Barnabus's grandparents on the eve of their wedding.

"The ability to walk in other people's dreams is an unexplained phenomenon that the Mirror has blessed our people with. Kassar took this gift and corrupted it for his own selfish purpose. In dreams, Kassar has manipulated our people and, in a brief period of time, caused many of our people to lose faith," Scatman explained.

"It's truly a beautiful concept," Abigail said. "I remember the dream when Charles came to me, and through the use of dream symbolism, he showed me the love he felt in his heart for me. It was a very special moment, one that I will not soon forget."

"It was for that very purpose that shadowtreking came to be. But now, however, because of Kassar, we must use the gift that the Mirror gave us to save our sanity, our lives, and our kingdom. This has become a very serious situation," Scatman said as he looked down upon the floor.

In his eyes, Abigail and I could see the emotions from his words, and a few tears began to trickle down his cheek.

"I feel so much pain and sorrow for all those people in our community who no longer trust the Mirror. Because of Kassar, there are many people who are just drifting like clouds, and they do not even attend worship services anymore. The Mirror showed us you, Charles, and how you could help us. We had our doubts, but we trusted the Mirror, and once your growth took root, our belief had been confirmed that we had heard the Mirror correctly."

Abigail looked at me with love, proud to be my girl. It made her feel good from within, but at the same time, she was afraid, for she knew that the role I had to play was important and dangerous. Impulsively, she reached for my hand and held it tightly in hers as she looked deeply into my eyes.

"Charles is a unique young man, for he is sensitive but is becoming increasingly strong in his heart's convictions. His moral creativity causes him to be more perceptive than a lot of people I know," Scatman stated with pride that was reminiscent of what a father would brag about his son.

"Sometimes I think Charles and I are soul mates," Abigail told Scatman with a deep sense of conviction.

"Maybe you are. Just maybe," Scatman replied in agreement.

"My friend, Charles, prepare yourself, for tonight, you will need all of your recourses that you possess to defeat Kassar. Abigail and I will be in the dream with you, but we will be unseen. Only by your thoughts and the events that might transpire will you notice our presence. Our ability to transmit words and ideas to your mind might be the deciding factor in defeating Kassar. It is our ace card."

"I didn't know that could be done," I said.

"Yes, you did," Scatman replied quickly and seriously.

"I did?" I questioned, quite puzzled.

"How do you think that you changed Kassar into a snake? It was your presence in Abigail's dream that saved her. In your dream, try to react rationally and try to be aware of the mental images placed in your mind from Abigail or me. It's for this reason that Abigail and I will be there with you. If Kassar changes into a horseman with an axe, trying to cut your head off, we will try to stay one step ahead of him and project an image in your mind, such as a gun to shoot him off the horse. This battle in your dream can be compared to a chess game. If your opponent comes after you with a knight or bishop, use your queen to stop them. Be patient, wait for him to make the first move, and use your imagination to counteract his aggression against you. We are going to be three conscious forces working together with the same goal: to stop Kassar. He allows his emotions to dictate his actions, for usually he does not think logically. I do not believe that Kassar realizes what he is getting himself into. Be patient, Charles, and he will fall," Scatman said, confident of his plan.

"Kassar said something very similar to those very words directed at Charles today," Abigail said, remembering the moment.

She had faith in Scatman's knowledge and wisdom. It was a peace within her that made her believe in Scatman's plan, along with sensing his deep faith. With the realization of this truth, she knew that they would be guided by the power of the Mirror.

"Our plan is set. We know what we must do, but now all we can do is wait. The time is not yet, but it is, however, drawing near. Let us enjoy these moments together with prayer and music, and before we begin our quest, we will have some refreshments. Abigail and I will have some herbal tea while you, Charles, will have a special glass of wine to enhance dreams. It will make you drowsy and cause you to sleep."

Scatman got up from the chair and left the room for a brief moment, and when he returned, he carried his banjo with him. The musical instrument had been like a dear friend to him, for it had helped him get through some rough times. When Scatman's wife died, it was music that sang comforting words to him. He sat down in his rocking chair, and we began to sing worship songs. He loved to play the banjo, for through music, his spirit was filled with joy and it brought him to a place of contentment. Watching Abigail and I reminded Scatman of his wife and, by indirect measures, how Kassar had killed her. Scatman knew that there was an element of danger in what we were about to embark upon, but life is about taking risks, and he believed that our faith would lead us to do the will of the Mirror.

"By the way," Scatman spoke up cheerfully, "you don't have to worry about school tomorrow. Barnabus made arrangements for both of you to be excused from classes. He knew that it was going to be a late night for both of you."

"That's a bit of good news," I said.

"Yes, it is," Abigail agreed.

"My young companions, in a time that is so very important for everyone who lives here, the events that will evolve around Charles's dream could alter our lives forever. Let us join our hands and minds together in prayer and petition our requests to the Mirror."

We formed a circle in front of the fireplace, and we bowed our heads in prayer. Scatman prayed first, and he gave thanks and asked forgiveness for his wrong thoughts, desires, and motives. He asked the Mirror for protection, guidance, and faith to accomplish the task that had been set before us. As Scatman concluded, Abigail spoke up, praying for wisdom and courage so that she could be a helping hand to me when I faced Kassar in dreams. When it was my turn to pray, I hesitated at first, until I asked the Mirror to forgive my doubts, as my inexperience led me to question what my eyes had seen. I also petitioned for Kassar to be forgiven, and I pleaded that he did not realize what the consequences of his actions might become.

"Most of all, my Mirror, I do not want to fail you, my friends, or the people who live here in Mimetus. Do not let me be a disappointment, and I thank you for your love. In your name, I seek the truth."

When we finished our prayer, we faced each other in a short moment of silence, feeling a joy that slowly came down upon us. A presence filled our spirits, which was confirmation that the absolute will of the Mirror would be done on that night. We felt that we were not alone, and an unseen presence was comforting and encouraging us, which gave us hope and confidence.

"Let's get our snacks and drinks," Scatman said, and he got up, knowing that the appointed time was drawing near.

"Sounds like a good idea," I replied, with Abigail in silent agreement.

We got up and followed Scatman into the kitchen, where he had a tray of cookies and sweet bread. He had arranged the snacks on an old, wooden serving tray lined with a fancy decorated paper doily and then carried them into the dining room and set them on the table.

Scatman went back into the kitchen, put a small pot of water on the stove for the tea, and then reached in the small cooler for the wine. Abigail and I sat at the table quietly while Scatman prepared the drinks. We looked into each other's eyes, searching for answers to the many questions arising from the emotions that were buried deep within our hearts.

"Are you scared?" Abigail asked, knowing that I had to be.

"Yes. Very much so," I told her with complete honesty.

"The Mirror will not leave you, and Scatman and I will be there to help. We won't let anything happen to you. I promise. Charles, I believe that there are many guardians in the spirit watching over us, and I know that we will be protected against any harm."

"I know, Abigail," I said as I took her hand in mine, which comforted me.

In her eyes, I saw her love for me, and without being aware of it, I seemed to be transmitting the same exact message. Love has many forms of communication. Some are visible, such as a special look in the eyes, while others can be audible or felt physically, such as a touch of a hand. It is a language that is beneficial for all to learn, as I did when I met Abigail.

"Here we go," said Scatman, and he set down the tray on the table next to the snacks. "Let us drink to the victory that we will accomplish tonight: the successful end to our long and agonizing problem. Let the spirits rejoice with what we will achieve," Scatman proclaimed in a salute to the heavens.

Abigail and I followed Scatman's gesture, and we toasted to our success. Everything had been said, we were prepared, and our faith in the Mirror was secure. We did not discuss the events that were forthcoming while we had comforting fellowship together.

In less than ten minutes, I began to feel the effects of the wine, and I began to grow drowsy and realized that the time to dream, walk, and fight was closing in on me. I began to tremble, as the unknown triggered fears of what I was soon to walk into.

"The time is close, Scatman. I'm starting to become extremely weary. That wine has quite a kick to it."

"Yes, it does," Scatman replied as a weak smile came to his face. "When you are ready, go upstairs to the room that you slept in on that first night. Good luck, and try to remember everything that you have learned. Abigail and I will help you where we can, but it will be your faith that activates the power of the Mirror."

When Scatman went into the kitchen to clean up, Abigail and I got up and faced one another. I stared deep into her eyes with tears slowly rolling down my cheek, for I was trying to memorize her face. I was trembling, as the evidence of doubt made me afraid that I might never see her again if our plans were unsuccessful.

"I love you," I said with heartfelt emotion.

"I love you too," Abigail passionately responded, as she felt my love for her.

We held each other in a tight embrace until I yawned and reluctantly let go of her embrace. I kissed her on the lips in a short and tender moment until I turned away from her and slowly started to climb the stairs up to the bedroom. I impulsively glanced back at her to look upon her face one more time, just in case. When I reached the top of the stairs, I walked into the bedroom, and kicked off my shoes, and I slowly lay down on the small but comfortable bed. Before I could realize what was happening to me, I began to drift away from reality.

Chapter 28

When I walked upstairs to sleep and dream, Abigail and Scatman went into the living room and sat in front of the fireplace.

"Will Charles be okay?" asked Abigail with loving concern for me.

"We won't let him get hurt, will we?" Scatman replied, sympathetic of Abigail's worried heart.

He knew they had some time to spend before they would need to enter my dream, and Scatman reached for his banjo once again. Music is a tool that can relax the nerves, and Scatman knew that it was a perfect time for some soft picking of the banjo.

After a few brief moments, Abigail seemed to become relaxed, until she responded in faith, "Charles will return safely and unharmed."

When the appointed time finally arrived, Scatman refrained from playing his music and sat down next to Abigail. He took her by the hand and looked deeply into her eyes in preparation for the journey into the tunnel of dreams.

"Abigail, I am going to explain to you, as I did to Charles, how to mentally prepare yourself to enter a person's dream," Scatman began to explain to her like a dear friend and teacher. "It starts with the act of your will joined together with someone else, sharing this gift that the Mirror has given to his children. Now, Abigail, you must concentrate from the deepest part of your heart and mind so that you can project your spirit into Charles's dream. Focus your mind upon his image, how he looks and talks, along with those peculiar mannerisms that everyone has, so that you can almost touch him. Hear his voice and feel his touch so that your soul can join with his, giving him a helping hand in this fight."

"I can almost see and hear him as if he was sitting next to me," replied Abigail after a few short minutes with an enthusiastic astonishment.

Scatman reached over once again and took hold of her hand, and together, in unison, they were lifted outward with the same distinct purpose.

Alone in one of the quiet corners of the castle, Kassar sat in an unconscious state of mind, searching for my presence in a dream. Anger and bitterness dominated his spirit for what had been allowed to come into his life. Kassar could hear my voice and sense my presence, and he raced toward the confrontation that he had waited patiently for. He possessed a deep concentration upon the destruction of the one who had been trained to stop him, and on that occasion, it happened to be me.

When Kassar entered my dream and became a conscious life force in its domain, it did not take long for him to find me. Immediately, he noticed that I was walking through some undesignated woodlands, as if I was looking for something or someone. Kassar planted a thought into the life of the dream and, with the speed of thought, changed into a giant mosquito. The insect was humongous, a freak of nature. From a distance, the mosquito appeared to be the size of a bat, and it flew around the trees until it focused its sight upon me. When I saw the strange flying, repulsive being coming toward me, fear confronted me. Scatman quickly noticed the weird phenomenon flying in my direction and promptly projected with his mind a baseball bat into my right hand.

"With the bat you now hold in your hand, strike down that thing of evil that intends to do you harm," ordered Scatman's voice with authority, giving the impression from the vocal command as if it had originated from another place or dimension.

I looked down at the wooden bat and felt its hard matter in my hand, and I quickly held it up as if I was a batter in a baseball game. The giant mosquito continued to fly toward me, and when it got close enough, I could see its eyes, and I knew they belonged to Kassar. At the appropriate instant, I swung the bat with all my strength, and it smashed the wicked deformity of nature directly on its head. Upon direct contact, the insect thing quickly flew through the air from the end of my bat approximately forty yards, until it landed against the trunk of a large tree, apparently hurt and disoriented.

The grotesque creature sat motionless for a brief moment until it slowly transformed back into its human form. Kassar had to adjust his vision, for the hard impact on the head had dazed his senses quite significantly, even in a dream. Finally, he got up off the ground and walked over to me, facing his enemy. Kassar's desired wish—a showdown in a dream—had finally become a reality. He had wanted to meet me in this arena ever since I had defeated him in chess the first time.

"Finally, we have the chance to meet in here. I have been patiently waiting for this opportunity, and now it is here. A short time ago, I rid myself of your dear old friend, Barnabus. And when I'm done with you, I plan to destroy Abigail and Scatman. By daybreak, I will be in control of the kingdom, with no one to stop me. I will proclaim myself as king, and I will rule with an iron fist," Kassar proclaimed, boasting proudly of his evil plan. "No one would dare to oppose me because of the staggering presence of fear I would plant into their hearts and minds, which would be enough to control any rebellious ambitions that they might fathom to begin."

"Kassar," I said with the voice of authority, "I hate to spoil your wicked plans, but you will not leave here alive."

"Charles, you and your precious little friends are so blind. They have no real choices, for the Mirror dictates their actions," said

Kassar with disgust in his voice, attempting to explain his beliefs to justify his motives.

"As I see it, Charles, these people can't really feel what life is, for there are no temptations of greed and anger or the many other things that can lead a person astray. Tell me, Charles, how can you really feel alive if you are never tempted by what is wrong? Depending upon your point of view, those who believe in the pure and unblemished life are the ones who are dead inside beyond all understanding."

"You are the one who is blind and dead on the inside," I began to tell Kassar through the voice of offense. "These people of the Mirror have their thoughts focused upon the many things in life that can bring fulfillment and joy to the heart of man. You, my friend, are the one who lacks what is worthy and good. Tell me, Kassar, is there any love at all in your being for your fellow man? Have you ever stepped outside on a beautiful day, took a deep breath, and realized how lucky you were to be alive? No, Kassar, I don't believe the presence of the Mirror is with you or in your heart."

"Shut your mouth!" Kassar yelled, and he became obviously frustrated by the truthful content of my argument. "I don't have time to waste discussing the virtues of what is right and wrong. I came in here to destroy you, and I am going to take pleasure in watching you scream in agony and beg for mercy."

"If you think you can Kassar, then do it," I said with a cold stare, inviting him to a challenge.

Kassar hatefully glared into my eyes for a brief moment, and as our eyes met, we looked upon each other's heart and mind. I was determined to give Kassar the fight he was looking for, and before I could ponder upon another thought, I encountered a giant grizzly bear that Kassar had transformed himself into, which grew into a massive creature over ten feet tall. It rose up on its hind legs and let out a loud, terrifying growl that temporarily froze me in the state of fear.

I was practically helpless until I heard Abigail's voice softly say, "Change into something bigger."

I smiled briefly at the bear just before I changed into a large Tyrannosaurus rex dinosaur with the speed of thought. The dinosaur let out a loud scream that was much more horrifying than the roar of the bear. Immediately, the bear began to run, and I began to pursue it as a dinosaur, for I was a lot bigger and faster. Just prior to the moment I would have captured Kassar, he quickly changed into a World War II Japanese fighter plane and flew up into the sky.

My humanity was restored in a blink of an eye, and I walked out from the trees and into a meadow. I searched the skies for the plane with Kassar in it. It did not take me long to find it, as it began an attack run at me, shooting with its guns. It missed me with every shot, and I began to think about how I was going to shoot him out of the sky. Barnabus's voice spoke softly to me at that moment of need from a place beyond this world with a solution to my problem.

"Shoot that plane out of the sky, just like they did during the big wars. You remember the history classes, the war movies. You know what to do."

He was right. I did know what to do. And with the speed of thought, I was changed into a soldier with several other men-at-arms. We were entrenched in a narrow burrow equipped with cannons and other big guns, each with the same desire: to shoot the plane out of the sky. While we waited for the plane to return, I remembered the last basketball game I'd had with Kassar and how I learned to control the direction and force of the basketball with my mind. I looked at the cannon, and with that thought in my mind, we aimed and shot the weapon at the incoming enemy plane. I watched it fly until it made contact and blew apart the aircraft. The explosion shattered the plane into many different pieces, and I saw Kassar floating down from the sky with a parachute. He landed on the ground with a hard impact, and as he separated himself from the parachute, I could see pain in his eyes.

Kassar quickly walked up to me with determination upon his face. "I'm tired of playing games with you," he said, raising his hands into the air. He looked at them with much concentration until, suddenly, his hands and forearms were ignited into torches of fire. Kassar stared deeply into my eyes and projected fear into my mind. Scatman's voice rescued me, for he must have seen that I was in trouble. Fear had a stronghold on me that left me slightly paralyzed. Without Scatman's intervention, I might have been burned to death.

"Anything your imagination can conceive will be granted to you by the Mirror," I heard Scatman's voice softly say to me. Upon hearing his instructions, I looked down at my own hands as Kassar advanced slowly towards me. He believed that he had me positioned exactly where he wanted me: scared and confused. If he could have read my thoughts at that moment, fear would have entangled him instead. The weapon the Mirror identified in my mind instantly came to life, and it bloomed like a flower into the presence of reality.

I began to feel the heat coming from Kassar's hands of fire when a majestic sword similar to the ones used during medieval times, except substantially smaller, appeared in my hands. It was a pleasure to see the weapon as it produced a glow that originated from somewhere within its purposeful element. I held the sword up in front of my face, and with a proud gesture of accomplishment, my mind became fixed upon ending Kassar's evil presence. When he saw what I held in my hands, his eyes turned from confident to fearful, knowing that what I held in my hands was a weapon that would ultimately bring upon his own destruction. I wasted no time, and I took firm and direct action, rushing toward him, knowing the victory was mine. After two precise swings of the sword, Kassar's hands of fire were upon the ground, detached from the rest of his body and still burning. He fell to his knees, crippled with pain, and he screamed out in mortal terror. Kassar looked up at me, astonished by what had transpired, as a devastating river of pain rushed through him like a current of electricity. Once again, he realized that I had beaten him.

"What have you done?" he yelled out in anger through his pain.

I smiled with satisfaction when I saw what I had achieved. I knew that I would have never been successful without help. I was about to try to help him when his physical presence slowly disintegrated in front of my eyes. Slowly, he vanished until he was gone. I suddenly felt a sadness come upon me until I heard Abigail's voice.

"Good job, Charles. I love you with all of my heart."

In my mind, I said, *I love you too, Abigail.*

I glanced down at my hand when I realized that I no longer held the sword. I looked up and noticed the meadow in which I stood, trying to memorize the picturesque environment that surrounded me. Serenity was all around me, and it came upon my being and entered my spirit, revealing to me that the will of the Mirror had been served on that night.

Part Four

The Price of a Resolution

Chapter 29

Choices have many repercussions with either good or bad results, and we are led down a path on which, usually, we stay for many years. In specific circumstances, we find pain in those places, and sometimes there is a destiny and a purpose in our suffering. It is through the trials in life that we come to find a revelation of the truth. The hands of fate that are guided by the eternal eyes of our lives always knows what is best.

The Mirror came into my life for a distinct reason, and although I was confused for a while, I did try to understand that there was something important that I could not see. It was my desire to accomplish the Mirror's will, which was the deciding factor in rendering Kassar his demise. Barnabus and Scatman were my good friends who taught me the way of the Mirror. Barnabus died by Kassar's hands, which the Mirror allowed for a specific cause. He served faithfully as a teacher of religious truth for many years, but his presence was no more, as a void had become apparent.

When I was pulled back from my dream, and returned to the conscious world, a strange phenomenon took place outside the castle walls and throughout the entire kingdom. Shortly after Kassar had died, a wave in the atmosphere swept just underneath the line of clouds like ripples on the sea. It was quick, and it traveled across the horizons from east to west and from north to south. Its duration was brief, and when it was gone and out of sight, a satisfying peacefulness fell upon the land. The presence of strife and turmoil had been washed clean by the wave, along with the entity of evil that was lifted from the core of the kingdom.

"Charles!"

"Charles, wake up!"

I slowly opened my eyes and lifted my head off the pillow at the sound of Scatman's voice. When I realized what had transpired, I smiled with joy with the satisfaction of what we had accomplished.

"We did it, didn't we, Scatman?"

"Yes we did, Charles. We were successful in what we set out to achieve," Scatman said, his voice seemingly more dismal than joyous. "Sometimes even in victory, there is a price to pay. I believe that Barnabus is dead. Kassar did say that he took care of Barnabus. I believe he probably killed him before he came after you. We must go to the castle immediately, for I want to find out what happened to Barnabus along with locating Kassar."

Scatman, Abigail, and I worked quickly together to secure the house by smothering the fire and putting away the leftover snacks in the cooler. Scatman had run over to the barn to quickly check on his animals while Abigail and I cleaned up the kitchen and dining room. We talked briefly of the dream while we waited for Scatman. I told her with heartfelt sincerity how thankful I was that she was there with Scatman to help me.

"I'm grateful that you got out of there alive, Charles," replied Abigail with a deep appreciation of my survival.

Scatman returned shortly after his brief check on his animals and promptly announced, "No time to waste. Let us get moving," and he quickly led us out of the house and toward the vegetable fields in the dark of night. It was very difficult to see, for in the woodlands, nighttime seemed to be much darker than it was close to the castle and village. Scatman did carry an old portable lantern, so Abigail and I just followed the light.

Using his keen instinct and much precaution, Scatman led us through the woods in the dark. After several miles of following his shadow from the lantern, we came to the top of a steep hill, where we could see the castle in the valley below. I remembered the exact spot, for it was just a few days before when Barnabus and Scatman had brought me to the castle for the first time. We stopped for a moment, just listening to the sounds of the quiet.

"Do you sense a change since you came out of your dream?" asked Scatman with curiosity, hoping he was not the only one who was feeling something out of the ordinary.

"Yes I do, but I can't put my finger on what it is or what it means," I said, without the knowledge available to explain or understand what I felt.

"To me, it feels as if peace has been restored to the land. I believe that the harmony that could be felt by every little thing has been restored to the kingdom, and you have done a great service to all the people who live here, Charles. Let us continue," said Scatman, urgent to find out what happened to his friend. Once we reached the steps just beyond the courtyard, we raced up the many steps. Scatman outran Abigail and me, being the first one to walk into the castle, and he instructed Abigail and I to search for Kassar.

"Look downstairs in the entertainment areas, especially the music room. Kassar loved music of all kinds, and I believe that was the only time when he was at peace with himself. I'm going to Barnabus's room. When you find Kassar, come and get me."

I took Abigail's hand and walked very slowly down the basement steps to the entertainment center. Scatman's idea seemed to be a good guess, for I remember seeing Kassar listening to music with his headphones on, seemingly lost in a trance of his own making. I opened the door, and when I did, the lingering presence of death greeted us. Abigail had a queer look on her face, for I could sense that she smelled the same thing as me. The aroma had a distinct similarity to meat that was just beginning to spoil. The room felt like a tomb, and as we began our search, we initially found nothing. I was about to abandon my search when I noticed particles of sand leading to the back corner of the library. When I followed the faint trail of sand particles, it led me to the back of the library, where many alternative styles of musical composition could be found. I yelled out to Abigail when I found what lay at the end of trail.

"Abigail, come here! Quick!"

Abigail was on the other side of the room when I called out to her. She promptly stopped what she was doing and ran to the sound of my voice to see what I had discovered. A small pile of clothes lay at my feet, and I knelt down to examine them. In our minds, we both knew whose clothes they were, for we had seen Kassar wearing them at school.

Slowly and cautiously, I began to pick up his clothes garment by garment. Everything he was wearing was there: shirt, pants, underwear, shoes, and socks. Underneath all of his clothing, we found a small pile of sand almost two feet high and wide. Partially buried in the small mound of sand, I found a bright silver ring with an emerald monkey as its centerpiece.

"What happened to him?" Abigail asked me, being truly amazed at what she saw before her. "Charles, those are his remains. He was wearing those clothes at school today, and that's his ring. I remember seeing it on his finger when he approached and threatened you about sleeping and dreams. He was caressing the centerpiece in a gentle sort of way, like someone might pet their dog or cat. Why he was doing it, I have no idea."

"I remember that ring," I said in agreement. "I especially noticed the monkey centerpiece. What happened to him, Abigail? Why the sand? Abigail, I don't understand," I said to her with many questions running through my mind.

"Let's find Scatman," urged Abigail with the assurance of hope in her voice.

"Good idea," I agreed, and I got up off the floor, took Abigail's hand in mine, and walked out of the music library, closing the door behind us.

Chapter 30

In the mysteries of death, there are usually unanswered questions that surround many random circumstances. Pain and sorrow usually accompany a person who lacks faith, but to those who believe in a better place after life, death becomes a celebration. It is the proclamation that the deceased has crossed over to the other side, free from all the concerns of human life. Peace prevails all around them, having been liberated from the mysteries of life that are no longer important, for they have reached their final destination.

Abigail and I had not come to that measure of faith in our short life. In the course of time, the Mirror would comfort our minds about what happened to Barnabus and Kassar. Quite often, explanations are not available for everything that happens, but through acceptance, we come to believe that it was part of the creator's plan.

When Abigail and I walked up to Barnabus's room, we found the door slightly open. Slowly, we crept into the room and saw Scatman on his knees, at Barnabus's bedside, quietly sobbing. He felt us enter the room in his spirit, and it comforted him to have us share his grief with him. He turned his face toward us, and as we saw his watery eyes, it was evident that the cause of his despair was that Barnabus had died.

"He was like a father to me. I hardly knew my real father, but Barnabus took me under his wing and treated me like a son. Even though he was old and I knew his time was short, something tells me it wasn't supposed to happen that way. I don't know why the

Mirror allowed this to happen, but I know there is a reason, one that I can't see or understand at this time. I am grateful that I had the chance to know him like I did. Oh, my Mirror, how I wish he was still with us!" exclaimed Scatman in a voice of despair as he looked skyward, until his emotions erupted into a passionate cry.

I felt bad for Scatman as I heard his sorrowful words filled with deep emotion. He started to reminisce about several memories he had with Barnabus. Abigail and I were also quite grieved by Barnabus's passing, and we felt compassion in our hearts for what Scatman was feeling. He had known Barnabus a long time, and he was not only his father figure in his life but also a good friend. I tried to comfort Scatman as he cried for his friend when I remembered that Barnabus was the first person of the Mirror who came to me. I recalled that day quite vividly, and it seemed strange, but I felt as if time had prolonged itself inside the Mirror.

"He will always be with us, Scatman," I told him with sincere sympathy. "His memory will be with all of us who knew him and what he believed in. I believe that Barnabus has found a freedom that we can only dream about."

"I know you are right, my little friend," Scatman said through tears that flowed in an abundance of emotion from the depths of his broken heart. "I will miss you, my friend," he expressed to the deceased body lying on the bed next to him.

Scatman took Barnabus's hands into his and placed them together so that it appeared as if Barnabus was in deep prayer. He began to walk away from his friend's corpse when he suddenly stopped and looked once again at the lifeless body on the bed. In that distinct fragment in time, Scatman suddenly realized that Barnabus was at peace. After Scatman had wiped the remaining tears from his eyes, he turned his attention to Abigail and I.

"I'm okay. I'm glad that I have the two of you," stated Scatman as he tried to recover from a temporary outburst of emotion.

We embraced each other in a group hug, with the sorrowful emotions that accompany the loss of a loved one. Abigail and I were needed by Scatman for support similar to how I needed Scatman when I first arrived inside the Mirror.

"Did you find him?" Scatman asked inquisitively.

"I believe we found his remains," I stated flatly.

"What are you talking about?" questioned Scatman, unable to comprehend what I was referring to.

Abigail immediately interjected, and quickly explained.

"Scatman, in the music library, we found sand where it should not have been, which also led us to a small pile of sand. We also found Kassar's clothes that he was wearing at school today, along with his ring, next to the pile of sand. We believe that the sand is the remains of what was once Kassar."

"Show me," said Scatman, directing us.

Abigail and I led Scatman down to the music library. When we approached the door, that same fowl fragrance welcomed us once again. It was a distinct odor that mimicked spoilage of some kind. We followed Scatman into the room and immediately showed him the random particles of sand that grew more abundant as we followed the trail. Scatman followed the faint path with keen interest until he saw the pile of sand that Abigail had told him about. He bent down on his knees to examine the sand and the clothes.

"He was wearing those clothes at school," I told him.

Scatman studied the sand for a few minutes with a puzzled expression on his face. He gathered a handful of sand and then watched as the fine granules of sand passed through his fingers. Scatman knew all too well that there were many unveiled secrets which remain hidden through the passageway of life. Life and Death share common distinctive factors that occur at random. It is faith in the Mirror that makes it easier to accept the acts of the supernatural. Scatman knew this to be true no matter what he felt.

"I know that's his ring," said Abigail. "He was wearing it at school. I remember seeing it on his finger because I thought, 'What a strange ring.' Does that monkey centerpiece mean anything to you, Scatman?"

"No, not really, but I'm sure it had a deep meaning to Kassar. I'm not exactly sure what happened to him, although I think we have seen the last of him," said Scatman as he got up and faced Abigail and me.

He became quiet when he realized that we were not meant to know the significant meaning behind Kassar's disappearance.

"The sand might represent symbolically what he came from and where he has returned to. I believe Kassar was quite different than we are, and I am not even sure if he was totally human. Charles, when you defeated him in the dreamscape, his will to live died and he withered away into dust and sand. So the ancient theory that if you die in your dream, you die in life is true."

"That's a good guess, Scatman," I said. "It's better than anything I can come up with. I'm sure that what happened to Kassar will remain a mystery for a long time."

"I agree," said Scatman. "It's important for us to praise the Mirror for our deliverance. I know we are all exhausted and need sleep, but I believe it would be wise to seal off this room for the night. Let us give thanks to the Mirror, who works all things together for the good of us all."

Abigail, Scatman, and I joined hands, forming a small circle, and our minds became unified in a prayer of thanksgiving.

"I thank you, my Mirror, for working your perfect will in the events that transpired on this night for the well-being of all who live upon this land. You have kept us safe from any evil that would intend us harm. Comfort us as we grieve over the loss of your servant, Barnabus. We thank you for your love. In your name, we seek the truth," concluded Scatman, and he rose his head out of prayer.

"Tomorrow will be a busy day for all of us, for there will be much to do, but most important is that we must say good-bye to Barnabus. The funeral to honor him will be a sad event for all who knew him.

Afterward, we will take Kassar's remains to the lake and scatter them upon the sands of the beach. I'm glad that we have each other, for we will be able to comfort one another as we pay tribute to Barnabus's life," said Scatman with tears in his eyes, embracing Abigail and me in a group hug that gave him some measure of reassurance.

Abigail and I said good night to Scatman, and we walked up to our rooms. When we held each other in a tight embrace, our hearts were forever thankful that we had survived. Scatman remained in the music library, for he wanted to secure the room so that Kassar's remains would not be disturbed.

Scatman wished that he would have had the chance to say good-bye to his good friend. He remembered that the last time he saw Barnabus, his mind seemed distant and alone, for I believe the possibility existed that Barnabus had a premonition of what lie in his future. Quickly, Scatman gathered his thoughts as he focused his attention to secure the music room and lock the door. He slowly walked up to the guest room, the sleeping quarters that he had used on many occasions through the years. Sleep was beckoning him, and the exhaustion from the intervention of my dream and the discovery about Barnabus and Kassar had put a strain upon his heart and mind.

Peace had been restored to the kingdom once again. It was a presence that was not only felt but observed. On that night, as a new wave of harmony swept through the land, all was quiet. It was a fresh attitude that came alive in the hearts of many, as love and joy that was becoming dormant rose up from the depths of numerous subdued souls. The darkness had been eliminated, for the light of the Mirror began to shine brighter than it had for some time.

In the morning, after breakfast, Abigail and I helped Scatman organize what was needed for the funeral. A wooden casket was placed in the courtyard, where it was garnished with many types of radiant flowers. It was a lovely blend of colors, which made the arrangement quite picturesque. Barnabus's body was carefully placed in the coffin, and the cover was placed upon it until the time for the funeral. There were no cemeteries in the Mirror, which I thought was strange, as a coffin was used in preparations for a traditional funeral. We began to set up folding chairs in a semicircle around the coffin for family, friends, and acquaintances. A small podium was brought down from the worship center for speeches. Most everything that had to be done was complete, and in a few hours, the funeral would begin. I remembered my grandmother's funeral a few years before, but that was back in Ohio, and I knew what I would soon experience, I would never forget.

Just prior to the funeral, Scatman opened the music library, where we found Kassar's remains exactly as we had found them the night before. Using a small little hand broom, Scatman swept up all the grains of sand. He emptied all the sand into a round metal canister and sealed it with a tight-fitting lid for safekeeping. Kassar's ring and clothing were also put into a small bag and securely sealed. Scatman looked down at the spot where the sand was and silently asked the question, *What is the significance of the sand?*

Scatman was glad that he was busy, for if he had not been occupied, he might have been vulnerable to depression. As he focused his mind upon helping with the funeral arrangements, waves of negativity tried to control and influence his emotions. Quickly, the day passed until the time for the funeral was upon him. He appreciated the fact that Abigail and I were with him, for it helped to be with other people.

The setting for Barnabus's funeral was lovely. It took place on a beautiful springtime day. The weather reminded me of early May in Ohio, and it had become warm without the intense heat of the summer months. The open casket was set up among over one hundred chairs, with flowers of many varieties that were artistically arranged around the coffin. When the appointed time came, people began to arrive slowly, walking up to the casket and symbolically gesturing to Barnabus a fond farewell.

After everyone had arrived and had the opportunity to pay respects, a few select people came forward to give their own personal experiences about Barnabus. Scatman was the first to speak, and he fought off the tears in giving his account of their friendship.

"He was a caring man, and he was like a father to me, along with being my best friend. Barnabus loved the Mirror and served the people here with respect, for he wanted what was best for the community. He is in better hands now, and the Mirror will shine brighter because of Barnabus's love for life," concluded Scatman, speaking briefly about his friend, and he slowly walked back to his chair next to me and sat down.

The head schoolmaster, Mr. Morgan, came to the podium next, and he recalled a memory about Barnabus. It was a time when he was younger and Barnabus was the head schoolmaster.

"Everyone loved Barnabus, the teachers and especially the students. He really knew what it meant to walk in love. When circumstances turned against him, he never lost that joy and peace. I was a student when I first met him, and when I became a teacher, he took me under his wing. I learned many things just by watching him, for it was his actions and not what he said that motivated my heart to be more like him. When he retired, I was the one chosen to take his job, but never could I ever think about replacing him. He has been missed at the school for twenty years and now that his presence is no more, he will continue to be missed by all the people who had come to know him."

When Mr. Morgan sat down, Victor Reuben, the spiritual leader of the kingdom, approached the podium to lead everyone in a short prayer, giving thanks to the Mirror for all the lives that Barnabus touched, developed, and changed.

"What we ask of you, my Mirror, is that you comfort all of these people who will miss your servant Barnabus. May his life be a testimony to all of us. I know that Barnabus spent hours a day in prayer, desperately seeking answers to everyday issues. May we use his example to come to know you that much more. In your name, I seek the truth."

When the testimonies had been spoken and a prayer had been offered up to the Mirror, silence loomed over the crowd of people for a few brief minutes. Without expecting it, I began to observe a small stream of pale yellow vapor that started to rise up out of the casket and reach toward the sky. The mysterious vapor rose for more than five minutes, and the horizons began to shine brighter than it had before. Barnabus had arrived at his final destination with the joy he possessed in life, which would be with him forever. All who had witnessed the great phenomenon that transpires at every funeral watched with curiosity and amazement.

As the funeral ended, everyone rose up out of their seats and walked around the courtyard, engaging in fellowship with others. The cafeteria had baked a large chocolate sheet cake for the occasion, and set it up on a table, offering it with drinks. Many individuals began to discuss and meditate upon the meaning and purpose of their lives. It did not matter how many funerals a person has attended; witnessing the transformation and the levitation skyward remains a miracle of the Mirror. To see it makes a person wonder, "Where did they go? When will I follow?" I believed then, as I do now, that in pursuing the knowledge of life, we find meaning in death. It is only for a brief fragment of time that we walk in this life when it is compared to the eternal timetable that our soul exists.

After the fellowship from the funeral had been disbursed, Abigail, Diana, Scatman, and I began to walk toward the woods. In silence we walked, knowing where we were going and what we were about to do. I suddenly felt bad about Kassar, for I knew that he had many pains that hindered him from living and loving in a healthy, natural manner. He wanted to be loved but refused to take the first step toward changing his heart and healing the hatred that dominated his thoughts and personality.

Scatman gave each of us small plastic ramekins, and then he took the metal urn of sand, giving each of us some sand that was once Kassar. It was on the shores of the lake that we spread Kassar's remains.

"From the sand Kassar rose and walked among us, and now that he is dead, we return him to the very essence of his existence. The sands of life, the story of Kassar," said Scatman with a somber proclamation.

"I do not totally understand why he came here," I said. "I do believe, however, that we are better off because of the lessons that we learned from his existence," I stated with a deep compassion for the departed.

While we scattered Kassar's remains along the lakeshore, Scatman made a small fire with some small bits of wood that he found. He burned Kassar's clothes, and as we watched the fire grow, a dark reality touched each one of us by the events that took place. I suddenly realized that it had been a week since I had come through the Mirror, and I quickly flowered into one of his children. I fought and subdued doubts and fears as I discovered what real love was. Abigail and I became friends with a mutual love that grew and developed between us. We trusted the Mirror and each other, and within our hearts was a compass to lead us down the pathway to our destinies.

Chapter 31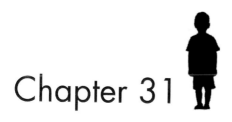

The spirit being in man is like a compass that orchestrates our lives to the truth, away from misdirection, by the divine word. Guilt and conviction arises from our spirit when it is necessary to reveal something to our hearts. To cleanse the conscious of guilt feelings, peace must be made with whoever we might have hurt due to our choices.

In the week that followed, I began to notice heaviness weighing down on the inside of me. I did not know what it was, where it had come from, or how to make it go away. In my mind, my thoughts were upon my mother and father back home in Riversville. I felt bad about leaving them in the manner in which I did, even though I believed that it was the permissible will of the Mirror. I wanted to tell them that I loved them. I thought it might remove the burden of guilt that housed itself within the barriers of my consciousness. The speculation rose up in me that I might feel better if I could somehow tell my mother and father that it was by divine authority that I was taken out of their lives. I knew that I had an important role to play inside the Mirror, and I did not want to feel bad anymore.

Slowly, depression became my companion, but I could not understand the reason why. We had just been successful in defeating Kassar, and even though Barnabus had been lost, there arose a new born conception of peace upon the land. It was something to be thankful and joyous about, but for some reason, I could not. I knew I could not trust in my feelings, for they can be very deceptive. I had dinner with Abigail and Scatman, and while we discussed events from the past week, I wanted to tell Scatman what I was feeling.

"Scatman," I said with a serious disposition, "I wish there was a way to return to Ohio so that I could tell my parents that I love them. I know I can't go back, but I wish I could tell them how I feel. I believe the Mirror brought me here for a purpose, but I still feel bad."

"Guilt is a hard thing to live with," replied Scatman sympathetically. "The Mirror can see your heart, Charles. Even though it was for the good of many that you came to live here, you still feel condemnation. You are very perceptive, Charles, for you probably won't find that peace until you tell them. I know, Charles, because I have been where you are now. I have been expecting you to become troubled from your past for a few days now. You can never return to Ohio physically, but your spirit can."

"What do you mean?" I quickly asked with curiosity.

"You can tell them in their dreams," answered Scatman, hoping that his reply would offer me some hope. "It's the same method you used when you shadowtreked with Abigail and I. The ability to tell your parents why you left has always been with you. You just did not know how to make the connection. In your spirit lies the capacity to cleanse yourself from your past. Approach the dream like you would any other, and you will discover upon your return that a gentle peace has replaced the guilt that is now causing you some concern. Many years ago, I had to do the same thing with my mother, and I am glad I did it. To this day, I have never looked back with remorse over the decision I made."

"Are you trying to tell me that it's that easy?" I asked, quite astonished about the simplicity of the solution to my problem.

"Yes, it is that easy," said Scatman. "Charles, before you enter their dream, make sure your focus is upon your parents as a complete unit. They are one. Your intention is to tell them both?"

"Yes, it is," I said in response to Scatman's query.

"I thought it was. You must visualize in your mind that they are one person even though physically, they are two. When you get into their dream, tell them what you feel. Only in this way will you be able to restore peace into your heart and mind," stated Scatman as he emphasized the importance of what he was telling me.

"Thank you, Scatman, for your wisdom and concern," I told him with a measure of happiness that I could not quite hold. It was a feeling of satisfaction that the deliverance from guilt was just a dream away.

When we had finished eating, Scatman returned to his little farm, and Abigail and I went for a walk around the castle and into the woodlands. Abigail had a heartfelt sympathy for me, and she listened to me pouring out my feelings. She tried to understand even though she had never experienced the emotions that I was encountering. I knew that she loved me and desired nothing more than to have me free from what was tormenting me.

As the day quickly transcended into night, and the majority of the people turned to their beds for sleep, I walked with urgent anticipation into the sitting room. I remembered that it was in that room, that I began my dreamwalk with Abigail. When I sat down on the couch that faced the fireplace, my eyes immediately were drawn into the active flames. Thoughts traveled rapidly in my mind until I took control of them and bowed my head down in prayer. I gave thanks to the Mirror for his will that had been done over the last week. I prayed earnestly for my heart and mind to be delivered from my past. My hope was that I would be able to have a successful link with my parents, which could only be accomplished with the Mirror's helping hand.

I lifted my head out of prayer, as my eyes focused upon the fire with my thoughts directly centered on my mom and dad. Memories that I had witnessed in my life with them skipped at random until I began to hear their voices, and as the vivid images formed into my mind, I could see their faces. The perception dawned upon me that the shadowtrek which I was pursuing, would be an experience in a dream like no other, and as those thoughts drifted inside my head,

I was pulled down the long tunnel of dreams. I knew where I was going, and my reflections from my past life was the connection that made it possible to accomplish my desires in the dream.

In the tiny village of Riversville, Ohio, at the home of Dave and Sharon Stormdale, all was quiet. My parents slept peacefully in the early hours of the morning. A dream had been placed into their subconscious minds in unison, a desire from their forgotten son, Charles. As I entered their dream, I saw them walking hand in hand through a small wheat field, surrounded by thick woodlands engulfed by a thick fog. A bright light suddenly cut through the fog and caused it to disintegrate. After following a short section of the trail through the thick woods, they entered a lush, green meadow, and that was when they saw me flying a kite, being raptured by the peacefulness of the moment. I could sense them watching me, and I almost could read their minds, what they thought as they observed me. I believe that at first, my parents did not recognize me, until I pulled the kite from the sky and approached them.

"Hi, Mom! Hi, Dad!" I said with an enthusiastic voice portraying that I was happy to see them.

"Charles, where have you been?" my mother asked, seemingly worried, which I thought was strange; for she acted like she knew who I was, although her memory had been erased.

"We have been worried about you," said my father with a concern for my welfare.

The only explanation I could reason in my young mind was that the Mirror restored some of their memories for the purpose of that particular dream. I was surprised by the reaction that both of my parents displayed at seeing me, because their actions were not like them, and I knew it.

"Do not worry. I'm alive, and I'm well," I said to calm their anxieties. "The reason I've come to you is to tell you that I miss you and I love you. However, after this moment, you will never see me again. I wanted to explain to you face to face that I was taken from you for an important cause by a divine authority. The two of you did not have true love in your heart for me in the way a parent should love their child. I loved the both of you no matter how you treated me, but you must learn that it is only by love that inner peace can be found. Your greed and selfishness was the motivating factor that brought the divine hand of all eternity to come down upon me with a future and a hope and took me away. I'm sorry this happened, but I just wanted to tell you that I still love you no matter how you treated me. Remember and learn, for a blessing will come around to your life once again and you will have another child. This time around, love him or her like you have never loved before. Somehow, I believe you will remember me, as I will remain a part of you for the remainder of your life."

When I finished telling them what I had to say, I walked over to my mother and father and, one at a time, hugged them with an emotional sincerity. I looked at their faces and studied them as if I was trying to memorize that exact moment in time. I backed away from them, turned around, and slowly started to walk away.

"Charles, my son, come back! Don't leave us! Please come back!" my mother shouted out in desperation.

I looked back briefly with tears in my eyes.

"I'm sorry. I really am, but I can't stay. I have to go," I said, and with those words, I walked into the woodlands and vanished from their sight.

My mother began to hysterically cry, and that was how she awoke from her sleep, wailing in her tears.

Sadness was upon my father as he awoke with the sound of his wife crying next to him. He knew why she wept. It was quite strange, he thought, how he perceived the knowledge behind her tears. The memory of the dream was fresh in his mind, and he started to wonder why he dreamt that he'd had a son.

A son? he questioned when he reasoned that both attempts to have children had failed, or so he thought. However, somewhere deep within himself, he believed that there was a part of him out there and it had been longing to talk to him. *Was that my child?*

He rolled over in their bed and put his arm around his wife to comfort her. *It was indeed a strange dream, but a dream is not real, not in this world,* he told himself. While thoughts filled with sorrow crept into his mind, his wife finally stopped crying, and he realized in his heart that they had experienced the same dream. Slowly and without realizing its implications, a deep conviction crept into his heart about their ambitions and desires.

"Honey," my father compassionately spoke softly, "I know what you dreamt. You saw the son we never had, didn't you?"

"Yes," she said through her tears.

"I believe we have been wrong about the way we have been living. It's time for a change. Do all these things make us happy? I want to walk away from our ways, our greed, selfishness, and the pride of all our possessions that reflects the manner in which our neighbors perceive us. The luxury vacations we take twice a year can be eliminated, for all of the stuff we own does not fill the emptiness that lives in us, does it?"

"No. Not for very long anyways," my mother replied sadly.

"I'm not sure where the strength will come from, but it is out there, and it's in us, and we need to walk away from the things that ruin our chances to experience any type of happiness."

"I know you are right, honey. The dream showed us that," she said after a moment of silent meditation.

When I disappeared from my parents' sight in their dream, I was immediately swept outward and down the long tunnel once again until I found myself in the sitting room at the castle. A gentle peace came alive in me, and I looked up and into the dying flames of the fireplace.

"Home," I said to myself. "Yes, I believe this is my home, and I will remain in the land of the Mirror for the rest of my days. My destiny is here, and the Mirror has a plan for my life," I proclaimed to myself as I came to a place of peace with my past, for I knew in my heart that all things work together for good.

The home of Dave and Sharon Stormdale did change since I had lived in their household. The dream seemed to change my parents' motives and desires, especially from the inside. It was a new beginning, one in which they treated each other differently, with a certain degree of love and respect. They were invited by one of my mother's acquaintances at work to begin attending church services as a weekly event. In time, their spirits were reborn and their minds were cleansed. My memory never returned to them, although somewhere within the deep regions of their souls, they knew I lived.

One solitary possession of mine remained in my parents' house. It was something small and insignificant that normally would be overlooked. Located in the basement, in the very room in which I slept night after night, displayed on an old wooden bookcase, was the 1969 New York Mets autographed baseball. I won that baseball at the fair on the first day that changed my life. The baseball sits there still, untouched and unnoticed, just an object to collect dust. There is no memory attached to the baseball, for it was something that was accidentally left behind.